ANNA DAUGHERTY

Before Grace

Black Rose Writing | Texas

ISBN: 978-1-68513-637-6

LIBRARY OF CONGRESS CONTROL NUMBER: 2025933753
PUBLISHED BY BLACK ROSE WRITING
www.blackrosewriting.com

Printed in the United States of America
Suggested Retail Price (SRP) $22.95

Before Grace is printed in Adobe Garamond Pro

*As a planet-friendly publisher, Black Rose Writing does its best to eliminate unnecessary waste to reduce paper usage and energy costs, while never compromising the reading experience. As a result, the final word count vs. page count may not meet common expectations.

Scripture quotations marked CSB have been taken from the Christian Standard Bible®, Copyright © 2017 by Holman Bible Publishers. Used by permission. Christian Standard Bible® and CSB® are federally registered trademarks of Holman Bible Publishers.

Edited by Denise Harmer

Praise for
Before Grace

"A heartfelt story about love, faith, and second chances (with all the feels)."
– **Lena Gibson, award-winning author of *The Edge of Life: Love and Survival During the Apocalypse* and *The Wish***

"Anna Daugherty delivers a tale of two journeys—recovering from tragedy when responsibilities leave no time for personal grief and the seemingly impossible path toward ever loving again. A beautiful story about faith, friends, family, and a path to the locksmith who will set you free."
– **Cam Torrens, award-winning author of the Tyler Zahn series**

"Packed with vibrant and compelling descriptions, Daugherty's writing will pull you deep into the lives of her characters and the struggles they face…I found myself with tears in my eyes as I cheered them on. It didn't take long to become my favorite of her books."
– **Barbara A. Luker, author of *Hiding In Plain Sight***

Before Grace

"But he said to me, "My grace is sufficient for you, for my power is perfected in weakness." Therefore, I will most gladly boast all the more about my weaknesses, so that Christ's power may reside in me."
–2 Corinthians 12:9

Chapter One

Chubby three-year-old hands smeared strawberry ice cream across the headstone, coating her father's name in his favorite flavor.

"Josie, get off," Katie said for the hundredth time, apologizing to the marker. Or to Aaron. Though if he were here, she imagined he might laugh and swipe a finger at the dribble. He had been the better parent.

Katie rubbed his name clean with a napkin while the October sun continued to beat down on their frozen treats. Baton Rouge missed the memo about autumnal weather. Katie caught a drop of ice cream on her daughter's chin before it made it to her dress. "Hurry and finish it, Jojo."

The blonde ball of energy seemed not to hear her, continuing her scramble over and around her father's headstone. Her twin sister heard, though. Sage picked up the pace, finishing her ice cream in two bites. She took a napkin from underneath Katie's purse and dabbed at her lips, then sipped from Katie's water bottle before returning to her spot, sitting cross-legged in the shade, her copper hair frizzing in the humidity.

Katie studied the scene, framing it in her mind's eye. She scooted the balloon bouquet closer. In the store, it made sense to Katie to bring balloons in lieu of flowers to a birthday party. Now that she saw it, the overall effect was more garish than festive.

If cemeteries required a certain etiquette, Katie wouldn't know. She hadn't been here since the twins were infants. Now, with careful timing, she managed to make a road trip pit stop here, on his birthday, in hopes that the balloons and ice cream could shield her from the suffocating darkness.

"Where's Daddy?" Josie asked.

Katie patted the ground in front of them. "In here. And in heaven."

"Why can't Daddy have ice cream?" she asked, repeating the same questions they covered at the store.

Katie sighed. "He can't eat ice cream in the ground."

"Can he eat ice cream in heaven?"

"Yeah, probably."

Josie's face wrinkled and she stomped her foot. "Den you shoulda boughted him some!"

Katie gritted her teeth and forced on a smile, trying to deescalate the little volcano. "The ice cream is free in heaven."

Josie stuck her face into her ice cream cone, trying to lick out the last bits without eating the cone. "I wanna go to heaven." Ice cream lined her cheeks and forehead.

"One day," Katie said.

Another foot stomp. "I wanna go now!"

Everything turned into a problem with this child. "Fine, go," Katie said. Maybe everybody would beat her there.

Josie looked around. "Where is it?"

Katie pointed up. Josie jumped as if trying to get there. It might be cute, but Katie couldn't care at this point. The cuteness lasted only seconds before the next tantrum started. Any sweet moments Katie spent in recovery.

Dressed in a rainbow tutu and hot pink shirt, Josie climbed back onto the headstone and jumped from it. Katie gave up correcting her and gathered their things instead. She carried her purse and water bottle to the car parked nearby, along with a stack of baby wipes, napkins, and Josie's soggy ice cream cone.

Josie zoomed around the headstones of varying sizes, shapes, and shades of gray, while Sage carefully studied the blank back side of Aaron's. Katie wondered if her child saw things others didn't—a thought too spooky for this place. She didn't care for ghosts.

Yet you're heading straight toward them.

Aaron's mother, Suzanne, called a few weeks ago and said their church needed a photographer for their fall festival. It happened to be right around the time her current lease in Birmingham ended and Katie owed Aaron's family a visit, so she agreed. A trip to the Texas coast sounded fun at the time. Now though, doubt built with every mile they drove closer.

"Let's go to the zoo!" Katie said, clapping her hands to distract herself and the girls. "Daddy loved zoos."

Josie cheered for the zoo and made a beeline for the car. "Sage!" Katie called over her shoulder. Sage didn't budge. Katie buckled Josie into her car seat and walked back to the grave site. "Sage, come on. I'm sick of this place."

Sage rarely fought her, but today she stood her ground. She pointed to Aaron's headstone.

"Aaron James Kaminski," Katie read. She didn't want to read the rest. The words felt sticky and heavy as the emptiness of his absence came racing back. She needed to leave. "It says his name so we know it's his. Can we go now?"

Sage turned big green eyes on her, then stared at the headstone some more. What did she want? Asking Sage to start talking was as useless as asking Josie to stop. Sage pointed at the dates.

"This one is his birthday. He would have been thirty-three today." Only a few months older than Katie. He never turned thirty.

Sage pointed to the other numbers.

The worst day of my life. "That's when he left. Um, you know, to heaven." A poor word choice, perhaps. Her kids would grow up thinking heaven was a euphemism for father abandonment. She'd have to fix that one day. But Katie couldn't stand here any longer. The weight of it pressed down. One balloon had flown away, and they had run out of ice cream. "Sage, it's time to go, I mean it."

Finally, the little girl followed her back to the car and Katie buckled her car seat. Their tires crunched over loose gravel as they exited. Katie risked one quick look in the rearview mirror before diverting her eyes back to the road ahead. No ghosts.

Just one day. She could get through one day here. One long day in their haunted former city before they headed out first thing in the morning.

She debated showing the girls their first house while in Baton Rouge, but decided against it. She didn't want to see it.

The beautiful, white-columned house had been their dream home when they bought it. It turned into a nightmare after Aaron died, as Katie struggled to keep up with the daily maintenance while caring for infant twins. In the haze of postpartum hormones and grief, she sold it—the place she wanted to both cling to and escape.

When she left, she leased an apartment near friends in Nashville for six months. When that got old, they tried Atlanta. Then Charlotte for nearly a year. Most recently, Birmingham. As long as she kept moving, she could survive. She could outrun the black hole chasing her.

Except this time, she ran straight into it. It had been nearly three years since she had been to Aaron's hometown of Ridley Bay. She had visited once since his death, only to find his family's grief compounded her own, and she couldn't bear it. Now, with three years of buffer time, she had regained some strength. Hopefully it would be enough.

Regardless, they only had to stay for a week. One week in a short-term rental, because Katie turned down Suzanne's offered guest room. She didn't want to sleep in Aaron's old room. After one week, she would figure out where they were going next.

Katie drummed her fingers on the steering wheel and took the next exit. "Look, girls, there's the sign for the zoo. We're getting close."

"I didn't see it!" Josie screeched, kicking her legs against the back of Katie's seat.

"Oh stop it. It's only a sign, you're fine."

It didn't help. After a few failed attempts to distract her, Katie turned up the volume on the Disney songs playing in the car to drown out Josie's cries so she could think straight. She grabbed her purse in the passenger seat and dug out an emergency lollipop which did the trick.

At a red light, Katie risked a quick glance back. Josie happily looked out the window with her lollipop. Silent tears slid down Sage's cheeks.

"Are you serious? You too?" Katie sighed as she emptied her purse to find the last lollipop for Sage. Anything to make the crying stop. Katie didn't have the heart for more tears.

When they reached the zoo parking lot, Katie hunted for a parking spot. She cruised past a young couple pushing a double stroller identical to Katie's. She almost wanted to roll down the window and ask if they wanted a couple more kids. "They're free," she whispered to herself, turning onto the next row. She wanted to be here with Aaron instead.

This life looked nothing like the one she had imagined for herself. And most days, she wanted nothing to do with it. But here she was. Trying her best.

She pulled into a spot and grabbed her camera from the front seat. The zoo promised a few good photos at least. "Let's find some elephants," she said. Tomorrow, they would find some ghosts.

Chapter Two

The "Welcome to Ridley Bay" sign greeted Katie and her girls on Saturday. She had an old picture of herself standing next to it; Aaron took it on her first visit here, when she met his family. He proposed on that trip.

Katie found their rental easily and the excitement of a new place kept the girls occupied while she unloaded the car. They traveled with half their lives stuffed into the back of the vehicle. The rest sat in a storage unit in Baton Rouge, waiting for the day they found a place worth staying.

When she finished unpacking the last bag, Katie called Suzanne to say they had arrived.

Suzanne sounded surprised. "Oh, wonderful! You made it in time for dinner."

"I said we would," Katie said.

Suzanne made a harrumphing sound Katie didn't care for. "You never know with road trips. But I can't wait to see you all, especially here on our own turf."

"Right," Katie said, far less excited than Suzanne. She excused herself from the call to get the twins ready. After a long day of driving, she'd rather bathe cats than get them back into the car. Eventually, with enough coercion, she had them in shoes and heading for the door.

It only took a few minutes to get to Suzanne and William's house—perks of a smaller town. Katie parked in front of the midcentury build, in the same spot as her last visit, while the neighbor's same gray cat watched once again. She remembered this place too well. Maybe they should have met on more neutral ground—a restaurant suddenly seemed like a wonderful idea, better than "on their turf."

The moment she unclipped the last car seat buckle, she heard the front door open and Suzanne's voice.

"My girls!" she called. She wore navy capris and a subtle floral top in two shades of blue. Her naturally blonde hair a touch whiter these days, though it only looked better for it. She could have just walked off a Land's End photo shoot.

Suzanne squatted to the girls' height for forced hugs. Sage and Josie didn't know their grandmother well, but Josie managed a hug without too much drama. Sage hid behind Katie's leg. Suzanne waved it off. "Oh, that's fine, you'll warm up to Nana quick, I know it." She winked at Sage, who hid further.

"Well, come on in," Suzanne said, ushering them all inside.

Aaron's dad, William, stood inside, waiting to greet them in a blue and white gingham shirt and khakis. His red hair had dulled and thinned a bit with age, but he still shared a strong resemblance with Aaron. He gave Katie a quick smile and a loose hug, and a head rub to the girls.

"Girls, you've actually been here before," Suzanne said, gesturing to the living room around them. "You were only a few months old. Right, Katie?"

"That's right." And from what Katie could tell, the furniture had never moved. The photos never changed either. They lined the walls, the bookcase, and the desk, featuring Aaron and his brother Tyler like a miniature museum. Was Katie imagining the dust?

Before she had to engage in too much small talk, William's brother and his wife arrived to distract her and set off another round of awkward hellos with the girls.

Though only a couple years apart, William's brother, JP, looked a decade younger, with a long, slender frame, light brown hair that hid any grays, and far less lines on his face. His wife, Tricia, greeted Katie like an old friend. She wore a flashy geometric dress and smelled like citrus as she wrapped Katie into a tight hug. Her bony arms could give a surprising squeeze. "Oh, I'm so glad you're here!"

Katie smiled her brightest. "We're glad to be here."

"Oh my goodness," Tricia exclaimed, kneeling to see the girls. "They are every bit as precious as in your pictures. Don't you adore her pictures?" She glanced at Suzanne. "I save every single one. The last one you shared with Sage on the swings—the expression you captured." She gave a chef's kiss in the air.

Katie laughed. "Thank you. Photos are the reason we're here."

"That and family," Suzanne said with a nod.

"True," Katie said. If it were just photos, plenty of opportunities paid more—especially in bigger cities. Her photography went viral years ago and she had enough of a fan base across the south to keep her busy.

"I see more and more of Aaron in her as she gets bigger," Tricia said, looking at Sage.

"Yes, they skipped out on my genes," Katie said. Sage was a girlish copy of Aaron, and Josie looked more like her Nana than either of her parents. Suzanne probably liked it best that way.

"What are they into now?" Suzanne asked. "I have a playroom all set up, but I had to guess at it, really. I raised two boys, the girl things are all new to me."

"A playroom? For a weeklong visit?" Katie asked.

"Well, I'm hoping there will be more," Suzanne said, reaching for the girls' hands instead of meeting Katie's eyes. "Besides, you might love it enough to stay."

Yikes. If Suzanne wanted to believe her own truths, Katie couldn't stop her. She followed Nana and the girls to the playroom, in Aaron's old room. Suzanne chatted about the toys she had pulled from the attic and the newer additions she bought. It all sounded like far too much for a short visit from the grandkids.

The moment she saw the room, overwhelm rolled through her like a wave pool starting in her stomach and ending in her chest. It looked...classic. Like a photoshoot backdrop. A daybed featured a trundle underneath, a small bookshelf held a row of books and several white rope baskets filled with toys. A dress stand held several princess dresses. A child-sized table offered art supplies freely at child-level—a certain recipe for disaster. One corner of the room featured a miniature nursery with baby dolls.

"Wow," Katie managed. "We travel with a bucket of toys," she laughed.

Suzanne clicked her tongue. "A bucket! These girls deserve the world."

There. The look Katie remembered from their previous visit all those years ago. Her mother-in-law's face expressed exactly how she felt about Katie's parenting. That disapproving look hid nothing. And Katie already knew she wasn't cut out for motherhood. She didn't need reminders. So despite her promises to keep in touch with the Kaminskis, they had slipped apart.

"They tend to make playthings from nearly anything," Katie said. "I love their creativity."

Suzanne clapped. "Well there's plenty to be creative with here!"

Josie dove into the princess dresses, while Sage stared at a basket of blocks.

Soon Josie had a running narrative entrancing both Suzanne and Tricia as she chattered all about her favorite princesses—largely based on the colors of their dresses.

"Jasmine is a worstest one, because her dress has pants," Josie explained, pulling dresses from the rack faster than Katie could re-hang them.

Suzanne laughed, following Josie's logic. "That's simply terrible, Josie. What about you, Sage? What's your favorite princess?"

Sage ignored her, deeply focused on lining up two building blocks now.

"She likes Wapunzel," Josie said. "Because Wapunzel wears purple."

"Is purple your favorite color, Sage?" Tricia asked.

Sage looked at Katie, then back at her blocks and pushed the top one a fraction of an inch to the left.

"It is," Katie answered. It might be wrong to admit, but Katie dreaded when others tried to talk to Sage. Did they think they would witness the magical moment when Sage decided to talk? They wouldn't. Instead, everyone would get to enjoy Sage's extreme shyness and the awkward silences in between.

A knock sounded on the doorframe and they turned to see William, barely poking around the edge. "Dinner's ready," he said.

Katie and Tricia followed William to the kitchen while Suzanne stayed behind to help Josie into a yellow princess dress.

"Does Sage ever talk?" Tricia asked in a low voice.

"Sometimes, at home. Only with me and Josie."

"Have you seen a speech therapist?" she asked.

"No, she can speak up if she wants something enough." Nothing was wrong with her daughter and Katie didn't care to talk about it. "So what are the best things to do here? Besides the beach, of course. I want to take the girls to something fun this week. Y'all have an aquarium, right?"

Tricia rolled with the change of topic, helping her build a list of things to do in Ridley Bay. It all felt like role-playing for Katie, trying to be the type of person who did family dinners. She hadn't been comfortable in this role with her own family, much less with her in-laws.

They settled around a large table. Suzanne even had booster seats for the girls, along with brightly colored plastic plates, sippy cups, and character forks and spoons. Katie eyed the table—a mouth-watering and truly southern spread of roast, potatoes, gravy, rolls, green beans, and not a single thing her children would likely eat.

"How was Birmingham?" JP asked, breaking through the dinner-time quiet.

Katie buttered rolls for the girls and rattled off her favorite things about their previous city. She praised the clientele and the gorgeous townhouse they had rented.

"What do the girls do while you work in other cities?" Tricia asked.

"Some places we have friends who help, or we can usually find a drop-in care place," Katie said. "We always make it work. That's a photography perk—I can schedule photoshoots whenever is best for me, and then do editing and social media after they go to bed."

She and Aaron had imagined it to be a perfect arrangement, allowing her to spend most of her time with the girls. That ideal hadn't panned out very well.

"Not much routine though," William said, in his quiet way.

"Do they do okay with so much change?" Suzanne asked. "I remember our boys hated change when they were young—Aaron especially. The day we moved the couch is infamous in our family." She laughed.

"That's the great thing," Katie said, brightly. "The girls are pretty flexible now. Josie sometimes throws a fit, but she gets over it fast. I think it's good for them."

"I wonder if Sage would come out of her shell a little with more consistency," Tricia said.

Katie cleared her throat, smiling. "She'll open up whenever she's ready." She didn't need parenting advice, especially not in front of Sage. And not from Tricia, who never had her own kids.

"Well, I know Suzanne would be happy to watch the girls if you want to stay in the area a little longer," Tricia said.

"Oh absolutely," Suzanne said. "And I bet you could find plenty of work here."

"Maybe so," Katie said with a smile. Truthfully, she had no idea where to go next. The openness both excited and bothered her. Any of Texas' larger cities could work. Her social media followers surprised her when she teased her coastal destination—apparently she had several fans even in Ridley Bay. It could be a fun place, if she didn't have the watchful eye of her mother-in-law here. If it didn't remind Katie every single second that Aaron should be the one here, handling all of this.

That thought itself revealed the problem with coming here. In the rest of America, she had handled everything on her own for three years, without giving it a second thought. But here, in Ridley Bay, the black hole she ran from got much closer.

Chapter Three

It cost Katie two gray hairs and a yogurt stain on her shirt to get to the church only twelve minutes late. She recognized the place from her one previous visit. Aaron's Uncle JP had helped plant the church and she and Aaron had promised to visit on their first Sunday. Aaron never made it, but Katie kept the promise alone—well, alone with infant twins in tow.

At one point in life, she and Aaron attended church regularly. But it hadn't been a big part of her life since his death. God hadn't done much for her lately, and she didn't need much from him. Plus, getting the twins ready for church proved to be as fun as eating nails.

The middle school where Grace Church met welcomed them with the smell of cleaning products and a faint whiff of preteen sweat. Faint strains of worship music came through the double doors straight ahead. Other than the greeter by the door, the hallway was empty. Just as Katie asked about childcare, Suzanne came around the corner.

"There you are!" she said, with a double-take as she saw the girls. She knelt for hugs, then stood to give Katie a polite side-hug. "The princess dress for church?" she asked. *Already judging.*

Josie still wore the princess dress she had borrowed from last night. Sage had dressed herself in a leopard-print top and zebra-patterned skirt over floral leggings. They were far from picture-perfect today.

Katie smiled as politely as possible. "I couldn't get her out of it." Did her words give away the fact Josie had slept in it?

"You look beautiful," Suzanne said, smiling down at Josie. "And I love your top, Sage."

Sage edged farther behind Katie, green eyes wide. "Thank you," Katie said for her. "She loves animals."

"Me too, sweetie," Suzanne said. "Well, do you want to use the childcare, or bring them into church with you?"

Katie about choked on her own spit. "Childcare," she said. Keeping her kids quiet for an hour would be the death of her. Besides, she desperately needed each little break she could get—they never lasted long enough.

Suzanne waved them down the hallway. "The childcare rooms are this way."

Katie tried to convince Suzanne to go ahead and grab a seat inside the auditorium. She declined. *Well. She signed up for this, then.*

"Katie, this is Ava, our pastor's daughter," Suzanne introduced when they reached the toddler room.

The young teen greeted the girls and Katie walked into the room with the girls held by each hand. Sage scooted herself to the far edge of the wall, to watch the other kids. Josie, however, sensed the coming separation and panicked. Her hand locked onto Katie's with a death grip. When Ava reached for her, Josie's legs gave out and she turned into a puddle of skin and bones. She let out a high-pitched scream.

"Oh my goodness," Suzanne said. "Should she stay with us?"

"She can't sit still for two minutes, much less an entire service," Katie said, above the din Josie created. "She'll get over this fast."

Katie scooped up her thrashing daughter. "She'll settle in a few minutes if you can wait it out."

"We've got it," Ava said, reaching for Josie. The other teen in the room stepped in to help as well. Together, they peeled Josie from Katie's arms like a leech. Josie managed to get a good grab on Katie's shirt, pulling it to the point of nearly indecent exposure. Three red claw marks marred her collarbone by the time they transferred her.

Katie and Suzanne walked back down the hallway to the auditorium, accompanied by the soundtrack of Josie's wild screams.

"She really has a hard time with that," Suzanne said.

Katie shrugged, trying to hold onto the happiness she shouldered for her entire little family. Neither of the girls contributed much. It all fell on Katie to wear a smile. "Separation anxiety is pretty normal for toddlers."

"At this age, still?"

"Yep," Katie said as brightly as possible. Being defensive wouldn't help. She needed a different read on Suzanne, a false one if necessary. *Nana* surely meant well. They had gotten along once. When Aaron was here. She mentally slapped herself. *Not that again.* She and Suzanne were perfectly fine.

They walked into the auditorium as a new worship song began. Katie followed Suzanne's lead through the dimly lit space to a spot on the left, near the front and next to William.

The lead pastor, Micah Sanford, spoke and Katie settled back to enjoy an hour of relative quiet, without small hands grabbing at her. It flew by, and when the service ended, the worship band sang another song before dismissing everyone.

Tricia found them, and she and Suzanne introduced her to another older couple. As a family member of the associate pastor, introductions slowed their progress out of the auditorium, but Katie didn't mind. She enjoyed the meet-and-greets.

They eventually gravitated toward the doors to exit the auditorium. JP and Micah stood at the doors shaking hands and JP reintroduced her to Micah—who, to his credit, remembered her.

A wail sounded from down the hall, with a uniquely Josie tune to it. She must have seen other parents retrieving their children. Katie tried to edge her way around the group in the doorway, but JP landed a hand on her shoulder and waved someone over with his other hand.

"Isaac," JP called. "This is my niece I told you about."

Katie turned, with a smile ready, and her eyes landed on an apparition. All the sounds around her disappeared, her smile froze into place, and her heart did the same swoop her stomach did on roller coasters. *Impossible.*

The past crashed into the present with such force, her mind scrambled to make sense of it. He couldn't be here. It couldn't be him. Yet... it was.

Isaac freaking Torres. He stutter-stepped and uncertainty flickered across his face too.

"Isaac, this is Katie. Katie, Isaac," JP continued introductions, unaware they were unnecessary.

His face, his name, so familiar, but in the wrong place. In Ridley Bay. In a *church.* She didn't know what to do. She simultaneously wanted to hug him like an old friend and run away with a paper bag over her head.

A decade had done nothing to age him. If anything, he improved with time, the way some men do, like a good pair of jeans. He still stood a few inches too tall and too wide for any man, with dark hair, only an inch longer than his previous military cut, and a new stubble beard.

The sounds around them came sweeping back in and Katie realized they were caught in a stare-off. She forced a handshake which he returned like a limp rope. "Isaac Torres." She had to laugh; what other option did she have?

Her name was a shape on his lips more than a sound. "Katelyn Lewis."

Ten years disappeared and the hand in hers suddenly felt like fire. She dropped her hands and laced her fingers together, subtly pinching herself. Could that really wake someone from a dream?

It didn't work. He still stood there. Not a ghost. Not a dream. Alive and in the flesh. "Kaminski," she corrected. His eyes locked with hers, dark as the night and intense as ever.

"Wait, do you two know each other?" JP asked.

Isaac's gaze drifted over her face, down her body, back up again. Katie straightened her back, cringing internally. The years hadn't been as kind to her as to him. A yogurt stain sat somewhere on her shirt.

"Sort of," Katie said. "I think we met back in Fairbanks, right?" She knew exactly where they met. She could pick out the very barstool.

"Right," he said. A line on his shirt pulled the wrong way at his hip—a concealed weapon. A small earbud sat in his left ear—his bad one. A tiny wire wove from the earbud into his shirt. Not a hearing aid, a radio. *Security?* That could help explain his presence in a church.

"Nearly ten years ago, if you can believe it," Katie added.

"Wow, what a crazy coincidence," JP said. More like a crazy trick. From heaven or hell though, she couldn't decide. JP looked between them both. "I guess you didn't know Aaron then."

Isaac stood at a slight angle, with his right side closer to them. "No," he said. Still a man of few words.

"Isaac moved soon after we met and we lost touch," Katie added. "I met Aaron a couple years later."

A scream from down the hall pierced the air and Isaac's eyes darted past Katie. She turned to it. "And that bloodcurdling sound is my cue. I'd better go get her."

Then she risked one more look at Isaac, still as a statue, laser focus locked on her. "I guess I'll see you later." *You.* A person she had never expected to see again in her life. She swallowed hard and turned.

Walking too fast down the hallway toward the children's rooms, Katie pinched her hand again. *What just happened?* She slowed as she rounded the corner, out of his line of sight, and pressed the back of her hand to her face. Her fingers cooled her cheeks as she forced herself to calm down. Her head felt like a soda can someone had shaken and she needed to crack it open and release the pressure. A laugh is what came out.

"Wrong ghost," she whispered, shaking her head. She had expected to find Aaron haunting this city. Not a ghost from an even more distant past, and certainly not her own past.

·   ·   ·

"We lost touch."

Liar.

Isaac hated being surprised. He saw every person who came in and out of this church. And yet, somehow, the woman who had slipped in and out of his life all those years ago had slipped through the doors today without him ever noticing. He cursed himself. *Critical error.*

His mind refused to accept it. This could not be Katelyn Lewis. He should have known if Katie entered the building—heck, the town.

JP had talked about his nephew's tragic death. He talked about his nephew's widow coming to visit, and how excited they were to see her two little girls. Never in Isaac's life would he have pictured Katie's face on that person. The woman he knew ten years ago swore she would never marry or have children.

Liar. Like all the others.

"How did you and Katie meet?" JP asked. They still stood in the doorway, Isaac staring down the hallway where Katie had disappeared.

"Mutual friends," Isaac said, dismissing the conversation with a pat on JP's shoulder. "Be right back."

Stepping outside, Isaac mentally shook himself. One critical error didn't have to be his undoing. He was a professional, and he had a job to do. Honestly, he would do anything right now to distract himself from Katie's sudden appearance.

Isaac worked here most Sundays, ever since a church shooting in rural Texas two years ago prompted nearly every church in the state to hire security. He had hours to fill in between shifts with the police department. It had been a good gig until now, the moment he found out *she* was the associate pastor's niece.

His mind wanted to reel at the revelation, at the three thousand miles and ten years that should have made this moment impossible, but he stopped it and forced himself to focus on a quick walk through the parking lot.

The sun glinted off car hoods and shiny tar cracks in the asphalt. Nothing looked out of place today, except for a white Lexus SUV with out-of-state plates, an inch-thick layer of dirt, and an inspection sticker a year past its expiration date. An expensive car should have legal tags, unless they were hiding something. He'd run the plates while on active duty tomorrow.

Isaac turned back to the building at exactly the wrong moment. Katie exited, with two small backpacks looped on her arms and a little girl in each hand. Twins, judging by size, though they looked nothing like each other or Katie. One had deep red hair, the other sported platinum blonde.

Before he could take a roundabout path to miss her, the blonde tripped and splayed onto the asphalt, pulling Katie's arm down with her. A sparkly backpack plopped on top of the child, knocking a metal water bottle into her head, like a bad game of Jenga. A high-pitched scream ripped through the air.

Isaac took two steps in the other direction before he felt the sting of his mother's wrath coming all the way from Phoenix. She had raised four boys with old-school manners and a wooden spoon in hand. Cursing his own upbringing, he about-faced and strode toward the miniature pileup. He waved a truck down another aisle instead of its current moronic attempt to squeeze past the Katie-sized disaster.

Katie mumbled a string of frustrated syllables as she dusted off the toddler. The redhead darted back to the safety of the sidewalk and watched in silence. Isaac grabbed the roll-away water bottle and scooped stray coloring pages and a unicorn dress back into the bag.

Katie didn't seem to see him as she grabbed the backpack from his hands and her eyes darted around the parking lot. "Sage?" she shouted.

Isaac pointed behind her. "Sidewalk."

Katie hauled the blonde onto her hip, waved an apology to the truck, and crossed back to her other daughter.

Her daughter.

He still couldn't reconcile that. This couldn't be the Katie he once knew. Yet, it was. Olive skin tone, black hair—cut to her shoulders now—and almond-shaped green eyes. With a squared-off jaw and petite features, she could have had a modeling career if it weren't for her diminutive height.

Katie lectured the redhead about running away, as if she had done anything wrong by retreating to the sidewalk. The redhead ignored her mother, staring at Isaac instead, with wide eyes. Both little girls had those same green eyes—their only resemblance to their mother. He tried a smile but she didn't return it.

"If you could learn how to walk, this wouldn't be so hard," Katie said to the blonde.

The harsh tone didn't sound like the Katie he once knew, though she had always said she lacked any maternal genes. "Need help?" he asked, interrupting her tirade and apparently alerting her to his presence.

She spun on him, eyes wide, like the redhead's. "Isaac."

"Katie." That's about as far as their conversations would be going today. Names, again and again, because neither of them could believe it.

Her eyes flicked from his to the girls and back again. "Here." She passed the two pink backpacks to him. With the blonde on one hip and the redhead held firmly by the other hand, she crossed the parking lot, knowing he would follow.

And he did, holding the extremely feminine backpacks a solid foot from his body. Not because his ego was particularly fragile, but he had nieces and a healthy fear of glitter. Katie led them to the white Lexus. No need to run the plates, after all. It belonged to a frazzled liar, not a drug dealer.

Isaac waited silently while she opened the car door—a kids cup and a pink sandal fell out—and buckled in the redhead and the protesting blonde. With her back to him, she sighed and her shoulders dropped before she squared up and turned to face him, a wide grin pasted on her face.

"Small world, huh?" she asked.

"Very."

Her eyes dropped to the backpacks and she suddenly laughed. "Are you worried the backpacks clash with your outfit?"

His jaw flexed.

"Pink glitter would really help soften your all-black look." Katie's gaze dragged over him. "Are you going for plainclothes or bouncer?"

He didn't answer.

"You're not in the army anymore."

He handed her the backpacks. "Police."

"Ah. Thank you, Officer Torres. Sorry about Josie, she's got some lungs on her. I think she'll make an excellent singer one day." She laughed at herself.

Little pitchy. Isaac kept his remarks to himself. They weren't in their twenties anymore, and he wasn't interested anymore. He needed to get back to the nearly-emptied school building and help lock up. Isaac nodded to her. "Katie," he said, a brief farewell.

"Good to see you again," she said.

He didn't answer. Because he didn't agree.

Chapter Four

The day shift kept Isaac busy in the most mundane ways—welfare checks, minor crime reports, and managing disputes between unreasonable adults. Isaac preferred second shift, but thanks to staffing shortages, nobody got the shifts they wanted anymore. At least days were easier on the body than night shift. He had just finished a three-month rotation on nights and it got harder every year after thirty. The younger guys handled it better, but Isaac wasn't about to admit he was getting old.

A call from a half-blind elderly man pushed his lunch break late, but Isaac finally met up with Officer Kingston at their usual burger spot.

"He was convinced someone had stolen his car from the grocery store parking lot," Isaac said, around a bite of burger. "Even when we found the stupid car, he wanted to file a report because he said someone moved it."

Kingston laughed and wadded up a paper wrapper. "Don't you get sick of this stuff? I swear, if I didn't already have some seniority here I'd move to a bigger city. The last SWAT call out was a month ago."

Isaac nodded. They were both on the SWAT team, but in Ridley Bay, it wasn't a dedicated team. Aside from the occasional training or warrant arrest, they spent most of their time on regular patrol. Isaac didn't mind it as much as Kingston. Kingston had a death wish and it would end him one day.

"Did you hear they're talking about redistributing the SWAT resources?" Kingston asked.

Their combined unit already covered multiple counties across the gulf coast. "They can't. We're the second closest team to the border."

"Second, though."

"Have you seen those guys?" he asked in a flat tone.

Kingston snorted. "The Ken dolls?"

Isaac dipped his head. "We're the first actual SWAT team."

"Let's hope this town gets a little more interesting to justify us."

"Is that really something to hope for?"

"Absolutely." Kingston lived for this. He spent every off hour with other officers, at every happy hour, every hangout.

Isaac had been like him once. The police force replaced the brotherhood he'd had in the army. But once he got engaged to Lauren, he started going home after every shift. By the time his marriage ended, he couldn't go back to those hangouts. He felt old and dissatisfied with those guys. So he drove home every day to an empty house.

A pretty brunette stopped by their table. "Are you guys police officers?" she asked in a high-pitched voice.

"No, this is Halloween prep," Isaac answered, glancing at his uniform.

Kingston shot him a Cheshire cat grin before turning his full attention to the girl, who had to be two decades younger than them. "Don't mind him, he gets rocks every year."

She laughed, tossed her hair back, and thanked them for their work. Kingston took over, smiling and chatting with her. Isaac had crossed paths with a few badge-chasing women and avoided them like the plague. There were plenty of other guys happy to soak up the attention. Kingston was one of them. The kind of guy who enjoyed the thrills of police work too much, and sought adrenaline in too many beds. A brotherhood wasn't necessarily filled with good guys.

Isaac's friend, and a former cop, Penn had once warned him against identifying with it too much and promised a better community at Grace Church. It was partly why Isaac took the security job there. And why he went to things like Tuesday Bible studies, regardless of his own opinions on the Bible. Penn told him it would be better for his marriage. Ironically, Isaac didn't need the advice. Lauren did.

When the girl moved on, Kingston and Isaac talked baseball for a while. Isaac stuck with his hometown team from Phoenix, while Kingston was a Houston guy. They ribbed each other for a bit before a radio call came in about a three-car pileup on the edge of town. They tossed their trash and headed for their cars.

The universe seemed intent on proving him wrong about the monotony of the day shift that day. A traffic stop turned into a warrant arrest, and Isaac hadn't even finished writing the report for it when someone called in a nasty car accident on the highway. The driver hadn't bothered to buckle her two kids. Isaac hated working wrecks with kids. He hated being one of the first officers there, and the eternal wait for the ambulance.

His shift ran late, and when he finally pulled onto his street, the lights were off in most of the houses, except for Vera's. His elderly neighbor had a habit of falling asleep in her recliner, with all the lights on and the television blaring.

Isaac grabbed the mail on his way in. He hooked his keys inside the door and flipped on the lights. He didn't judge Vera for sleeping with the lights on. After some shifts, he did the same. Some nights he couldn't close his eyes without seeing the same gruesome images over and over. Incidents with kids always seared into his brain like a branding iron.

Why couldn't people just use car seats? Yes, kids cried in the car. *Get some earplugs,* he wanted to shout at them. He always ticketed drivers who didn't buckle their kids. But it didn't matter. Some kids would still suffer; some would die. It all felt so powerless, so pointless.

He poured himself a bowl of cereal and flicked through the mail. Advertisement. Car warranty alert. Electric bill. A letter from his ten-year-old nephew. He slid the envelope open. He had ten nieces and nephews, one of whom had appointed Isaac his pen pal for a school project. Apparently writing letters was an old-school skill they taught for history's sake.

Isaac scanned the letter and the sloppy handwriting even worse than his own. His nephew Crew outlined the gritty details of fourth grade flag football and the politics of team captains who chose all the wrong players. He stuck it to the fridge. He'd write him back before the school deadline. His brother Cristian said the cop stuff in his last letter gave the kid a few popularity points.

A creak sounded in the house and Isaac felt every nerve stiffen. He listened for another second, like a kid scared of the dark. The old house made too many sounds. Every time, he wished he had a dog to blame them all on. He had mentally picked and named one a dozen times. But he couldn't keep a dog with the shifts he worked. He couldn't keep a wife, either. So it was just him and this creaky house.

Isaac set his cereal bowl in the sink and leaned over it for a minute, dropping his head, shoulders hunched, his ears ringing. Maybe he should tell his nephew the truth: Isaac would never wish this job on anyone he loved.

His phone buzzed with another text from his oldest brother, Andres—the third text today. Isaac picked up the phone and called for an update on Mom.

"How's she feeling?" he asked.

"She won't eat," Andres said. "She's got mouth ulcers from the chemo, I guess. She says everything hurts or tastes bad. Dad's frustrated, so we're taking over for now. Mia cooks extra for dinner and I take it over every couple of days."

"Thanks for doing that, man."

"Have to. You and Oscar bailed out."

Andres and Cristian, the oldest two, had stayed in Phoenix. Isaac and their third brother, Oscar, had both landed in Texas. Now Andres and Cristian, along with their wives, took on the brunt of supporting their mom through breast cancer. And they each had a bunch of kids to take care of too.

"Didn't mean to. I moved here way before cancer showed up."

"Yeah I know, I'm messing with you. I don't mind doing it. I did hear the Phoenix Police Department is hiring though."

"I don't think big city PD is for me." Ridley Bay wasn't exactly a small town, but it certainly had less drama than a city like Phoenix. Besides, Isaac was a third of the way to retirement here and he didn't have time to start over again.

"So you stayed in the same city as your ex. Do you ever run into her?"

Isaac puffed out a breath. Being the only brother with a failed marriage wasn't exactly a badge of honor. "Nah. Every officer knows her, and her car."

Andres laughed. "How many tickets have they given her on the witch broom?"

Isaac grinned. "Only a couple. Mostly it helps me stay out of her path."

"Good. If mom makes it out your way again, Lauren might need a security detail."

It didn't matter that he was thirty-nine, or that his mother had hit seventy-two, the woman was fiercely protective of her youngest son. And she didn't know the half of what Lauren had done.

Isaac listened to more updates on Mom's treatments, wishing he could offer something. Some of his family believed in prayers, but Isaac didn't. "Do you think Mom's still awake?" he asked. "I should probably call her."

"You probably should. But no, she goes to bed early most days."

"I'm off tomorrow, I'll call her."

When they ended the phone call, Isaac leaned against the kitchen counter, looking out the window at Vera's house. The elderly woman had one adult son in Miami who never visited. As much as Isaac disliked that, he didn't do much better himself. He tried to balance out the scales by helping Vera when he could, while his brothers took care of his own mother.

Before heading to his room, Isaac ordered a book to be shipped to his parents' house. Mom always asked for police thrillers—anything that kept the cop alive and had clean language. She wanted to know more about Isaac's job and claimed he didn't talk enough, so she learned about it through reading.

Isaac ordered another for himself. He wouldn't normally spend his off time reading about his own work, but they had formed their own little book club in which he had to answer all of her "was this realistic?" questions. "They left out all the paperwork," was his typical review. And they made police work sound more exciting than the reality. More heroic. Most of his days were either boring or depressing.

In the shower, he scrubbed his skin raw, but somehow he could still smell gasoline and blood.

•　　•　　•

When Isaac woke, the dull thumping of Vera's television penetrated the thin walls of their houses. He hadn't slept well, though he rarely did. Pulling on athletic shorts and a black *Ridley Bay Police Department* shirt, he headed out the door for a run. His chest pack multitasked as a weighted vest, hydration, and a place to stash the handgun he never left behind. He never knew when he'd find another fan of the police.

After a slow start, Isaac worked his way back into his regular pace. At mile four, he reached the bay and turned back around. Running worked wonders for clearing his mind.

Once he had showered and smelled better, Isaac headed over to Vera's house. All the lights were still on.

He knocked loudly on the door and announced his name. Then he waited two long minutes as she shuffled to the door.

She answered with a smile, her thinning white hair twisted into a pink clip. "Isaac, what are you doing here? Come in, come in." She waved her cane toward the living room. "Why aren't you out there keeping our streets safe?"

"I'm off today." His eyes swept over the house. Vera still took good care of herself and her home. She was the dutiful, rhythmic kind of person who would dust the shelves long after she forgot her own name—rather like his mother, though at least a decade older. "Can I do anything for you while I'm off? I'm planning to mow later and I'll get your yard too."

She sat in her recliner and motioned for him to sit too. "You can talk to a lonely old woman, that's what you can do."

Vera could talk for hours. Isaac settled onto the couch and asked about her son, preparing himself to hear the same stories again—about her son as a child, about her husband, his tenured career as a university professor, and that cruise they once took to the Bahamas.

Vera praised her son's wonderful accomplishments in advertising. The man was her pride and joy, and she never said a bad word about his failure to visit, other than occasionally admitting she missed him. Isaac wondered if the man knew about his mother's slow and steady mental decline.

"Have you talked to him recently?"

"We talked just the other day. We had the longest chat on the phone. He has a baby now, you know? A little girl."

Isaac had heard about the baby girl for a couple years now. There was no telling when they had last talked.

"Oh, enough about me," Vera said, shushing herself and waving her hand again. "How is your wife doing? Why don't you bring her over?"

They had been divorced for two years, though their marriage really ended a year before the divorce. It happened around the time Vera's symptoms worsened and she had frozen them in her mind as a couple.

"We got divorced," Isaac said. He didn't want to pander to a false reality, but he never pointed out her forgetfulness either.

Vera's hand fluttered to her mouth. "Oh, dear. Now why would you go and do a thing like that?"

Isaac grinned at her shock, every time. He had tried out a few replies but preferred a simple, truthful answer that justified some of his anger. "She cheated on me." It happened after the original problem. But he didn't like to explain that one.

She gasped. "No!"

Isaac nodded. "Yes."

Vera shook her head, absolutely scandalized. "Oh dear, I'm so sorry. You'll find someone better, I know it."

Isaac laughed and scratched at the stubble on the side of his face. "Nah, I think I like being alone."

Vera clicked her tongue. "No, you do not. Nobody likes being alone."

"What do you mean? You and I are both on our own and doing fine."

Vera shook her head as tears sprang to her eyes. "Young man, we are not fine and you know it."

Isaac frowned. He enjoyed their good-natured ribbing and hearing her old stories again and again. But he didn't particularly care for this.

"You are too good of a catch to give up just yet," Vera said. "You have to try again. You'll get it right next time."

"I seem to only pick the bad ones," Isaac said, with a wry smile.

"Well, you bring the next one to me and I'll let you know if she's good or not." Vera tapped her head. "God gave me the mind for that sort of thing."

"He gave you a good one, Ms. Vera," Isaac said as he stood and gathered a couple of dirty dishes in the living room. He meant it, despite the hints of dementia. He had seen elderly people become wretched as they lost control over their minds and bodies. Few stayed as positive as Vera. "I better get to the yards. You still have my number, right?"

She waved him off with a pshaw. "Yes, yes, but I'm the wrong age. You ought to be giving your number to ladies a bit younger than me."

Isaac laughed. "Call me if you need anything." He liked to offer the promise, though he knew it might be empty.

"You'll be in my front yard if I need anything."

"For now, yes." But he wouldn't always be around. If she ever did call, he would probably be at work. Lauren loved to remind him of that.

Chapter Five

Josie had been begging to go to the beach ever since they first arrived, so Monday morning they set out with towels, swimsuits, beach toys, and camera in hand. Their rental had a nice view of the bay—the area Aaron had once described as a kid-friendly favorite, with small, shallow waves. Katie wanted better pictures though, and headed out of town toward an island with more wild, rugged beaches.

After crossing a large bridge, they reached a quiet beach with only a couple of families around the area. Mild, humid weather made it a decent day for an autumn swim. Katie snapped on life jackets and Josie took off, running to the water. The first wave sent her screaming and running back to her mother. Sage put her hands over her ears and stood back by the car while Katie set up their spot.

Using sand, water toys, and a bag of snacks as weights, Katie pinned down the picnic blanket against the never-ending wind. Sage took a seat on the blanket. Then Katie chased Josie back and forth between the waves for a few minutes, until Josie tried to turn it into a game of splashing muddy sand at each other. Not Katie's favorite.

She headed back to Sage's side, where the little girl worked on a sandcastle, but Josie followed. Now it turned into a game of keep-away between the girls. Josie begged and screamed to tear the castle down while Sage let out her own wails anytime Josie got close. There was never enough of Katie to keep everyone happy. She always had to choose between kids. And as the louder and more persistent twin, Josie got more attention.

Katie built small sandcastles for Josie to smash, to keep Sage's castle safe. The bigger Katie's reaction, the harder Josie laughed. So she dramatically cried for every bucket of sand lost to the stomp of a toddler. Until one stomp, when the wind caught the sand and tossed it into Josie's face. She screeched and tried to wipe it away, smearing sandy hands over her eyes. The howling started and Katie could feel frustration building.

"Seriously, Jojo," Katie mumbled, pouring water onto her own hands and trying to clean Josie's face.

The second she let go of her daughter, Josie stormed over to Sage's sandcastle and smashed it before anyone could stop her. Sage let out a scream and pushed Josie back.

"Sage!" Katie snapped. She got to the girls and grabbed one in each hand. "What is wrong with you? Don't push your sister."

Sage tried to wipe away her tears, ending up in the same sandy predicament Katie had just rescued Josie from. Katie groaned. "You guys make everything miserable." She swiped a towel across Sage's face.

Sage turned and pointed to the sandcastle.

"I know, baby," Katie said. "Build another one. Make it better."

Sage didn't try again; she sat on her towel while Josie played at the edge of the water. Katie didn't have time for moping. She grabbed her camera and decided to take a few shots instead.

Behind the lens, the tightness around her throat began to loosen. In photographer mode, she didn't mind the childish antics—she could turn them into something photo-worthy. Splashing water, wind-whipped smiles, and closeups on dimpled, sandy hands—she could make it all feel magical, instead of like a suffocating weight on her chest.

Katie wondered if one day the girls would remember it as magical, if they remembered anything at all. Would they be like Katie and forget it all? That might be for the best. But Katie wanted someone to know about these moments—someone to share a memory with. So she posted it all online. A million strangers held these memories with her. A million strangers took Aaron's place.

She coaxed the girls back into playing together and grabbed a few sweet photos of them holding hands. Josie even managed to get Sage to the water's edge, and they both dipped their toes in.

It didn't last long. Two moms and a group of kids showed up at the beach and Josie darted off to meet the new friends. Katie returned her camera to its bag and stood in between the girls, trying to watch them both.

Over the next few minutes, the other moms drifted closer to Katie. It certainly wasn't her own doing.

"Are they twins?" one of the moms asked. She wore athletic clothes and a baseball cap.

The other mom wore a wide-brimmed hat and a dress flowing over a pregnant belly. Katie looked away from her and focused on the athletic mom. "They are," Katie said with a smile. She introduced herself and her kids, explaining they were just in town for a few days.

"Where are you from?" asked Sundress Mom, one hand on top of her belly.

"We lived in Baton Rouge for a while," Katie said, her eyes on the girls. "But we've traveled all over the south the last few years."

"I can't imagine all that travel with littles," said Workout Mom. "My kids cry on a drive to the grocery store."

Katie laughed. "Movies in the car help."

"Really? We didn't start any screen time until ours were older," said Sundress Mom.

"Ah." Katie shaded her face with one hand, watching Josie splash in the waves and Sage bury animal toys in the sand. This is why she didn't do mom friends. Too many opinions. Too many babies. "Well, if it's between screens or screaming in the car, I'll choose my sanity."

"A movie in the car makes sense," said Workout Mom. "Some people use it as a babysitter, you know?"

Katie laughed. If screens could babysit, she would have saved lots of money over the last few years. "Oh yeah. I can leave them for days at a time with the television and a bag of fruit snacks."

Workout Mom frowned and Sundress Mom narrowed her eyes. "You're joking, right?"

Katie arched an eyebrow. Apparently the sense of humor in Ridley Bay ran low. She pointed to Josie. "That kid would burn the house down if left alone for three seconds. Of course I'm joking."

"What about her?" Workout Mom asked about Sage. "She seems calm."

Sage stood a few awkward yards from the group of kids playing in the water, watching them. Social situations were not her forte. "She is. She'd probably be fine on her own. Maybe better off."

The women switched to spouting off tips for getting a few seconds to oneself with little kids in the house. Tips that avoided screens, and almost all required a husband. Katie excused herself to check on Sage. She didn't fit into those circles.

Thanks to her father's complexion, Sage's nose already sported a new shade of pink. Katie reapplied sunscreen and dug up the ocean animal toys Sage had buried around their blanket, ignoring Sage's protests.

"Is that all of them?" Katie asked.

Sage shook her head, silent tears on her cheeks.

"Will you help me find them? Or are they staying here?"

Sage stomped her foot. "Stay."

"Sage, we're going to run out if you keep burying them." It happened at parks. In gardens. In trash cans. Sage was worse than a dog with a bone.

Katie found a couple more before giving up. Soon she pried Josie away from the friends she had found and piled the sandy crew into the car. Hopefully the beach had exhausted the girls enough to earn a solid hour or two of nap time. If not, she might hire her favorite babysitter, the television.

Katie sighed and glanced at the camera bag in the front seat. It held proof of a lovely visit to the beach. She relied on that. This could be a good week, she just had to see it that way.

Chapter Six

Suzanne and William invited Katie to join them at the lead pastor's house on Tuesday for a Bible study, and she rarely declined invitations. Katie arrived at Micah Sanford's house ten minutes late, and it took at least another five to get the girls out of the car. Somehow, they made it here without Josie's shoes. Sighing in surrender, Katie headed in with Josie on her hip and Sage held by the other hand.

Micah's wife, Rebecca, greeted her at the front door and Suzanne joined her, ushering Katie inside. The moment she walked into the living room, her eyes caught Isaac and her heart jumped. He stood in the far corner of the room, talking to another man and eyeing her above his glass of iced tea. His eyes darted away the second she spotted him, apparently still feeling as antagonistic as he had on Sunday.

She hadn't expected to see him here—a Bible study didn't need security. Was he here of his own free will? Before she could pester him with questions, Rebecca and Suzanne began parading her around the room for introductions. She greeted a dozen people with smiles, introducing her girls and nodding along to all the gushing over their cuteness. *Just wait until you see the fits they can throw.*

Katie met a couple of other young women—Cora, freshly out of college, and Brielle, who seemed younger than Katie but was probably close in age. Brielle hadn't carried twins, likely enjoyed a full night of sleep most nights, and wore clothes that had been updated sometime in the last three years. Toddlers aged Katie.

She stepped away from them at the same moment a woman walked in from the backyard with warm, brown skin and curly black hair that fanned around her face. "Hi! You're new," she said, with a bright smile and a bounce in her step. "I'm Zoe." She stuck a hand out, fingernails painted lime green.

Katie liked her immediately. "Katie. It's nice to meet you."

"And who are these beauties?" Zoe asked, smiling at the girls.

"This is Josie, and this is Sage." Katie tried to gesture to the girl hiding behind her leg.

Zoe squatted down. "My daughter has a unicorn dress *just* like yours, Josie. She'll be so excited to meet some new friends." She stood again. "I have four, they're all running around in the backyard to get their crazies out before dinner. They're ten, seven, four, and one."

"Wow, four? I can't imagine. I only have two and feel like they're about to destroy my sanity."

"Oh, well, go ahead and let that go. Then parenting gets easier."

"Thanks for the tip," Katie said, laughing. "I'll try it out."

Katie followed Zoe outside, where Josie joined in a game of tag (barefoot), while Sage sat on the porch and watched. Micah's daughter Ava held a chubby, honey-toned baby who hopped out of her arms and waddled up to her mother. Zoe lifted her and pointed out her kids, naming them off. "That's Landon, Lincoln, Lainey, and this is Serena."

"Ran out of L names?" Katie asked.

Zoe laughed. "We're in the process of adopting her, so we didn't get to pick."

Serena had a different look, but she still fit into the family. Before Katie could ask, Zoe explained. "My cousin lost custody, permanently. The whole situation is sad, but we're grateful to have this sweet girl."

"Wow. And even with three kids, you took her in. Good for you."

Zoe nuzzled the little girl. "Look at this chub. I have all the baby fever."

Katie laughed. She had nothing to say. Babies only reminded Katie of the worst year of her life.

The door behind them opened and Zoe's husband walked out. Zoe introduced him as Penn and Katie recognized him as the same man speaking with Isaac earlier. He sported an academic look, with a shaved head, tawny beard, and square glasses. But he carried himself like a cop.

From what she saw in her stepfather, a detective, law enforcement officers never lost that.

"What do you do?" Katie asked.

"I teach criminal justice at the local university." *Academic, check.*

"Oh, wow. That sounds interesting. Do you work with the police department any?"

"Yeah, I was a police officer up until a couple years ago. I stay in touch with them."

There. Her instincts about people continued to serve her well. "Thanks for your service."

"Did you meet Isaac?" Zoe asked. "He's a police officer too."

"Oh yes, we met on Sunday, for the second time. We actually met a long time ago in Fairbanks. Small world, right?" She had been in college, he had been in the army, fresh off a deployment. And she had fallen fast and hard for him. Then life brought that chapter to a quick close. He moved to a fort in Texas, and she graduated and moved to Louisiana. And yes, she had ended things over the phone and it wasn't pretty, but that didn't seem worthy of the cold shoulder treatment he gave her now.

"Fairbanks? Like, Alaska?" Zoe asked.

Katie grinned. "Alaska. There are actually people up there." And Katie never wanted to go back.

"I didn't know Isaac was ever in Alaska," Zoe said to Penn.

"I forgot." Penn shrugged. "You know how much he talks about himself."

Katie laughed. "True. I'm surprised to see him here tonight. Is he a Christian now?"

Penn and Zoe exchanged a quick glance. Penn shook his head. "Nah, he's just smart enough to come for the free food."

Katie's heart sank a bit. Before she could give it a second thought, Micah gathered everyone for a quick prayer and they soon settled into a potluck dinner together. Isaac took a seat in another room with a few other people, while Katie, the Kaminskis, and Zoe's crew filled the dining room.

Zoe peppered her with questions about bears and frostbite and dark winters. "Did you grow up there?" Zoe asked.

"In Juneau," Katie said. "I went to Fairbanks for college."

Her stepfather had offered to pay for university anywhere in the state. She went as far as she could. The seventeen-hour drive to Fairbanks guaranteed her mother would never attempt a visit with six kids ages eight and under.

"Then you came to the south because you realized humans need the sun to survive?"

Katie laughed. "All the fuss about the heat made me curious, so I found a photography job with a marketing firm in Baton Rouge." She wanted to get as far from Alaska as possible.

"That's where she met Aaron," Suzanne said, joining in.

Katie nodded. "At church." Aaron had gone to college in Baton Rouge and stayed in the city for an internship which turned into a job.

By the end of dinner, Zoe knew most of Katie's story and Katie had learned a thing or two about her as well.

Micah's daughter Ava gathered kids to head upstairs so the adults could do their Bible study. Ava carried Serena while Zoe's other kids and Sage followed quietly and dutifully. Josie clung to Katie, as she carried her upstairs after the others.

"Come on, Jojo," Katie said as they reached the play area the Sanfords had set up. "You remember Ava, from church on Sunday." She tried to engage Josie in a coloring book, but as soon as she stood, her daughter clung to her knees again.

"She calmed down quickly on Sunday," Ava said, walking over to her. "Why don't we try it for a few minutes today?"

"Okay, let me know if you need help," Katie said.

"I'm sure you'll hear if we do." Ava grinned.

"True," Katie said, returning her smile.

Ava situated Josie on her lap and distracted her with the toys while Katie slunk away. Only two steps down, she heard Josie's scream pierce the air. Katie hurried downstairs, where she found a living room full of adults, almost all of which had their eyes on her—all except Isaac. Perhaps she should have anticipated a cold welcome, if she had ever imagined seeing him again. But she hadn't.

"I'm guessing that's yours, not mine," Zoe said.

"Yeah, you know, I got the buy-one-get-one-free special and I'm pretty sure I got a defective model. Terrible return policy though." Most of the group smiled or chuckled, except for Isaac and Suzanne. "She should settle down in a minute. If not, I'll get her. Sorry for the interruption."

"No problem," Micah said, in the way someone does when they literally don't have problems. Then he led another round of introductions for Katie's sake. She had already memorized almost everyone's names, but enjoyed a chance to review.

The only part of introductions Katie disliked was when the word "widow" came up and she got pitying sighs and sad eyes. On her turn, she skimmed through with the lightest tone possible. "I'm William and Suzanne's daughter-in-law. My husband—their son—died about three years ago. The girls and I travel for my photography now and we are super excited to be visiting the beach. Huge thanks to Zoe for suggesting the wetlands too, I am definitely adding that to my list."

The quick redirect kept pitying glances away and Katie had gladly mastered the art of it. Though death might be the most universal human experience, nobody knew what to do when it came up. Grief was a spectator sport, and people loved to watch from the sidelines with morbid curiosity. Katie found a bright and light disposition earned far more friends than the sad widow title ever could.

Soon the group finished introductions and they could still hear Josie crying. "Maybe Nana can help," Suzanne said, patting Katie's knee and heading upstairs.

She doubted it. Josie didn't know Nana well enough to care. But sure enough, a few minutes later, all had quieted upstairs. Katie settled in, finally not the only one responsible for Josie. A weight lifted off her shoulders.

Micah led a discussion about prayer and Katie jumped in at times with the right answers or a funny story. Her own ease here surprised her a bit. Even after all this time, she could easily step back into it.

Growing up, Katie's stepfather forced her to go to church every Sunday and Wednesday. Despite her dutiful teenage protests, she enjoyed it and got saved at fifteen. Though she hadn't been in church much lately, she still believed.

"Prayers don't all get answered," William said, thumping his Bible against his knee. "We prayed nonstop for three days for Aaron and he didn't make it."

Katie grimaced inwardly. She didn't want to go there. She had already been once and clawed her way out of it. "But prayers can be answered in other ways," she said, deflecting. "It's better to focus on that."

"Like what ways?" Micah asked.

She hadn't expected to be questioned; he should have just agreed. Katie gave whatever random answers popped into her mind. "I mean, I guess it was God's plan for Aaron, right? So it must be okay. The girls and I are fine. We've traveled and seen new places. It's all worked out." She didn't believe anything she said.

"That's a positive outlook," Micah said in a measured tone.

Katie laughed. "Why not stay positive?"

"Joy is a great thing, if we're finding it at the feet of Christ," Micah said. "But sometimes to get there, we have to bring him our sorrow first."

She wasn't sure she understood what he meant, but Zoe saved her and cut in with her own thoughts. *Thank goodness.* Katie nearly offered to stand up and juggle for the sake of a distraction. Anything but this.

•   •   •

Isaac didn't go on Tuesdays for the Bible study. He went for the free dinner. Rebecca was a fantastic cook and always sent him home with a box of leftovers. Isaac had never put much effort into learning how to cook. He had relied on mess halls in the military and microwave dinners ever since. He only stayed for the Bible study part to be polite.

When the group ended, Ava brought the kids downstairs. The blonde toddler seemed to have realigned her attachment to Ava and had no interest in Katie. The redhead made a beeline for an armchair in the corner of the room with a book in hand. Honestly, Isaac had the same inclination.

He stuck around to chat with Penn, standing a couple inches closer than he might otherwise, to hear him over the group noise inside the house. Penn understood. They had met in Afghanistan and both felt the aftershocks of a few too many explosives.

They had stayed in touch over the years, with Penn convincing Isaac to try out Ridley Bay when he discharged. They might have little in common personally, but police and military work could bond even the strangest pairs. And Penn understood him. If Isaac ever didn't come to Bible study, Penn would text him. *"Put the beer down and get out here."* Isaac appreciated it, despite grumbling about it.

"Any update on the crash victims?" Penn asked. He was still friends with everybody at the department and had a bad habit of listening to a police scanner.

Isaac shook his head. He could easily find out if the kids made it, but he hadn't asked because he didn't want to know.

"I'm sorry," Penn said. "Those are the worst wrecks."

Isaac nodded, watching Penn's one-year-old toddle down the hall. "Your daughter's eating a shoe, by the way."

Penn tilted his head and studied her for a moment. "What doesn't kill ya…"

Zoe joined them, forcing a hug on Isaac. "If she'll stay an adventurous eater and not turn picky like the rest, she can eat all the shoes she wants."

Isaac snickered and shook his head.

Katie interrupted their group as she said goodbyes to everyone with the blonde kid on her hip. She wore jeans and a graphic tee featuring a camera and the phrase *"Don't be negative."* And of course, she had charmed their entire group. Luckily Isaac had gotten the Katie shot years ago and had immunity now.

"We're heading out," she said. "The leeches are tired."

A flinch passed over his face and anger flashed through him. He wanted to remind her of her own shirt: "Don't be negative."

Suzanne came up to Katie and rested a hand on her arm. "Did Josie have shoes? I checked upstairs and the backyard and didn't see any."

"Oh, no," Katie said. "Somehow we made it here without any."

"Impressive," Isaac said, earning a glare from Zoe and Katie both, though Katie's eyes lingered. She seemed more confused than annoyed.

"I'll just carry her to the car," Katie said.

"Don't forget that one," Penn said, pointing at the redhead, passed out on the chair.

"I'll get Sage," Suzanne offered. She scooped up the tot and balanced her in her arms with a grunt. "Goodness, I forgot how heavy a sleeping child can be."

"Isaac, why don't you help them out?" Penn asked.

"We're okay," Katie called over her shoulder, already heading toward the front door.

Isaac took her at her word.

When Penn stepped away to gather his own herd of children, Zoe turned on Isaac and wagged her eyebrows. "I heard you two met before," she said in a sing-song tone.

He said nothing.

"She's cute," she said, dragging the word into three syllables.

"She's a terrible person," he said. A liar, a bad mother, and a woman he had once been interested in. The unholy trifecta.

"Oh, come on. Why do you say that?"

"She doesn't like her own kids."

Zoe shrugged. "We all have bad days."

"I think it's every day." Based on the little he had seen.

"Hmm. Maybe she needs help. Or a moms group." Zoe's eyes lit up.

Isaac shook his head. "I think she needs more than that."

Zoe ignored him. "She's only here for a week though, I'll have to work fast."

How much damage could Katie cause in a single week? He honestly didn't know. She had done a number on him in two months flat. "She's a bad influence."

"I can handle her," she said confidently.

Once Zoe made up her mind, only a fool would argue. "At your own risk, then."

"Not everyone's a monster, Isaac. I know it seems that way when you're a cop, but it's not true. Besides, I have a good feeling about her."

"That's what she does to people."

Zoe laughed and patted his arm, her eyes following one of her kids as she stepped away. "One day, I want to hear this story."

Not from me.

Chapter Seven

Every day they managed to find something new to do. For a mid-sized town, Ridley Bay offered a great selection of beaches, wetlands, parks, restaurants, and more. Katie had a list she wouldn't be able to finish in a single week, which tempted her to stay another week. But the thought of Suzanne's gloating and rejoicing kept her from booking it.

Wednesday morning, Katie drove the girls to Suzanne's house. Their nana had offered to watch them while Katie worked, and she never turned down free childcare. Her mom called while they drove and Katie ignored it. She didn't need to hear any stories about her wonder-siblings, or listen to another pleading reason she should visit Alaska. Not happening.

Suzanne met them at the door, propping the screen open and releasing the smell of fresh cookies. "Come in," she said, welcoming them with hugs. The girls warmed to Nana effortlessly and hurried inside, heading straight for the play room. Katie followed awkwardly, unsure if she should drop and dash, or stay and chat.

"How's Tyler?" she asked, passing pictures of Aaron's brother in the hall. "Think he'll have any kids one day?" Katie hoped this entire play room wasn't just for Sage and Josie.

Suzanne smiled and shook her head. "I'm not sure. Tyler thinks he's Peter Pan and never plans to grow up."

Tyler was four years younger than Aaron, and Katie had always liked him, though he all but vanished after Aaron's death. "Is he still in Boston?"

"Yes. He hardly visits since Aaron died. I think it's too hard for him, you know?"

Katie nodded. She agreed with Tyler.

Suzanne pointed out a toy castle and small soldiers. "That was his. I pulled it from the attic. I know the girls might not like soldiers, but I think I can buy a couple of princesses to add some appeal."

The Kaminski house wave of overwhelm started again. "I think you've gotten them more than enough."

"Oh, but it's so fun to shop the little girl aisles," Suzanne said, giddy as a kid herself. "I never got the chance to buy things like baby dolls before."

Katie laughed. "I wouldn't call toy shopping fun, but sure."

"Reliving your childhood is part of the fun of raising kids though."

Katie's brow furrowed. "If you want to relive it." Was that her problem? Perhaps others could find joy in childhood that she couldn't.

"You wouldn't?" Suzanne asked.

"Maybe parts," Katie said. Truthfully, she didn't remember her childhood. Surely she'd had baby dolls and such. She just didn't remember them.

Her own father had died in a car wreck when Katie was five. A few years later, her mom married an ultra-religious man. They had six more kids who were so much younger than Katie, they never felt like siblings. They had Old Testament names, wore long skirts, and homeschooled. But not Katie. She didn't fit into their plan, so they left her in public school to handle herself. Some people looked at their childhood and found memories; Katie found a void. What would the twins one day find?

"This might be a good time for me to go," Katie said quietly, taking a step back. "While they're busy playing."

"Oh, sure. Here, let's get you a cookie first." Suzanne shuffled by Katie and toward the kitchen. Katie followed her, passing bookshelves filled with scrapbooks, photo albums, and picture frames. Guilt poked around the edges of her chest. Where Suzanne had enshrined her children, Katie tried to ignore her own. Perhaps this is how Aaron had remembered so much. Sure, Katie had photos, but they lived online, not in their real lives.

Suzanne held out two chocolate chip cookies, wrapped in a napkin. "I can't send you out empty-handed."

Katie smiled. "Thanks. And thanks again for watching the girls."

"No problem. I'll keep them however long you need."

Forever? "I appreciate it," Katie said as she headed for the door.

"Should you say bye to the girls?" Suzanne asked.

"It's easier if I don't."

"For you or them?"

Katie shrugged. "Both. They do nothing but slow me down."

Suzanne sighed. "Katie, if your children are in the way, perhaps you need to change course."

Katie turned and stared at her for a second. *Seriously? Go ahead and say it. You think I'm a bad mom.* A dozen defenses ran through her mind, but Katie knew better than to engage with Mother Suzanne. She forced on a plain smile instead. "Okay. Thanks for the advice." And she let herself out the door before Suzanne could say anymore.

•   •   •

A few minutes later, Katie pulled up to a coffee shop, two blocks from the bay. It had an over-the-top surfer theme. Surfboards lined the walls, many signed by names Katie had never heard of. A surfboard-shaped menu featured drinks with titles she assumed were surfing maneuvers. After ordering a cutback vanilla latte and a scone, she took her laptop to a small table and connected to the Wi-Fi. Password: *Kahuna10.*

Katie closed her eyes for a moment, inhaling latte and exhaling Suzanne. She opened her eyes and her editing software, ready to focus. After this week's travels, she was behind on edits. She had done a set of fall mini-shoots before they left their last apartment in Birmingham and the photos at the pumpkin patch had turned out great.

Working quickly, she soon had the first few albums uploaded and sent to the families. Then she switched to managing her online content and social media. She had offered one full photo session on the beach here in Ridley Bay, hoping to make a little extra income while here, and the response shocked her. The session booked in minutes, and a waitlist extended down the comments section. People from Houston and San Antonio said they would drive in for it.

Katie tapped her finger on her coffee cup and watched traffic pass outside the window. She liked this town and could easily imagine grabbing an apartment here and setting up shop for a few months, like they had in so many other places. But she would probably get better business in a bigger city, like Houston or Austin. She had free childcare here, at the cost of judgmental comments from Suzanne.

She needed to look at her budget and figure out their next move. Thankfully Aaron had been a careful planner with a good life insurance policy. His foresight saved Katie and the girls from a financial fiasco that first year. Now Katie's work covered most of their expenses, while the money from his insurance and the sold house helped fill in the gaps when needed. But she didn't want that fund to run out. She wanted to keep enough back for a down payment in case they found a place they loved. Though the more they traveled, the more she doubted it would happen.

A text from an unknown number came through on her phone.

Hey Katie! This is Zoe, I got your number from Tricia, I hope you don't mind.

I wanted to invite you to our MOM group. We have a playdate this Friday!

Katie frowned at it. She had never been in any sort of mom group before. It seemed so… matronly. She preferred to drop the kids off and do something on her own. Why would they even invite her? She was just a visitor.

Katie: I gotta know, is MOM an abbreviation or are you super excited about it?

Zoe: It used to be Minivans on Mondays, but we switched to Fridays. Now it's Minivans on Mission, but the mission is just to survive.

Katie chuckled. She liked Zoe. If they were okay with welcoming a visitor, she could make friends for a day.

Katie: I drive an SUV, do I still qualify?

Zoe: Don't judge our cars and we won't judge yours! Buena Vista Park at 9. Or whenever, because we'll all be late.

Speaking of being late, the time at the top of her phone caught her eye. Katie needed to meet Micah for lunch and talk about fall festival photos. She tossed her phone and laptop into her bag and grabbed her keys.

Chapter Eight

Isaac parked at the back of a deli near campus, where he was meeting Micah during his break to go over security plans for the fall festival. He stuck his aviators onto his shirt collar and headed inside, taking a quick scan of the small dining room. Several eyes met his and quickly went back to their companions. Two Hispanic guys with neck tattoos were sitting to the left, watching Isaac. He didn't mind tattoos, he had a couple of his own. But he hid them in places where the average street rat wouldn't see them and be able to identify him.

Isaac ordered his food and joined Micah, swinging a seat around to the end of the table so he could face both the door and the gangsters.

"How's it going?" Micah asked.

"Good. Ready for the festival?"

Micah glanced at his computer. "I think so. Should be our biggest yet." Grace Church partnered with another church in the city to host the largest fall festival in town.

"Got all the guys you need for security?"

"I did, but Officer Langley just called out, his kids have the flu. I'm open to suggestions, or I can call around." Micah had once been a chaplain for the police department, and still had connections there. Isaac had known of him for years, but didn't talk to him personally until three years ago, when he needed marriage counseling. Since then, their connection had morphed into something between friendship and work.

"Does Penn want to work as civilian security?"

"He said he had to help wrangle his own kids there."

"Have you asked Dempsey? She's on nights, so she might have to leave a little early. Could be good for bag check though." She usually picked up extra work.

"I'll try her next." Micah jotted down a note.

Next they reviewed the layout. The church oriented the festival to make the most of natural boundaries at the park, reduce the expense of rented fences, and ensure everyone entered through one gate. They needed two officers there checking bags, two more patrolling the festival, and one directing traffic.

Isaac alternated between looking at Micah's map and watching a third man join the tattooed table. This guy had tattoos covering his bald head; Isaac recognized a few as gang symbols. The guy shot him a couple ugly looks.

"Thanks for your help on all this," Micah said.

Isaac leaned back in his chair, pushing it back on two legs. "I don't mind." He had nothing better to do than work, on or off hours.

The front door opened and Isaac's eyes darted over to find none other than Katie Kaminski entering, wearing denim shorts and a *Nashville Fun Run* shirt. His teeth clenched. The woman was everywhere.

Micah waved her over. He stood and gave her a half hug. Isaac remained seated, feeling the scorn of his mother from a distance.

"Hey Isaac," she said, brightly. As if she could find him on the moon and not be surprised. Her eyes drifted over his uniform and snapped up again.

He dipped his head in a single nod rather than answering.

She took a seat across from Micah and immediately started chatting about photography. "I can't wait to do the fall fest. I mostly do family lifestyle portraits now, but I love events, they can be so much fun."

She had an infinity symbol tattooed on her ring finger. *Ironic.*

"I was really impressed with your portfolio," Micah said. "Isaac, have you seen her work?"

Not in a decade. Unwilling to get into their messy past with Micah, he shook his head, hoping Katie wouldn't correct him.

"Show him your latest post," Micah said.

Katie reached for her phone—sporting a fuzzy lime green case—then hesitated and set it back down. "I doubt Isaac is interested in toddlers on a beach."

"True," Isaac said.

Micah raised his eyebrows. "Then be interested in good photos."

Isaac dutifully took the neon phone. He swiped through the three photos in the post, planning to not look too closely. He knew they would be good. In the first, the blonde twirled, with a towel stretched across her arms; the sun shone through the weave of the towel. The second showed a close-up of the redhead, grinning with a smattering of sand across her nose and eyelashes. The third showed both girls holding hands, toes in the water, their reflection outlined in the shallow water around them. Her photos always had a dream-like quality to them, and she had only improved with time.

"I like my photos to feel like a rose-colored memory," Katie said to Micah. "All the best parts, the things you want to remember."

Isaac passed the phone back.

"You definitely capture the feeling," Micah said. "If you can stay in Ridley Bay any longer, we have beach baptisms coming up. The church could really use some quality photos of those."

"That sounds fun," Katie said, practically bouncing in her seat. "I've never done baptisms, but I do have an underwater housing for my camera that is sorely underused."

"Here—" Micah passed her the church credit card. "Get your lunch order in and we'll chat festival shot list and maybe baptisms."

When Katie walked away, Micah turned to Isaac with a slight smirk dancing on his lips. "Warm welcome for our guest."

Isaac's eyes wandered over the deli. "Sorry," he said dutifully, not remorsefully.

Micah crossed his arms. "I heard you two met a long time ago. You know her well?"

He knew Katie Lewis quite well. The same didn't ring true for Katie Kaminski. "I know she refers to her children as leeches."

Only two people understood Isaac's irritation at that—and Micah was one of them. "Well, I'm sure she has work to do, like the rest of us." They'd had these conversations before. Micah called it grace, Isaac called it excuses.

"It shouldn't be hard to avoid calling your children derogatory terms." Especially for a Christian, though Isaac had noticed few lived up to their own standards.

Micah tilted his head each way, as if weighing the sentence. "I'd imagine being a widowed mother could stretch someone thin."

The slightest hint of guilt crossed his mind. Obviously she had been in a difficult situation. And he had once cared deeply about her. But Isaac didn't want to justify any of Katie's behavior—past or present. He glanced at his watch. His lunch break ended in two minutes. "You're good at reading people, I'll let you reach your own conclusions."

Katie walked back to their table as Isaac stood to leave. The tattoo table had recently exited, splitting up their group. The new guy and one of the original guys climbed into a lowered truck and drove south, while the third walked north.

"Can I pray for you before you go?" Micah asked.

Katie set down a number tent and looked up at him.

"Maybe next time." He rarely said yes. But there had been days he needed it, even if he didn't believe in it. On those days, he preferred to go to Micah than the new chaplain.

"I'll see you later," he said. He gave a nod to Katie too and headed to the squad car to run the truck's license plate. The registered owner had two warrants. Isaac drove north.

Chapter Nine

It shouldn't have surprised him to find an illegally-parked white Lexus SUV with an expired inspection sticker at the kids' Bible club. Katie's aunt and uncle ran the group, of course she would be here this week. He couldn't escape her. Isaac briefly debated leaving, but he didn't run from Lauren and he wasn't running from Katie either.

The Kaminskis hosted the after-school program for kids at a north side elementary school as part of Grace Church's local mission efforts. Isaac timed his arrival to the end of the meeting. Kids worked to wrap up their final craft and Katie zipped around them snapping pictures of messy hands and toothy grins. A few of the friendly kids ran up to him for high fives and fist bumps. Some waved. Others avoided looking at him.

He came for those kids. The ones whose parents hated or feared cops. He wanted those kids to know where and how to get help. It had saved lives before. The police chief encouraged community engagement, so whenever he had a slow day, Isaac tried to swing by to make those connections.

JP, Tricia, and the student volunteers all said hello. Katie grinned and waved. Isaac didn't bother returning it. He focused on the kids who would talk to him and tried to hang out near the ones who wouldn't. He knew them all by now.

The kids showed off the T-shirts they painted—apparently recreating Joseph's coat of many colors. Between his mother occasionally dragging him to church and the years of doing church security, he had heard enough of the Bible stories to recognize this one.

After complimenting several designs, Hendrix shoved his shirt in Isaac's face. "I did it all red because they put *blood* on the coat!" he shouted.

Isaac tried not to laugh. "Of course you did."

"What's the most blood you've ever seen?" Arjun, another fourth-grade boy, asked.

"I've seen enough," Isaac said.

"That's not a real answer," Arjun said.

"Hey, I shoot people for a living, why don't I get any cool questions?" Katie asked, lifting her camera.

Hendrix and Arjun rolled their eyes at her. Their friend Tarek looked concerned. Katie demonstrated, raising her camera to eye level and adding a "pew pew" sound effect as she clicked. Tarek joined the other boys in the eye roll.

"Nothing," Katie said to Isaac, with mock despair.

"Everybody's phone has a camera," Hendrix said. "But *he* has a gun!" He looked at Isaac's duty belt with awe. They had gone over strict no-touching rules a long time ago.

"And a car," Arjun added. "Can we go see it now?"

"You guys done here?" Isaac asked.

"Go ahead," JP said, over the general hum of noise a group of forty kids always raised.

Isaac headed to the car, followed by a long trail of kids. He reached inside for a pack of hand wipes and made the kids wipe off paint, dirt, snot, and God knew what else before they took turns flicking on the overhead lights, touching buttons they weren't supposed to touch, and making their own siren noises while pretending to steer.

The boys asked to sit in the back, behind bars. They asked to be handcuffed too. "Against the rules, sorry," Isaac said.

"If we do anyway, then are we real arrested?" Tarek asked.

Isaac grinned. "Nah, we try not to arrest kids. I'd be the one in trouble."

A few kids stood back and watched from a distance. Isaac passed around sticker badges and even the more reluctant kids snuck forward to grab one. Katie came too, taking photos. He forced himself to ignore her and act natural.

When it was time for the kids to head home, he flicked on the siren for a second. Some loved it, others covered their ears. Then the group started to disband. Parents walked the smaller ones home, the college volunteers walked with a few, and the older ones ran off to their houses.

Only one kid remained near Isaac. The little redhead. Several yards away Katie fixed the blonde kid's shoe, and the redhead stood there on her own. He had heard her name, but he preferred the distance of remaining nameless.

Isaac squatted to the little girl's level and pulled off his sunglasses, tucking them into his shirt. "Do you want to turn the lights on?"

She nodded but didn't move.

Isaac pointed inside the car to the small switch. "Just push this to the side, okay? Don't press these buttons." He backed up a foot away from the door, clearing the path.

Slowly, she edged toward the car, keeping her eyes on him as if he were a snake. Without turning her back to him, she eased into the car. She gently nudged the switch over and looked at Isaac again.

"Knock it over one more spot. There you go. You can climb out and see."

She leaned out the open door, craning her head to see without getting all the way out of the car, and plastering little hand prints on the window. A few more among the dozens.

Repositioning herself inside the car again, she looked around it, studying it all. Isaac pointed out a few things, explaining the computer, the bars, and the siren switch. Then the redhead's eyes snapped behind him. He glanced back to see the blonde sister running for them, with Katie following.

"I wanna do it!" the blonde wailed, throwing herself face down onto the grass next to the car.

"Whoa. Okay. You're next," Isaac said.

The redhead climbed out silently. The blonde climbed in, trying to turn the steering wheel and making vroom noises. "Wewoo!" she shouted.

Isaac obliged with a quick flick of the siren. The girl squealed, while her sister covered her ears.

Katie joined him, standing on his right side, a foot shorter. She wore white shorts and a black T-shirt featuring a cat wearing neon sunglasses. No jewelry, save for a fitness watch on her wrist. Her hair was pulled back into a short ponytail. Beauty came effortlessly to her.

"I love that you do this," she said. "The girls have never seen a police car up close."

He didn't say anything.

She carried on anyway. "So when did you get out of the army?"

"Seven years ago," he said. When he turned thirty and found himself already sick of life, he knew he needed a change. He finished out his contract and followed Penn's example, heading into the police force.

"How did you end up in Ridley Bay?"

"They were hiring."

She breathed out a laugh and shook her head. "Oh, Isaac."

So it wasn't the whole truth, but he didn't want to explain it. Fort Bliss had looked too much like Afghanistan and Isaac needed to get out of the desert, which ruled out returning home to Phoenix. But he didn't want to go too far from family, either. When Penn suggested his own hometown in Ridley Bay, it seemed like a perfect solution. Whenever Isaac retired, he'd already be on the beach.

The blonde tried to push the redhead farther away from the car and Katie stepped forward. "Josephine Kaminski, no pushing!"

The blonde turned her attention back to the car, while the redhead plopped onto the grass with crossed arms and a scowl.

Katie turned back to him. "Her name's just Josie. Not Josephine. But it sounds better when she's in trouble. Luckily Sage never gets in trouble because I've tried to find a longer word for her and nothing begins with Sage."

"Sagebrush," Isaac said. "Sagacious. Sagittarius."

"Thank you, walking encyclopedia, you can power down now." She turned her whole body toward him and looked up. "Could I please talk to the non-robot Isaac?"

"Go for it."

"No, I mean really talk. We need to catch up. Like old friends."

"Is that what we are?"

"Not by how you're acting. Which makes me think we remember things differently."

How many ways could there be? Before he could ask, the blonde hopped out of the car and came skip-running to them. "Mommy, did you see?" she said, her voice at least two levels too loud.

Katie sighed before kneeling to give her a high five. "You make a great police officer, Jojo."

The redhead moved to the doorway of the car, alternating looking inside and back at Isaac. He was about to tell her to climb in when his radio blurted out a non-urgent request for a second officer at a nearby neighborhood.

"Sorry kiddo," he said, walking up to the car. Without another word, she scampered back to her mother's side. He reached inside for the roll of badge stickers and squatted down to the three-foot height everyone else was on. "Do you want a badge?" He held out a sticker.

The blonde ran up and got one. He held another out, waiting. The redhead tugged on her sister's sleeve and the blonde ran back to get the sticker for her sister.

"What do you say?" Katie prompted.

"Tanks!" the blonde shouted, skip-running away already. The redhead turned tail and ran after her.

"Thanks, for her too," Katie said, with an apologetic shrug. He stepped away but she stopped him with a hand on his arm. "Isaac, I really do want to talk soon."

One glance back had guilt niggling at his chest again. He remembered those green eyes, much closer, outside of her apartment in Fairbanks, with tears. He had kissed her then. Could he really just ignore her now?

"Please?" she asked. "Before I leave town."

He had once promised to be there for her anytime, anywhere. He could handle a few minutes tonight. "Fine. I should be off by six tonight."

A smile lit her face. "I'm free."

"Text me," he said. She could easily get his number from any of the Kaminskis. She nodded. Then he climbed into the car and settled his hands onto a sticky steering wheel.

Chapter Ten

It took Suzanne all of two seconds to readily agree to babysitting this evening. She didn't ask why or what Katie had planned, and for once, Katie didn't volunteer any extra information. For some reason, it felt weird to tell her mother-in-law about her meeting with Isaac. It shouldn't, but it did.

Then she got Isaac's number from JP under the pretense of sending him a few photos from the afternoon. She would, eventually, just not today.

At a quarter till six, she dropped off the girls at their nana's house and drove to Burger Bay, the diner Isaac had suggested. In a town this size, without five o'clock traffic, she managed to actually arrive early.

Isaac, however, was fifteen minutes late.

"Sorry," he muttered when they met at the door. He wore dark jeans and a gray henley. Katie almost missed the uniform, but she welcomed the fresh soap scent. "Needed to wash up. Gross day."

"Gross?" Katie asked. She had upgraded her cat tee to a red blouse.

"Not a good story before dinner." He pulled the door open and held it for her.

She walked up to the counter and ordered a basic burger and fries. Neither offered to pay for the other.

Isaac took a table in the back corner and sat facing the door. A familiar routine to Katie, after growing up with her stepfather in law enforcement.

"Great day for a run," Katie said, looking out the window.

He followed her gaze as a shirtless man with dreadlocks went jogging by. "You're a swimmer, not a runner."

"I was. But it's much easier to push two kids in a stroller than a life raft."

Though he still faced the window, she could see the side profile of what appeared to be a hint of a smile. He turned back to her. "Is that what you wanted to talk about? Weather and exercise?"

Katie grinned. "Only if we were old friends. But apparently you don't think we are."

He appraised her, then let his gaze roam around the diner before returning to her. "Do you kiss all your friends?"

Oof. Heat climbed into her face but thankfully her skin tone hid it, and Katie could too. "Fair enough. Maybe it would be more accurate to say we were the right people at the wrong time." She had always thought of him fondly as an Almost. And Almosts were never meant to be.

He nodded slowly and crossed his arms. "Interesting. I'd say you were a liar."

Katie's eyebrows shot up. "A liar? I never lied to you."

"Funny how memories work."

Katie stared at him, trying to imagine what he could possibly mean. A waitress interrupted them, dropping off their meals and buying Katie some time.

"How did I lie to you?" she asked.

Isaac shook his head. "I don't think it matters anymore."

He started to chow down on his food, but Katie let hers get cold. "No. No clamming up. I have one hour and you're going to talk. I'm an honest woman and I need to know what lies I may have accidentally told."

Isaac snickered. "There's no such thing as an honest woman."

"Wow, harsh words from Officer Torres. I know you meet some characters in your line of work, but surely you know good people too. I mean, you go to Grace, don't you?"

"I work with them," he clarified. Then he shrugged. "They might be honest for a little while."

Katie raised her eyebrows. She did not remember him being nearly this cynical. She must not be the only woman he treated like an inconvenience. "That's quite the judgment to pass. I'm sorry, Isaac, I honestly do not remember lying to you. I thought we were clear on where we stood."

"So I misread your interest?" he asked.

Katie mixed her own fry sauce on her plate, pushing ketchup, mayonnaise, and mustard around with a french fry. "Of course not. I was crazy about you."

He chuckled. "Which explains why you told me not to call you anymore."

"I had to. We wanted completely different things. We were a dead end." They knew they wouldn't work out together, but knowing wasn't enough to keep them apart. While he was in Alaska, they were like magnets, unable to deny the attraction. Once he moved, Katie finally had the clarity of mind to end it. She deleted his number and tried to delete the memory of him, though it proved an impossible task.

"That's part of the lie," he said. "You told me you never wanted to marry or have kids." He gestured toward her as if she wore the very proof of her children. She probably did around the middle. *Thanks a lot, Isaac.*

"That wasn't a lie. That was immaturity." He was seven years older than her, and in their twenties, those years mattered more than they did now. He had wanted to settle down—words which struck fear in Katie's twenty-two-year-old bones.

"And you outgrew it in, what, three years?"

"Four," Katie mumbled, feeling momentarily beat. But she hadn't lied. It had been true at the time she knew Isaac. She had met Aaron two years later, and married him two years after that.

"What?"

She straightened. "Four years. And that wasn't the only reason. You weren't—aren't—a Christian." Her faith may have its own weaknesses, but she had known better than to continue dating him for that alone. Katie looked him squarely in the eyes. "I told you I couldn't date you."

"Because of God," he sneered.

"It's important to me. Respect that."

"It didn't seem important. You said one thing and did another, Katie. Is that not a lie?"

Ouch. After two dates, she had insisted they couldn't date—so they "hung out" nonstop for two months. And on his last night in Fairbanks, she ended up crying in his arms. And kissing him.

Katie tapped her fingers against her thigh, feeling more and more like a child caught with her hand in the metaphorical cookie jar. "I wasn't a liar. I was selfish." She hadn't been willing to give up her Almost, even when she knew she should.

"Is there a difference?" Isaac asked.

Her shoulders dropped in defeat and she sighed. "Maybe not." She knew he wanted more from her than she could give, and she let him leave Alaska with a faint hope of a future. Without ever intentionally telling a lie, she had betrayed him.

Isaac glanced at his phone and Katie's eyes darted around the room. This hadn't worked out the way she had hoped. He placed unfair blame on her. She *had* told him all the reasons it wouldn't work. He shared an equal role in their relationship progressing anyway.

Isaac finished his meal in record time and they hadn't found any middle ground. If they couldn't reconcile their past, maybe they could at least be friendly now. "I'm ready for your gross post-dinner story," Katie said, cranking up her own smile.

He studied her for a moment and shook his head. "What changed your mind about settling down?"

Okay, never mind. "Aaron," she said. After growing up in a family where she never felt welcome, she couldn't wrap her mind around domestic life until Aaron showed her the beauty of home. Without him here, she struggled to see it again.

"Good for him," Isaac said gruffly.

She realized her short explanation might be rude to the guy who had loved her unsuccessfully. And to be fair, Isaac had played a role in changing her mind too. It was hard to remember, faced with his harsh rejection now, but he had once made her feel like she truly belonged. "And you, honestly. You made me question it for the first time. Then I graduated, moved out of Alaska, and grew up a bit. I guess marriage wasn't such a hard sell after all."

"And kids?"

"I wasn't sold. I was surprised." Birth control failed her doubly.

Isaac leaned back against his chair. He gave her another cop stare for a moment, before standing and taking his cup for a refill. When he came back, he set the cup down and stood beside the table for a moment.

"Is this a power pose?" Katie asked, looking up. His interrogation tactics didn't work on her. "Because I will gladly stand on this chair to get taller than you."

She shifted to stand but Isaac chuckled and pulled out his chair, taking a seat. "It's not a power pose, I'm thinking."

"Hard work."

He gave her a smirk in reply. "If the twins were a surprise..." he drummed his fingers on the table. "Why did you keep them?"

"Keep them?" Katie's eyebrows shot up. She might not be in the running for any Mom of the Year awards, but he had just implied something incredibly offensive. "They weren't lost puppies, Isaac. How could you say that?"

Isaac put his hands up. "I'm not—I wasn't trying to imply anything. But... Some women don't."

Some women? And he thought she was one of them? Anger rendered Katie speechless for once. No, she had never come around to the idea of raising kids, but she did it anyway, with whatever amount of success her two healthy children proved. Yes, some days she hated it, but it hadn't been her choice. She blamed her misery on fate. Abortion had never been an option. Was he trying to suggest she had an out? That she had brought this upon herself somehow? She visualized dumping the rest of her fries in his lap.

Then she did the inappropriate thing she always did when emotions overwhelmed her: she laughed. "That's an awful thing to say to a mother."

He studied her. "You're right."

Katie shook her head and words came tumbling out. "I thought it would be okay. Aaron's excitement was contagious and I figured we could do it together. And we did, for two months. And for two months we were both exhausted and one day we had a stupid fight and I said he shouldn't be so tired since I got up with the babies all night. Turns out he had a heart defect we didn't know about and it killed him a few days later. Does that answer it for you? How Katie Lewis Kaminski ended up on her own, trying to raise two kids she never expected to have?"

Someone at a nearby table stole glances their way. Katie may have raised her voice a touch too loud but she was too shaken and angry to care.

Isaac kept his eyes down, his arms crossed. "What if you had known he wouldn't be around?" he asked softly.

Katie's brow furrowed and she glared at him. *What a stupid question.* "He would still deserve to have his children live."

Isaac turned toward the window, elbows propped on the table, resting his mouth against his hands.

Silence engulfed them. Katie wanted to fight it off, but after a conversation like that, she couldn't just bring up the weather. Maybe immigration policy or capital punishment. Conspiracy theories. Anything would be less combative than this.

Isaac cleared his throat. "You made the right choice."

"Obviously. So apologize for being rude."

"I wasn't rude, I was curious."

"You were rude," she said.

"I'm sorry."

"Fine. I forgive you. And tell me you're sorry for my loss. For Aaron."

"I am," he said. "I really am."

"Thank you." Katie studied him for a moment, trying to find a way to turn this evening around. "Now, tell me your gross cop story, I've been waiting this entire time."

"You're still eating."

She pushed her plate away. "I'm done. Tell me."

He narrowed his eyes at her. "You're bossy."

"I'm confident."

"Always have been." He grinned at her and she found him rather easy to forgive.

"So this story?"

He eased back in his seat, draping one arm along the back of his chair. "We got a call about a weird smell in somebody's alley."

"And you answered it? That's not an emergency."

"Wait for it," he said, with half a smile.

Katie settled her chin on her hands and listened to the terrible tale of the stray dog and the poorly-buried cat—a story equally hilarious and disgusting. Then she matched it with a twin potty training tale which managed to get a full laugh out of him. And for one fleeting moment, she felt young again.

Chapter Eleven

Josie and Sage woke earlier than usual on Friday. Katie tried to placate them with a few episodes of their current favorite television show while she whipped up pancakes.

"Breakfast of champions," Katie muttered, sliding plates to each girl and dousing her own in syrup.

Then she slipped back into her bedroom to get dressed for Zoe's MOM group today. A Texas cold front had blown in overnight, bringing the temperature to the 50s—jeans and T-shirt weather.

Before long, they were on their way to the park. Josie dressed in another princess dress, and Sage had picked purple pants and a sweater in another shade of purple.

They got to the park to find four other moms and what felt like a dozen kids running around. Katie got introductions all around—Zoe, Flora, Ginny, and a very pregnant Madelyn. She tried to keep track of the kids' names too, but made no promises. The other moms wore coats and parkas.

"So what are we doing today?" Katie asked, swinging her arms back and forth into a clap.

Madelyn gave her a funny look. "Watching the kids."

"That's it?" Katie asked, her arms stopping.

"That's it," Zoe said, sipping her coffee. "Because it's easier to do in a group."

"Gotcha." Katie didn't get it. It sounded terribly boring. She struggled to form close female friendships, either because she kept them all at arm's length, or because she liked to move faster than most women.

"We do have a mom's day out planned for tomorrow though," Zoe said. "I'm pretty sure I can add you in if you want to join. But you might need a background check."

Katie laughed. "Okay, this sounds serious. What's the plan?"

"We're going to a gun range."

"Are you serious?" Katie asked. "Do you have pent-up rage to get out or something?"

Zoe laughed. "No, I just want my own chance to mess things up and be loud. My kids get to do it all the time."

"Cheers to that," Ginny said, lifting her own paper coffee cup.

Huh. Maybe these ladies were more interesting than she initially thought.

"I'll miss out," Madelyn said, rubbing her belly.

Katie turned to Zoe. "I haven't shot a gun in nearly twenty years," she said. Not since her teen years, when her stepfather forced her to learn.

"No worries," Zoe said. "Flora has never shot before, so I figured we'd have somebody come and teach—oh, wait, you know Isaac! Perfect. I bet he'll be fine with adding you. He's going to help out and give some instructions."

Katie's stomach rode that weird drop again. Last night's conversation seemed to end on a friendly note, but that didn't guarantee niceties tomorrow. The quiet strength she had once seen in him had been replaced with quiet anger. "Why not Penn?" she asked.

Zoe gave her a look. "Who do you think will be wrangling all my kids?"

Oh boy. Katie puffed air into her cheeks and blew it out. "Okay. Ask him if it's okay if I come. If not, that's fine too."

Zoe laughed at her. "Why would it not be? Don't tell me you have some sordid criminal past. I'm having trouble picturing it."

"No, we knew each other a few years ago," she explained for the others. "And he's not my biggest fan now."

"Knew each other in the friendly sense or the biblical sense?" Ginny asked.

"Oh, good grief," Katie laughed. "Friendly!" Or something in between, to be honest.

"Well, don't take his bad attitude too personally," Zoe said. "His ex-wife messed with his head pretty bad."

"Ex-wife?"

"You didn't know? He got divorced two years ago."

Katie tucked away the annoyance that arose. She had spilled everything about her past and he never mentioned a marriage.

She turned her focus to the kids. Josie ran around with the others. They all mixed in fluid games Katie didn't understand. All except Sage, who seemed equally confused by the setup. She sat on a swing, not moving, only watching. It looked so ridiculous and pitiful, Katie couldn't stand it anymore. "I'm gonna go give her a push," she said, excusing herself from the semi-circle of moms.

"Sage, why don't you go play with the other kids?" Katie asked as she got closer. *Like a normal child.* Sage stared at her.

Katie swallowed hard. She wasn't sure why she had this kid. This kid that looked exactly like Aaron. He should be here to raise her. Because Katie certainly didn't know what to do with her. "Want a push?" she asked. Sage gripped the chains of the swing.

Katie gave her a few pushes before returning to the other moms. "I don't know why she's like that," she said.

"Like what?" Zoe asked. "A kid?"

"A quiet and antisocial kid."

"She'll outgrow it," Zoe said.

Katie sighed. "I don't have a clue what I'm doing."

"None of us do," Ginny said.

They were being too nice. "I feel like I started out a step behind and never caught up," Katie said.

"You got knocked a solid few steps back, girl, don't discredit yourself," Zoe said. She filled in the other moms on Katie's widowhood. They gave all the usual gasps and apologies.

"How did you survive infant twins on your own?" Ginny asked.

"I don't actually remember much of it," Katie said. That was the dark year, when time had stood still after Aaron died, yet somehow the girls had grown into toddlers. Afterwards came the numb year, then the recovery year. She hadn't titled this year yet.

"Well here you are now, with two happy, healthy, sweet girls," Flora said. "You're amazing."

Katie laughed. "I believe you mean the screaming tornado and the kid who doesn't talk."

"You mean the toddlers," Ginny corrected.

If they didn't want to see her ineptitude, Katie wouldn't force them. "Maybe I just need a break."

"Every mom needs help," Flora said. "Motherhood is so constant, it's hard to catch a breath."

"But what if I want the break to last forever?" Katie asked.

The group quieted and Katie realized she had probably pushed the limits on mom confessions.

"Have you ever put them in daycare?" Madelyn asked.

"No. Aaron and I had it all planned out. I was going to stay home with them. So I'm trying to stick to it, at least most of the time."

"You can change the plan if it isn't working for you," Ginny said.

"I know." But for some reason, Katie didn't like the idea of full-time care either. She needed to hold to the original vision she had shared with Aaron. "I really do want to make this work though."

"Then try to find joy in what you can," Zoe said. "It's there, if you look for it."

"I always have to give myself and the kids plenty of grace," Flora said. "Let them make mistakes, and let yourself make a few too."

"I make plenty," Katie said.

"So we apologize and try again to get through by the grace of God," Flora said.

"I'm pretty sure motherhood is designed to drive you to your knees in prayer," Ginny said. "Every time I think I can't make it another minute, I dig a little deeper and find enough grace to go on."

Katie nodded as if she understood, but she didn't. "Do you really think God cares about toddler tantrums though?" she asked.

"Absolutely," Zoe said. "If he cares about the hairs on their heads, I think he cares about the playground fights too."

"And the Bible says he 'gently leads those with young,'" Ginny added.

"Thank goodness," Madelyn laughed.

From there, the conversation somehow took a swift dive into birth stories and whether the twins' movements were distinguishable in the womb (yes).

To her surprise, Katie didn't mind it much. Though she preferred to orient her life around other things, it was nice to connect with people who understood temper tantrums and snotty noses. These women didn't make trite comments or ignore the harder moments, but they didn't wallow in them either. They even watched Sage while Katie took Josie to use the restroom. Not having to drag both kids everywhere helped too. She would stay in Ridley Bay if only for that.

•   •   •

That evening, Katie headed to the Ridley Bay photo session she had booked. She dropped the girls off with Suzanne and William and drove to a remote part of the Ridley Bay beach with a bag full of lenses, charged batteries, memory cards, and a backup camera, a second bag for lighting gear, and a third bag with props.

The cold front ruined any notion she'd had about kids splashing in the waves, so she decided to aim for a less traditional beach photoshoot. She brought a cozy blanket and s'mores supplies and picked up firewood and fire starters on the way to the spot.

She had a small fire going steadily when the Jameson family showed up. They wore warm, coordinating colors, following the advice and tips Katie had emailed. Katie chatted with everyone first, memorizing names, getting the ages of their three kids, and feeling out the subtleties of their interactions. She took mental notes on all the little details—the older daughter's too-cool-for-pictures attitude, the way their middle daughter held onto her father's hand, and the curly hair whipping around their youngest son's face.

They gathered around the fire pit. Katie pulled out a woven blanket and sat the kids in the middle, bookended by parents. She spread the blanket across everyone's shoulders. It forced them in close to one another, and sibling hijinks started immediately.

Perfect.

Katie prompted tickles and told jokes as she snapped photos, catching the exact moments the family relaxed. Getting "lifestyle" shots required helping people look natural, and there was nothing natural about it. It was a lot of posing, directing, and then backing off at just the right moment to catch the movements in between. Katie captured every grouping— siblings, daddy-daughters, mom and son, and every other mix. Family dynamics shifted with each person added or removed.

The timer on her watch vibrated, alerting her to wrap up their session. She instructed everyone to relax for a bit, while she pretended to scroll through her photos. She did this often enough, the shot list lived permanently in her brain. She knew exactly what she had so far and what she still needed. This was a stalling tactic.

Once everyone had settled down, she asked the kids to repeat after her: "Supercalifragilisticexpialidocious."

The kids tripped all over their own tongues and Katie swung her camera to the parents, catching just the moment she hoped for. She had noticed them exchange "the parent look" earlier—the look when someone's child does something cute and they look at their spouse to confirm they too appreciated their adorableness. The shared smile agreeing, "Yes, our genes are the best combination." She had exchanged it a few times with Aaron. When she had no one to share it with, it got harder to notice the cute moments.

But the littlest started to get frustrated he couldn't say the word, and pushed his sister, who pushed back. The mom jumped up to intervene and swoop up her son. "I'm so sorry," she apologized to Katie. "He missed a nap today and honestly I'm surprised we made it this far."

"No worries. Why don't we finish with a cuddle? Or whatever calms him down."

The mom pulled a water bottle from her bag and he sipped on it, leaning his head onto her shoulder.

The setting sun provided warmer colors and Katie adjusted her shutter speed to play with the light from the fire pit. They ended on a few perfectly cozy, sleepy toddler photos. If that was their stage of life, no matter how stressful and terrible the days could be, Katie would make sure they had rose-colored memories. Even if they wanted to escape it in the moment.

Katie helped the family load up and then put her gear in the car. She cleaned any sand off her camera before starting the car. Her phone buzzed with a text from her mom. Grimacing, Katie opened it.

Mom: I would love to see you around the holidays if possible! Esther and Samuel will be performing in a strings concert the weekend after Thanksgiving.

Katie deleted the text. Another invitation to care about her marvelous half-siblings went in one ear and out the other. She wasted no time on frustration and didn't bother to give it a second thought. She currently felt great and wouldn't let her mother's text bring her down.

Photography sessions put her on a high. A high where she could do anything. Where two whining toddlers didn't hold her back. Where crying kids were her forte and not her curse. Somehow, she didn't mind when it was someone else's kids.

But her kids awaited. So Katie drove to Suzanne and William's house to retrieve them.

Suzanne welcomed her into a house smelling of sausage. "We have leftovers if you want some," she offered.

"No thanks, I grabbed a quick bite on the way here."

"The girls have been in the playroom ever since dinner. I hardly heard a peep out of them while I cleaned up. They love it."

Suzanne ushered Katie into Aaron's childhood room, where Sage cradled a baby doll while Josie stacked blocks and knocked them down repeatedly.

It was idyllic. A memory in the making. Katie's traveling bin of toys had never looked so paltry. Suddenly, Katie feared they would want this too. What if her girls began to realize all the ways she was failing them? At least before now they hadn't known. They hadn't had something to compare to. Now they would.

Katie's throat tightened. She needed to plan their next destination. Ridley Bay couldn't last forever.

Chapter Twelve

Isaac stood in the bathroom, hands braced on the countertop, staring down at the open drawer and the stick with two lines on it. He had landed here too many times since having dinner with Katie on Thursday. Her words floated through his brain like lost puzzle pieces. *"He would still deserve to have his children live."* Aaron had deserved something Isaac apparently didn't, something that outlived him. Nothing would outlive Isaac. His life was a closed circuit.

And he had offended Katie with his questions about the twins. Maybe he should have been honest about why he asked them. But nobody knew about the abortion besides Lauren and Micah. He didn't go around sharing that story. It wasn't his favorite.

His phone beeped with an email from Micah and he slammed the drawer shut. He had to meet Zoe—and Katie—at the gun range in an hour and he still needed to dress and eat breakfast. Isaac pulled on a shirt and checked his phone.

Micah: Katie gave the rights for these, if the department wants to use them. (Told you she was good.) He attached six photos of Isaac at the backyard Bible club.

The different point of view caught Isaac's attention. The only photos he had in uniform were headshots or body camera footage in negative situations. These, however, were happy. Smiling, he stuck a badge on a little boy, while other kids blurred, running around him. In another, he served as a human jungle gym, dangling kids on each bicep. A close-up showed his aviators in a child's hands—her smile reflected in the lenses, his uniform in the background. In another photo, from a child's perspective, he loomed like a giant, resting an arm on the car door. Crisp and colorful, each picture played with the sunlight in various ways.

Isaac forwarded them on to the department's public relations person, along with the photo release Katie included. He passed them on to his mom too, just because she would love them. Then he emailed Micah a quick thanks for sharing them.

A reply came back instantly: *Thank Katie.*

He probably owed her at least that much after being a jerk all week. Maybe Katie had lied to him a decade ago, maybe not. But four years ago, she made the right decision—the one Lauren couldn't.

In the last few years, they had both had their lives ripped apart, and she had to carry two kids through it all. Katie didn't deserve to be treated like dirt if she struggled to pick up the pieces. Besides, she was only here for a couple more days. He could be nice for that long without getting burned.

Isaac loaded the back seat of his truck with a pistol case, a bag of gear, and a few boxes of ammo before driving to the best spot in town for breakfast tacos. His phone rang as he started the drive to the gun range. "Hey Mom," he answered.

"There's my baby." Her voice shook.

"You doing okay?" he asked.

"I am, I just saw the pictures you emailed, oh my heart. Thank you for sharing, those are wonderful."

"I figured you'd like them."

"You're a good man. Who took them?"

He hesitated. "A friend of mine."

"They're very talented," she said. Like everyone said.

A brief flash of possessiveness passed through his head. *I knew that first.* He had seen her talent years before the world had. "Yeah, I know."

"I started that new book you sent," she said. "But the main character is a woman." She sounded disappointed.

"What's the problem?"

"I raised four sons, I can tell you there are some differences between a man and woman."

Isaac laughed. "Please don't go into detail. This one has really good reviews. All the police work is the same."

His mom sighed. "I'll read it. But I'm trying to get into your head, so it won't be quite the same."

"I thought you wanted to know about my job. Is it that hard to get in my head?"

"Yes. Oscar is an open book. I see Andres and Cristian almost every day. You were always the quiet one."

"What's wrong with the quiet ones?"

"Nothing. They're God's gift to the world, if we'll only slow down and listen."

Isaac gave a grunt. His mother had become a Christian when he was a child. Andres and Cristian had joined her over the years, while Oscar and Isaac ignored it all.

"Are you coming to visit anytime soon?" She asked so often.

Isaac kept close tabs on her health, through Andres. She had been more tired lately, but Andres didn't seem worried. Still, Isaac watched flight prices to Phoenix. He needed to visit sooner rather than later. "I might be able to make it for Thanksgiving. Or Christmas. I should be able to get at least one holiday off."

"Oh! Make it Thanksgiving. Oscar is coming for the week. We could all be together again."

"Sounds fun. And loud. Very loud." Isaac had thought it loud growing up in a family of six; now with his brothers, their spouses, and their kids, there were nineteen of them when they all got together and he couldn't follow a conversation in the middle of that crowd.

"Yes, it will be. But you'll have the guest room and we'll padlock the kids out so you can escape."

His parents had downsized to a small two-bedroom house in a historic neighborhood not long after Isaac had graduated. It was too small for Oscar and his crew, so Isaac got priority booking.

"Perfect. I'll request the time off."

"That makes me so happy."

"Me too, Mom."

"Now how are *you*, besides work?" she asked.

"I'm not sure there's much to me besides work."

"See? This is what I mean about getting inside your head. I'll have to go down the list now. Physically? Mentally? Emotionally?"

"Good, good, good."

"Thank you for the details," she said, to prove her point. Isaac could picture her eyebrow raised. "Personally? Friends? Community?"

"Good." Well, good enough.

"Spiritually?"

"The same."

"Hobbies?"

Isaac pulled onto the dirt road leading to the gun range. "Well, I'm teaching a group of moms how to shoot this morning, if that's the kind of fascinating update you're looking for."

She chuckled. "It is. Is this a self-defense class?"

"Not really. Just Zoe's idea of a good time."

"I like her," his mom said. Isaac mentioned Zoe and Penn enough, she recognized their names.

"One day, you'll feel well enough you can come and meet them."

"Yes, I will," she said. "In the meantime, I'm praying for you, sweetie."

"Shouldn't you be praying for yourself?"

"I have plenty of people doing that. And I'm not out doing dangerous things every day."

"Neither am I."

"I don't believe you," she said. "Stay careful out there."

"I always am."

•　　　•　　　•

Texas cold fronts never lasted long, and by Saturday the sun warmed everything up again. Katie followed the directions Zoe texted for the gun range, driving several miles outside of town to a deserted-looking place with a weather-worn sign marking "The RB Gun Club." Driving between sandy dunes to a parking area, she soon found Zoe, Flora, and Ginny already there, hanging around a concrete bench in front of a long range.

"Sorry I'm late," Katie said when she joined the group.

"No worries," Zoe said. "Isaac's just now here too." She waved to a black truck as it pulled up next to where they stood.

Isaac climbed out of the truck in olive green joggers, a black long sleeve top, and his signature aviators. He walked up to Zoe and gave her half a hug. Then surprised Katie with one for her as well. He wanted to be friendly today?

He introduced himself to Ginny and Flora, then glanced around the range. "I thought we were shooting handguns today," he said.

"We are!" Zoe patted the small, locked case next to her with her own weapon.

"You're at the rifle range. You planning to shoot your Glock a hundred yards?"

"Oh." Zoe turned and looked around them. Isaac laughed and she smacked the back of her hand against Isaac's chest. "I haven't been here since I had Lainey and I gave her all my best brain cells."

"Clearly. Come on, let's drive to the other side."

Zoe clapped her hands together. "Can we ride in the back of the truck?"

He raised his eyebrows. "Suit yourself." Then he opened the tailgate and held a hand out, helping each woman up. Katie went last, and he gave her hand a slight squeeze. Some sign of forgiveness, maybe? He seemed more himself here, like the Isaac she remembered.

They rattled around on the loose dirt road, getting a coating of dust on themselves as he drove through sand dunes to another section, with much shorter shooting ranges. He parked near a few short concrete benches and helped everyone out. Then he hauled out a large black duffel bag from the back seat of the truck.

Once they were settled, a different side of Isaac came out, a side that spoke far more than usual. He gave them all a talk about gun safety and range rules.

"And never point a gun—empty, loaded, or otherwise—at anything you don't want to shoot. Which reminds me—" He paused and aimed a look at Katie. "Are we good, Katie?"

All three of the other women snickered like school girls. Katie narrowed her eyes at him. "We were."

One side of his mouth lifted and he finished going over general rules. Then he pulled out two small guns, making snarky remarks about the value of a Sig versus a Glock. Katie didn't understand any of it, but Zoe bantered back. He went over a few starting tips and passed out magazines and a box of bullets to everybody and instructed them on loading the magazines. He finished at least five while they struggled to feed bullets into theirs.

"Ready," Zoe said, lifting hers.

"Come on, let's get targets up," he said.

They clipped four paper targets onto large wooden easels that somehow still stood despite the thousand bullet holes they each sported.

Back at the tables, Isaac pulled earplugs, earmuffs, and safety glasses out of the duffel bag. "Ears on, so you don't end up like me. Eye protection if you want it." Flora doubled up on everything. Isaac pulled out a separate set of electronic ear plugs for himself.

Zoe went first. Isaac walked with her toward the target, stopping a few yards away. She didn't seem to need much instruction. Then Ginny went, and her ten shots took much longer, as Isaac suggested minor changes between each, working on stance and aim. Then he repeated it with Flora. Each woman came back to load another magazine.

Isaac stood in the range, holding the emptied handgun Flora had finished off. He waved for Katie to join him. But he didn't hand her the gun when she arrived. He seemed to weigh it in his hands a moment, stepping closer to her. "I've been rude this week."

Katie feigned a gasp. "You don't say?"

He grinned. "I'm sorry."

"I think I get it now. I'm sorry I didn't handle things better back then."

"Well, the past is past." He put the gun in her hands. "Friends?"

Katie looked at the weapon. "Is this how we seal the deal?"

He laughed. "Insert the magazine like I showed you." He walked her through racking the first bullet, then put a hand on her shoulder to direct her stance and hold on the gun. After a couple tips on using the sights, he took a step back. "Take a shot."

Katie blew a breath out and squeezed the trigger.

She blinked one eye open, then squeezed a little tighter. Still nothing.

"What's wrong with this thing?"

"Whoa, don't swing it around." Isaac caught her arm and laughed at her. "Safety's on. It was a test. Keep your eyes open."

This time he took the gun from her, released the magazine and the bullet in the chamber, and handed it back empty.

"Hey, I just loaded that," Katie said.

"Yeah, and you're gonna do it again. Now dry fire a couple times until you can keep your eyes open and hand steady."

The second time, Katie saw what he meant. Not only did she involuntarily squeeze her eyes shut, she also jerked her arms away as soon as she tugged on the trigger. After a few more tries, she stayed steady.

Isaac reloaded the gun and flicked the safety off. He handed it to her. "You're hot."

Katie bit down on her smile and cleared her throat. "Thank you."

"Wipe the smirk off, Katelyn. I meant the weapon."

"Your words, not mine."

"Two shots, aim for the center."

Katie shot twice and then paused. They studied the target, less than four yards away. Not a single hole.

"Okay. Let's try home defense. We're moving closer." They closed half the distance. "Two shots."

This time she got one on the paper, but not even in a ring on the target. Isaac's mouth twisted. He adjusted her stance and hold again. "Okay, the perp is in your house and he's heading straight for your kids. Two shots, now."

"What? Don't say stuff like that."

"Shoot, Katie!"

She shot twice. One shot landed a couple inches away from the red dot, near the seven ring, the other another inch over.

"Whoo!" She pumped a fist up.

"Gun—" Isaac reminded, catching her arm and pushing it down.

"Sorry."

"Not bad. Take three steps to your right. You're in the kitchen, behind a wall. You're going to shoot at an angle."

She took two more shots. One landed in the six ring, one didn't make it onto the paper.

"He's in your hallway and he's got body armor, go higher. You see the ten-ring marked at the top? Shoot him there twice."

She readied her sights.

"He's gonna get the girls. Now or never!"

Bang. Bang.

Both landed within an inch of the ten marked at the top ring.

Katie cheered and Isaac took the emptied gun from her before she could swing it around again. He grinned at her. "You've always done best under pressure. Sorry for the kidnapper story, I couldn't think of anything else that would scare you."

"Nothing?" Katie raised her eyebrows. Plenty scared her.

"You nearly fought a moose over a camera."

She laughed, surprised he would bring up the past. "Admit it, those photos were worth it."

His smile spread. "Still think guns aren't fun?"

The fact he remembered such a small detail shocked her. "I'm a changed woman," she said.

He chuckled and nodded to the benches. "Go reload."

She retreated with the magazine in hand and the women continued taking turns until they each emptied their boxes of bullets. Then Isaac took a turn to show off, shooting rapid-fire, from various defensive positions, and walking sideways as he landed a shot in the dead center of each target, ten yards back.

"I'm getting there!" Zoe claimed.

He dropped the magazine onto a concrete table and pulled off his ear protection. "Once you can tell the rifle range from the handgun range, you can join me on the SWAT team."

Zoe made a face behind his back, clearly a skill she picked up from her kids.

He coached everybody through cleaning the guns, disassembling them and pulling out rags and tiny brushes. The weapons fell apart like miniature 3D puzzles.

"Do you know how to put these back together?" Flora asked, catching a spring from rolling off the table.

Isaac sighed. "Ten years in the army, seven on the police force, most of those on the SWAT team, and this is the treatment I get. I can assemble that gun blindfolded and in handcuffs."

"Now that I'd like to see," Katie said.

Isaac grinned. "Your enthusiasm for handcuffs and blindfolds has been noted."

Zoe cackled, and Ginny and Flora snickered.

"Ladies," Katie said, in her most scolding tone. "Don't encourage him."

"What? We're all married—or have been," Zoe said. "Can't say anything we haven't heard."

"Some of us are happily single now," Katie said.

"You don't want to get married again?" Zoe asked.

Katie felt her face warm. She kept her eyes on the tiny metal tube she brushed off. "And give up having the whole bed to myself? No, thanks. I don't miss arguing over the thermostat or toilet seat position."

Flora laughed and Zoe tsked, but Isaac raised an eyebrow at her. "Really?" he asked. His familiar laser-focus warmed her cheeks. He'd always had a knack for seeing through her. Everyone else gladly took happy Katie at face value, while Isaac read between the lines, and called out her deeper side.

Jokes came easily, but it discredited Aaron and her guilt won out. "I mean, we had a good marriage. Aaron was great. But it's still a lot of work. I gave it everything, then had it ripped away. I don't want to do that again."

What could they understand about it? These women likely took their husbands for granted, seeing only the little annoyances and losing sight of the joys. Katie knew what a relationship could be—the shared memories and dreams for a future—but it didn't make her want to do it again. It made her dread the thought of going back to square one, to awkward first dates and uncertain small talk.

"What about you, Isaac?" Zoe asked. "Would you get remarried?"

"Ditto Katie, minus the good marriage and great spouse." He arranged gun parts in front of him and pulled a beanie from the duffel bag. "Now, Flora, this is for you." He tugged the beanie over his eyes and assembled the handgun, blind, in a minute flat.

After the short drive back to the front of the gun club, Isaac pulled up next to their vehicles and opened the tailgate. He helped each woman down. Katie went last, and his hand landed on her back as she hopped down.

Everybody headed for their cars, saying their goodbyes and thanking Zoe for an unconventionally fun mom's day out.

"Katie," Isaac said, as she reached her car.

She stopped. They waited while Zoe pulled her vehicle out from between them, with a trail of dust. Only Katie saw her wiggle her eyebrows at her. Katie rolled her eyes back at the woman.

The space cleared, he walked over to her car and stood at the back of it, keeping a few feet between them. "Micah sent over some of the Bible club pictures. Thanks for those."

"Always happy to share pictures."

"Do you ever get tired of hearing how good you are?"

She laughed. "I don't know, do you?"

"Touché," he said with a smile. "Are you going to stay and take the baptism pictures next week?"

"I'm not sure." She didn't have a good reason not to, except the restlessness that came with being in Ridley Bay.

"Where are you and the girls going next?"

"We might stick to Texas for a little while. Maybe Austin." She needed to look for an apartment. Honestly, the constant moving felt more exhausting than exciting.

"Not going back to Alaska?"

"Never. I don't go to the same place twice."

He chuckled. "Sounds like you."

"Besides, it's already snowing in Juneau, while I'm taking the girls out for a picnic lunch today."

He nodded and took a step back. "Sounds good. Enjoy your picnic."

"Wait," Katie said. She wasn't ready to let him go. "I have a question. Zoe said you were divorced."

He frowned. "Yeah."

"You didn't tell me you got married. What happened?"

He stuck his hands into his pockets and leaned back slightly. "I worked a lot of nights. She didn't want to spend her nights alone. So she found somebody else to spend them with."

Katie sucked in a breath through her teeth. "Yikes. Thus, all women are liars, huh?"

He looked away. "I know it's not right."

"But it's safe."

"Yeah."

"I'm sorry," she said.

"I'm sorry for your loss, too. I really am. I've heard great things about Aaron."

"They're all true." He hadn't been perfect, and they had their share of married spats, but he had been a wonderful man.

"Then I'm glad some part of him gets to live on in the girls," Isaac said. "I'm guessing they're copies of him, since they didn't get much from you."

Katie laughed and glanced down at her crossed arms. "Yeah. They're all Kaminski."

"It must be hard, raising them on your own."

She nodded. She had nothing positive to say to that.

"You're doing good, Katie."

She met his gaze again. "No, I'm not."

"You're doing the right thing, no matter how hard it is."

"I don't always do it the right way."

"None of us do. But I have a feeling you'll get there."

Why did that make her emotions turn upside down? She swallowed. "Thanks."

Then he really surprised her by moving closer and wrapping his arms around her. It sent shockwaves through her. She hadn't had someone's arms around her like this in so long. It felt strange. Familiar from too long ago. Different from Aaron. Somehow comforting and safe. Katie chided herself for thinking of the word. She hadn't felt *unsafe* before. It was just hormones. Hormones she thought had long since faded away. Maybe she needed more hugs in her life.

They both stepped back and Isaac glanced at his watch. "I guess I'll see you at the festival tonight," he said.

"Yep. Hopefully I'll be the only one shooting anything."

He grinned. "Let's count on it."

"Thanks for the gun lesson."

"You need another," he said, stepping away.

"Next time I'm in town," she called back.

He shot her a grin over his shoulder before disappearing around the truck. The twenty-two-year-old inside of her squealed but Katie shut her up. What in the world was she doing? She didn't make the same mistakes twice.

Chapter Thirteen

Why in the world did he hug her? There should be a name for it: The Katie Effect. The green eyes turned men—or at least Isaac—into gluttons for punishment. Ever since that hug, he'd been thinking of more. Of his last night in Fairbanks and a kiss he couldn't forget. Things he didn't need to think about.

Isaac ate a late lunch and mowed his yard, then pushed the mower to Vera's yard. He should probably save this for tomorrow but he needed to keep moving. By the end of the festival, he would be exhausted. Maybe he would finally get a good night of sleep tonight.

Vera knelt outside by her garden bed. She raised a hand to him and struggled to stand. Isaac jogged to her side and helped her up.

"These old legs," she muttered, shaking her head. "One day I won't be able to get up again."

Isaac glanced at the pile of weeds on the ground. "Can I do that for you?"

"No," she snapped. "I need to know I'm still good for something."

"Me too."

"Wait until you retire," she said. "It gets worse."

"I'll work until the job kills me." It would kill him one way or another. Everybody knew cops died soon after retiring. Sitting around with all that junk in their heads and bodies always killed them. He'd rather die in the line of duty than in a recliner.

Vera scoffed. "I'm not sure whether to laugh or scold you. There are other things to live for. You'll find yours."

Isaac adjusted his sunglasses and glanced down the street. He needed to finish this yard sooner than later. "I guess."

"What about your wife?" Vera asked. "When will the two of you have some children?"

Here we go again. "We got divorced." And his child was long gone. Dumped in the trash. He tried to shake off the thought but it stuck like a thorn.

She gasped and wagged a finger. "I knew that girl was no good. I tell you, you can trust my intuition." She pointed at her head.

They repeated the usual conversation for a little while before Isaac excused himself to mow her yard. Vera shook her head, looking down at her flower bed. She pointed down at a purple flower. "You know, those asters make a good tea for treating fevers, if you ever need some."

"They make medicine for that now."

Vera patted his arm and gave him a weak smile. "I just wanted someone to know. My son doesn't care either." Then she turned and hobbled up the steps to her house.

Isaac sighed. He could feel bad for hurting her feelings or he could mow her lawn. The latter would accomplish something, so he did that.

An hour later, he had finished all the chores, showered, and changed into his police uniform for the festival. He drove his patrol car to the event two hours before they opened the gates for the evening.

A frenzied pace greeted him as volunteers rushed around to get everything set up. None of the other officers had to arrive for another hour, and Isaac sat in his patrol car to wait most of it out. This is what his mother didn't understand about his job—the waiting outnumbered the excitement ten to one.

When it got closer to festival time, a few early birds started waiting at the gate and the other officers showed up. Isaac went over the layout and stations for everyone. The festival space held a game area with everything from a dunk tank to pumpkin decorating, a large white tent featuring a craft market, four food trucks, a concert stage, and a petting zoo at the back.

Shortly before the gates opened, Katie and the Kaminski family bypassed the line and entered through the volunteer entrance. The girls both wore monkey costumes, and Katie had a shirt that said, *"This is my circus, these are my monkeys."*

"Hey," Isaac said to the group, walking up as Officer Dempsey began a thorough search of Katie's backpack.

Katie barely lifted her eyes to him. "Do we have to take all the lenses out?" she asked. "I have a media pass, this seems excessive."

"We're checking everyone's bags," Dempsey answered patiently.

"Careful—" Katie put her hand under Dempsey's as she lifted another lens. "Those are really expensive."

"Don't worry, Katie. Butter Fingers here hasn't dropped anything in twelve minutes." Isaac patted Dempsey's shoulder.

Officer Dempsey snorted as she settled the last lens into the bag. "She's good to go."

Isaac picked up the bag and passed it back to Katie. "Why is this thing heavier than a full duty vest?"

Katie situated the bag on her shoulders. "Fancy cameras. I don't let anyone touch them." Her eyes skimmed over Dempsey for a split second and Isaac couldn't help but grin.

He turned to Suzanne, holding a little monkey by each hand. "You guys ready? Got a leash for that one?" He indicated the blonde.

Suzanne laughed. "Jojo? No leash, but a firm grip. And man-on-man coverage."

Isaac knelt to monkey height. Josie, who could barely see past her monkey hood, only now noticed him. Her face lit up. "Wewoo!" she shouted.

"Yeah, that's my car." He grinned. "Girls, I don't think we've officially met. I'm Isaac. You must be monkey Josie, and you're monkey Sage?" Both girls nodded silently. "Nice to meet you. Have fun tonight. You can come get any one of us 'wewoos' if you ever need help."

He stood and pointed out the lost child area to Suzanne and William. "You might want to show it to the girls and review a plan with them in case."

Katie elbowed him. "Could you stop scaring poor Nana and Pop? My children aren't feral."

Isaac's gaze ran down her. "You happen to lack natural fear. Is it genetic?"

A smile split across her face before Katie ducked her head to hide it and clear her throat.

"We did get our two boys safely through childhood," Suzanne volunteered.

Isaac held his hands up in innocence. "Okay. Not my circus." Until somebody gets lost and he was the one to deal with it.

Katie pulled on her *"Media Team"* lanyard and wove a camera strap over her shoulder. "*This* is my circus. I've got pictures to take." She kissed her girls and flashed a quick smile and head shake at Isaac before stepping away. The Kaminskis took the twins in the other direction.

Isaac turned around to find Dempsey's eyebrows halfway up her forehead. "What?" he asked.

"I hope you're not that chatty all night, we'll never get through the line."

Isaac zipped his lips. He blamed the festival cheer.

•　　　•　　　•

Katie would have guessed Isaac's smile had entirely different effects on young children than it did grown women, until she heard even Josie go silent in the introductions. Maybe that smile froze them all. And where did nice Isaac come from? Introducing himself to her kids like he was... *something*.

It didn't matter, she had a job to do. Her favorite job.

When Suzanne and William disappeared with the girls, Katie popped the lens cap off and headed outside the gates to where a crowd already formed a line. Children stood on parents' toes and rode on shoulders. There were costumes of all kinds—except anything gruesome, a Grace Church rule to keep it kid-friendly. Katie's favorites were the homemade ones—the kid in a cardboard box jail cell, the stroller turned into a pirate ship, or the teen in a Santa Claus outfit, handing out candy in a reverse-trick-or-treat move.

Life looked brighter through a camera lens and Katie caught it all.

She stood just inside the gates when it opened, catching the wonder and finger points of excited children. She could easily fill her camera with these moments. However, she avoided the grumpy parents and eye-rolling teens. She didn't need reality. She needed happy. Happy photos created happy memories, regardless of the reality surrounding them.

She headed to all the little kid spots first, before the kids got too overstimulated. She captured evening sunlight sparkling on the duck pond games, the upside-down grin of a kid in a corn pit, and a festival worker handing out fistfuls of candy.

For the most part, she made sure to stay away from her own kids, to prevent a Josie meltdown. But at one point, she spotted them across the way and snagged a picture of Sage getting her face painted—her wide, serious eyes focused intently on the mirror in front of her.

Making her rounds, Katie caught a few snaps of almost every performance on the main stage. Middle school choirs and high school bands provided the soundtrack for the evening. As the sky darkened, string lights took over, creating a sparkling background.

Later, she came across Josie eating funnel cake with William. "Where's Sage?" Katie asked, slightly annoyed at Isaac for making her feel paranoid.

"Bathroom trip with Nana," William said.

Satisfied, Katie grabbed a picture of powdered sugar on Josie's cheeks and gave her a kiss. Josie watched her mom leave without protest this time, happy to stay with Pop for the sugar.

A minute later, she crossed paths with Isaac. He stopped and gave her a funny look. "What?" she asked.

He reached over and swiped a thumb at her nose. "No drugs, Katie," he said.

Katie pulled back and rubbed her nose. "I kissed a little monkey."

Isaac tilted his head, wearing half a grin. "These street names are hard to keep up with."

"It's powdered sugar, you nut."

He grinned and licked his thumb. "Didn't think you seemed like the type."

Katie laughed. Was he flirting with her? Or trying to make up for being rude all week? Nice Isaac could mess with a girl's head. She should know. She took a step back. "How's security going tonight?"

He glanced around and leaned his good ear slightly toward her. "I'm not bored."

Katie frowned. "I don't think that means anything good for the rest of us."

His half grin stayed in place. "Dempsey and Zapata just arrested someone violating a restraining order."

Katie's eyes went wide. "Are you serious? And I missed all the excitement?"

"That's the goal."

"Sometimes I regret not going into news. The pictures I could get…"

He chuckled. "I'm sure you have better stuff than an angry ex on there." He gestured to her camera. "How's your job going?"

This was the guy she had met a decade ago, not the cynic she found a week ago. The past and present started to blend, to swirl and ignite. Katie leaned back against the magnetism, pretending to scroll through photos on her camera. She knew exactly what she had. "Yeah, I think so."

"The little monkeys seem to be having fun."

Katie glanced at him. The man was fire: mesmerizing, gorgeous, and untouchable. She needed to escape. "They are."

"I saw them dunk a high schooler in the tank earlier."

"Oh! The dunk tank. I still need to photograph that. Thanks!" Without waiting for a goodbye, she whirled around and headed toward the tank, as fast as she could. She already had dunk tank photos.

Chapter Fourteen

The night had nearly ended and the crowd thinned out to mostly older kids and their families. Suzanne and William found Katie, each carrying a little monkey. When Josie saw Katie walking up, she threw herself toward her mother and wailed, kicking at William.

Katie quickly pulled off her camera and zipped it into her bag before reaching for Josie. "I'll take the tired monkey."

With Josie settled in her arms, Katie listened to Suzanne rattle off all the girls' favorite things—the donkey they had petted, the carousel they rode, and the hay bale maze Sage had mastered. Suzanne made a fall festival with toddlers sound magical, almost more fun than photography. Katie felt a tinge of jealousy.

"I think we're ready to call it a night," William said. "Do you want us to take them back to our house?"

"Or if you give us the key to your apartment, we can put them to bed," Suzanne offered.

Katie didn't want either. While she deeply appreciated their help, she was used to doing things on her own and had never missed her kids' bedtimes. Some days she might resent that fact, but today, she didn't want them to leave without her. She had festival FOMO—fear of missing out.

"No, thank you so much though. I'll take them from here."

"Are you sure? Are you done?"

"I have more than enough pictures," Katie said.

"Do you want us to help you to the car?"

"No, really, I think we might walk around a little more. We'll be fine."

Suzanne glanced at her watch and pursed her lips. "It's getting late."

Katie bit her tongue and forced herself to reply nicely. "It's a special night. I want a few minutes to enjoy it with the girls."

Suzanne sighed. Reluctantly, the grandparents finally left Katie with her little monkeys held by each hand.

She made her way back to the petting zoo, where both girls perked up. It was quieter now, only a couple of other families hung around when they headed inside. Josie made a beeline for the bunnies, while Sage stopped at the first goat she found. Katie squatted down to her level, free of the camera for a moment, and watched as Sage flashed her a mile-wide smile which Katie freely returned. The goat stood a bit taller than Sage, with floppy ears and those crazy slit eyes. He nudged at Sage and Katie leaned forward to block him from getting any more aggressive but Sage only giggled.

"You're the goat whisperer, huh?" Katie asked.

Sage nodded, running a hand down his long, hairy nose. "He likes me."

Katie's chuckle escaped as air. She glanced around, but no one was near them—no witness to Sage's voice. *It does exist.* And Katie loved the sound of it.

"He sure does," Katie said. She reached a hand out near Sage's and the goat nudged her, still looking for food. "Do you want to feed him?"

Sage's eyes lit up as she looked at Katie and nodded.

Katie stood and passed Josie on her way to buy a cup of feed. "Don't strangle the bunny, Jo," she said as she walked past.

The middle-aged woman manning the table of feed cups took Katie's money and passed her two cups. She wore a "Peterson's Petting Zoo" shirt.

"How much does a goat cost?" Katie asked, taking the feed cups and change.

The lady laughed and didn't answer. It might be a rhetorical question but Katie would take a goat home tonight if Sage liked it so much.

She returned to her daughters with the feed cups and Josie and two more goats joined. Sage and Josie both giggled to the point of hysterics when the goats slobbered all over their hands.

"Sage, wook," Josie said, pointing as nearby goat droppings fell from one.

"He needs a potty," Sage said, all but cackling.

That's it. I'm buying a goat. "Girls," Katie scolded their potty jokes, though she couldn't hide her smile. She needed this moment. She needed to capture it. Katie slipped her camera out of her bag and backed away a few steps to get the right angle.

Their monkey suits were dirtied with goat slobber and old powdered sugar and it wasn't picture-perfect, but their smiles more than made up for it. Sage's hand looked so tiny beneath the goat's fuzzy lips and Josie's eyes twinkled with mischief as she lifted a goat's ear to peek underneath. Katie needed a wider angle to catch the full scene. "Keep feeding that one," she said to Sage as she backed away to one side of the fence.

Behind the lens, she tweaked her camera settings when she heard a scream—not one of her own kids. Through the lens, she saw a little boy running up to their group, startling the goats. Katie lowered her camera in time to see Josie's goat back-step into the goat Sage was petting. It swung up to headbutt at the goat but crashed down onto Sage. With a thunk, she landed in the dirt as the goats scattered.

Capping her camera, Katie jogged over to Sage. "You okay, kiddo?" Sage's wide eyes stared up at her but she didn't move. "Here you go." Katie held her hand out to her, waiting.

Sage's mouth opened and for a second nothing came out. Maybe it had knocked the wind out of her? Then her piercing scream filled the air.

Katie dropped onto her knees. "Whoa, Sage, shh, you're okay. The goat got scared, it didn't mean to hurt you."

Sage clutched one arm around her chest and screamed louder. Katie's heart rate began a rapid climb. "Sage, honey, what's wrong?" She ran her hands over her daughter's body, gently lifting her head to check for blood or anything she might have hit.

"Mommy, watch me," Josie said, twirling in Katie's periphery.

Sage screamed again and tears trickled down her cheeks. The woman who had sold Katie the feed reached them. "Is everything okay?"

"No, I think she's hurt. A goat knocked her down."

The woman reached for Sage, who arched away silently. "Those goats are just playing, you don't have to be afraid of them."

"She's not afraid, she's hurt," Katie said.

"They wouldn't hurt a fly," the woman said.

Tears trailed down Sage's dirty cheeks and she struggled not to cry in front of the woman. Sage's mouth pressed into a tight line and her body shuddered. It didn't look like a seizure but Katie's panic kicked in and she couldn't tell what was happening apart from what she feared.

"Mommy, did you see my spin?" Josie asked.

"Not now, Jojo!"

"Here," the woman said, putting a hand on Sage's shoulder. "Let's sit you up." The moment the woman touched Sage, Sage screamed, and the woman's hand flew back.

"Don't touch her," Katie said as her panic skyrocketed. Nothing was visibly wrong with Sage. *Just like Aaron.* She reached for Sage's pulse, losing her last bit of control. Katie needed help. She needed Isaac. "Get security. Now."

The woman scurried off.

"Mommy! You didn't wook!" Josie stomped her feet near Katie.

Katie gritted her teeth together, her focus blurring and her mind filled with hay and dirt. Sage's heart rate seemed high but not dangerously so. "Josephine Erin. Your. Sister. Is. Hurt."

"Watch dis." Josie did another spin.

"Okay." Katie flashed her the only smile she could muster before turning her attention back to Sage. "It's okay, baby, we're going to help you feel better soon."

"I sorry," Sage said between sobs.

Katie's heart broke into a thousand pieces. What had she done to make her child think she had to apologize for getting hurt?

"It's not your fault, angel." If it was anyone's fault, it was the little boy's, but he was gone. Or maybe it was Katie's, for being behind the camera lens when it all happened. For choosing a perfect picture over being in the moment. Guilt ran over her like rain. She should have stayed closer to the girls. She should have been able to reach Sage sooner.

"I sorry, Mommy."

"Stop saying that!" Katie snapped. Sage's eyes filled with fresh tears, while the burning guilt and panic filled Katie's chest with intense pressure.

Nobody else remained in the petting zoo pen. The festival was closing and Katie was here, alone, on her knees. The pressure grew to a tipping point until she heard the pen gate slam and the voice of someone stronger than her. "What happened?"

Oh, thank God. She dropped her shoulders, absurdly relieved at the sound of Isaac's voice. "A goat got spooked and head butted her—" Katie tried to retell it but Isaac barely listened as he dropped onto his knees.

"Hey, little monkey," he said softly as he looked her over.

"She has the same heart defect Aaron did," Katie said, close to his ear.

"Tell me more," he said, smiling at Sage as he took her pulse.

"Arrhythmia, it goes too fast. Seizures can be part of it too, but she's never had any."

"Which of those bullies needs a timeout?" he asked Sage, gesturing to the goats in a little herd near them.

Sage turned her head and tried to point at one, but lifting her arm made her face crinkle up. She used every fiber in her being to fight her tears and Katie leaned down to kiss her face and hide her from the world so she could cry.

Isaac rested a hand on Katie's back and she lifted. He turned toward Katie's ear, directing his voice away from Sage. "Heart rate seems okay. Something might be broken though, I think she needs an X-ray."

"How do we get her to my car?"

He rubbed her back and held her gaze, obviously trying to bolster her before making his suggestion. "We don't. I'll call an ambulance."

"An ambulance?" Katie asked, unable to keep the rising pitch out of her voice. Did he not want to move her? Was he suggesting a spinal problem? Or did he think they needed something faster—or a transport option with defibrillator?

He took both of her hands in his. "She's gonna be okay. But if she doesn't want to move, I won't force her."

"But Josie…" Katie said, glancing at her other daughter. The petting zoo attendant entertained her with bunnies and cast nervous glances at Katie and Sage.

"I'll call William and Suzanne too."

Katie nodded and Isaac radioed for an ambulance. Somehow he also placed a phone call in between singing lines of the "Five Little Monkeys" song to Sage and messing up all the lyrics. Katie sat on her heels, useless, holding Sage's hand and mentally grasping at something—she didn't know what.

People filed into the petting zoo. JP and Micah both arrived. JP took over entertaining Josie. Someone else helped the petting zoo attendant load animals back onto the trailer. They began to clean up while Sage lied in dirt, hay, and animal waste. Eventually, enough people surrounded her that Sage tried to move toward Katie, trying to sit up, trying to hide, and crying at the effort. Katie cradled her arms around her until the paramedics arrived.

The paramedics asked the same questions as everyone else and did the same assessment as Isaac. Katie gave them more information on the heart condition. They looked serious as they took notes and she wished they would tell her it wasn't related. A broken bone shouldn't have anything to do with Sage's heart, but it still put stress on her little body. Katie tried to fight fear with logic, but fear was never perfectly rational.

The EMTs set a stretcher next to Sage. A horrible, oversized, metal bed too large for a toddler and Katie hated it. "She doesn't need that, does she?"

"It's just standard," a female EMT replied, in the same overly nice tone Isaac had used.

"Isaac…" Katie said. She couldn't see him, but she could feel his presence behind her.

He put his hand on her shoulder. "It's okay. I'll close out here and meet you at the hospital."

She shouldn't have needed to hear that, but she did. She nodded, leaning into his hand and trying to absorb all the strength she could.

Suzanne and William arrived as the EMTs loaded Sage into the ambulance. Katie passed her car key and camera bag to Isaac, gave Josie a quick peck on the cheek, and dove behind the growing crowd to avoid interacting with her in-laws. She could see Suzanne's panic a mile away and didn't need an ounce of it near her right now. She had enough of her own as she climbed into the ambulance next to Sage.

Chapter Fifteen

It took another hour to clear the festival area. Josie had long since gone home with her grandparents, JP had filed incident reports with the petting zoo company, and the other officers had taken off. Isaac walked out to the empty parking lot with Micah.

"Are you going to the hospital?" Micah asked.

Isaac glanced at his watch, beginning to regret his offer to go with Katie. In the moment, she needed it. Now, it felt too personal, and he was selfishly exhausted. "It's way past visiting hours."

"You think they won't let you in?" Micah asked in faux innocence.

Isaac knew most of the nurses at the hospital, he had been there on official duty often enough. They wouldn't question him. And he had promised Katie he would go. He blew out a breath of resignation. "I'll go check on her." It might soothe his own guilt over the situation. He couldn't keep everybody safe, but he hated ending the night with an ambulance. Even more, he hated putting Katie and Sage in it.

"Keep us updated," Micah said.

"Will do."

Isaac climbed into his patrol car and took the familiar drive to the hospital. He brought plenty of people here, took reports here, and escorted a few convicts here.

One of his favorite nurses, Patty, was working at the desk when he arrived. "Officer Torres," she said, with a toothy smile. "What can we do for you?"

"Hey Patty. I'm here to check on a friend."

"Sure, who is it?"

"Katie and Sage Kaminski."

Patty put a hand to her heart. "Oh, that little redhead is so darling."

He wanted to tell her she should see the twins together, but he only gave her a half smile instead. She left to find Katie, while Isaac sank into a cold plastic chair in the waiting area two seats away from an elderly man. A pair of college students sat in a far corner, heads together, whispering. Doubts about being here and exhaustion from a long day crowded any other thoughts.

He crossed his arms and closed his eyes for a second until he heard footsteps. Katie followed Patty into the waiting area, her eyes red. She looked as tired as he felt. Isaac stood and met her halfway.

"Hey. Are you okay?" he asked.

"Fantastic. Never better." She let out a breathy laugh and gestured down the hall. "They have an ice cream vending machine. Did you know that exists? I bet it scares people into thinking they've died and gone to heaven."

She needed that—a quick deflection, a joke. Isaac held her gaze. "How's Sage?"

Her shoulders dropped, her eyes darted away. "Broken collarbone and two cracked ribs."

"Ouch."

Katie nodded, unusually silent.

"What's wrong?"

"I want to go home. To our apartment. Wherever. But we have to stay overnight."

A slight shake in her voice grabbed his attention. "Because of the heart condition?" He had to admit she freaked him out with that comment at the festival. His first aid knowledge didn't include heart defects.

"Yeah. They ran a couple tests…" Her voice trailed off.

"And?"

"She's okay. Thank God." Yet her voice sounded robotic—not particularly thankful or relieved.

Isaac doubted God had much to do with it. "That's good news, right?"

"I know. It's just… Aaron and ICU and hospitals. I don't like being here." She pressed her pointer fingers to the bridge of her nose.

A story hid somewhere in those words but he could read between the lines. Katie's head was partly here and partly in the past. He needed to bring her back. "That was Aaron. This is Sage. She isn't in ICU, is she?"

Katie shook her head.

"And the doctors said she'll be okay."

She nodded, still not meeting his eyes. "I know." Her voice cracked and she crossed her arms tightly around herself, as if she might be able to hold herself together from the outside in.

For a moment, he felt ten years and one divorce younger, and he cared about the woman in front of him. Maybe because they never had any real closure, he suddenly realized some part of him may have never stopped caring.

Katie broke the silence with a whisper and the weakest smile, barely capable of lifting the corners of her mouth, much less her eyes. "I should probably get back to her."

"Do you want me to come with you?"

Her eyes jerked up to his, a washed out, pale green color. "You would do that?"

"Of course." Why did he offer that? He hadn't even been with Lauren when his own child died. And this wasn't his kid. It was Katie's and Aaron's. And Aaron was dead. The world had scrambled all the pieces and dumped them at his feet.

She reached a hand out to brush his elbow, some sign of gratitude or "follow me" perhaps, then led him down the hall. Isaac nodded at Patty's raised eyebrow as they went past—a silent no-visitors reminder she wouldn't enforce. He almost wished she would.

Katie cracked open the door, slipping into the dark room where Sage slept, her monkey outfit traded for a child-sized hospital gown. Now a brief flash of anger replaced his moment of doubt. These people believed in God, yet lived in a world where child-sized hospital gowns existed. He swallowed and silently lifted a chair over to the bedside, next to the one Katie sat in.

"I don't know if it's a good record or terrible one, but we've only had one other emergency room visit with the twins before this," Katie said.

"Josie?"

She gave him the briefest of smiles. "How'd you know?"

"A hunch."

"She tried to fly off a playground when she was two. Got four stitches on her forehead. Her hair covers the scar." Katie shuddered. "You have no idea how horrible it is to see blood on your kid."

Debatable. Maybe he hadn't seen it on his own child, but he had seen worse things than a forehead cut on others. "Does Josie have the heart defect too?"

"Thankfully no."

Isaac hesitated, wanting to know more, but not wanting to push her too far. "What does it mean for Sage in the long run?" he asked.

"It's just something to manage," Katie said simply. "We know what to look for and what to do. She should be fine. We just didn't know Aaron had it."

Realization settled heavily around Isaac. Aaron's death was preventable. He could only imagine how many nights that had haunted Katie. "I'm sorry."

She shrugged. For a moment, only the steady beep of a monitor kept them company. Hair stuck to Sage's sweaty forehead, one arm slung out to the side, while the other rested against her chest in a sling. Katie brushed her hair back. "I hate seeing her in pain. She's limited on what medication she can take. If she moves the wrong way, she cries, and then the crying hurts her even more. I'm used to Josie's crying, but it freaks me out to hear it from Sage."

What could a three-year-old understand about pain management and hearts and broken bones? Did anyone know what Sage could or couldn't understand? "Does she ever talk?" he asked.

"She talks to Josie and me. You should have seen her with the goats. She said a couple of full sentences. I nearly bought one on the spot before it tried to take her out."

Isaac tilted his head toward Sage, trying to imagine her voice. Similar to Josie's, he assumed, though more calculated. "It's not related to the heart condition, is it?"

"No. Just who she is."

"But is it who she wants to be?"

Silence followed for a moment. "I don't know. She balances out Josie and I figured that was a good thing. Maybe not."

"The quiet ones usually have the best things to say. Sometimes they need help getting it out though."

Though they had been talking side-by-side, she turned to face him now and he met her gaze. What a mistake. Even in a room illuminated only by the flashing lights of medical equipment, Katie could still take his breath away. Those ten years and all they held seemed to vanish.

Katie must have felt it too, because she leaned her head on his shoulder. Instinctively, he dropped his arm around her. In an instant, Isaac knew he was in trouble. He would repeat the past without hesitation with this woman. She was his drug of choice.

The shrill ring of his phone broke the quiet and he grabbed at it like a man lost at sea, reaching for a lifesaver. A police department number lit the screen. Isaac walked toward the door, as far from Sage as possible, though she hadn't stirred at the noise. "Torres," he answered.

A dispatcher's voice snapped through the line. "We're activating the SWAT team, we need all officers to respond immediately."

His Katie-drunk mind snapped to attention, immediately sobered. "Where?"

"Salville. Possible hostage situation, suspect exchanged fire with officers."

A police shootout in a tiny town fifteen miles north of Ridley Bay. The truck was already heading there with their gear. "I'll be there in twenty. Send me the location."

He ended the call and stared at the door for a second before turning back to Katie. Something was wrong with him. He felt more comfortable rushing into a SWAT call than being in this room. Lauren had accused him once of preferring a stranger's emergency to a loved one's personal problems. Maybe she had been right.

Katie stood with one hand on the bed and the other on the back of the chair. "You're leaving?"

"I'm sorry," he said. "It's a SWAT call."

"Okay."

"I have to go."

She nodded, her bold, fearless demeanor temporarily replaced with insecurity.

Regret built in his chest, both past and future, as he walked out of the room without another word.

•   •   •

A thousand emotions coursed through her. Shame over how desperately she wanted Isaac to stay. Anger at Aaron, for not being here with her. A familiar, crushing loneliness. A touch of fear over whatever had called Isaac out the door.

Katie stood, staring at the door he had disappeared through for far too long. As if by staring at it, the moment of his sudden departure might rewind and play out differently. Her stepfather had been an investigator— his work usually took place after the immediate danger had ended. Watching someone rush into an active situation felt different. She wanted to know what was happening. Penn and Zoe might know, but she couldn't text a friend at this hour, much less a new acquaintance.

Finally, Katie pulled back her shoulders and lifted her head. She had enough to worry about with Sage. She didn't need anyone else to worry about, and she certainly didn't need anyone else here at the hospital. "You've done this on your own since the beginning," she muttered. "You can do it tonight too." She had weathered stomach bugs and colds and Josie's four stitches alone. She would survive this too.

Katie dropped onto the small, cold, leather sofa in the room, tucking the thin fleece blanket provided around her. She tried to rest, but before she could settle in, Sage woke up crying.

"Oh, baby, shh. It's okay." Katie climbed into the bed with her and cuddled her close. Sage wasn't loud like Josie, but every cry filled the cracks in Katie's soul with guilt and regret like lead. Somehow, this was her fault. Her mind could easily conjure up Suzanne's disappointed look when she found out the circumstances of the injury. Would Aaron wear it too if he were here?

Sage's cries increased in intensity and Katie's own panic rose as she tapped the nurse call button. They had to keep Sage's heart rate regular and it required a fine balance of medication—not too much or too little. Katie rocked and shushed Sage until the nurse arrived.

Finally, they gave Sage another dose of pain medication and strapped her arm sling a bit tighter to prevent any more movement. After what seemed like an eternity, Sage quieted and drifted back to sleep—her eyes closed, her face relaxed again. The cut of her cheekbones and jawline so closely resembled Aaron's.

He never would have let this happen.

Katie squeezed her eyes shut for a moment, then looked around the room. She needed a distraction. At times like this, she would normally plan an imaginary vacation to anywhere happy. But tonight, nowhere seemed happy enough. Because despite being here, in a hospital, on her own, there was nowhere else she could imagine being than by her daughter's side. Katie tucked herself around Sage on the bed, pressed her lips to her forehead, and started to pray.

She prayed for Sage, and she prayed for Josie, spending the night with her grandparents. She prayed for the Kaminskis and for Grace Church, and for herself. The only prayer she wouldn't whisper was one for Isaac, no matter how often he came to mind. She had prayed for a man before and it hadn't ended well. She refused to open herself to that pain again.

Finally, exhausted, she fell into a light and frequently interrupted sleep.

Chapter Sixteen

Isaac took over as tactical lead on what had started as a domestic violence call. The suspect opened fire on the responding officers, immediately turning the call into a critical situation. The caller said she and two children were in the house in what was now a hostage situation.

A media drone hovered over them like a vulture, with a news truck parked a block away, no doubt housing a reporter giddy over fresh blood.

They had the cops cleared out of the area immediately and the closest neighbors had been evacuated. It had taken two hours but SWAT had free rein now. Their negotiator worked on the megaphone, cooing every reassurance, many of them lies. Isaac tired of the chatter. Adrenaline had sustained him until now; listening to the droning voice over the megaphone pulled the life out of him. He shook his head and pinched his eyes closed and open, trying to clear the sandy feeling from them.

Two snipers held rooftop positions on nearby houses. Repeated radio checks confirmed they had no chance of taking a shot. The blinds were all closed, the lights were out, they had nothing.

A call came through dispatch. The same number that had made the original call, likely the woman inside the house. But she didn't say anything. The call clicked off moments after ringing.

Isaac looked to their team commander, who nodded. "Let's get them out," he said, activating the breach team.

Officer Langley stumbled through putting on his gear, dropping his helmet. The man had responded to the SWAT call with a full-blown flu and raging fever. Isaac stood a safe distance in front of him as Langley stooped to grab his helmet. "What's wrong with you?"

"Nothing." Langley's eyes could hardly focus, sweat lined his forehead.

"Take it off."

"You need me," Langley said.

They did. They had a SWAT officer out of town on vacation and another recovering from surgery. "You're a liability," Isaac said.

"You can't send in three of us," Kingston said, already geared up.

"I can't send in *him*." Isaac jabbed a finger at Langley as if the flu were the man's own doing. No doubt he had picked it up from one of his three kids at home.

Langley swayed on his feet. He looked like he hadn't slept in days. "I can do it."

Isaac braced his hands against a cabinet and sighed. He was a weapons expert, not a raw force guy. He hated breaching, but he could do it. "Sit down and stop breathing on our gear. I'm going."

"You sure?" their team commander asked, not even looking over.

"I'm sure."

Moments later, Kingston took point, two other officers were the breachers, and Isaac provided rear cover. It was a scrappy team, but it would have to work. One sniper and one ground officer already covered the back of the house in case the guy tried to make a run for it.

A fresh burst of adrenaline heightened his senses as they made their approach. The negotiator backed away from the scene as the breach team crowded the front yard, black as the night around them.

Kingston and Zapata placed a small explosive on the door. A standard door, they could probably kick it open easily, but they weren't taking any chances on looking like idiots in case the guy had it fortified.

The bang set off a high ring in Isaac's ears as they all burst forward—Kingston, Zapata, White, and Isaac. Screams and crying came from upstairs. It sounded like kids.

They cleared an office on the first floor. Then the dining room. The hall opened to a kitchen and living room, with stairs on their right. Multiple points of access and one tiny team—

A flash of light and a shot rang out in the house and all hell broke loose.

White and Zapata dove behind the kitchen island. Officer Eckhardt burst in from the backyard. Kingston fired upstairs. Isaac took a corner angle, spotting the perpetrator on the stairs, using a pony wall as cover. They didn't have many options. The victims could be right behind the guy for all they knew. Every shot they took from here risked lives.

The second the suspect popped up again, countless shots exploded from both sides. They had no choice but to defend themselves at this point. Warmth spread through Isaac's arm. "Go!" he shouted when the shooting stopped.

Kingston and Zapata charged upstairs, ballistic shields raised to cover them and Isaac. It was a vulnerable position but they had few options. White and Eckhardt would have to cover downstairs.

They turned the corner on the stairs to find the perpetrator curled over himself, bleeding from somewhere, still holding his gun. He fired a wild shot.

With a swift kick, Kingston disarmed and restrained him. Kingston called for immediate medical evacuation for the man while Zapata and Isaac cleared the rest of the house. Isaac tried to shake out his arm and struggled to maintain his hold on his gun. He switched to his left hand.

They found a woman and two children tied to chairs in a bedroom. Before they even entered the room, a call rang over the radio, loud and clear. "Officer down." Was that Eckhardt's voice? Isaac's blood ran cold. All of him ran cold.

Zapata swore and grabbed his radio. "Make that two officers down."

Confusion spun in Isaac's mind for a moment before realization crashed down on him, along with burning pain, and the room tilted sideways.

Chapter Seventeen

Katie woke at the crack of dawn when a shift change brought in a new nurse. She did a quick check on Sage while Katie glanced at her phone. Dead as a doornail. "Do you happen to have a phone charger?" she whispered. She only had her purse with her. The Kaminskis had her car, and everything else was at the apartment. An apartment they only had for one more day.

"Sure, hon." The nurse reached for the phone. "I'll charge it at the nurse's station and bring it back once it's up and running again."

Not ideal, but beggars can't be choosers. Katie passed off the phone and stretched out her stiff body, gently climbing off the crowded bed.

Sage had woken once more in the night, and nurses had woken Katie twice. Luckily, Katie knew how to survive on little sleep. She had struggled with insomnia ever since the twins were born. Or maybe since Aaron's death. Those events all ran together too tight to tell.

The energy of the morning crew buzzed in and out of the room. A doctor stopped by and said everything looked normal. He promised to get them out of there soon. Katie would need a ride from the Kaminskis. She asked for her phone to make the call and the nurse soon brought it back.

When she handed the phone to Katie, a shocking slew of notifications lit up the screen. Suzanne, Micah, JP, and Zoe filled her phone. Were they really that worried about Sage? Katie called Suzanne.

"He's okay," Suzanne answered breathlessly.

Katie squeezed her eyes shut and opened them again. What in the carnival world was going on? "*She's* okay, yes."

"Oh, Sage? Yes, thank goodness."

"Wait, who are you talking about?" The moment she asked, Katie knew. It came back to her like a ton of bricks. Isaac and the SWAT call. Katie nearly dropped her phone, fumbling for her texts. The dozen of texts from Zoe had nothing to do with Sage. Katie didn't hear Suzanne's rambling as she scanned the texts—*Isaac. Shot. Arm. Hospital.*

"He's here?" Katie demanded, ear to the phone.

"I suppose. It's all over the news, Katie, really, you should turn it on."

"I've been a little busy taking care of my child," Katie snapped back.

"Of course you have," Suzanne consoled. "I didn't mean—anyway, yes. I'm so glad Sage is okay. Are they releasing y'all?"

"Yes." Katie wasn't paying attention anymore. She stood on tiptoe trying to reach the remote underneath the television in the room. "Can you pick us up soon?"

"I'll send William so I don't have to bring Josie."

"Sounds good." Katie flicked on the television. Freed from the phone call, she quickly found the news station. Glancing back at Sage, happily eating a muffin, Katie muted the television and turned on closed captioning to protect little ears.

Aerial footage showed a dark street filled with SWAT vehicles and flashing emergency lights. Katie watched with one hand over her mouth. The camera switched back to two morning reporters in a news room, smiling inappropriately in the face of the dark topic. "A domestic violence call quickly escalated into a nightmare in Salville, Texas, when the suspect opened fire on first responders. Two members of the Southern Coastal SWAT team were shot. We received reports that one is stable, while another remains in critical condition."

Katie returned to the long text threads on her phone. Micah and JP had both included her in group texts asking for prayers for Isaac. Neither offered many details. Zoe, however, had insider knowledge.

Zoe: Are you awake?

Isaac is in a SWAT call, Penn's listening on the radio, just thought you might want to know

Two officers down

Isaac's hit

Shot in the arm.

Are you okay? Call me anytime, I won't be sleeping

Isaac's at the hospital

Wait, you're there too, right?

He's stable but we don't have any other info

He's not answering his phone

Sorry, I'm being rude, is Sage okay?

Katie texted her back, apologizing for the dead phone. She thought about offering to hunt down Isaac's room but hospital security might chase her out. Besides, Isaac wouldn't want her to see him like this. The man was—or had been—impenetrable. This would shake him to his core. Katie switched the television to a kids show and ran her hands over her face.

She should have prayed for him last night. Did a curse hang over her? She seemed to be a black widow—dooming the men closest to her.

The doctor returned, a large woman whose presence filled the room. She dismissed Sage with extremely specific instructions regarding medication, as well as follow-up appointments and care.

"Thank you." Katie took the handout of notes from the doctor. "Hey, I think my friend is here. Isaac Torres. He's one of the officers who was shot last night. Do you know how he's doing?"

The doctor smiled a patient, professionally distant smile. "We're giving him our full attention. He'll be fine."

"Can you tell me where he is?"

"Sorry," she said with a shrug. "Privacy laws."

Katie nodded. When the doctor left, she texted Isaac.

Katie: You're bulletproof

Don't make me a liar

Then she pocketed her phone and its partially charged battery. "Ready to go home, sweetie?" Katie asked, forcing her attention back to the room and her daughter.

Sage looked at her. "Where?" she asked softly.

In one word, Sage had settled the weight of the world squarely on Katie's chest. Where? Their apartment rental that ended tomorrow? The

Kaminskis' house? The next place? Katie swallowed and smiled. "I'm not sure," she croaked.

Everything was breaking down.

•　　•　　•

When Isaac woke, it could have been the next day, three days later, or three years later for all he knew. He felt eighty years old and weak. A dense fog surrounded his brain. A high sun shone through cracks in the blinds and his first thoughts were curse words. He'd been shot.

He tipped his head back and closed his eyes again. What kind of idiot gets shot?

He tried to replay the shooting, to see if it made any more sense now. From the sound of the first shot to the last, time played games with his memory—it seemed to have lasted either half a second or half an hour. Somehow both at once, though the truth was likely around a minute. When had he been shot? He remembered a warm feeling, maybe even a sting, but it didn't register as pain. His adrenaline had been running too high.

"Officer down." The first crackling voice on the radio had to be Eckhardt's. Which meant Officer White had been shot? Isaac needed updates. What had gone wrong? Was it a tactical error? They had been overexposed when they reached the center of the house, but what could they have done differently?

Glancing around the room, he saw two IV lines connected to him; one held a clear liquid, the other blood. Gauze covered everything from his right shoulder down to his elbow and he couldn't identify the actual injury.

All his life, through multiple deployments in the army, through multiple SWAT calls on the force, Isaac had been untouchable. He had come to believe he would either die on the force or retire from it. This—a show of weakness, a failure, a slow demise—had never been an option.

A knock sounded on his door.

"Yeah," Isaac called out, his throat dry, and his voice raspy. He cleared his throat.

The door cracked open and the police captain stepped in. "They said you were asleep," he said.

"And you couldn't let a sleeping dog lie."

Captain Watts grinned. "I'll harass you until you're in the afterlife, Torres."

"I'm sure you'll be harassing me there too."

"If we end up in the same places."

Isaac dropped his head back on the thin pillow and stared at the ceiling tiles; the speckled pattern seemed to dance. He didn't want to think about the afterlife right now. "Am I late on filing my reports?"

The captain snickered. "I'll give you a pass. You gonna pull through?"

Isaac tried to shrug but his right arm didn't move like it should. Instead, a stinging pain shot through it. He gritted his teeth and swallowed. "Ask the doctor, I guess."

Watts patted his good arm. "Glad you're okay."

"We screwed up."

"Not really. That guy put up one heck of a fight. Kingston said his insides were nearly his outsides and he was still shooting."

"Did he make it?"

"Still in critical condition. You guys shot a little too true."

Isaac nodded. He didn't remember much after they rushed upstairs. "How are the kids?"

"They're okay. So is the woman. They're all here at the hospital too, minor injuries. Most of the work's gonna be up here." The captain tapped his head. Psychological trauma.

"Who was the other officer shot?" Isaac asked.

"White. Couple of good chest shots. The ballistic vest caught them but he's got broken ribs and a bruised lung."

Isaac glanced down at his arm, covered in too much gauze for a minor scrape. "What do I have?"

"A real shot. I'll get your doctor in here to go over it. You might want to call your mom too, she somehow found my number."

"How does she know?"

"It's all over the news."

The drones and the news truck came back to him now. Details felt fuzzy. How had a bullet to his arm damaged his brain? "Right. Sorry. My mother is an amateur detective."

"I'll keep her in mind if we're ever hiring."

Isaac grinned. "Hey, that reminds me. Can I have Thanksgiving off?"

The captain snorted. "You can have whatever you want, Torres."

Oddly, Isaac didn't care for the way that sounded.

Captain Watts promised a return visit and debrief soon to come, then stepped out as a doctor walked in. The rundown on his arm didn't sound good, but the doctor played it up like Isaac should be happy.

"It's just an arm," the man said.

"Right. Like a lizard tail. I'll grow a new one," Isaac replied.

The doctor smirked and flipped through Isaac's charts. They all spoke the same dark humor. They had to in jobs like this. "As in you can live life with a hole in your arm, but you can't live with a hole in your head."

If the shot had been farther left, it would have hit his vest. If it had been higher up, it would have been the last thing Isaac's face ever felt. "I'd rather not have a hole in my arm."

The doctor raised his eyebrows in amusement. "We stitched it closed."

"Okay, be straight with me. How hard is life going to be with a hole in my arm?"

The doctor dropped the chart and squared up with Isaac. "It's going to be painful for several days, or weeks. You're going to have limited mobility. Your right arm may atrophy a bit. You'll probably need some physical therapy. But this doesn't have to retire you unless you want it to."

"Not a chance."

"Then you'll be back out there in a matter of weeks."

"Okay. But what's wrong with my head? I can't focus." Following a train of thought felt like hopping between clear patches in the fog.

"Blood loss," the doctor said simply. "You'll have some weakness and fatigue for a while, but you'll get your strength back."

"Okay. Thanks."

The doctor turned to leave. "By the way, someone dropped off a phone charger for you. The nurses unplugged their landline because of your mother."

Isaac choked back a laugh and glanced at his phone plugged in next to the bed. "I'll call her."

"Thank you."

When the doctor left, he reached for the phone with his left arm. Every inch of the movement sent pain radiating from his arm through his chest and back and down his legs. Was that normal?

His phone held messages and missed calls from everyone. Mom, Dad, Andres, Cristian, Oscar, Micah, JP, Penn, William, Dempsey, Zapata, Katie, even Lauren—which amused him. *"Semper fi,"* she wrote. Lauren had a remarkable ability to get under his skin, to simultaneously check in with him and irritate him. She wasn't dumb; she purposefully texted the former soldier a marine motto. *Always faithful*, a perfectly ironic thing for his unfaithful ex to send. He deleted the message.

His thumb hovered over Katie's text. *"You're bulletproof. Don't make me a liar."* If he texted her back, she would say something to make him smile. She still had that ability and he still had an addiction to her. And once again, they had a deadline on their time and a God in between them. Had he learned nothing from the past? This time would be worse; there was more of her—two little girls he already cared about. Last night at the hospital had reminded him not to walk down the same path again. With Lauren's *"semper fi"* fresh on his mind, he deleted Katie's text as well.

She should be leaving town any day now and he could carry on with his life. Today, he needed to call his mother, and he knew it might take a while. He already wanted a nap. Eighty-year-old Isaac needed lots of naps.

"Isaac Torres!" she answered, launching into a tirade against his delayed phone call, but it quickly turned weepy. "You said you were always safe. Why were you running into a house with a madman?" Her words choked over. Isaac waited it out.

"To save people," he said calmly.

"That's not your job!" she nearly screeched. It didn't sound at all like his mother. No wonder the doctor and captain had both begged him to call her. "Your job is to be on the ground and tell the other guys what to do."

"And sometimes, my job is to get the job done, whatever it requires."

Just tears.

Isaac sighed. "Mom, I'm okay. You're talking to me right now. I'm fine."

"*I'm* not," she said. "I would fly out there right now but my doctor doesn't want me to, he says I'm too weak. Well, he's never met a mother then. I can do anything for my children."

"Stay in Phoenix, I'll be there in three weeks for Thanksgiving."

"*Three weeks*," she groaned. "But you're in the hospital *today*."

"And you're in the hospital every week."

"Not for being shot. I called Micah Sanford, he should be there soon."

Isaac choked, trying not to laugh. "How do you have Micah's number?"

"I found your church's information online and they put me in touch with him." She sounded smug, proud of her amateur detective skills.

"Micah and I are friends, he was probably coming anyway."

"I made sure of it."

Isaac smiled and shook his head. "I love you, Mom."

She sniffled. "What if I had never heard that again?"

"You're hearing it now."

"Why couldn't you be an accountant or librarian?" she pouted.

"Come on, I thought you were proud of me."

"Yes, but you need more time. No matter how many good things you do, you still don't believe the truth, and the clock is ticking."

If a man had hackles, Isaac's raised. His mom frequently reminded him about her prayers, but otherwise left religion out of their conversations. He took a breath. She was shaken; he needed to let it go. "Okay."

"Oh, don't shut me down."

Realization dawned. "You didn't call Micah to send a friend over. You called Micah to send a pastor over."

She sighed and her voice dropped. "I called Micah because I'm scared for you, Isaac. I trust the Lord's timing, but sometimes I think you're fighting him a little too hard." Her voice cracked.

She really and truly believed this, and she believed Isaac was running out of time. Or maybe she believed *she* was running out of time. He shifted, trying to relieve a growing discomfort radiating up his arm, into his neck and head. "I think the doctor wants to talk to me," he lied. "I need to go."

She sighed. "I love you."

"I love you too."

Isaac ended the call and dropped a hand over his eyes, exhausted but now in too much pain to sleep. He glanced at his arm, the IV, and the nurse call button. He might as well get used to pain.

•   •   •

Isaac woke to a nurse carrying in a tray of food. He didn't recognize her and he immediately didn't like her. Maybe he shouldn't have that response to so many people.

"Are you having any pain?" she asked with the most patronizing smile.

Was she serious? How could he *not* have pain? "Yep."

She patted his foot. "We'll get another round of medication going for you."

"Thanks."

She looked at him for a moment, as if waiting for something more. He had nothing more. "The chaplain is here to see you," she said.

"Fine. After the pain meds."

She nodded. "We'll be right back."

"Right back" in hospital speak wasn't the same as "right back" for everyone else. Eventually they returned with a round of pain medication. Shortly after, and long before it kicked in, the door opened again and Micah Sanford walked in.

Irritation flashed in Isaac's core as he remembered his phone call with his mother. "You're not the chaplain anymore," Isaac said.

Micah paused at the door, a flicker of a frown danced across his brow. "You're right. I guess I'll see myself out." He turned and stepped out.

Genuine shock held Isaac still for a moment. Did Micah just leave?

Fine. If he only wanted to visit as a chaplain, Isaac didn't want him here. He glared at the food tray the overbearing nurse had left. He didn't want food. He didn't want anything to do with this place. He wanted to be as bulletproof as Katie claimed. He wanted out. Fear tainted his anger and it all blurred in his mind, along with pain meds. His chest felt tight and he wondered if it stemmed from the injury or the medication.

A knock sounded on the door and this time Micah only stepped in halfway. "Can I visit as a friend?"

Isaac shook his head, feeling raw and foggy. "Do whatever you want. I don't care." It might be petulant. But Penn had already said he couldn't come by until tomorrow. And Isaac knew now that Micah was only here on a holy mission from his mother. These people didn't really care.

Micah walked in and dropped onto a chair in the room, near the window. He crossed his arms and stretched his legs out long in front of him.

They sat there in silence long enough, Isaac almost forgot about Micah. He dropped his left arm over his eyes to block out the light beating into his skull and drifted in and out of consciousness like a boat at sea, vaguely aware of his surroundings the entire time, while his body tried to rest.

Time didn't seem to be moving, but the light through the window said otherwise. The annoying nurse entered the room again. They had stopped the blood transfusion at some point and only a regular IV line pierced his hand now.

"Oh, you're still here?" she asked Micah.

"I have permission to do whatever I want," Micah replied. A quick glance confirmed the grin Isaac heard in Micah's voice.

The nurse turned to Isaac. "You didn't eat anything. Who doesn't like roast beef and potatoes?"

Isaac had never skipped a meal in his life but he couldn't stand to look at the tray. "Somebody else's blood is pumping through my stomach right now—ask them."

She did the foot pat again and Isaac wished his bones could shrink away inside of his skin. "It's normal to not have much appetite in these circumstances."

Isaac stared at her. Nothing felt normal about this situation. She did a quick check of his blood pressure and clicked around on a computer for a minute, then turned to Micah. "He'll probably need to rest soon," she said.

"He has been," Micah said.

She smiled and left.

"You don't have to stay," Isaac said.

"Do you want me to leave?" Micah asked.

Isaac knew the answer, but he didn't like admitting it. He shook his head. "I know my mom sent you to save my soul. You can start saving."

"I can't do the saving."

Isaac groaned. "We're going to be literal? Fine, try to get Jesus to save me."

"I've been trying for seven years, Isaac."

"Then maybe your prayers aren't as strong as you think they are."

Micah stared at his hands for a minute. That might have shot a little too directly. "I'm choosing to trust God's timing and his answers."

"I trust no one."

"I know," Micah said. "But I think it's hurting you more than it's protecting you." Micah had the ability to speak to a room and change the entire atmosphere of it, energizing it, bringing it down, or layering it with gravitas as he did today. Isaac wasn't sure if—or how—Micah's words could be true though.

"What good is trusting a God who lets babies die and men kill each other?" Isaac asked.

"I trust a God who will bring about justice eventually. One day, the murderers and abusers will have their day in court, like your shooter. If it's justice you're after, God's your guy."

"How can you know? We can't know anything about what God's doing or not doing."

Micah rested a fist under his chin. "You're agnostic now?"

"I'm not anything."

"You have to be something. Everybody believes something, even if it's believing there's nothing." Micah tapped his fingers against his leg for a moment. "You're a smart guy, Isaac. And you've listened to my sermons for two years, so I'm curious. What do you believe about God?"

Sure, Isaac had been in the room for two years of sermons and Bible studies, but he didn't know the first thing about God. "He might exist, but I don't think I like him much. He's supposed to be good, but I don't see it. If he's all-knowing, he made us knowing we were doomed from the start."

"Is there only bad here?"

The evil seemed endless, but Isaac knew the answer. He could picture the answers, like Katie's rose-colored photos. Monkey-clad toddlers with powdered-sugar noses, backyard Bible club kids with sticky hands, and Vera tending her garden bed of fall flowers. Good still existed. If there was only evil left, Isaac wouldn't be a cop. He did this job because some part of him—lately buried in his subconscious—believed in fighting for whatever good still existed. "No."

Micah reached into a leather messenger bag by his feet. He pulled out a camouflage Bible Isaac recognized. The chaplain gave them to lots of guys at the police department. A couple of officers carried them around.

Micah stared at it for a moment. "Believe it or not, this one's yours. I make notes in it every time I pray for you. All those weak little prayers I send up." He raised a brow at Isaac. "I've been waiting a long time to give this to you. I know you might not want it, but could you give it a try? Consider it a temporary loan."

Isaac sighed, tired of his own behavior. He didn't want to push everybody away. So he took the Bible and thumbed through the pages. He had looked up a few Bible verses online to argue with Micah about, but he had never read a physical Bible. There were highlights and notes in the margins throughout the book. "That's a ton of prayers."

Micah shrugged. "I pray a lot."

"I wouldn't know what to read."

"Pick any highlight. Or start at the beginning. You can't really go wrong." Micah grinned and stood. "I've got to get back home soon, but I'm available any time, Isaac. I mean it. You can call."

Isaac swallowed his pride and muttered the truth: "Thanks for coming."

Micah squeezed his good shoulder. "Of course."

When the door closed behind Micah, Isaac lowered the bed, exhausted again. He didn't care what time of day or night it was, he wanted sleep. Somewhere in his dreams, he heard a Jumanji drum beat emanating from the Bible on the table next to him. The ringing in his ears seemed to keep time with it.

Chapter Eighteen

When William arrived to pick up Katie and Sage, he brought a small sequined bag and an outfit for Sage, so Katie didn't have to march her poor child out of the hospital in a dirty monkey costume. Katie lifted a tulle dress from the bag. "Where did this come from? I don't recognize it."

William's hands stayed in his pockets as he shrugged. "Suzanne bought a few things for the girls."

"How much did she spend on all these 'few things'?" Katie asked, twirling the tag around to reveal a boutique store name. "I keep discovering more."

"She loves those girls more than she knows how to express. It comes out in all sorts of ways."

Katie nodded. Maybe she should be grateful for an overly welcoming grandmother. Instead, she felt suffocated. Katie would normally point out the temporary nature of their visit, but a new smothering blanket settled around her—the realization they couldn't leave anytime soon. She couldn't strap Sage into a car seat and drive who-knows-where with her daughter in pain.

"I think I need to extend our rental," Katie muttered, mostly to herself as she pulled out her phone.

"You are welcome at our house."

Katie looked at him. "You've had Josie for a solid twelve hours now. You sure you want to offer that?"

William grinned in a way that reminded her of Aaron. "She slept most of that time."

Katie laughed. "Let me get Sage changed and then please get us out of here."

In a few minutes, Katie had managed to carefully change Sage into clothes without making her cry. Next she called the rental company. At first they offered her another apartment nearby. But with a bit of explanation, a bit of begging, and some influencer marketing nonsense, they agreed to move their next reservation and let Katie stay in the apartment another week. Another week didn't give healing bones much time, but it bought Katie enough time to figure out their next step. Now she could tell Sage where "home" was for another week. Guilt over it all sat like a stone in her stomach. Something had to change.

Soon, she and Sage were alone at their apartment. William had dropped them off and gone to get Josie, suggesting they have a few quiet moments alone first. The exhaustion must be as evident on Katie's face as on Sage's.

As soon as they walked through the door, Sage headed to the kitchen and started pulling cabinets open.

"Are you hungry?" Katie asked. No response. "Let me see what I can find, sweetie." They didn't have much. She had been planning to leave soon, and Katie had mastered the art of shopping for exactly one week's worth of groceries, thanks to their frequent moves.

The refrigerator was empty, save for a tiny bit of milk and two juice boxes. The cabinets held some staples Katie liked to travel with—lollipops, granola bars, cheese crackers, and dried fruit. She pulled out the snacks, put a little bit of everything on a plate, and brought a juice box to the table.

As soon as Sage saw the offering, the tears started. "Nuggets," Sage cried. These meltdowns weren't like her, and each one stressed Katie out more and more. A broken bone could heal, but had something broken on the inside? What was happening to Sage?

"Shhh," Katie whispered in vain. "I'm sorry hon, this is all I have right now. We can get nuggets later." They couldn't even leave to get any right now if she wanted to. William had taken the car, operating as chauffeur with the only car seats available. If she ordered delivery, it would take half an hour—a lifetime in toddler tantrums. "Sage, please, there's nothing I can do."

"I wanna go home," Sage wailed.

Katie didn't even know where she meant. Stress tipped over, sloshing against her sides. "Please stop," she begged. Sage kept crying. The doctor had said keeping Sage calm was key. Crying put pressure on the cracked ribs.

"That's it. You need sleep."

"No!" Sage screamed.

Katie pressed her palms to her eyes. This wasn't Sage, unless some twin magic happened when the goats butted heads and it gave Josie's personality to Sage. She lowered her hands and let out a long, slow breath. Kneeling, Katie gently framed Sage in her hands and waited for the crying to slow down. "Sage, love, how about a lollipop and a cuddle?"

Sage nodded. She still had festival dirt on her face. They both needed a real shower and a real bed. The shower would have to wait. Katie grabbed a popsicle, led Sage to the girls' bedroom, and they both climbed onto the twin bed.

•　　•　　•

The next thing Katie knew, someone was knocking on the door. She glanced down at Sage, still fast asleep in bed, wearing the tulle dress. Katie eased out of the bed and headed for the front door, bracing herself for Suzanne and Josie to make their appearance. Instead, she found Ginny, holding a large paper bag.

"Hey," Katie said, blinking against the sunlight as she swung the door open. "Sorry, we just crashed for a little nap, did I miss a call or something?"

Ginny nodded, smiling as wide as the ocean. She didn't move to come inside. "Sorry to surprise you. Zoe texted us about Sage's accident and I wanted to do something. I tried to call, then I talked to Suzanne and she gave me your address. I wanted to drop off some food and games. Kids with broken bones get bored fast, ask me how I know." Ginny gave her a sidelong glance

Katie blinked and tried to find words. "Thank you so much… I really—I don't know what to say."

"I know it's not much, but sometimes even the little things help, right?"

"It's a godsend. We weren't planning to stay another week and now that we are, we desperately need to make a grocery run."

"Really? Sunday afternoons are my grocery day, let me pick some things up for you."

She barely knew Ginny. She didn't deserve this. "You don't have to do that."

Ginny waved dismissively. "It really isn't any hassle. Let's make a list."

"Sure, sure," Katie's brain started to catch up again as she pulled the door wider. "Come on in."

They stepped over a living room bombed with stuffed animals on the way to the kitchen. "Sorry for the mess," Katie said, trying to clear a larger path.

"I have three kids, it's nothing I haven't seen before." They reached the kitchen and Ginny pulled a notepad out of her purse. "What snacks do y'all like?"

Together, they made a list, including frozen chicken nuggets, in a few minutes.

"I'll be right back with this," Ginny said.

"Here, take my card," Katie said, reaching for her purse.

"Broken bones can get expensive," Ginny said. "Let me cover this."

"Are you sure? You hardly know me."

"Moms have to stick together," she said.

Katie's hand dropped and her dusty old tear ducts considered brushing themselves off. She had needed this. "Thank you, Ginny. You are too sweet."

"I'll be back soon." And then Ginny left as fast as she had come.

Katie dug into the bag and pulled out a plastic container of what looked like chicken and rice and a frozen pizza. Score for Sage. Beneath that were a couple of classic children's games. Katie hadn't thought that far ahead—what would Sage not be able to do now? How was she supposed to keep a three-year-old from moving her arms too much?

When Sage woke up, she accepted a slice of cheese pizza as a placeholder until Ginny returned with nuggets. Ginny popped in only long enough to stock the things into the kitchen for Katie and then she left again.

Shortly after she left, another knock sounded on the door. For some reason, it made Sage start to cry. Katie sighed and answered the door to find Suzanne, Tricia, and Josie. She felt tired before the first hello.

"Mommy!" Josie shouted, launching herself at her mother.

Sage's crying increased to a screech. Suzanne and Tricia looked alarmed as they glanced past Katie, who tried to unwind Josie's arms from her waist.

"She's feeling a little sensitive today," Katie said, trying to step toward Sage as Josie wrapped herself around Katie's leg.

"I'll get her," Suzanne said.

Katie wanted to protest, to refuse Suzanne's help, to prove she could do it all herself. But the truth was, she couldn't. And her own shortcomings seemed to become more and more apparent every day.

Eventually, she and Josie made it to the table, where Suzanne cradled Sage in her lap. Sage's sling held her arm close to her body and she took shallow breaths against Suzanne's chest. Suzanne glanced at Katie. "Do you think she can be around Josie? What did the doctor say about recovery?"

"Rest, pain medication, and keeping her shoulder stable. There's not much else we can do other than wait, I guess."

"William said you're going to stay here a little longer?" Suzanne asked, the glee on her face at odds with the circumstances.

"I have to," Katie retorted a bit too harshly. "I can't toss a broken child in the car, can I?"

"Hush that—" Suzanne stood, with Sage in her arms, and scowled at Katie. "She isn't broken. Learn to speak life over your children, Katelyn."

Then she turned and disappeared down the hall with a still-whimpering Sage in her arms.

Josie squealed as she tossed a stuffed animal into the air, and Katie leaned over the table to bury her face in her arms. Overwhelm seeped out of every crevice.

Tricia rubbed Katie's back. "It's okay," she whispered. "She's just in pain."

Katie wasn't sure whether Tricia meant Sage or Suzanne. Maybe both.

"Mommy help me!" Josie called from the living room.

With a deep breath, Katie stood, forcing herself to dig a little deeper, like Ginny had once said. Somewhere inside of her, she had to find another ounce of patience and joy for Josie's sake. She sank onto the floor in the living room to help Josie create a stuffed animal school. The effort squeezed the last bit of life from her.

Josie patted her face. "Smile, Mommy."

Katie blinked back the growing tension on her brow. "I'm sorry sweetie. Mommy needs a minute. You can play with Auntie Tricia."

"No! I want Mommy!"

Katie kissed Josie's head. "I'll be right back.'

Tricia hurried to the floor to take over, instantly distracting Josie from a potential tirade. Katie slipped down the hall, needing a moment to compose herself, but her steps stilled outside of the girls' bedroom. Through the closed door, she heard Suzanne singing. The faint lyrics of "Amazing Grace" drifted out.

"Through many dangers, toils and snares, I have already come."

The song came like a punch to the stomach. Katie braced herself against the doorframe. Aaron used to sing it to the girls when he rocked them. She heard it dozens of times in those earliest weeks. And she had forgotten about it until now. Did he learn that from Suzanne?

"'Tis grace hath brought me safe thus far, and grace will lead me home."

Hurrying to the bathroom, she locked herself inside and leaned against the door. She closed her eyes and tried to remember it for just a moment. The gray rocking chair. How he cradled a baby in each arm. She couldn't remember his voice exactly, but it was deep, with the slightest hint of a southern accent.

Going back there was dangerous. There was nowhere to go; like so many things in her life, it was a dead end. The black hole closed in around her; Katie could feel its hands around her throat. She should have known she couldn't fight it off in Ridley Bay.

She turned on the tap and leaned over the sink, splashing her face with cold water. She rubbed it onto her neck and tried to wash it away. But she kept picturing him, again and again, leaning over those two babies, singing to them. *"And grace will lead me home."*

"Oh God," she whispered, sinking to the bathroom floor. She had said Aaron's children deserved to live. Is that all she had given them? His children deserved to be delighted in. Sang to. Cherished. Katie didn't have it in her. She couldn't love like that. She was failing her children, but she didn't have a clue how to fix it. "God help me."

Chapter Nineteen

Suzanne and Tricia set up a rotation to keep Josie occupied while Katie stayed with Sage. Neither Nana nor Aunt Tricia wanted to be left with the hurt one, and Katie couldn't blame them. She didn't really either. Seeing Sage cry throughout the day left her feeling empty.

Monday, Tricia took Josie to the park all morning and brought them all lunch. That afternoon, Katie had Josie in the apartment for the first real stretch of time. It proved to be both wonderful and challenging. Her contagious delight at every little thing lightened the mood; Sage smiled more with her sister nearby; and Josie's mile-long blonde eyelashes smoothed over a multitude of little sins. However, she played too roughly, constantly forgetting to be gentle and crashing onto the couch too close to her sister and causing a fresh round of tears and stress.

The next day, Katie felt restlessness building up inside of her, ready to overflow. She had agreed to letting Suzanne and Tricia use her car instead of moving Josie's car seat back and forth. Now Suzanne had Josie for the morning and Katie was stuck at the apartment. They should have rearranged the car seats after all. She hated not having her car.

"Let's go for a walk," Katie said.

Sage shook her head.

"Come on, your legs aren't broken." Katie went to their patio door and slid it open. "It's a beautiful day, kiddo, I think you could use a little sunlight."

Sage shook her head again and went back to playing a solo game of Candy Land. Katie sighed and picked up her laptop. With nothing else to do, she could at least get a little work done.

First, she emailed Micah that she would be in town for the baptisms after all and could gladly take pictures. Then she turned her attention to managing online content and finishing edits on her last photoshoot. The festival photos were next on her list, but those would take several hours to get through.

Katie opened her calendar. No new work scheduled would make a dent in their monthly budget. She needed to figure out their next step. Just as she pulled up a list of Texas cities and the cost of living, she heard Suzanne knock on the door.

"Come in," Katie said, clearing a path through the living room minefield of toys.

Suzanne carried a large brown paper bag from an Italian restaurant and it smelled like heaven. "I didn't know what you liked so I got a sampler," she said, setting it on the countertop. Josie trailed in behind her Nana, focused on peeling stickers off her hand.

Katie peeked inside the bag. "That smells delicious."

"Josie decided to tattoo herself with stickers, by the way," Suzanne said. "I hope that's okay."

Katie laughed. "You managed to keep her entertained all morning. She could have come back with a real tattoo and I would have turned a blind eye."

Suzanne scoffed as she turned on the kitchen faucet. "I hope that isn't true. We did have fun though. I introduced her to our library. What'd you think of that, Jojo?"

"Good!" she shouted, running for a second bag Suzanne had set by the door. She started pulling out a stack of board books.

Suzanne smiled after her, then shook her head and scrubbed a bowl in the sink.

"You don't have to do that," Katie said.

"I don't mind. I like to help. You and the girls can go eat."

Katie hesitated. Nobody else had washed her dishes in years. "I know it looks like a mess in here, but I can get to it all, I promise. I was going to clean while the girls napped."

Suzanne raised her eyebrows at her. "Have you ever tried a quick catnap while the girls nap? It always worked wonders for me."

"Not really. People always say to sleep when the baby sleeps, but I never could figure that out. Am I supposed to do the dishes when the babies do the dishes?"

Suzanne laughed and shooed her toward the table. "Go eat."

Katie pulled out the food and spread an entire feast across the small dining table. She dished up plates for the girls and herself, and invited Suzanne to join them. Josie chattered about her day while they ate, and soon the twins had finished, long before the adults, and run off to play.

"That was scary about Isaac, wasn't it?" Suzanne asked as she packed up leftovers.

Katie pushed a lone noodle around on her plate. "Mm. Yeah." She didn't really want to talk about Isaac. He had never texted her back, and the entire incident reminded her how dangerous it could be to care. "But he's fine."

"I guess so," Suzanne said. "He's just now leaving the hospital."

Katie's head came up. "Really?"

Suzanne nodded. "JP said he's on medical leave for the foreseeable future."

That would kill Isaac as surely as a bullet. He existed for work. But Katie didn't have the capacity to care right now. Caring meant pain and she couldn't carry any more pain for anyone.

"Were you two close back in Fairbanks?" Suzanne asked, her tone overtly casual. She was digging.

"We didn't know each other long, only a couple months."

Suzanne gave her a sideways glance. "Sometimes it doesn't take long."

Suzanne, coming in hot today. "True." Katie stood and stretched, ready to change topics. "I should probably get the girls down for their naps."

Suzanne clapped her hands together. "I'll do it. You go lie down."

"Are you sure?"

"Absolutely," Suzanne said. "Don't make me tell you again."

Katie laughed. "A mom doesn't need to be told twice to take a nap."

"Then go," Suzanne said, taking Katie's plate from her hand. "I've got this."

Soon, Katie found herself in bed, staring at the ceiling in the too-bright room. She hadn't done this in ages. Did she remember how to catnap? Her mind drifted to Isaac, to Sage, to Aaron, to Josie, to her mother, her younger siblings, and finally to nothing.

An hour later, the sounds of Suzanne playing with the girls woke her. She hadn't felt this rested in… as long as she could remember. In no rush to rejoin the chaos she could hear outside her door, Katie sat in bed scrolling through apartment listings on her laptop. They only had a few more days in this rental. She didn't want to keep living week to week, it was too stressful, even for Katie. She needed a longer plan.

Katie poked around on a map, taking quick looks at every Texas city, but moving to a new city right now, with an injured child severely limiting her childcare and work options, seemed foolish. It would be easier to stay put. Besides, she needed a little more time before picking their next place, and promoting it on social media. Her followers already knew she was here. She could find work here, and she had free childcare. Maybe they could stay another week. And another.

Before she could do anything rash, Katie snapped her laptop shut and headed out of the bedroom to find the girls showing off their best ballet moves to Suzanne.

Their Nana's eyes sparkled. "They're so precious," she said to Katie. "Have they taken ballet before?"

"They did for a couple months last summer. Josie loved it." Sage only watched from the back of the room, so Katie withdrew her.

"Mommy, I want bow-way class again," Josie said, accentuating every word with a twirl.

Sage tugged on Katie's shirt. She looked back at Suzanne, then up at Katie again, debating whether to speak in front of someone else. Katie knelt so she could whisper it. Sage leaned into her ear. "Me too," she breathed.

Katie kissed her forehead. "We'll find another ballet class soon." Here or somewhere.

Josie cheered, Sage smiled, and Suzanne clapped. Katie joined her mother-in-law on the couch to watch a few more twirls. Until Josie's next spin ended with her arm knocking into Sage's chest.

"Oh dear—" Suzanne said, popping up from the couch as Sage burst into tears.

Katie sighed. Everything ended this way. She scooped up Sage and carried her into the kitchen, grabbing an ice pack and a popsicle. Of course, Josie wanted one too. After several minutes, she settled both girls in the kitchen, dripping sticky red juice onto the floor.

Suzanne tidied toys in the living room and Katie plopped back onto the couch. "The doctor said to try to keep her still for the first two weeks. I don't think she had ever met a three-year-old before in her life."

Suzanne gave her a pitying look. "It's hard."

"Even with the sling, she still bumps it and moves it too much." Katie sighed and leaned her head back, staring at the ceiling. "We're stuck in this tiny apartment trying not to bump into each other and I think I'm losing my mind."

Suzanne joined her on the couch and patted her knee. "You are always welcome at my house."

Katie nodded. She didn't like to spend her time in that haunted house.

"Why don't you come to Bible study tonight?" Suzanne asked.

Katie looked at the girls sharing their popsicles and making a giant mess. "Is it already Tuesday again?" How had this been the longest and shortest week of her life?

"It is. And I'm sure we can keep Sage happy and safe if you want to join us tonight."

Katie watched her daughter try to lick cherry popsicle off her chin. She needed an escape, if only for a couple of hours. "Sure. I could use some Bible-ing."

Suzanne chuckled. "We all could."

•   •   •

Katie spent the afternoon debating her agreement to join the Bible study. There would be questions about Sage and her injury, which Katie didn't want to talk about. Questions about how long she was staying in Ridley

Bay, which she didn't know the answers to yet. And worse, she knew everybody would be talking about Isaac. She didn't want to hear that.

By the time Suzanne returned to pick them all up, Katie's nerves ticked in her chest like a time bomb. The girls absorbed Katie's energy too, and refused to get into the car. Sage parked herself at the front door of the apartment, a statue. Josie wanted to bring everything she owned with her, like she thought they were moving out.

"My bunny!" Josie wailed, turning back.

"We will come back for the bunny," Katie said, partially begging. Suzanne stood a few feet back, still trying to coax Sage out the door.

"Don't weave him!" Josie screeched.

"It's just for two hours!" Katie yelled back. They had already compromised on a dozen animals, filling the back seat with stuffed creatures of all shapes and sizes.

Josie broke out of her grasp and barreled into the apartment. Suzanne barely managed to block Sage from getting plowed over. With a hand against the side of her head, Katie stared at them all. "I don't think we're gonna make it," she said.

"I think we have room for a bunny," Suzanne offered gently.

Katie's hand flew out to the side. "It'll be another thing after that!"

Suzanne nodded silently.

Katie swiped her hand over her face. "I'm sorry for yelling at you," she mumbled, walking back inside to follow Josie to her room.

Josie burrowed into bed, tucking her face into what looked to be an uncomfortable mix of books, plastic animals, and blocks. Only her bottom stuck out of the pile and Katie blew out a breath. *She's three, you're thirty-two.* Time to be the bigger person.

Katie rubbed her back. "I'm sorry I yelled, Jojo."

Josie popped up. "I not," she pouted, then shot back down.

Katie kept up a circular pattern on her back. "That's okay. I want to save room in the car for you and Sage. Can you pick one last toy? I promise we'll come back for bedtime and you can have all the toys in bed with you."

The tears started anew. "I can't find bunny."

Katie hadn't paid attention to what Josie was asking for until now. The only bunny she knew of was a small, white, plastic bunny. She clarified Josie's target with her and began the search. Not in the pile on the bed, or any on the floor. Sage had been playing with the animals earlier today.

With a sigh, Katie headed into the living room, where she found Sage still in the doorway and Suzanne kneeling in front of her, whispering all sorts of encouragements.

"Sage, have you seen the little white bunny?" Katie asked her.

Sage stared at her with wide eyes. She hadn't spoken a single word in the last few hours.

Katie suddenly realized what happened to the bunny. "You buried it, didn't you?" When Suzanne glanced up at Katie, she ignored the questioning look. "Where is it, Sage?"

Sage shook her head and Katie grit her teeth. "Go and get it." Sage didn't move a muscle.

Katie groaned and headed for the couch, peeling off cushions. She found a handful of blocks and an embarrassing amount of cracker crumbs. This apartment was too small to have many hiding places. She peeked under the couch and in the kitchen cabinets. *Where would you bury a bunny?* She checked the trash can and the toilet. Nothing.

Meanwhile, Suzanne managed to get Josie into the car and even Sage seemed to be making progress, two steps outside of the door. Katie stopped them, squatting down by Sage. "Did you bury the bunny?"

Sage nodded.

"Can you show me where?"

She shook her head.

The inside of Katie's head was screaming. *What is wrong with you?* Did she not remember? Or did she refuse to help? Katie had taught them the rule about Aaron: buried things don't come back. Why was her daughter obsessed with it?

"Josie seems to have moved on," Suzanne whispered.

Katie nodded and stood up. She hadn't. She needed to find that bunny more than Josie did. But they were already running late. She would have to find it tonight. "Okay. Let's go."

With careful movements, they buckled Sage into the car seat without any discomfort and took the short drive to the Sanfords, arriving only a few minutes late, despite the bunny crisis. A new crisis started upon their arrival though. While Josie hopped out and into Suzanne's arms, Sage cowered in her car seat, crying.

Katie stayed back, trying to coax her out. "What's wrong? Does your arm hurt? Your chest?" Katie gently pointed out places, trying to find the problem.

Sage shook her head. She pointed at the house.

"You're not hurt, you're scared?" Katie asked. "You don't have to go upstairs with Ava if you don't want to. You can stay with me."

Sage ducked her head and folded over herself. She sniffled and pointed to her arm. "They see my arm."

"Baby, what's wrong with that? It's nothing to be embarrassed about. Everybody gets hurt sometimes." Isaac came to mind as a prime example.

It took a little more coaxing, but Sage finally, reluctantly, allowed Katie to pull her out of the car. She hid behind Katie all the way through the yard and up the porch steps. At the door, Katie glanced down to see Sage pulling the bottom hem of her shirt up and over her sling, hiding her arm and exposing her little, round toddler belly.

Fresh cracks split across Katie's heart. Sage's protests weren't as loud as Josie's, but she was struggling just as hard. Her struggles were quiet, buried inside, only visible in moments like this. Katie dropped down to Sage's level, unable to take another step. "Oh, sweetheart," Katie ran her hand over Sage's furrowed brow. "We don't have to go inside."

Sage stood in between the front door and the porch steps, head swiveling between them. She looked trapped. The pressure of Sage's pain and crying had built in Katie's chest for the last few days and now it spilled everywhere. Something had trapped Sage inside of herself for her entire life. The realization sent Katie's heart crashing to the ground. Sage needed help.

Katie sat on the porch step, fighting the pain for both of them. She held her arms out to Sage who quickly climbed into them. Katie cradled her and rested her cheek against Sage's head. She would spend the entire meeting on this porch, if that's what it took. She would do anything. But whatever she had been doing, it wasn't enough.

The lyrics to "Amazing Grace" came to mind and Katie sang them softly, watching as the street lights came on. Last week, Micah mentioned finding joy in Christ after bringing him the sorrow first. Katie preferred to skip the pain and sorrow and jump straight to the joy. She wanted to fast forward the process. But tonight, it became abundantly clear she couldn't. The pain and sorrow were inevitable.

Katie kissed Sage's head and started to pray. She wished she had prayed more for this little girl over the last few years. Katie's prayers had been so selfish for so long, focused on her own pain, she missed the struggle happening right in front of her eyes.

Suzanne texted and asked if she needed any help. Katie told her they were going to enjoy a quiet evening outside for now. A few minutes later, the door opened and Katie glanced back as Sage burrowed into her mother's chest. Penn stepped out, with a tower of containers in his arms, and jerked to a stop when he saw her. "Oh, hey," he said.

Katie cleared her throat and hoped her voice came out normal. "Hey. Stealing leftovers?"

"Taking some to Isaac." He hesitated at the door. "Are you coming in?"

Katie shook her head. "Sage needs a minute. We'll see."

"Want me to bring you a plate?"

"That'd be great."

"I'll be right back." He set down the stack of boxes and disappeared inside. He returned with a plate large enough to feed an entire family.

Katie smiled. "Thanks."

"I heard about the accident. How's she doing?"

Okay. Fine. Good. Katie didn't know which lie to choose and she only found a shrug instead. "How's Isaac?"

Penn gave the slightest grin. "About the same." Then he grabbed his tower of food and waved goodbye.

Katie sighed and adjusted Sage on her lap so they could eat. It might be weird, showing up to the Sanfords' house only to eat on their porch steps. But it didn't matter anymore. What mattered was something had to change. Sage needed to be set free.

Chapter Twenty

Cartoons blared in Isaac's living room as he paced across the house, as weak as his elderly neighbor. He poured a glass of water, trying to follow the doctor's instructions about hydration, and collapsed on the couch with a thud that resonated throughout his entire body.

He poked at his phone. The texts slowed down once everybody knew he was alive. It was Tuesday night and he knew the Grace Church group was meeting at the Sanford house. After two years of Penn's annoying text reminders, Isaac stared at his phone, wondering why none came tonight. He couldn't go in his current condition, but Isaac still wanted an invite. Or at least an annoying "we're praying for you" text. Instead, his phone sat silent.

An obnoxious theme song about rescue dogs suddenly filled the room so nothing else could live here with him. He picked this trick up years ago from his nieces and nephews by chance. He had been visiting after working a particularly traumatic car accident, and their shows proved so mind-numbing and silly, it eventually tuned out the disturbing videos playing in his head.

All the dogs had snappy little catchphrases and Isaac started to think the department could use some of those. Several officers from the squad had come to the hospital that afternoon to debrief in Isaac's room before he was released. They brought his truck and one of the officers drove him home while several others surrounded them in patrol cars like a ceremonial parade. Isaac kept his mouth shut, but he wanted to point out the idiocy of it all. He wasn't dead and he hadn't done anything heroic. They brought in a madman with a few bullet holes and temporarily saved a woman and two kids. But if the woman didn't get serious help, they would likely end up back in a similar situation. That's how these things always went. Isaac couldn't really save anyone.

He couldn't save his baby or his marriage. He couldn't save his mom from cancer. And he couldn't stop the anger tearing him apart.

Bitterness filled his mouth like copper. Or was it blood? Isaac swiped at his mouth. There were moments when it all felt futile—when arrests were overturned and abusers walked away. But it never felt more pointless than today. If the bullet had gone a few inches over, it might have finished Isaac, and he was both okay with that thought and terrified by it.

While the cartoon dogs managed to save a wandering cow, they failed in their higher calling of distracting Isaac. The house felt emptier than ever and Isaac was rapidly growing annoyed at them. His ears rang and the mental image of kids tied to a chair forced its way into his head.

Isaac needed something stronger than water, regardless of what the doctor said. Forcing his aching bones up, he headed into the kitchen and grabbed a beer to work out the details of a drinking game based on the kids show. This would be his life now. He was on administrative leave until he healed and a regulatory board finished reviewing the incident. All he wanted was to get back to work, but all he could do was sit here.

Half an hour later, the anthropomorphic dogs howled again and Isaac ticked the box on his mental drinking card, draining the last of his beer. He crunched it in his left hand, while his right remained mostly useless. The same moment he crunched it, he thought he heard a sound at the door. Isaac waited, testing control in his right hand, squeezing his hand into a fist repeatedly. The knock sounded again.

With a heaving sigh, he set down the beer can and pushed himself upright. His body craved sleep, but his mind wouldn't let him yet. He wasn't going to bed until he knew he would pass out the instant he laid down. Most likely, he'd sleep on the couch with the television on.

Out of habit, he tucked the handgun in the front hall into his waistband. He needed to practice leftie more. He pulled open the door to find Penn standing there with a miniature tower of plastic containers in his arms.

"I come in peace," Penn said. "Rebecca Sanford sent me with food."

"Come in," he said, swinging the door wide to let Penn through. He followed his friend to the kitchen, glancing at the time on the microwave clock. "Shouldn't you still be at Bible study?" Isaac asked.

"Wanted to bring you dinner before you went to bed, old man," Penn said. "Nice sling, by the way. You match Katie's kid."

"Sage?" Isaac had briefly wondered about her in the last couple days, but never texted Katie. "How is she?"

Penn paused for a second. "Seemed to be having a hard time tonight. She refused to go inside, so they ate on the porch."

"You could have sent Katie with the food if you're just gonna make her eat outside."

"Dying to see her?" Penn asked, with a smirk.

"Better than your ugly mug."

Penn laughed and popped lids off the containers. "Have you eaten anything yet?"

Isaac shook his head as a mouthwatering scent filled the room. He hadn't eaten much at the hospital. His favorite nurse, Patty, called it a childish protest. He called it microwaved cardboard.

"It's Mediterranean night," Penn said. "Chicken shawarma and rice."

Whoever packed it included pita, a bean salad, falafel, bruschetta, baklava, yogurt, and more. Isaac had to laugh. "How much do y'all think I eat?"

"Not enough, apparently," Penn said. "But these are southern Christians. They cook for an army."

Isaac grabbed two plates and heaped food onto one. He pushed the other toward Penn. "Wanna join me?"

Penn patted his stomach. "I already ate at the Sanford's."

Isaac slowed down, drawing out the visit for a moment longer. Penn would have to leave any minute and get back to the community he was part of—not as a paid contractor, but as an actual member of it—and the family waiting for him. Penn had other people. Isaac nodded. He didn't really know how to be good company.

"Sorry I forgot to send you the weekly text," Penn said, a grin on his face. "Looks like my assumptions were right. You do just sit around and drink." He glanced at the living room, where Isaac's beer sat on top of Micah's Bible. He didn't really need the reminder of his pathetic life.

"It's okay," Isaac mumbled around a bite of pita. "You didn't want to witness the hero worship if I showed up. It's hard to be the little guy."

Penn chortled. "I had to witness it anyway. You're the star tonight, whether you're there or not."

Isaac grinned at him. "So you left."

"Yep. Couldn't handle it. They think you're so fantastic, but they've never seen you try to arrest a naked man with a fake eye."

Isaac choked on his food hard enough that Penn smacked his back a couple of times. Tzatziki sauce nearly came out of his nose. "The look on your face when his eye fell out—"

"*Your* face, man!" Penn cackled. "I can't decide if I'm happy or sad we didn't have body cameras yet."

"Sad, only sad."

They swapped a couple of old cop stories from Penn's days on the force while Isaac ate, until the body cameras came up again. "Have you looked through anything from Saturday night?" Penn asked.

Couscous puddled on his plate, mixing with bean juice and dripped tzatziki. Isaac stabbed at the baklava, reaching the point of overstuffed, and without regrets. "No."

"Is it under review?"

"Yeah. I'm on administrative and medical leave." Anytime they fired a gun, they went on administrative leave until the situation could be reviewed. "Now a bunch of people who have never been in that situation get to sit in the comfort of their desks and try to find something we messed up." Mistakes could cost cops their jobs.

"Did you mess up?"

Isaac shook his head. "I don't think so." But adrenaline could easily erase details.

"They know real life doesn't always go by the book."

"I hope so." Isaac wiped his hands on a napkin and stole a glance at the clock. "Can I be honest with you?"

Penn waited.

"I keep thinking, what if we had killed him?" Isaac said.

Penn studied him. "What if?"

"I don't know." Isaac didn't have the answer. Every time his mind wandered in this direction, he steered it back. But part of him wondered if it would have been better.

"Do you wish you had?"

Isaac would never wish that. If he did, it was time to retire and sell his guns. "No. But he's a family abuser and cop shooter. Would the world be better without him?"

"But he's made in the image of God."

Isaac scoffed. "Some image."

"A flawed, broken likeness, made for more."

"Now you sound like Micah."

"Well, we read the same Bible."

Isaac shifted and crossed his arms tightly. "But why? Why read it?"

Penn clasped his hands behind his head and stared at the light fixture for a moment. "Because life makes more sense when I do."

"Abusers make sense?"

"Pain makes sense. It brings us back to Christ and reminds us we need him. It reminds us we were made for an eternal home where this stuff doesn't happen."

"Seems like a cruel teaching method," Isaac said.

Penn shook his head. "Look, I'm not Micah. I'm not trained in this stuff." He tilted forward, resting his elbows on his knees. "I'm just saying, when life gets hard, I still have hope because of what I believe. What do you have?"

"Baklava," Isaac mumbled, poking his fork into another piece.

Penn snatched the fork out of Isaac's hand and popped it into his own mouth. "Now what do you have?"

Isaac stared at him. "I have a psychotic friend."

Penn's cheeks stuck out with baklava as he talked. "I still have Jesus. And I know he's going to carry me through this and shape me to be more like him." Penn swallowed. "Or I could let all the junk in the world make me bitter."

"You ate my food. He's about to have to carry your broken face back to your family."

Penn laughed. "I'm trusting our friendship to carry us through this one."

Isaac shook his head. "It's feeling the strain."

Penn stood from the table and headed to the living room. He gathered the beer can and Bible and returned to the kitchen while Isaac stowed the remaining food in the fridge. Penn plopped the Bible onto the countertop and tapped it with one finger. "Start at the beginning," he said. "It's not like you have anything else to do for the next few weeks."

"Thanks for the reminder."

"Don't worry. You won't be lonely. The ladies at church have already organized food drop offs for the next few weeks."

"Should we tell them I live off microwave meals anyway? I can do those with one hand."

"Nah, you take a bullet, you get a free meal. It's how it works."

"Should have told me sooner, I could have gotten shot a long time ago."

Penn laughed. "I've got to get back to the family and wrangle a bunch of kids into bed. Enjoy your quiet nights while they last."

"Are they ending?"

Penn shrugged and grabbed his keys. "Who knows? Things can change in a heartbeat."

Whatever Penn meant, it sounded ominous. The door closed behind his friend, and for a moment, it was all Isaac could think about. How much could have changed the other night?

The military cured him of any youthful belief in his own immortality. He had lost friends both in the army and the police department. Yet somehow, he always believed he had time to figure things out. Now, Isaac truly understood he might not have tomorrow, and he had to admit, it scared him.

Chapter Twenty-One

The next morning, a storm rolled slowly along the coast. Isaac had, predictably, fallen asleep on the couch, though he moved to his bed in the night. When he woke, his body felt stiff and his arm throbbed with pain. His throat was dry and his eyes filled with sand as he downed a glass of water and pain medication while watching the rain fall steadily outside.

Isaac headed to the couch. Bed. Couch. Bed. Couch. He could see why retirement killed cops. He cracked a window to listen to the storm, and after a moment of hesitation, grabbed the Bible. He couldn't handle any more cartoon dogs this morning.

Thumbing through the book, he stopped at Micah's random highlights. Partial thoughts trailed along the margins, scribbled like tiny addends to the verses next to them: *"To forgive is to be set free"* or *"Christ is the standard of justice."* Some were prayers: *"For peace and protection"* or *"Bless him with new beginnings."* Dates accompanied them, dating back several years, some back to when Micah had been the police chaplain Isaac avoided. More seemed to be dated within the last couple years, since he started working for Grace Church.

There were too many to catch flipping through, so Isaac took Penn's suggestion and started at the beginning. He didn't read it straight through, but he read wherever there were notes, and if something caught his interest, he'd read more for context.

He got to Leviticus and had been in church long enough to hear a few jokes about these early books. The endless laws and punishments bored everybody else to tears, but Isaac found himself fascinated by the justice system, at least from a historical perspective, if nothing else.

Over the next couple of days, reading filled Isaac's time. He had nothing else to do, besides a couple of meetings with the police department and a physical therapist. He was nearly useless around the house, and under strict orders not to do any strenuous workout yet. So he sat around, ate rich southern food, and read the Bible.

He read more of it than he ever intended to.

He liked the Old Testament God. That God didn't get as much pulpit time as Jesus and the New Testament. The Old Testament God knew about anger and justice. Some stories and verses in there surprised Isaac. Absolute depravity of man matched by the full wrath of God. Maybe that's why these weren't the stories told on Sunday—they weren't feel-good tales. But Isaac appreciated them. They matched his reality.

Just when he thought he could get along with that God, he reached the end of Micah's Old Testament notes. Isaac set the Bible down. He could be on the same team as God, but he wasn't interested in Jesus.

When Saturday came, he had absolutely nothing to do. He could ease back into light workouts, with one arm. The workout resembled more of something Vera might accomplish than his usual routine, and nothing like the boot camps he had survived time and time again. No matter how angry he got at his body, he couldn't get it to function any better.

By that afternoon, he was so sick of himself, he couldn't take another minute alone. He called each of his brothers. Oscar didn't answer, *the jerk*. Andres and Cristian each chatted for a bit and passed the phone around to their kids.

Cristian's wife, Sara, snatched the phone as soon as their youngest son finished talking.

"You're in trouble," she said. "Now Crew thinks it's super cool to get shot. What do you have to say for yourself?"

Isaac snickered. "Sorry, I can't help being his coolest uncle."

"You're a bad influence." She laughed. Sara was Isaac's favorite sister-in-law. She and Isaac had been friends since grade school; she developed an inexorable crush on his older brother in high school. "And I heard you're coming up for Thanksgiving?"

"Yep, full Torres reunion."

Sara groaned. "Please bring a woman. It's such a boy's club around here."

"You should be used to that."

She sighed. "A girl can always dream. Send me the flight details and we'll pick you up."

"Will do, thanks."

Oscar finally called back, so Isaac switched calls to talk baseball with his brother. Their home team hadn't made it to the World Series and Oscar couldn't let it go. They griped about pitchers and injuries for a bit before Oscar had to get back to work.

When the calls ended, silence filled Isaac's house again.

He sighed and flipped on the television. A bilingual kids' show came on but he found it insufferable and turned it off. He scratched at his jaw and grabbed the Bible on the side table. He flipped it open and stared at the beginning of the New Testament. The beginning of Jesus.

Isaac read a few chapters with distaste, then glanced at the clock. He had killed a couple more hours. It was almost dinnertime, and he had copious amounts of leftovers from a week of food supplied by Grace Church women. He would never be able to eat it all, and had already gotten into the habit of packing some up to take to Vera's house. He headed to the kitchen and slowly, left-handedly, filled a container with the latest casserole.

Outside of his front door, he spotted her immediately, piddling in her garden again. She wore a large nightgown and her white hair piled on her head. They called out a familiar greeting, but she gasped as he got closer. "What happened to your arm?" she asked, for the third time this week.

"I got shot," Isaac said, with a slight grin.

Her hand flew to her heart. "Oh My-lanta. What in the world happened?"

Isaac explained it again, losing some of the anger and shock every time he told her. Vera was exposure therapy.

"You didn't *know* you had been shot?" Vera asked, her eyes looking up at him with a disbelieving tilt of her head. Her tone implied he might be lacking in brain cells.

"Adrenaline does funny things to the body," he said. "I was too focused on the mission."

She made a humming sound of clear disagreement. Then she clipped off a few gray-green stems of a leafy plant. "This is antiviral," she said. "You make a tea with this, to help with that." She waved a hand at his arm. Then she waved at his head. "I don't have anything to help with *that.*"

Isaac laughed. He didn't point out any of modern medicine's advancements this time. He put the stems in his pocket. "Yes, ma'am. Should I take this food inside for you?"

"Why don't we eat together?" Vera asked, eagerly. She likely forgot they ate together yesterday and the day before. But Isaac needed it too.

"Sure," he said. "Let's do that."

For the next hour, Isaac listened to Vera prattle on about her nearly-estranged son, her granddaughter of unknown age, and her church she rarely visited anymore. She had been homebound for two years now. Occasionally people from her church would give her rides, but he knew it didn't happen often. Maybe she forgot to ask. Either way, it made him dislike her church.

"Where do you go to church?" she asked earnestly, prepared to share the gospel with him if he named a denomination she disliked.

Isaac reminded her about the church he worked for, and Vera waved a dismissive hand at him.

"Oh, it's one of those new churches, isn't it? With loud drums and boys with mohawks. You know, everybody wants to change everything, but there is nothing wrong with a traditional Baptist service and choir, thank you very much."

Isaac grinned. "I have yet to see a single mohawk at Grace Church. But your church sounds nice."

"Oh, it is. Maybe you could go with me sometime."

"Maybe." He didn't tell her he only went to church to work.

"I think I missed last Sunday, come to think of it," she said, a distant look in her eyes. They tended to cloud over in moments when she recognized her memory problems. She was happy enough when she didn't realize her own struggle.

"That's okay, I did too," Isaac said.

"What's today?" she asked, quickly growing agitated.

"Saturday," Isaac said.

Vera snapped her fingers. "I need to find a ride. Can you find my glasses and my phone book?" She tried to stand, pushing up on the table for strength.

"Why don't I take you?" Isaac offered. "I'm off work for a while."

"Really?" Vera frowned at him. Not the happy response he expected. "But don't you have your own church to go to?"

She could be sharp sometimes. "That's okay, I can skip it."

The frown stayed in place. "Then you'll come to mine?"

"Tell you what, I'll drop you off, go to my church, and pick you up when we're done." He wouldn't, but she didn't need all the details.

Vera's wispy eyebrows danced up and down. "Worried what my friends would think of the tall, handsome man on my arm?" She gave him a wink.

Isaac let a laugh burst out. "Find someone your own age, Vera."

She giggled and hobbled off to clean up dinner. "Church is at nine," she called over her shoulder.

Chapter Twenty-Two

Sunday evening, Katie drove along the coastal edge of Ridley Bay, past the boardwalk, through a quiet suburb, and to the edge of town. The main street veered away from the coast, but a quiet single-lane road led to a row of houses that looked one hurricane away from vanishing. She had agreed to taking baptism photos tonight and extended her rental another week.

Living week by week stretched Katie. She hadn't packed to stay this long. Though moving was a small affair for them, she did have a portable storage box holding their things—including more clothes. What did a photographer wear for water photos anyway? A swimsuit seemed weird, and her go-to jeans and blouse combo wouldn't work. She settled on bright pink running shorts and a black top, with a nicer outfit to change into later.

She parked behind Suzanne and William's car, right on time, a rare feat for Katie.

Lugging her camera gear, Katie walked up to a pastel-colored house. Sage and Josie tagged along slowly behind her, holding hands and having a private conversation, though Katie couldn't hear any of it. Despite the beautiful weather, Sage wore a jacket to hide her sling. They had compromised on the disguise. They also skipped church that morning, for Sage's sake.

A chalkboard sign at the door said *"Come around back"* with an arrow. Katie followed it and the mouthwatering scent of charcoal grills. They walked along a short path between the house and a garage until they found themselves in the back—also known as the beach.

This stretch of the beach might not win any awards, but Katie could appreciate the view. Low waves, an endless sea, and a pink-tinged sky would make for some nice baptism photos.

"Katie!" Tricia called and waved at her. The other Kaminskis turned to greet them, along with the Sanford family and an older couple.

"Nancy Newton," the older woman said, shaking her hand. She wore cream slacks and a light pink blouse, with her short, thin gray hair blown out.

"Katie Kaminski. It's nice to meet you."

Nancy introduced her to her husband Richard. They tried to meet the twins, but the girls both hid behind Katie's legs.

"Really, Josie?" Katie asked. "You're not even the shy one."

Nancy laughed. "That's all right. I heard one of these girls took a hard fall at the festival." She bent over to smile at the girls.

Katie let them hide. "She'd rather not talk about it."

Nancy stood with an "oops" look on her face and put her finger to her lips, promising silence. Katie smiled at her.

"You ready?" Micah asked, joining them with a wide grin.

"I think so," Katie said, motioning to her camera gear. "What's the evening look like?"

Micah gave her a brief rundown of the plans. They had four adults getting baptized first, then three kids. JP would baptize the kids, except for Penn's son—Penn would baptize Landon himself. Afterwards, they would have a picnic on the beach.

Katie nodded along, mentally categorizing the shots she wanted. Thankfully she traveled with all her camera gear, including the underwater setup. One never knew what opportunities might arise. "Got it," she said, as Micah finished the overview. "Do you want just the baptisms or the whole event?"

He grinned. "How much extra will that cost me?"

Katie smiled. The festival had been a paid gig, this was volunteer. "I'll trade a free photo shoot for signed photo releases and marketing rights." She planned to get a few beach photos for her own advertising if she decided to stay here a little longer.

"Deal."

JP clapped a hand on Micah's shoulder and leaned in. "Sounds official over here."

"I get the feeling your niece didn't build her business on free photo shoots," Micah said.

JP laughed. "Shrewd business woman, huh?"

Katie rolled her eyes. "Aaron was the business one. But he taught me a few things."

Other families arrived now, one by one, filling in the beach backyard. Katie greeted Zoe, Penn, and their kids. Ginny and her family came as well. Katie took in the names and faces of the other families, but she did a double take when Isaac's dark countenance entered, a few inches over the rest. Her heart skipped in surprise. What in the world was he doing here? A crowd swarmed around him immediately.

Zoe had invited Katie to contribute to the meal arrangements for him. For reasons she couldn't quite explain, Katie declined. She didn't want to see him in pain. She couldn't handle it.

Now he showed up in decidedly un-beachy jeans and a black and gray flannel, his arm strapped to his body in a black sling. Her heart gave a squeeze. Hearts always squeeze. But she felt it that time. Maybe she should get her heart checked out.

Katie skirted the group for a moment, pretending to check on the kids while she tried to gain her bearings. Two Sundays in a row—he had absolutely shocked her. Ridley Bay had that potential. She needed to get over it. Forcing a breath, she straightened from Josie's sandcastle and scanned the group. Half a dozen people crowded around him, yet his eyes were on her—they flicked away when she caught him.

"What are we doing?" Katie mumbled to herself. She had to face this—whatever this was. She shied from nothing. She took a direct course through the growing crowd and caught up to him in time to see Brielle reach him with stars in her eyes. Katie slowed her roll for a second, eavesdropping to the praise. *How brave. How strong.* Isaac glanced at Katie, and she could see his discomfort from here. She felt it too, every time somebody used those words to describe her widowhood. Survival wasn't brave or strong, it was an instinct, not something they chose.

"You must have been terrified," Brielle said, gently touching his forearm. "How are you feeling now? Emotionally and everything?"

Katie had no problem with Brielle touching him, she laid no claim to the man. But the *Please Help Me* look in Isaac's eyes caused her to interrupt. "What are you doing here?" she said a bit too loudly, stepping into the mix.

Slight amusement lit in Isaac's eyes. "It's a free country."

"Thanks to you," Brielle said.

Something closer to disgust than a smile crossed Isaac's face. Katie put on her best puppy dog eyes. "So true. Hey, can we talk? I need to file a complaint."

His mouth twisted, trying not to smile. "Sure." Isaac gave a nod to the small crowd around him and followed Katie off to the edges of the event.

"You looked like you needed rescuing," she said.

"By a shrimp of a woman. I've sunk low."

"Rude." She flicked his good arm.

He grinned. "Sorry. I've been trapped inside all week. I forgot my social skills."

"You never had any."

"Look who's rude now."

"Whatever, I really do have a complaint," she said.

"Really?" he asked, his mouth lifting ever so slightly at the corners.

"Yes! Why didn't you tell me you had a sling?"

A slight V formed between his eyebrows. "What?"

"You knew Sage was in a sling, but you never said anything to me. You could have sent me a picture or something."

"I'm not in the habit of texting you selfies, Katie."

"Shut up, not for me. This is about Sage. She's been so self-conscious she won't leave the house. Look at her—" Katie gestured to where her girls played in the sand. "She's using one hand and keeping the other inside her jacket. She's so embarrassed. Please show her your arm. She needs to know it's okay to get hurt."

"I'm not sure it is. I'm pretty embarrassed too."

"Whatever. You don't care what anyone thinks of you."

"The quiet ones always care," he said in a low voice.

Did he just align himself with Sage? Her heart gave another squeeze and Katie felt breathless. These were definitely the signs of a heart condition. She knew some good doctors for this. "Can you at least show her?"

He nodded. "I'll go talk to her."

Katie nodded and watched him walk away. Toward her daughter. Should she be walking with him? Did she need a doctor's appointment? Shaking herself off, Katie tried to catch up to him without jogging.

A few other kids had joined the sandcastle building and Sage did her normal abnormal thing—she sat a solid yard back from the rest, playing silently by herself. Isaac squatted beside her, not facing her. Sage ignored him for a moment.

He said something, but Katie couldn't catch it over the wind and hungry seagull cries. Sage stopped what she was doing and slowly turned her head to him. Katie stepped out of Sage's line of sight. Isaac seemed to have a pretty good handle on this. He laughed about something. Sage studied him. Then, she tugged at her jacket sleeve and let her own sling flash into sight.

Katie sucked in a breath. In one minute flat, Isaac got her to open up in a way Katie couldn't. Jealousy struck her. Why couldn't she do that? What was she doing wrong?

The kids near them jumped up in a sudden game of tag and Josie took off running with them. Behind Katie, the Kaminskis all played various roles in the gathering. The entire scene suddenly hit her mind's eye, like a drone camera floating above it all. The games, the friends, the family, the beach—this place and pace felt so different. In a matter of days, she felt less alone in Ridley Bay than she had anywhere else. While she ran amok, chasing happiness like a child trying to catch a lost balloon, happiness here felt like the winter sun—something to wait for and bask in, rather than chase.

Longing filled her lungs. Katie wanted to fit here so badly, she forgot everything else for a moment. She forgot she struggled with family rhythms and slow living. She wanted what they had. She wanted her kids to know where home was and who their friends were. She wanted whatever made Sage giggle right now. She wanted to stay in Ridley Bay.

Sage caught her eye and made a small "come here" motion, forcing Katie back into her body. Katie joined them in the sand and Sage gave her mother a silent, meaningful look, then pointed at Isaac's sling.

Katie grinned, scared to say the wrong thing and make her daughter clam up again. "I see that."

Sage pointed to her own sling, now on display.

"It looks like yours, doesn't it?" Katie asked.

Sage nodded and handed Katie her jacket. Katie's throat felt tight with both joy and jealousy.

"Turns out we both got hit in the arm," Isaac said, studying Katie. "But it's kind of cool because now we get to match. I just need a purple shirt too."

Sage straightened her purple floral shirt and gave her mom a tiny grin.

"Yeah, you do," Katie said. She smiled at Isaac and hoped he caught her silent gratitude.

With a bit of effort, he shifted and sat on the sand, reaching for a shovel next to Sage. "You're taking pictures tonight?" he asked, scooping sand into Sage's bucket.

Katie snapped back to the moment and straightened. She could see Micah rounding up people. "Yeah, I better get ready. I'll see if Suzanne or Tricia can come get Sage."

"We're okay," Isaac said. "Between the two of us, we have two good arms to build with now."

Another heart squeeze. Katie might be dying sooner rather than later. "Thanks." With one last glance, she left them.

•   •   •

From their safe and quiet distance, Isaac and Sage watched the baptisms begin. Katie charged into the water first, wielding a camera in a large plastic case. She let out a whoop when a wave hit her core. Micah and a man from their church waded in more hesitantly.

Isaac buried his laugh as he turned his attention back to the sandcastle. He had seen Katie invent Alaskan swimming, jumping into a snow pile in a swimsuit to prove a point. She could easily handle an autumn plunge in the ocean.

He hated when Katie said Sage was embarrassed. He understood the feeling, but he didn't want Sage to feel it. Agreeing to come and talk to her was the easiest, most natural thing he could have done. And it obviously mattered to Katie.

Isaac glanced around him and shifted his seat. "Where's our shovel?" he asked.

Sage stared at him with green saucer eyes, too big for her face, like she had come out of a cartoon. She looked away from him and went back to patting her sandcastle.

He often had to distract kids from trauma—from seeing their father arrested or their mother battered and bruised. He could easily talk to a kid. But he hadn't expected to care about this one so much. She seemed like a tiny, fearful version of Katie. Of course he wanted to help.

Still moving stiffly, Isaac glanced behind her and all around them both. A green shovel shouldn't be hard to find. "Sittin' on a shovel, kiddo?" he asked.

She shook her head and patted the sand next to her, where a small lump rose. Isaac shifted and reached for the pile. Sage put her hand in his way, stopping him.

Isaac grinned. "You hid the shovel?"

She shook her head.

"It'll be easier to build a sandcastle with a shovel," he said, reaching for the lump again.

"No," she said firmly.

She does have a voice. Isaac studied her for a second, unsure of what to do. "Why not?"

Sage stared at him for a moment, then patted more sand over the buried shovel.

"You know, Sage, your words are important."

She nodded, looking sad, and dumped another bucket of sand on the disappearing shovel. She knew her words were important. That's why she was so careful with them.

"I like to hang onto my words too," he said. He wasn't used to being the one to carry on a conversation. Maybe Sage was quiet because her mom and sister always did the heavy lifting in conversations.

He, on the other hand, could enjoy silence too. He helped Sage bury the shovel even further. If it were his brothers and their kids, they would probably dig it up and handle the tantrum that followed. But that wasn't Isaac's place, so he would buy somebody a new shovel.

"It died," Sage said quietly.

Isaac barely caught her words, turning his good ear closer. Had he heard her right? He opened his mouth to say something, then closed it again. *Huh.*

The adults finished their baptisms, and Katie and Micah both came back to the shoreline for a moment. Rebecca Sanford handed them towels. Isaac's attention turned from them when he caught Josie in his peripheral, scrambling his way.

"Wewoo!" she shouted, skidding to a halt and barely missing their admittedly ugly sandcastle. "I wanna make too!"

"Come on, little monkey," he said, moving back to make more room.

Suzanne caught up to Josie, out of breath. She bent over, her hands on her knees. "I thought she was running for the water," she huffed.

Isaac forced himself up, silencing the grunts of effort. He brushed off his jeans. "I'm impressed you've kept them dry this long."

Suzanne looked down at Sage. "What are you two doing?" she asked. Her tone made him self-conscious. Was it weird to help somebody else's kid build a sandcastle?

"Katie asked me to show Sage my sling," he said.

"I see." She clearly disapproved.

Isaac stepped away, ready to excuse himself. "If you've got an eye on her now, I promised Penn I'd head over…"

"I've got her," Suzanne said.

Isaac took another step, then stopped. He lowered his voice to try to keep his comment away from Sage's ears. "She buried the shovel. It's next to her but she won't let me get it."

Suzanne sighed, her defenses seeming to drop for a moment. "I've noticed she does that."

"This isn't the first one?"

"It's not only shovels," Suzanne said.

Isaac nodded and walked away. He had nothing helpful to add. Maybe it was normal. Maybe not. He'd leave that one for the experts.

Penn and Landon stood by the water's edge, ready to trade out with JP and the last kid. Isaac headed for Zoe's family. She held Serena on her hip while the middle two ran wild. Penn's parents were here too, and his mother held her phone out, ready to record.

Isaac was here tonight because of Landon. He had known the kid since birth and attended plenty of his birthday parties and soccer games. When Landon asked Isaac to come to his baptism, he agreed without giving it much thought. Now, he realized it didn't make much sense.

"So they dip in the water and his soul is saved?" Isaac asked Zoe, a question equal parts genuine and sarcastic.

Zoe poked her elbow out at him. "You haven't been listening all these years?"

"Not really."

"'By grace you have been saved, through faith… not by works,'" she quoted. "It's an outward expression of faith. Something to show others you're on their team."

"Can't you say it? Why get wet?"

Zoe laughed. JP walked to the shoreline while Katie waited in the water as Penn and Landon approached. "It's symbolic," Zoe said, her eyes trained on her son. "Death, burial, and resurrection. It's hard to hear from here but they always say you're 'raised to walk in newness of life.'"

Isaac nodded. He should stop interrupting the moment. He had already read about Jesus' baptism in the Bible and he didn't see that line in there.

He had to admit, he liked Jesus more than he expected. Jesus held others to an even higher standard than the Old Testament God. According to him, every hateful thought equaled murder. And it made Isaac both dislike and respect the man, somehow simultaneously. If Jesus was real, which based on his research seemed highly likely, Isaac understood the message: He could never save himself.

Isaac watched as Penn dunked his kid under the water. People cheered. Katie dipped around them, clicking. Isaac glanced around at the crowd. They seemed to easily accept all the Bible stuff. Could they really grasp how radical the story was though? They hadn't fought evil; they hadn't looked it in the eye the way he had. But God had, and he didn't just want to punish it, like Isaac. God wanted to redeem it through his own blood.

"I'm glad you're here," Zoe said, turning a smile to Isaac. "It means a lot to Landon."

Isaac watched the kid walk back to the shore. "I'm not sure why. We're not even on the same team." Or maybe they were. Isaac had too many questions and too few answers.

Zoe's smile faded. "I know. But he really admires you. Please be careful with that."

His friends rarely expressed doubt in him, but Zoe's message came loud and clear. Her son was on her team, and she didn't want him getting too close to the other side.

Landon ran to them and gave his mom a wet hug. He gave Isaac a lopsided pre-teen grin and fist bump. His family and friends congratulated him, and Isaac didn't know what to say, so he kept quiet. Penn joined them, with a towel around his shoulders and one for Landon.

Isaac glanced up and caught Katie's dripping wet form reach the shore, silhouetted in the fading light, her black shirt clinging to her sides. He pulled his head back to the crowd around him. After a bit of small talk, Rebecca Sanford invited everyone to join them for dinner and they all headed for a couple of long tables set up close to the house. Isaac followed a step behind.

He didn't need to be here anymore. He came for the part Landon wanted him to see, and now they would do the church thing—eat, talk, and somebody would probably bring out a guitar.

Isaac excused himself and headed toward the house and the path that skirted around it. A few steps from the house, Micah exited, a plate in his hand, stuffing the rest of a hamburger in his mouth. He nodded at Isaac and they met on the foot path.

"You call dibs on the burgers or what?" Isaac asked with a grin.

Micah held the back of his hand in front of his mouth, answering around a bite. "Gotta eat fast so I can go chat." He had changed after his part of the baptisms and wiped his hand off against the jeans he now wore. "You returning the Bible yet?"

Isaac shook his head. "Not yet."

"Read any of it?"

"Most of it."

Micah's eyes went wide. "In a week?"

Isaac shrugged. "I've been bored."

"What'd you think?"

Isaac glanced behind him. Nobody else was near them. He didn't know why this felt secretive but it did. It embarrassed him to feel confused. Like the sling, his words revealed his vulnerability, proving he wasn't as bulletproof as Katie and others might believe. "I think I need it, but I don't understand it."

"What do you not understand?"

"It's too easy. You just say you believe in Jesus and that's it? It's not enough."

Micah weighed his words for a moment. "You're right. I mean, even the demons believe in Jesus. The redeemed declare him as Lord of their lives."

That step still bothered Isaac. He didn't want to give up control. "Okay, so explain the criminal on the cross next to Jesus. He asks Jesus to remember him and Jesus hands him a free ticket to heaven. He didn't do anything. That doesn't seem fair."

"He submitted to Christ's authority," Micah said. "If it took more, it would mean Jesus dying on the cross wasn't enough."

Isaac didn't have a retort. Did he really think he could do anything to add to that ultimate sacrifice? What actions could top it? Either it was enough or it wasn't. And if it wasn't, they were all doomed.

"Do you want to talk inside for a minute?" Micah asked.

Isaac glanced behind him. "You need to go make the rounds."

"Nah, JP's got it. I have time."

Isaac snickered. Micah always said stuff like that. God must adjust clocks for the man. Regardless, he took Micah at his word and followed him into the Newton house. It had a distinct retirees-on-the-beach atmosphere, with paintings hung by rope and bowls of seashells adorning the side tables.

"So you tried the Bible," Micah said as they walked into the living room and sank onto the couches.

"I tried praying too," Isaac said.

"How'd that go?"

Isaac shrugged. "Don't know yet. I didn't ask for chips and candy."

Micah laughed. "Because God's not a vending machine." He preached a sermon on it once. Isaac did listen, sometimes. "Can I ask what you prayed for?"

"Help with the anger…" He could admit that emotion easier than the next. "And the fear."

"What are you afraid of?"

He couldn't pinpoint it. Some might say dying, but Isaac didn't fear death itself. He feared meaninglessness more. A meaningless life that could have ended before he ever made it count. "I can't save anyone. No matter how hard I try. Even if I save a life in the moment, I didn't save it forever." People still went back to bad situations, they still chose crime again, and he might not be there to save them the next time.

"You're afraid you can't be Jesus?" Micah asked with a grin.

Isaac returned the grin. "Now it sounds dumb."

"No, it's smart. You know the problem, but it scares you to trust someone else to be the solution."

Isaac pointed a finger at him. "Exactly. I keep thinking I might believe this, but I kind of want a two-week trial period or something."

Micah laughed. "It's not a subscription service. There are no temporary contracts. You either believe it or you don't."

Isaac thought he might believe it, but he didn't know how it might change his life if he admitted it. And he hated unknowns.

A door opened down the hall and Katie stepped out, wearing jeans and a striped blouse. One hand towel-dried her hair, the other held a phone she stared at. Oblivious to them, she wandered into the living room, then glanced up and jumped at the sight of them, eyes wide like a deer in headlights. "Oh, hey guys."

"Sorry to scare you," Micah said.

"No, it's okay, I'm just... distracted. Sorry. It looks like I'm interrupting something. I will just..." Katie stepped away, then back in the other direction, heading nowhere.

"You're good," Isaac said, standing. "I think I know how this one ends anyway."

"Really?" Micah asked, rising to his feet.

Isaac nodded and shook his hand. "Yeah, just give me a little time to think."

"Let me know if you want a dunk tonight," Micah said with a grin.

Isaac laughed. "Slow down."

Micah headed out the back door to join the picnic, while Katie ducked into the bathroom. Isaac waited a moment until she reappeared, with her phone still in hand.

"Sorry," she said, pocketing her phone. "You didn't have to stop talking because of me. I didn't hear anything, really. I was totally lost in thought."

"It's okay. What's all the deep thinking about?"

She pulled a hair clip out of her backpack and twisted up her wet hair. "Don't tell anyone yet... But I think we might stay in Ridley Bay."

Isaac's defenses jolted awake. He could resist The Katie Effect for a week or two, but *staying*? "For how long?" he asked.

"I'm not sure..." She stared into the distance, apparently working the details out in her own mind. "Maybe a few months. I was looking at furnished apartments online and found a couple options…" She glanced at him. "And you don't have to look so horrified."

His jaw couldn't possibly be wound tighter. He swallowed and tried to loosen it. "No, I just…" He just *what*? He was just a moth to her flame and would get burned by this? "Okay."

"'Wow, welcome to Ridley Bay, Katie,'" she mimicked in a deep voice. "'This is a great place for the kids. The Kaminskis will be so happy.' Honestly, Isaac, any of those would work."

He nodded. "All of those, then."

"Gee, thanks. Your sincerity means a lot."

He dipped his head. He wasn't a stupid moth. He could do this. "Yeah, no. That's great."

She gave him a wry look. "You're about as warm and welcoming as an ice bath."

And you're fire. He hoisted her camera gear bag onto his good arm. "You can handle it. You did the ocean polar plunge."

She started toward the door and he followed. "Better than Alaskan swimming," she said, glancing over her shoulder with a magazine-worthy smile.

He was a dead man walking.

Chapter Twenty-Three

Katie found the needle in the haystack: a furnished, two-bedroom apartment in Ridley Bay. The style and price point were geared toward snowbirds—rich northern retirees who came here to escape the cold—rather than young families, but it was available immediately and Katie took it.

Suzanne's ecstasy over Katie's decision to stay almost pushed her away. The teenage rebel inside of Katie wanted to leave, to prove she could. But she stayed the course and Suzanne watched the girls while Katie moved everything on Tuesday.

It only took a few hours to pack and clean their short-term rental, then to unpack and settle into the new place. These were only their travel things. Now that they had a six-month lease, Katie planned to have their moving pod shipped here. It held more clothes, toys, and creature comforts like their own pillows and blankets.

One day, she would have to face the stuff she had left in Baton Rouge—the furniture, paintings, and the symbols of a permanent home. But she wasn't sure when they would find a new home for it all. Hopefully before they drained Aaron's life insurance funds.

Katie crafted a couple of posts for her social media accounts about her extended stay on the coast. A boutique in Ridley Bay had already reached out to set up a collaboration. And she opened photoshoot slots for a few more fall sessions. She still had a couple of brand sponsorships in the works as well. With a little more hustle than she'd shown lately, they would be fine here.

That afternoon, when Katie drove the girls to their newest apartment complex, she pointed out the playground near their unit. "Look how close it is, we can walk over there all the time." The girls strained against their car seats to see.

"Mommy, pool!" Josie shouted, pointing it out.

"How fun," Katie said. She didn't bother telling her they would be gone before summer came. Future Katie and future Josie could handle that problem.

Inside, the girls ran around the place, exploring their new home. It held a queen bed in one room and two twin beds in the second.

After only a couple hours in the new place, someone knocked on the door. "Wow, someone found us fast," Katie mumbled. Vague memories of Aaron's few complaints about small town life came back to mind.

Those complaints disappeared when she saw Tricia at the door with grocery bags full of paper goods—toilet paper, paper towels, paper plates, and more.

"How did you know we needed all this?" Katie asked, as Tricia unloaded everything on the kitchen countertop.

"I've moved a few times in my life."

"That's right…" Katie put the pieces together like a toddler with a wooden puzzle. "You grew up a military brat, didn't you?"

Tricia nodded, her springy curls bouncing around her face. She wore a bold, primary-colored dress draped over her figure. "We moved every year."

"Did that ever bother you?"

Tricia laughed. "Oh yes. It's hard to leave every home you ever had, isn't it?" She reached down and patted Josie's head. The little blonde adored her Auntie Tricia and hung on her leg. "I learned to be tough though. You gotta do what you gotta do," she said, her signature resiliency on full display.

Katie didn't have to move. It was a choice.

"Did I hear you found a ballet class?" Tricia asked, already opening cabinets and finding spots for everything she brought.

"I did," Katie said. "Suzanne is taking the girls tomorrow to pick out ballet shoes and leotards."

"How fun. I know she is loving every minute of having the girls here."

Katie laughed. "I think her years as a boy mom left her pink-starved. You should see the dresses she got the girls. They're the frilliest things you can imagine."

"Oh, she loved raising boys too," Tricia said. "She just loves it all."

Katie smiled. "The ultimate mom." Suzanne bested Katie at everything.

Tricia made a little humming noise that sounded doubtful. "A good one, sure. But she had her difficult moments too, you know."

"No, I don't know. Aaron acted like she was perfect."

"Aaron made everyone feel that way."

"True. Aaron saw the best in everyone."

Tricia patted her cheek. "And in you too."

"I know. I miss that. There are some days when I could really use that boost."

"Then let me fill in a little bit," Tricia said, planting her hands on her hips. "You are a powerful mother who has been through unimaginable stress and is trying to do and be her best for her children. You are a talented photographer who manages to balance a business and motherhood and make it look easy, even though it isn't."

Katie laughed. "Who are you talking about?"

Tricia bopped her nose. "You."

"I *want* to be that person but I'm not."

"You're becoming her every day."

Katie sighed. The girls grew bored of their conversation and ran off to their room to play. Katie lowered her voice so they wouldn't hear. "I'm worried about Sage," she said.

"What about her?"

"I don't think she's just quiet. Sometimes… I think she's trapped inside herself." Katie struggled to get out the sentences she had avoided saying for so long. "I think she needs help."

Tricia put her hand over Katie's. "It's okay if she does."

"I wish she didn't."

"I know. We all have things we wish were different. But wishing never changed a thing. Some things only get better once you face them."

Katie sagged and dropped her head onto Tricia's shoulder. "I don't know where to start. I'm scared they're going to say she's broken." Or worse, that Katie had broken her. That her total lack of maternal warmth would ruin her children.

"Oh, honey, they won't. You don't have to get her evaluated for anything if you don't want to. You could start with something like play therapy or family counseling and see how that goes."

Katie straightened. "Family counseling? You think we all need it?"

"I don't think it would hurt. You said you wanted to grow as a mother, and sometimes we need a little guidance in those efforts. Besides, did you ever talk to a professional after Aaron died?"

"No. That was the last thing on earth I wanted to do. I don't want to sit around and focus on what's messed up." Not to mention, it scared Katie to welcome all these voices into her life. All these people to tell her how much damage Aaron's death had done and how she failed as a mother.

Tricia nodded slowly. "Well, sometimes that's where we have to start. Only after we take a good look at the problem can we start focusing on solutions."

Katie drew a long breath. "I guess so."

"Look, I know you're not staying for long, and these things can take time. Why don't we make a few calls and see who has the earliest availability?"

Katie nodded. "Okay." It felt like stepping into the void. A black hole into which Ridley Bay might suck them and never let go. She hated the feeling. But more than anything, she wanted to get better.

•   •   •

While the talk with Micah helped, Isaac truly met Jesus in his bathroom, standing over the drawer and the pregnancy test. His anger had no other outlet. He tried to control everything and he failed. He was ready to give up control.

"What kind of cop needs a savior?" he muttered to himself, pinching the bridge of his nose and closing his eyes against a building headache.

Penn. Zapata. Langley. Plenty of men and women at the police department. A lot of people Isaac respected. If he thought he was the savior, he had been kidding himself. But how could anyone save a world this broken?

Trust Him.

That's what it boiled down to. Isaac could either keep trusting himself—and letting himself down—or he could trust someone far, far greater than himself. He closed the bathroom drawer, picked up the Bible with his good hand, and took a seat on the foot of his bed with a heavy sigh.

He flipped through Romans again, where Micah highlighted several verses. *"For all have sinned and fall short...There is now no condemnation for those in Christ..."* The last one read like a how-to guide on salvation. *"Confess with your mouth that Jesus is Lord, and believe in your heart..."* Isaac read it over and over until he had it memorized and the words swam in his eyes.

Did this make him an idiot? To believe in a big guy in the sky?

He shook his head. He had been through it all a hundred times. And every time he ended up here. This wouldn't be his first prayer, but it was the most important.

Without a clue on how to do it, Isaac tried to copy some of the phrases he heard in church, but he bumbled them and rattled off his random thoughts instead. It all came together at the foot of the cross. It ended with the realization that he wanted to be part of this. He believed it and he needed it.

Isaac pressed his hand over his eyes and pulled in a breath. For the first time, he started to realize giving up control might be the best thing he could have ever done. Because for the first time in as long as he could remember, he wasn't racked with anger and regret. He had hope.

An hour later, when his phone buzzed with Penn's weekly text inviting him to the Bible study that night, he was already dressed and ready to go. He made it to the Sanford house a few minutes early.

Micah opened the door and gave him a hug. "How you doing?" he asked.

Isaac lifted the Bible in his hand. "Finished this."

Amusement lit Micah's eyes. "And?"

"Can I keep it?"

"It's yours."

Isaac nodded. "I think I'm a Christian."

A wide smile split across Micah's face. He gripped Isaac's good hand and pulled him in for a second hug. "You have no idea how long I've been praying for this."

Isaac tapped his finger on the Bible. "I saw the dates."

Micah laughed. "Okay, that long."

They stood on the porch and talked through it all for a few minutes until more people began to show up. Isaac wanted to make sure he did it right, but Micah didn't seem to have a doubt in his mind. Isaac envied that kind of assurance. Perhaps he would have it one day.

William and Suzanne arrived, and while William stayed outside to chat for a minute, Suzanne skirted them with hardly a smile, heading inside.

"How long are you out of work?" William asked, after the prerequisite niceties and asking after his arm.

"My medical leave goes another week," Isaac said. "I have some vacation time after that. And then they'll probably bring me back for desk work until I can go out on patrol again."

"Have they finished the formal review?" Micah asked.

Isaac nodded. "Mostly. Last I heard from my captain, there were no problems. I think we're getting off a little easier since the perp pulled through. If we had a dead guy on our hands, we'd be in far worse trouble."

William huffed and stated his defense of cops and all the logical problems with the justice system. Isaac nodded, wordless. He gave up complaining about it a long time ago. When Zoe and Penn and their crew arrived, William moved inside.

"You guys the welcome crew?" Zoe asked with a smile. She juggled Serena in one arm and a potluck dish in the other, while Lainey hung onto her leg as she walked. Micah took the potluck dish and Isaac took Serena.

"You beat me here," Penn said, eyeing the Bible in Isaac's hand.

"Yeah, I came of my own free will this time."

Penn gave him a crooked smile and head tilt as they followed the others inside. "Really?"

"Really."

Once they got the dishes and kids settled, Penn and Isaac each grabbed an iced tea and headed for the back porch. Landon and Lincoln raced outside after them, tossing a football to each other. Isaac told Penn about his decision.

Penn hugged his neck. "I'm happy to hear that, man. Welcome to the club."

"Think fast," Landon called, throwing the ball to his dad.

Penn handed it to Isaac. "How's your leftie throw?"

"Abysmal." Isaac tossed it and Penn laughed at his attempt.

"Have you told your family you're a Christian now?"

"It's literally only been a few hours."

"Hey, I didn't know, you got all that free time sitting around."

Isaac snorted. "It's torture."

"I'm sure Zoe would take you up on some babysitting if you're bored."

Isaac rotated his bad shoulder. "Too bad this arm keeps acting up."

Penn dropped his head back in a laugh. "Convenient. Speaking of your arm, I heard you're getting a medal?"

Isaac chugged his iced tea before answering. He had mixed feelings on the award. "They scheduled a ceremony for Thursday."

"Uh oh," Penn said.

"What?"

"You're not going."

Isaac shook his head. "Not planning on it. It doesn't make any sense." Medals like this never did. Isaac had one from the military as well. *Bravery.*

Valor. Vain words meaning someone had been through something traumatic and survived. He did his job, nothing more and nothing less.

"Just go. Accept the medal and give it to your mom for all I care. But do it."

That wasn't a bad idea. She would love it. "I don't even know why I'm getting it."

"Because this is what we do."

Somehow, that reasoning worked. Penn was right. This is what they did. This is how things went, in the army, in the police force. They lived and died by honor; by following the book and doing the right thing, even when it didn't make any sense.

Rebecca announced dinner and Penn gathered his boys to join in the line. Isaac couldn't help but notice Katie's absence tonight. Did she end up leaving Ridley Bay after all? That would be best for them both, but he doubted it.

Only a second later, he caught her name in someone else's conversation. Isaac turned his head, trying to focus on the words and tune out the droning ring in his ears. Suzanne was talking to Rebecca about Katie. Before he could decipher what she said, Zoe sidled up to his side. "So Katie moved into a new apartment today," she said.

Darn her and her mind reading. Isaac dropped his focus to his plate and loaded it with tonight's baked potato bar. "Really?" he asked, trying not to sound too interested.

Zoe nodded smugly. "She's staying for at least six months. I had a feeling she would catch onto the Ridley Bay charm."

"Mm."

Zoe laughed and reached past him for cheese. "It looked like you bonded with Sage at the baptisms."

It was true. When he and Katie joined the others for dinner, Sage silently followed him like a little shadow the rest of the evening. "I tried to convince her arm slings are the new thing."

Zoe turned her back to the countertop, Serena in one arm, her plate in the other. "Did it work?"

"Guess not. They're not here tonight."

Zoe laughed. "It's probably the move keeping them busy today. I know you could talk my kids into nearly anything." Zoe raised a warning eyebrow at him.

"Chill out, mama bear, we're on the same team now."

"Wait—what?"

Isaac laughed and carried his plate into the dining table while Zoe scrambled after him. He updated her and quickly shushed her when Brielle joined their table. He didn't need any more fawning from her. He wished her all the best, but her sugary sweet vibes made his jaw hurt. Isaac expertly directed the conversation away from himself and let Zoe's kids interrupt his few sentences.

When they all moved to the living room, Isaac hung back to clean up plates and let the others get settled. He and Penn took barstools behind everyone else. Tonight, he belonged here.

Chapter Twenty-Four

A wall of small play figurines and a sandbox greeted Katie at the family counseling office. She took a seat in a green chair, wondering if they had confused this for an appointment with kids. A few minutes later, a student counselor named Holly entered the room. She had been the first available counselor. Katie shook her hand and they quickly reviewed the paperwork.

Holly asked Katie what she wanted to work on. Katie didn't know. She only knew being a mom was hard, and Holly looked too young to understand that.

"Why don't you show me what a day looks like for you?" Holly pulled the sand table to the middle of the room and gestured to the wall of plastic toys. "Can you pick out some things that represent your day?"

"Seriously?" Katie asked, with a laugh. "I spend all day with kid toys."

Holly shrugged. "But not these."

Oh boy. She was serious. Katie hid an inward grimace and turned to the figurines. She wanted to grab the giant spider and the green alien to see what Holly would say to that. The fear of ending up in a room with soft walls stopped Katie.

Instead, she found two little girls, a miniature playground, and a church. She found a few trees. Miniature toy blocks. A little couple could represent Suzanne and William. A princess worked too, because her days were filled with puffy dresses and tea parties. She set them up in a corner of the box. "There."

Holly asked Katie to explain all the pieces in the sandbox so far. Katie followed orders, feeling like a child.

"Is that everything?" Holly asked.

To be polite, Katie studied it a little longer. "I don't think we really have 'normal days,'" she said. "I find routines suffocating, so we tend to switch things up a lot."

"Okay. Maybe a recent day, then? Today even."

Katie looked through the wall of figurines for something relevant. She found some dollhouse furniture. "We just moved to a little apartment," she said, arranging the furniture in the sand. "Honestly, if you have a moving truck though, that makes more sense for us."

"You move frequently?" Holly asked.

"Every few months."

"Why is that?"

"I need to stay mobile," Katie said, not exactly sure of the answer herself. "I worry if I stop for too long, the pain will catch up to me."

"What pain?"

"The dead husband," Katie said wryly. She pointed at Holly's clipboard. "I put it in my notes." They never really read that stuff.

"Do you want to talk about him?"

Katie gave her the brief overview she had memorized and could rattle off in her sleep—the story compartmentalized away from the pain so she could keep living.

"Is there anything else you want to add to the sandbox?" Holly asked. "Anything that represents your life."

Holly's tone implied Katie's failure with the project. She glanced at the wall of random figurines, finding tiny soldiers, a variety of television characters, and a tombstone, but Aaron wasn't a regular part of their life. Or was he? She added it to the mix. Then she found a wounded soldier amongst the toys—his head wrapped in gauze, his leg in a cast, his hands gripping crutches. She added it.

"Okay, my daughter isn't quite this bad off," Katie said with a laugh. "But she is wearing a sling right now."

"What happened?" Holly asked.

Sitting back in her seat and dusting sand off her fingers, Katie explained the goat incident. She mentioned her photography—the way she always preferred life behind a lens. "I know I should have been closer. But sometimes I'd rather back away. I'm constantly overwhelmed."

Holly made a quick note on her notepad. "How is your daughter doing now?"

Katie figured this was a safe place, so she let out all the fears. All the worries about Sage's heart, the injury, and worse—the silence and the way she buried toys. "I know it's not normal. But I've been ignoring it and hoping it gets better."

"Has it?"

"No. That's why I'm here. I want to be a better mom."

"You keep implying you're not a good mom. Why do you think that?"

Katie fidgeted in her seat and turned to the wall of figurines again. This time, her eyes landed on a tiny camera on the top shelf. She picked it up and turned it in her hands. "I don't know. I don't feel like a mom at all. My husband was the one who wanted kids."

"You didn't?"

Katie shook her head. She hated to talk about it though. She wanted them now, but her past self and her present reality still felt at odds. "I think the life I envisioned for myself is so different from my reality, it's hard to accept it sometimes."

"Maybe we can paint a new vision that matches your reality."

"Maybe." Katie shrugged. "Most days I'd rather escape it."

Holly nodded but Katie could tell she didn't understand. She decided to switch topics, lifting the camera in her hand. "I found this for my photography."

"Would you like to add it?" Holly asked.

"Sure." Katie leaned over the table. Her miniaturized Suzanne and William stood by the church, the girls were by the apartment, with the tiny toys and the playground nearby. Something was missing.

Then it dawned on her. She had nowhere to put the camera, no one to hold it. She stared at the sand box for a moment. "I'm not there," she said.

Holly gave her a faux-understanding, mostly-patronizing smile. "Do you want to be?"

Her throat felt tight. Katie swallowed. "I guess I should be."

She grabbed a peg doll in a dress from the shelf and stared at the box. She didn't want to be anywhere in there. She looked at the shelf again, tempted to grab the airplane. She wanted to be far, far away from here. "I'm not sure I fit in there."

"Into motherhood or life altogether?"

"Depends on the day," Katie said with a weak laugh, staring at the sandbox. "It looks better without me though."

"A day in your life looks better without you?"

"I guess I did that wrong."

Holly clicked her pen. "There's no right or wrong, really."

Katie's hand hovered over the sandbox before setting the peg doll down in a corner, far from the other things. She pushed everything else into the opposite corner, staring at the two tiny girl dolls. "I think the twins are happier there."

"Without you?"

Katie nodded.

The concern on Holly's face came straight out of the psychologist's playbook. "Are you happier without them?"

"I don't know," Katie breathed. "Sometimes I think I might be. Sometimes I want to walk away and find out. Every time I get a break, I feel more like myself and I wish the break lasted forever." It was word vomit—the stuff that stirred in her stomach, uncomfortable, destined for release.

"Are your children safe there?" Holly asked, studying the figures crowded into the corner furthest from miniature Katie.

"Yes."

Then Holly pointed her pen at the miniature Katie. "Are they safe with you?"

Katie thought about Sage—her fears, her silence, and the way she covered her sling with her shirt at the Sanfords' house. The sling that she had been terrified to reveal until Isaac made it okay. "I don't know."

Holly glanced at the clock, then laced her fingers together and studied Katie. "Tell me what you mean."

"I mean I try, but I'm not perfect. And obviously Sage is struggling. And maybe Josie is too. I probably could have prevented the broken collarbone. Or that time Josie got stitches. There isn't enough of me. I can't be everything they need, so sometimes I don't even want to try."

"How often do you feel that way?"

"Every time I give Josie the wrong color of cup," Katie said jokingly, trying to lighten the mood. It felt dark and heavy in here, with all her worst thoughts spilling out and filling the room.

Holly nodded solemnly, opening her portfolio. She pulled out a business card. "We're almost out of time, but I am concerned, Katie. I think you and your girls might benefit from more serious help. This is a psychiatric center here in town, they are a wonderful resource."

Holy smokes. It was happening. The room with soft walls. Holly wanted to send her to a psych ward. "Oh, no, really I'm not—" Katie said, wishing she could rewind a bit of their conversation. "I need a break, but not, like, a *forever* break."

"I understand. But I think it would be best for your children if you were in a more secure frame of mind. I know we both want to keep your children safe."

"They are safe."

"Wonderful," Holly said in a patronizing counselor tone. "Let's keep them that way. It's okay to need help sometimes."

"Right, that's why I'm here."

"And that's why we're here. And the state is here." Holly covered Katie's hand with her own. "I do need to let you know, I am required to report any suspected neglect."

Katie rose from her chair, her voice rising as well. "I have never neglected my children. They're not in danger."

Holly stood, her tone robotically level. "But they could be."

"No, they aren't." Katie's heart raced. She wasn't a good mom, but that didn't mean she was a bad one either. Heat spread from her chest to her head.

"Please consider checking in with the psychiatric center. We just want what's best for you and your children."

"You completely misunderstood me."

"Maybe we can try again next week," Holly said, with a calm, veiled smile.

"Maybe so." *Absolutely not.*

Holly opened the door and Katie nearly bolted. Her heart thudded against her ribs. *Required to report?* She wouldn't. She couldn't. Wasn't it her job to listen to people's worst thoughts? To listen and provide guidance? Katie wanted to fix the problem, but the problem was herself. *Oh, God.* What had she done?

Chapter Twenty-Five

A dark cloud of stress followed Katie after the counseling appointment. Any mom guilt she carried tripled. Even the counselor thought she failed as a mother. She replayed the conversation in her head, rewording and restating it to make more sense.

When she woke the next morning, she struggled to move. Everything that sounded fun now seemed too hard. Parks, beaches, libraries, museums, and aquariums all awaited, but Katie didn't want to do anything. A heavy weight dragged her down onto the couch, where she lay in defeat, putting a movie on for the girls.

This could easily spiral out of control. A mountain of pain waited, ready to collapse on top of her if she let it. When the movie ended, Katie forced herself upright and washed her face in the bathroom. "Okay girls, let's go," she said.

"Where?" Josie asked.

"I don't know."

"Nana's house?" Josie asked.

Katie checked the clock. They had a couple of hours before nap time, but they could find something else to do besides spend them with Perfect Suzanne. "Maybe. Let's get dressed and then we can decide." Mid-morning pajamas were not a good look for Katie.

She took a single step toward the bedroom when a knock on the door stopped her. Katie glanced at the girls, as they squabbled over the last of the popcorn. Her phone had no messages, and she wasn't expecting any visitors.

Wearing pajama pants and an oversized tee, she answered the door to find two people in business attire with clipboards. Katie opened her mouth to start the "I'm not buying anything" speech, but the woman interrupted.

"Are you Katelyn Kaminski?"

"Yes, and you—"

"My name is Yvette, we're here with Child Protective Services to investigate a report concerning your children."

A vacuum sucked the air and noises out of her head as the world dropped around her. Katie's grip on the door handle tightened until her hand hurt. She had convinced herself Holly was all bark and no bite. This couldn't be happening. Behind her, at exactly the wrong moment, Josie started to scream. Yvette and the man with her tried to peer around Katie. Katie pulled the door tightly to her side, trying her best to fill the small gap.

"Can we come in?" Yvette asked, trying to ease into the space. Katie doubled down on her grip and stance. "We'd like to talk to you about our concerns, and walk you through the first steps."

"No." Katie knew little about CPS, but she knew to keep them out. "No, I'll be contacting my lawyer." She didn't have a lawyer. She would soon.

"We'd like to set up an appointment within a couple days. It might be most convenient if we go ahead and talk here—" Yvette still peered over her shoulder as Josie screamed.

"No, thank you." Katie's death grip on the door nearly numbed her hand. She risked a quick look back to make sure nobody was hurt. Just a fight over popcorn.

Yvette nodded. "That's fine." She passed Katie a business card. "We'll reach out later today to set up an appointment."

As quickly as possible, without slamming it in her face, Katie shut and locked the door. She turned her back to the door, the business card trembling in her hand. Sage and Josie pulled the popcorn bowl back and forth until Josie overpowered Sage and the bowl flipped over, spilling popcorn on the floor. Sage screamed.

"Girls, stop," Katie said.

They ignored her.

She sank to the floor. This couldn't be her life. She wasn't a bad mom. *But you're not a good one either.*

"Oh God," Katie whispered, pleading, as she dropped her head onto her arms. She had reached into the black hole and now she would pay the price.

·   ·   ·

Katie once believed that because she had survived the worst experience possible—losing her husband—nothing else could shake her. How wrong she had been. It took hours to scrape herself together after the CPS visit, but she eventually swallowed her pride and called Suzanne and William.

"I need help," she said, her voice shaking as she admitted what happened.

"We have a lawyer," Suzanne said immediately. "Don't do anything."

The day passed in a flurry of phone calls. The Kaminskis' lawyer, Patrick, called Katie and then CPS to arrange the mandatory appointment.

Friday they all went to the local CPS office, with the girls in tow. They wore matching outfits and braided hairdos—a feat that involved a few screams and tears. But everything about her girls now came under a critical eye. Sage's sling looked like a glaring red flag.

At the CPS offices, Katie had a lawyer and a meager list of potential character witnesses. CPS outgunned her, with a child psychologist, an abuse specialist, a pediatrician, a lawyer of their own, and two case workers.

They reviewed the case with Katie and Patrick while William and Suzanne waited in another room and Sage and Josie went off to a "play room" which Katie suspected was more of an interview room. Her stomach knotted so tightly she thought she might be sick.

When Sage's medical history came into the conversation, Katie mumbled answers about the heart defect, the frequent moves, the lack of a regular pediatrician, the date of her last annual check-up—more than a year ago. None of it reflected well on her.

Yvette suggested placing the kids with someone else until they could investigate further and Katie couldn't hear the rest after that. Sand filled her head.

But the Kaminskis hired the best of the best and Patrick didn't back down a single inch. He came back with arguments and legal terms Katie didn't understand, eventually threatening a lawsuit. And he won—she would have daily visits instead. CPS could show up any time they wanted, walk into her house, and evaluate her.

By the time they left, Katie thought she might be having a heart attack. The pressure around her lungs squeezed so tightly she couldn't take a full breath.

"I doubt this investigation will last for more than a few weeks," Patrick said to them all in the parking lot. "We'll set you up for a psych evaluation, get medical records, take a parenting class, go through a few house visits, and CPS will see that your children are perfectly safe."

Katie nodded, speechless for once. *What if CPS is right, though?* The thought tore at her chest. Something she had done or said warranted this. She brought this on herself. Somebody, at some point in the next few weeks, would find proof Katie was a bad mom. She would lose the girls. And if she lost the girls, there would be nothing left of her.

This is why she never wanted to love again. Even loving her own children proved too risky.

That night, Katie held the girls a little longer than usual at bedtime. She sat on Sage's bedside and ran her fingers through her copper locks until she drifted off. Josie still squirmed in bed, so Katie went there next. She sang a quiet lullaby to Josie, who tried to sing along without knowing the words. Katie smiled at her beautiful blonde angel. That someone believed she had wronged. Katie's heart felt raw. Fierce motherly love poured out of it. But Katie fought it, trying to build a stone wall around herself, to hold her together in case she shattered.

Katie began singing "Amazing Grace" and thinking of Aaron. She tried to remember the life they once dreamed of. The vision they once had for their family, however naive it may have been. But she found nothing.

They had started a parenting journal; it might still be in storage in Louisiana. Katie wanted to go get it, but she couldn't just leave town. She was trapped here, where the black hole had caught her. And she would give anything to hear Aaron, just once more, tell her she would be okay. *Anything.*

Chapter Twenty-Six

By Sunday morning, Katie's nerves were shot. They survived their first CPS visit yesterday, after Suzanne helped her scrub the entire apartment. Patrick even came to direct their preparations, advising them on every child-safety improvement she needed to make.

In an apartment meant for snowbirds, there were plenty of changes to be made. Katie's bottle of wine got sent to the Kaminski house. They moved up knives and glasses and added child locks to everything. They scrubbed and cleaned and stocked the pantry. Things Katie had never been great at.

Katie debated skipping church on Sunday, simply because she couldn't handle anything extra in her life right now. But Patrick encouraged her to maintain her regular routine and it meant a break from the apartment where she felt completely trapped.

Swallowing the ever-present drowning sensation, she loaded her arms with a bag full of crayons, coloring books, Play-Doh, and emergency snacks. She had given the girls a talk about how they were so big, they could go to "big church." In reality, she wasn't sure if childcare drop-offs were allowed. She could ask the caseworker, but preferred to interact with her as little as possible. Besides, Katie didn't want to let them out of her sight. It might be unreasonable, but the thought of someone showing up to take the girls while they were out of sight terrified her.

If she found motherhood stressful before, it was nothing compared to her life now. She wanted to scream at Holly. At least hourly.

They got to church only a few minutes late and took seats at the back of the church, in case Katie needed to take a noisy toddler out of the service. Micah walked down the row between two worship songs and stopped at various places, shaking hands. He greeted Katie with a bright smile.

"I hope it's okay if the twins stay with me today," Katie said. She made a slight gesture toward Sage's arm, as if that were the excuse. Katie had asked the Kaminskis to keep it quiet. Suzanne wanted people to be praying, but Katie wanted to limit the spread of information regarding her failures as a mother.

"Kids are always welcome," Micah said. "I don't mind a little noise."

Katie's return smile felt weak and hollow.

Tricia spotted her at the back and moved from her spot by JP to come and sit with Katie. She took a seat on the other side of the twins. Even with the extra help, Katie struggled to follow the service, either lost in her own prayers, or distracted by keeping the girls quiet.

When the service ended, Katie breathed a sigh of relief. She had never been more stressed in a church than she had for the last hour.

"They did so well," Tricia said, as the lights came up and people dispersed. "And so did you. You were quite prepared." She gestured to the bag of activities Katie now repacked.

"Thanks," Katie said, struggling to find the smile she needed. "I'm trying."

Honestly, the girls had done well. Katie never even hustled a child out of there. She thanked God for it. She might need people here as future character witnesses. She and the girls had to be on their best behavior now, every second of every day.

At the auditorium doors, she found Isaac talking to JP. Her eyes ran over him—no ear piece, still carrying a concealed weapon, but on the left-hand side. Surely he wasn't back to work already. Why was he here?

Before she could ask him, Brielle caught up to him and started chatting. Isaac always looked like he had something caught in his teeth around her. Katie ducked her head and tried to navigate the girls around them without being noticed.

"Hey," he said.

Katie glanced up and tried to feign surprise before remembering she was a terrible actor. "Oh, hi."

"Kept the girls with you?" he asked, gesturing to the twins.

"Oh, yeah. Wanted to keep them close." Katie tried to paste on a smile. She might win a Golden Raspberry for this performance—the opposite of an Oscar. A slight pinch formed between his eyebrows as he picked up on her lie. Brielle still stood there, waiting to get in on the conversation and Katie needed a distraction *now*. "Don't tell me you're working security with that thing still on," Katie said, gesturing to the sling.

Brielle laughed. "I asked him the same thing."

"I'm a decent leftie," he said, his tone clearly returning a lie for a lie.

She didn't have the capacity to deal with it right now. "Good," she said. And not a moment too soon, Josie saved her from needing to say anymore, with a sudden cry for the bathroom. Katie waved to Brielle, avoided Isaac's eyes, and walked the girls to the restrooms.

Sage changed her mind four times on whether she needed to potty, and by the time they finally exited, most of the Sunday crowd was gone. Tricia, JP, and the Sanfords all carried armloads of church supplies outside, Suzanne and William visited with a couple of worship leaders, and Isaac stood talking to Penn—who Katie now realized served as the substitute security guy.

Suzanne waved to Katie and caught up to her. "Why don't we go out for lunch?" she asked, bright as daylight, as if the world still held joy.

Keeping the girls quiet for another hour sounded impossible. "I don't know…" she said. When CPS asked about her regular routine, she struggled to answer. They didn't follow much of one. But Patrick said to stick to what she could. If CPS found an empty apartment at every visit, they might accuse her of avoiding contact.

"Oh we should, I realized we haven't taken you to this spot on the docks yet, they have the best seafood—"

"I don't know if I can," Katie said, her words full and hinting. She didn't want to talk about this in front of others, and from the corner of her eye, she could see Isaac walking toward them.

Suzanne gasped and touched her arm. "Is it because of the case? Goodness, it's almost like house arrest."

"Who's under arrest?" Isaac asked, reaching her side.

Katie shook her head, her composure slipping. She felt exhausted, as if every night of insomnia combined into this moment. She hardly wanted to stand anymore. "Doctor's orders," she said, her tired brain searching for some fragment of truth to turn into a lie. "The sling and all. We're just getting bored waiting, I guess." She didn't bother meeting his eyes.

"That's it," Suzanne said, with a strange look on her face. Katie couldn't tell if it was disapproval at the lie, or something else. But she turned and left them.

"I hear you," Isaac said, dropping to a squat next to Sage. "How's your arm feeling, kiddo?"

Sage stared at him.

"Sometimes I get tired of the sling and take it off," Isaac said. "But I never last long before the pain makes me put it on again."

"How much longer do you have in yours?" Katie asked.

"A week or two," Isaac said, still talking to Sage. "How about you?"

She held up two fingers on her other hand.

"We really are sling buddies," Isaac said. "Healing takes time. It gets hard to wait, though, doesn't it?"

Sage nodded her head solemnly.

"It's impossible," Katie said. "We can't do anything too active for Sage, but it has to be engaging enough for Josie. We've played so many rounds of Candy Land, I dreamed I turned into a peppermint."

Isaac stood, keeping his eyes on the girls. Josie twirled around them and Katie pulled Sage closer to avoid a potential hit.

"You could go fly a kite," he said. "That's a low-impact kid classic."

That honestly sounded so fun, for a split-second light danced through her world again. "With one hand?" Katie asked, trying to picture it.

"She can still hold a kite spool."

Katie's mouth twisted to the side, trying to picture it. "Really? I guess I've never seen one up close. I've never flown a kite."

"You've never flown a kite?" Isaac asked, his voice raising a notch. "How is that possible?"

Katie shrugged, suddenly feeling awkward about her admission. "I don't know. Nobody ever took me as a kid. Once I was old enough to take myself, I never thought about it. Do you know any adults who go fly kites by themselves?"

"But you have kids now, you have to teach them how to fly a kite."

"Where do I learn how to do that? Are there tutorials on YouTube or something?"

Isaac swiped a hand over his face. "Are you serious?"

His disappointment annoyed her and a flash of fire reentered her soul. "Okay, Mr. Expert, if you're so passionate about kite flying, why don't you teach us?"

He raised an eyebrow. "I'm not an expert, but I didn't know someone could go their whole life without flying a kite."

Katie latched onto the idea now. She needed this distraction. Sure, Isaac might not be her biggest fan, he hadn't seemed happy she was staying in town, but he started this conversation and he was at church of his own free will today. Things could be changing.

"You're the one who suggested it," she said. "We're both bored to death, you're not working, you and Sage are sling buddies, and you probably have a weird knowledge of kites. So say yes." Besides, she might score points with CPS for hanging out with a cop—proof she lived on the right side of the law.

Josie picked up on the conversation and tugged on Katie's hand. "I wanna fry a kite!"

"*Fly*, sweetie. And we will, if Mr. Isaac will teach us how." Katie gave him a long, slow couple of blinks.

He laughed. "This is pitiful. Fine, for their sakes."

Josie began to cheer and Katie smiled. The soul-crushing restrictions she lived under faded as energy sprang back into her. So what if they missed a visit? "Tell me when," she said.

Isaac stared at Katie for a moment, then glanced down at the girls. "Tomorrow afternoon."

Katie clapped her hands. For a fleeting moment, the outside world wasn't crumbling around her. "Perfect, it's a date," she said. Isaac's eyebrows shot up and he opened his mouth but Katie quickly corrected herself. "A non-date. With two toddlers."

"Right." He still wore a wary look, though a smile teased the corners of his mouth.

Chapter Twenty-Seven

Isaac questioned his sanity on the drive to Katie's apartment. She needed a ride because William had taken her car for an inspection—finally. And he needed a mental health check because he was repeating the past.

They believed in the same God now, the deadline on their time had been extended, and two kids were tagging along. Despite all the changes, a non-date with Katie felt too familiar. Why did he agree to this?

Because Katie's never flown a kite. That bothered him. And it reminded him of something he learned about her years ago: that Katie's bubbly exterior made it easy to believe life had handed her sunshine and rainbows, when in fact she wielded the sunshine like a weapon. And yesterday, that sunshine appeared to have darkened. So he caved. And now they were going kite flying. Like the cute little family they weren't. He rubbed his eyes and pulled into the apartment complex.

Just fly a kite and walk away. He could do that.

He knocked on the door and Katie answered in jeans and a *"Running on Jesus and Coffee"* T-shirt. "Hey, come in," she said. "We're almost ready to go."

Isaac walked into a spotless apartment, save for a handful of wooden blocks Sage stacked on the floor. It hardly looked like anyone lived here. "How long have you been here?" he asked.

"Nearly a week."

"It's clean."

Katie smiled. "I know, it surprises me too."

She sounded offended. Before he could stick his other foot in his mouth, Josie came running down the hall wearing a yellow dress like a headdress and waving a wand. "Wewoo!" she shouted.

"Isaac," Katie corrected. "Mr. Isaac. He has a name, Jojo. And let's leave your Rapunzel hair so it doesn't get sandy. Come on."

Apparently "almost ready to go" meant packing a bag, removing Josie's headdress, taking an honorary photo of Sage's block tower, bathroom breaks for everyone, and hunting down shoes. Isaac began to understand why she ran late.

Katie handed him two bulky car seats and he hauled them to the truck. Cracker crumbs spilled out of one along the way, so he stopped to shake them both out. He didn't judge a parent for having a messy car, but he didn't particularly relish sharing in that situation.

"Need any help?" Katie asked, walking out with the girls. She now sported a yellow ball cap with a smiley face on it.

Isaac clicked in the last strap. "They're all set. Took longer with one arm."

"Sorry, I guess I should have done that," she said. "Thanks again for the ride."

"No problem," Isaac said. After she buckled the girls in, she climbed into the front seat. His eyes caught on a large princess sticker covering her bicep. "Nice sticker."

"Thanks, it gives me special powers. I think I can freeze you."

"Scary."

"Here, you could use some special powers." Katie peeled the sticker off and stuck it onto his shirt.

Isaac glanced down at the princess decorating his chest. "Does it make me look stronger?"

"Definitely. Masculinity works best in contrast."

Isaac grinned as he pulled out of the parking lot. He had plenty of contrast in this truck right now. "Okay, ladies, to the store."

"Wait, why the store?" Katie asked, with a quick twist in her seat.

"To get a kite."

She frowned. "You don't have one yet?"

"Nope. Figured we'd let the girls pick one. I didn't think it would be a problem."

Katie checked her watch. "It's not, I guess… I figured you already had your carefully-researched, number-one rated, highest-flying kite."

"They all fly about the same."

"Really?"

"I think so. We made our own growing up. Paper, string, and sticks. Old school. I figure if I could make those fly, we can make any store-bought kite fly."

She settled back into her seat. "Okay. Let's make it quick."

"Are we on a schedule?"

Katie shrugged and didn't answer.

"Hot date tonight?"

She gave a small, half smile. "Nope. I'm stuck with you today."

"Don't act like that's a downgrade. In your own words, this is peak masculinity." He flexed and pointed to the princess sticker. If he was flirting with her, he didn't mean to be. He only wanted to make her smile.

Katie snickered and rolled her eyes at him. "Shut up."

"Don't say dat, Mommy!" Josie called from the back seat.

"Yeah, *Mom*," Isaac said.

She shook her head, but she wore a genuine smile this time.

He drove them to a sports store on the island. Inside, he guided them all to the large nylon kites, though the girls stopped at every colorful bit of plastic on the way.

They finally reached the end of the store where enormous kites in dozens of shapes and sizes hung overhead. Dinosaurs, pirate ships, dragons, mermaids, and more. Isaac studied them for a moment, then reached for a box with a red octopus pictured on the cover. "How about this one?" He turned to show the girls, but somehow, they already held one.

Shoulder to shoulder, the girls balanced a long box with a picture of a giant, pink, glittery horse with wings and a crown. The words "Pegasus Princess" decorated the front of the box in a curly script. "Dis one," Josie said, patting the box.

Isaac grimaced and glanced at Katie, who tried not to laugh. He held up the octopus. "But look how cool the octopus is."

The twins shook their heads in unison. "We want da pony," Josie said, her platinum pigtails bobbing.

He turned to Katie. "I can't fly that thing."

She shrugged, her eyes dancing. "They all fly the same, right?"

Isaac frowned. Two pairs of wide, green eyes stared at him. Josie looked completely confident in her ownership of the pony. She patted the pony again and smiled at it. "Her name is Tinkle."

"Tinkle?" Isaac asked.

"Twinkle," Katie said. "I don't know, girls. I think Mr. Isaac wants an octopus. Maybe we can name the octopus Twinkle."

Sage's face fell and Josie stomped her foot, her bottom lip jutting out.

Isaac laughed. "No, I know when I'm outvoted." He squatted to face the pink flying horror again. Its wings had rainbow-colored tips. Heaven help him. "Okay. Twinkle the Flying Pony it is."

Josie squealed and hugged her sister.

"Pegasus," Katie corrected.

"I'm not going to use that word," Isaac muttered. If his brothers could see him right now, he would never hear the end of it.

They bought the kite and soon were back in the truck, heading for the beach. "Tanks for my pony," Josie said from the back seat.

Isaac turned to smile at her and caught Sage grinning too—her own thanks. "You're welcome. Now, let's go find a quiet spot far away from people to fly that thing."

"Oh, and you might want to give up your sticker too," Katie said.

One look down confirmed the blue princess still marked his chest. Isaac buried a groan. He had completely forgotten about it and worn it through the store. "But you said it gives me powers."

"Not powers of observation."

He peeled the sticker off and smacked it onto her knee. "You ladies are really gonna test my ego today."

She laughed. "Is it going to survive?"

He grinned. "Barely." He had to admit this was better than sitting around the house, watching cartoons or working out with one arm.

After a round of "Old MacDonald Had a Farm" performed by Josie (in which she insisted chickens say quack, and Katie had to convince Isaac to let it go), they reached the thankfully deserted beach.

The girls were so excited for Twinkle to fly, Isaac hardly had enough elbow room to get the kite out of the box. Katie helped tie the knots while Isaac coached her and they soon had it ready for launch.

After a few failed attempts with Katie holding the spool and Isaac lifting the kite, he walked back to her. He put a hand on her lower back before quickly redirecting it to the string. "Trade with me," he said. "I think you have the wrong job."

"Agreed."

She took the giant horse and lifted it as high as she could. She tossed it up and ducked as it crashed down next to her.

"Maybe if you jump you'll get as high as the average adult," Isaac called to her.

"I'm not that short, you're just a giant." Katie marched the kite toward the truck and climbed into the bed. A memory flashed in his mind—watching the northern lights in a truck bed—like his mind had stored every single day of those short months in Alaska and kept the files readily available.

Isaac swallowed. "Let's try again."

With a few extra feet of height, she raised the kite again. A gust of wind caught it and it finally lifted and gained height as Isaac unspooled it.

Katie and the girls cheered. Then Katie pulled out her phone and snapped a few photos before joining him. "What a glorious moment—Isaac Torres flying the majestic Pegasus Princess. I wish I had my real camera for this."

"Why don't you?" he asked.

She hesitated. "I don't know. I'm taking a break from it. Trying to learn to stay in the moment more. Hey, look at that, we're both taking a break from shooting." Katie laughed at herself. "Sorry. Too soon, isn't it?"

He snickered. "It'll always be too soon. Learn to say less, Katie."

Her face fell and she surprised him with silence.

He elbowed her in the side. "Hey, I'm kidding. What's wrong?"

Before she could answer, Josie tugged on her mother's shirt. "My turn. I wan' my turn."

Isaac squatted down to Josie's level. She grabbed for it, trying to wrest the spool away from his hold. "Let's fly it together," he said.

"No, I do it!"

"Okay, don't let go." Isaac gently released it but hovered his hand nearby. Katie snapped pictures.

When Josie predictably dropped the string a minute later, he managed to grab it before the kite met its demise in the ocean. He had to laugh as she scampered off to chase a seagull. To have a fraction of that energy for himself again.

He held the spool out to Sage. "Want to give it a try?"

She shook her head but stayed in place.

This could take a while. He dropped his knees to the sand and sat back on his heels. "Are you sure?" He continued to hold it out.

She stared long and hard at him before taking one step forward. He waited as she eased forward, inch by inch.

"Either you do or don't, Sage," Katie said, peeking at her watch again.

"It's okay. I've got time," Isaac said.

Sage glanced at her mother and back at Isaac.

"You can do it," he said.

She touched one side of the spool. They each held a side for a moment. Then she turned those big green eyes on him again and studied him squarely. Slowly, she moved her hand over to grasp it in the middle.

"Hold on tight," he said as he moved his hand out of the way. Isaac still hovered nearby, not because he thought she would drop it, but because she looked tiny enough that the pegasus could take her kite surfing on accident.

"Sage! Come get birds wiff me!" Josie yelled.

Sage held out the spool to Isaac. He took over and she ran off to chase seagulls with her sister.

"Sorry, they have the attention spans of goldfish," Katie said.

"That's okay, it's your turn anyway. Trade you the kite for the phone." He held out the spool and Katie took it, passing off her phone. Isaac stepped back to grab a couple photos and videos of this quintessential experience she had never had.

Isaac remembered what she once told him about her childhood, spent either grieving her father or avoiding her stepfather; and about the six younger half-siblings who led a separate life. Isaac never truly considered what that meant for her. What she might have missed. And now he wondered what the twins might be missing without a father.

Raucous screams and squeals caught his attention. Both girls were running away from a seagull hopping toward them. The bird apparently decided to stand his ground. Sage laughed as she scurried away, while Josie looked mildly terrified, pumping her legs as fast as she could. She tripped and tumbled into the sand, but popped back up like a jack-in-the-box and carried on.

Katie laughed at them. "This is actually fun."

"You sound surprised. Were you planning to hate kite flying?"

"No, but the beach can be a disaster with toddlers," she said, watching the girls run around the birds nearby. "I think I'm always bracing myself for the next tantrum or injury. It's hard to enjoy things when I know it will end with someone crying."

Isaac nudged her arm. "Aw, don't cry, Katie."

She grinned. "It's not usually me, but I won't say never."

"Maybe you can accept there will be a few tears, and focus on the good parts."

"I guess." Katie checked her watch for the hundredth time since they left their apartment. Her sunny side wore a shadow again today.

"Everything okay?" he asked.

"Yep. Great." She smiled and it barely reached her eyes. She was lying, but he found some relief in knowing she was terrible at it.

Twinkle flew for another half hour, while the girls took several short turns holding the line. Then the winds changed and darted their kite in the other direction before sending it twirling to the ground.

"Should we get her flying again, or take a snack break?" Isaac asked.

"Snacks!" Josie shouted. Sage nodded her agreement.

He and Katie had both brought snacks and they laid out the assortment in the truck bed. Katie lifted both girls onto the tailgate, then took Isaac's hand to climb up after them. She kept a hand on Josie's shirt, trying to convince her that leaning over the edge and face planting in the sand wouldn't be enjoyable. Isaac distracted her with a bag of cheese crackers.

Soon, everybody settled in with a snack. Josie sat at the edge of the tailgate with Isaac, her legs swinging over the edge. Katie sat cross-legged in the middle of the truck bed, with Sage's head in her lap as the girl lay on the hard metal.

Josie tried to get Isaac to kick his legs in time with hers. "No, dat one," she instructed, patting a cheese-dusted hand on his jeans. They swung their right legs out, then left, in time. She nodded happily and gave him another cheese pat. "Good job."

Isaac laughed. "Thanks. You're a good teacher."

She nodded again. "I ams."

Isaac glanced back at Katie. Her eyes were on Sage, passed out in her lap, and she ran a hand over her daughter's copper braid in a distinctly motherly move. For a moment, he desperately wished their timelines had collided differently.

What if the same people who snuggled into blankets to watch the northern lights could be the same people who now flew kites with toddlers on the beach? If he had gotten saved sooner, could this have been his life? Could he have changed Katie's mind the way Aaron did? Maybe they wouldn't have ten years of pain between them.

Katie caught Isaac looking at her and he didn't hide it. Whatever she saw on his face, she must have mistaken for concern because her eyes dropped back to Sage. "Her ribs and collarbone are healing fast, but she still gets tired easily," she said.

He turned his focus to Sage. "She seems to be doing great."

Katie sighed and mumbled something he couldn't hear over the wind. He hated asking people to repeat themselves.

"Is she not?" he asked.

Katie faced him and spoke up. "Yeah, no, I guess she is. In some ways. What about you?"

"I'm good," he said. It was more complicated, of course, but he counted on her not to ask.

Josie jumped up and Isaac held out his arm to keep her from tumbling off the tailgate. "I wanna fly my pony!" she shouted.

Katie checked her watch again. "I think we need to head home, Jojo."

"Aww," Josie pouted. "Pwease? Five minutes?"

Katie looked from her watch to Josie to Isaac. He put on a matching pout. "Just five minutes?" he asked.

Katie laughed. "Okay. Five minutes and no more. I mean it."

"Ten!" Josie shouted.

Isaac hopped off the tailgate and reached for Josie. "Gotta take what you get, kiddo. We've got five minutes, let's hurry."

Chapter Twenty-Eight

Back at Katie's apartment, she seemed more anxious than ever. Isaac helped unload the girls and carry car seats inside the apartment while Katie started slicing up fruit for kids who were somehow still hungry. She barely noticed him as she wiped down kitchen countertops, put the knife back in a child-proofed drawer, locked the front door, checked the patio door lock, and tested the knife drawer again.

"You okay?" Isaac asked.

She nodded.

It might be his signal to leave, but her demeanor set off alarm bells in his head. Isaac caught her arm as she walked by, wiping the countertops again. "Can we talk for a minute?"

Katie glanced at his hand on her, his eyes, then over to where the girls sat at the small dining table. "With or without interruptions?" she asked.

Isaac grinned. "Did you find a secret switch?"

Katie gave a pointed look at the television.

"Ah. That one. Without interruptions, if that's okay."

She flipped on the television, with the volume low, and edged toward the back of the kitchen, to create a few feet of space between them and the girls, while still supervising. "What's up?" she asked, without meeting his eyes.

"You. Something's wrong."

She crossed her arms and shrugged. "I'm great."

"Oh, okay. Good. Now try again, this time with the truth."

She laughed and looked down at her feet. She sighed. "I don't know. I'm a little stressed."

"What's going on?"

Katie flicked a speck off her jeans and shook her head, avoiding his gaze. He waited. Katie always caved to silence. "You're going to judge me," she finally said, her voice pointed downward. He strained to hear her.

A faint twinge hit his conscience. He deserved it, but still, he didn't like it. "I won't," he said. "I might have a few weeks ago, but not anymore."

Her bottom lip rolled between her teeth. "I went to see a counselor last week."

"You think I would judge you for that?" he asked. "I *have* to see one weekly if I want my job back."

She shook her head. "It's not that. It's what happened after. Something I said made her think the girls weren't safe with me." Katie's voice cracked and it hit him in the gut. "She reported me to CPS."

Oh, Katie. "When did this happen?"

With a deep breath, she updated him on the investigation so far. From what she said, Isaac agreed completely with the lawyer. She had a few long weeks ahead of her, but she would absolutely prove them wrong and get this expunged from her record. Then, he thought she should sue them anyway, for fun.

"I think I can only sue if they cause unnecessary harm," Katie said.

"They already have," he said. "I've seen abused children and their abusers. So have they. They know you're not one. This is a waste of your time and theirs."

Katie rubbed her arms and mumbled something he didn't hear.

"Katie?"

She looked up at him, apprehension in her eyes. "What if they're right?" she said. "What if the girls would be better off with someone else, like Suzanne?"

"You know that's not true."

She raised her hands in a helpless gesture. "I want to be a good mom. I thought a counselor would help but I guess I'm hopeless."

"Hey—" He reached for her and she stepped into his side. He wrapped his arm around her shoulders. "Just because it's hard doesn't mean you're a bad mom. If anything, it means you are a good one. It means you're doing your best."

"What if my best isn't enough? I love them but I still get frustrated and overwhelmed."

"That's normal." He squeezed her arm and she leaned in closer. "I think every parent gets frustrated and overwhelmed."

"I bet Suzanne doesn't."

"I bet she does."

Katie studied the girls for a moment as they traded fruits at the table. "They're okay, aren't they? I mean, Josie's a little wild and Sage is stuck in her own world, but there's nothing wrong with them."

"Of course not. They're great. And you're a good mom." He was tempted to march into the CPS offices and tell them the same thing.

She turned her head into his chest and he held her tighter. He wanted to shield her from this, to take it away. She had faced enough.

After a moment, Katie pulled in a breath and leaned back slightly to look at the television. "They love this show," she said, still under his arm. "But it doesn't make any sense."

"What do you mean?"

"Only the dogs can talk, none of the other animals can."

"I have a theory on that," he said.

"Really?" She tilted her head to look up at him. She was beautiful all the time, but absolutely stunning up close.

"Nuclear incident," he said. "It took out the actual first responders, along with most of the town, and mutated the dogs. The other people and animals who survived were mentally handicapped by the radiation."

Katie laughed and stepped out of his arms. "What on earth? Why do you know this show so well?"

"Did I mention I've been really bored since the shooting?"

She was still laughing at him when Josie stood up in her chair and started doing a potty dance. Katie paused the show and Isaac waited in the kitchen, watching Sage. She sat with her back to him, swinging her legs over her chair and stealing two of her sister's strawberries. Then Katie came back and swapped kids, taking Sage to the bathroom next.

Josie didn't take a seat though; she climbed on top of the table. Isaac went to stand next to her to prevent a fall. "What are you doing, little monkey?" he asked, steadying her elbow as she stood.

"I big as you," she said, with her button nose lifted high. Up here, she stood at her mom's height, and about a foot short of his.

"Wow, you grew up fast."

She giggled, her smile squishing her cheeks up into her eyes, wrinkling bright green eyes into slits. He had ten adorable nieces and nephews, but the twins were probably the cutest kids he had ever seen. He would never admit that to anyone else.

"Josie Kaminski!" Katie called when she walked back in.

Josie jumped onto Isaac, bumping his bad arm, while his good one wrapped around her as she squirmed to hide from her mother. He lowered her back to her chair.

"You know tables are not for climbing," Katie scolded Josie. She held her daughter's face in both hands. "You have to be safe, Jojo. You can't do this stuff right now." Josie writhed away and Katie sighed.

When she had Josie settled, she came back into the kitchen and filled two glasses with water and passed one to him. "So tell me why you were at church yesterday. Besides it being a free country and all."

"Which I single-handedly uphold, according to Brielle." It was an innocent comment, and most days he appreciated the support, but most days he did his job *without* getting shot. Now, he made a mistake and everyone wanted to praise him for it.

Katie put her hand over her heart. "Thank you again," she said, with mock sincerity.

He chuckled and shook his head. "I wanted to be there."

"Kid shows and church? The boredom must be pretty bad."

"It gets worse."

"Do tell."

"I've been reading the Bible."

Her eyebrows shot up. "I definitely wasn't expecting that."

He set down his glass and stretched his legs out in front of him, leaning back against the counter. "Turns out I believe all that stuff. And I realized I needed Jesus too."

A wide smile lit her face. "What? Are you messing with me?"

He held up three fingers in a pledge. "Scout's honor. Or do I swear on the Bible now? What do Christians do?"

"Did you just— Really?"

He nodded.

"Isaac!" She grabbed his arm. "We need confetti! Cake! Champagne! Is champagne an acceptable way to celebrate? Wait—Jesus made wine. He approves. We need wine!"

Isaac laughed. "Micah gave me a handshake. I got shortchanged."

"Do you feel all—" She waved her arms in a weird dance. "Holy Spirited up?"

"Don't do that."

"I bet you do."

He felt something. Not like wiggling in a tube man dance, but like he had dropped weights he hadn't even realized he carried. "I do. I mean, it didn't instantly fix everything else."

"No, I know. But now you can take it all to God. And that's worth celebrating. We weren't meant to carry this stuff on our own."

He nodded but he had already lost Katie's attention. She was rummaging through the fridge. "I don't have wine, it would look bad to CPS, but I do have cookie dough."

"Cookies!" Josie shouted from the living room.

"Cookies sound good," Isaac said with a grin. Right now, he didn't care if he was playing with fire. He loved being here and he would trade the future burn for this moment.

Chapter Twenty-Nine

The next day, Suzanne babysat the girls at her house while Katie worked from home. She posted a photo of Sage flying the kite, though she carefully cropped and edited any evidence of Isaac out of it. She only wished she could give her brain the same treatment.

Yesterday afternoon had been perfect. Too picture perfect. There had been a moment when Sage and Josie were comparing their cookies to the size of their faces. Sage had pressed her face into a cookie, leaving chocolate marks all over her face. Katie smiled, heard Isaac laugh, and glanced at him. And they shared *the look*. The parental "aren't they cute?" look. The look that made her heart realize how desperately hungry it was. It shouldn't have happened. She didn't need that. He had no right to parental looks. Katie searched for the delete button in her memory but couldn't find it.

Katie cranked up a song on her laptop to force her mind to focus. She opened booking slots on her website for Christmas photo shoots, and worked out the details of collaborations with two local brands. While Katie talked on the phone with one of them, her mom called and she sent it to voicemail.

Once she finished her more lucrative tasks, Katie switched over to editing the baptism photos. The murky Texas coast hadn't allowed for the underwater shots she hoped for, but she still had a few interesting ones. She caught better shots in the moments Micah lifted a person from the water—droplets slinging from their hair, laughter on their faces.

She opened a wide shot of Penn hugging Landon, their bodies a dark silhouette, with a cheering crowd on shore behind them, and a red sunset in the background. She made a few edits and the picture quickly became her favorite.

Her mom called again and Katie ignored it. Whatever exciting update about her half-siblings could wait. Somebody had probably gotten into college. Or got a first job. How old was Thomas anyway?

Outside, thunder rumbled and Katie only now noticed the fading light. She sat back, stretching her arms and studying the popcorn ceiling above her. She needed to pick up the girls and anxiously await the next CPS visit.

Katie stood, stiff from hours of sitting, and grabbed her keys. A few fat raindrops hit her face as she ran to the car. The moment she put it in reverse, her phone rang again. *Mom.* Katie sighed.

"This is Katie Kaminski," she answered. "Please state your emergency."

Her mom laughed. "Katelyn, do I need an emergency to call you?"

"You called three times, seems pretty urgent."

"You always answer on the third."

Dang. She needed to switch that up. "Touché. What's up, Mom?"

"I'll try to be quick. Do you remember the land your father left you?"

Whoa. Blast from the past. "I almost forgot about that. A few acres, outside of Juneau, right?"

"Twenty acres. We've been keeping an eye on it for you."

Katie inherited it when she turned eighteen, but she left Juneau shortly afterwards and never looked back. Her mom and stepfather had managed it her entire life. Surely land didn't need much babysitting. "Okay…"

"There's a company interested in building a resort there. They've sent a couple of letters about it. They're making a pretty good offer."

"Really? A resort?" Why did that bother her? She never planned to return to Juneau. Selling it made sense.

"Yes, and I'll admit, it is nice land for it," her mom said.

"I don't think I've ever seen it." Katie slowed as the rain increased.

"Yes, you have."

She searched her memory. "I don't think so. I guess I should sell it, huh? What do they need me to do?"

"You'll have to come and get the deed—"

Katie cut her off there. "Come? To Juneau?"

"Well, yes. It's all in your name, Katie. I can't handle this for you."

"I'm sure it can all be done remotely."

Her mom hesitated. "Well, maybe. I guess you can sign some papers and scan them in. But to get the documents… You'd have to appoint someone as power of attorney. Why don't you come up and see it one last time?"

Because CPS is monitoring my every move. "The girls can't do that flight, Mom."

"Can they stay with Aaron's mom?"

Katie shifted in her seat and flicked the windshield wipers up a notch. Could she leave the state with the ongoing case? "Maybe. That sounds like such a hassle just to sign some papers."

"It's not just for the papers, Katelyn. You need to see the land before you sell it."

"Why? Are you trying to get me to move back to Juneau?" What a unique ploy to get Katie to visit.

"No, I think your dad would want that. He loved going out there."

Her dad was a taboo topic between them. Once her mother remarried, Katie's dad had been erased from her life. She didn't know much about him and never felt comfortable asking. "He did?"

"Yes," her mom laughed. "We took you camping out there several times. I guess you don't remember."

"I was five, Mom. No, I don't remember."

"Come and see it before you sell it, Katie. One last time."

Katie pulled up to Suzanne's house and tilted her head back against the headrest. "When do they need an answer about selling it?"

"I'm sure they'll work with whatever timeline you need."

"I'll think about it. Can you forward me the offer letter?"

"I will."

Katie ended the call and stayed in her seat for a moment, staring out the windshield without seeing anything. She tried to picture the land, but kept drawing a blank. She tried to remember a camping trip. Nothing. Thunder shook the car.

Katie unbuckled and dashed to the front door. Suzanne opened at the first knock and ushered her inside. Josie popped up from where she sat by the coffee table. "Mommy, look!" She held a paper with watercolor squiggles all over it.

Katie tried to muster up some energy. "Wow, Jojo, that's great." Sage lifted hers, with all red shapes. "Very nice, Sage."

Suzanne tidied paintbrushes. "Sounds like a good storm rolling in," she said.

"Mhmm." Katie followed her to the kitchen, where rain spat against the windows. *Twenty acres. Power of attorney. Fly to Alaska. Fly far, far away.*

"Are you okay?" Suzanne asked as she started washing paint supplies in the sink.

"Yeah, no, I'm good. Thanks for watching the girls."

"Of course," Suzanne said. "Is the photography business going well?"

"It's good," Katie said, her mind still far away. "But I got a weird phone call."

Suzanne's hand stilled. "Is it CPS?" she whispered.

"Oh, no, nothing like that. It was my mom. My dad left me some land in Alaska and apparently a company is wanting to buy it."

Suzanne's eyebrows shot up. "Well, that's exciting. Are you going to sell?"

"I guess so. There's no point in keeping it." She had no idea what it was worth, but anything she gained could help her buy a new home one day. "My mom wants me to come do it in person. She thinks I need to look over the land first."

"That's a good idea," Suzanne said. "It'll be much easier to handle in person, I'm sure."

Katie hesitated. "I don't think I can go in the middle of the CPS case."

"They might let me keep the girls." Suzanne smiled and lifted her shoulders back. "I started the process of getting certified, so I can be ready."

Katie's scattered thoughts came into sharp focus. *Excuse me?* "Certified?" The word rolled into her mind with its own dark cloud.

"In case they need to do a kinship placement or something."

Thunder rumbled a little more closely this time. "You're getting certified to foster my children?" Her voice raised a touch too high.

"I figure it would help streamline things if needed."

The mental cloud burst and a downpour started from the inside of her scalp down to her toes. "How could you?" Katie whispered.

Suzanne's smile vanished. "I only want to help, Katie. If anything happens—"

"You think I'm going to lose custody?"

"No, I really don't. But just in case..."

Lightning flashed outside and Katie's heart thundered. She pressed her fist to her mouth and turned away. One thought dominated all the rest: she hated this stupid town. They never should have come here. Everything went wrong the moment she walked inside this black hole. She wanted to scream.

"Katie, I'm sorry. I didn't mean to upset you. I thought you'd be happy. They'll stay in our family no matter what."

No matter what they decide about me. Because everybody knows Suzanne is the obvious alternative. Katie forced a breath, her back still turned. "Okay," she said. Her voice sounded tight and choked.

"I really don't think they'll take the girls, honey. I needed to do *something.* You know?"

Forcing on a smile, Katie turned back to her. "Am I not doing enough?"

"You are," Suzanne said, gripping her hands. "You're doing so much, I felt useless standing around watching."

"Well, you're not useless. Thanks for watching the girls today." Her robot smile felt entirely unnatural. It hurt her cheeks. She walked into the living room. "Sage, Josie. Let's go, girls. Grab your pictures."

Sage ran over and hugged Katie's leg, but Josie instantly threw herself on the floor. "I don't wanna go! I wanna stay with Nana!"

"Oh, Josie—" Suzanne started to move toward her.

Katie put a hand out. "I've got this." Pushing through the waterlogged feeling in her bones, she sank onto the floor next to Josie and rubbed her back. "Come on, baby," she whispered. "We need to get home, it's storming."

"No. I not a baby!"

"Then come home with momma, big girl."

"I wanna stay with Nana!"

Katie didn't dare look at Suzanne. If she saw an ounce of smugness in Suzanne's face, they would never come to this house again. Katie would steal her own children away, and take the next flight out of the country. Anywhere would be fine. She closed her eyes, unable to bear another second. *Please, God.* She didn't know what to beg. For her own child to love her?

"Come on, sweetheart," Katie said, standing and lifting a writhing Josie. She draped her over her shoulder and spun around to distract her. "You're mine!" She turned and blew a raspberry into Josie's side.

Josie laughed, screeched, and laughed again as Katie carried her outside. Rain fell on them both, momentarily distracting Josie and soaking Katie as she forced Josie into her car seat. Josie fought the buckles and screamed for Nana again. Katie caught one swinging fist and kissed it. "No," she said. "You're mine."

Chapter Thirty

Katie had stepped onto a carousel of interventions—play therapy and speech therapy for Sage, parenting class for Katie, and another counseling appointment—this one with a specialist Patrick recommended.

Instead of going in with the hope of finding help, she went in terrified. This wasn't regular counseling, it was a test. One she couldn't study for. And she had to pass to ever get out of this CPS case. If she failed, she would ruin all their lives.

A strip mall housed the psychiatrist's office, which featured a simple "Ridley Bay Family Counseling" sign. Inside, a dimly lit waiting area held two futons and a buzzer, with another door beyond it. Katie pressed the button, her heart racing. A portly middle-aged man opened the door to the other side of the waiting room.

"Are you Katelyn?" he asked, extending a hand. "I'm Dr. Payne."

"Dr. Payne?" Katie said. *Don't make fun of his name!* She needed him to like her. She put on her most charming smile. "Call me Katie."

He led her to a small office, with a leather loveseat and two armchairs. Pictures of palm trees and the ocean decorated the walls. Dr. Payne took one chair, while Katie sat across from him on the loveseat. He flipped open a notepad and reviewed Katie's story. All the details were right. Aaron's death, the frequent moves, Sage's injury, the CPS case. Did the details alone make her unfit?

He guided her through a series of questions and she gave all the right answers. But Dr. Payne kept poking and prodding and breaking down her answers until Katie finally admitted what she had told Holly. She admitted her reality didn't match what she wanted, and she sometimes wished she could escape her life.

"But I would never, *ever* abandon or hurt my children," she said.

"I don't think you would," he said, tapping his pen on his chin. "So if this isn't the life you pictured—tell me what you *did* picture."

"Obviously life with my husband still around." Katie paused to think about it for a moment. What *had* she envisioned? Maybe she never fully built out that picture at all. "I guess doing photography and having a couple kids, like I do now. But happier kids who don't throw ketchup at each other."

Dr. Payne laughed and the skin under his chin wagged. If he had a white beard, he could pass for Santa. "Kids have a way of shocking us all."

"How do people adjust?"

"Well, I think an entire life vision is a broad goal for today, but let's try something smaller," he said. "What do you want tomorrow to look like?"

"Is hopping on an airplane and flying to Paris an option?"

"Is it?"

Katie smiled and shook her head. She stared at her shoes, imagining tomorrow. "I guess… I want to do something fun with the girls and be all there. To play with them and for once not be stressed about everything else."

"All day?"

"Well, no. I'd like to get a couple hours of work done. We'll make some meals, do some dishes, and wipe a few tears too. It won't be perfect."

"Most days aren't," he said. "But tell me something that will be better about tomorrow because your girls are there."

Katie thought about it for a minute. "Sage will slow us down and point out some tiny detail I wouldn't notice without her. And Josie will have us all giggling over something silly."

Dr. Payne smiled. "Who else appreciates those things like you?"

His words rang through her. Suzanne might be an ideal mother, singing hymns and stocking a playroom, but did she hear Sage's quiet questions? Could she see past Josie's mischief to find her magnetism? Katie might not be the best, but she was still their mother. And she knew from experience, substitute families were never the same. "Nobody," she said.

Dr. Payne clicked his pen twice. "I know it's been hard, but I really think you're going to be fine, Ms. Katelyn."

He sounded convinced of her sanity, yet she felt the need to make one last plea, a final statement. "I really do love them," she said.

"I think you love them so much it scares you."

"Love never gave me a great return on investment. But I keep trying anyway. I would do anything for them."

Dr. Payne pointed his pen at her. "That's what makes you a good mom."

Katie laughed. "So you think I pass the sanity check?"

"Yes, I do," he said. Then he shook his head. "Besides, I don't report stressed mothers." He muttered it under his breath, and it made Katie like him a whole lot more.

•   •   •

When Vera asked Isaac for another ride to church, he couldn't turn her down. Her church had an early service and Isaac could take her, endure the fawning from older women, bring her home, and still make it to Grace only a little late, voluntarily doubling up on church attendance. He never expected that day would come. He climbed out of his truck as Katie pulled into the parking lot in a finally legally-tagged car.

"You're late," he said, walking toward her as she got out.

She lit up when she saw him, as she likely did for everyone. She wore wide-legged pants and an emerald top that matched her eyes. "I know, but we're late because of donuts, so how wrong can it really be?" Her black hair danced in waves above her shoulders and a pair of turkey earrings dangled at her jawline. She reached back into the car and grabbed a small box. "Donut?"

Isaac took one. "As long as you promise not to make a cop joke."

She laughed and put the box back in the car. "I make no such promise. Why are you late, Officer *Churros*?"

He poked her in the side and she yelped and swatted at his hand.

"I went with my neighbor to her church first," he said around a bite of glazed goodness.

Katie turned around and blinked. "Oh. Okay."

Isaac grinned. "She's eighty-four."

Her eyebrows shot up. "You should lead with that."

Isaac chuckled. "You get jealous fast." And he liked it.

"Surprised, not jealous," she said, before sticking her head back in the car. "Here, hold this." She passed him a heavy full-sized backpack and went to unbuckle the girls.

"Did you pack rocks?"

"Waters, snacks, and every quiet activity I could find to keep them still in church."

The girls climbed out of the car in sparkling dresses, Josie in pink and Sage in yellow. Josie shouted "Wewoo!" at him.

"Mr. Isaac," Katie corrected, holding onto each girl's hand.

"Don't want to use childcare anymore?" Isaac asked as they walked through the parking lot.

"Not right now. I'm being paranoid, I guess, about letting them out of my sight."

Isaac pulled open the door for them. "That's okay. You're allowed to be."

At the same time, Zoe approached from the childcare rooms holding Serena. "Look who got kicked out of childcare again," she said, kissing the baby. "Little biter. Now I have to keep her with me in church."

"I've got snacks and board books," Katie said, gesturing to the backpack Isaac carried.

He didn't miss the way Zoe's eyes flicked between them. She gave a slight eyebrow raise to him and smiled. "Perfect, come sit with me."

And because he carried the backpack, he landed in the row of babies and toddlers. The double church attendance ended up being a blessing, because he couldn't pay any attention to Micah's sermon today. He held Serena while Zoe went to the restroom. Then he retrieved Sage's roll-away water bottle (and crayons and dropped coloring book), and let Josie put stickers on his pant leg. His jeans were soon redecorated with an entire fairy garden scene. As soon as the service ended and Josie got distracted, he pulled them all off before walking out of the row.

Katie met up with Suzanne and William, while Zoe went off to collect her older kids from childcare. Somehow, Isaac still carried the backpack.

He chatted with Micah and a few others in the church. A couple of people congratulated him on getting saved. It seemed everybody knew now.

"Might as well have another baptism soon and dunk this guy too," Penn said, joining them.

"Let's wait for the spring," Micah said. "I like baptisms, not polar plunges."

"By the way, nice purple fairy pants," Penn said, glancing at Isaac's leg.

There, on the back of his leg was one more sticker. He must have sat on it. "Thanks, it was that or my unicorn pants."

"Can I record you saying you have unicorn pants?" Penn asked.

Isaac peeled off the sticker and pointed at him. "Another couple weeks and I'm coming back for my job. You'll have to sit with your own kids again."

Penn nodded toward the door. "What about them?" Katie and the twins were heading outside and Isaac still held the backpack.

"Oh, shoot. Hang on." Quickly excusing himself, he caught up to her in the parking lot. "Hey, don't forget your bag of rocks."

"Oh, my bad, thank you. We need this." Katie reached for the bag.

"I've got it," he said. Her hands were already full with kids. He followed her to the car.

"Thanks for your help this morning," she said. "Sorry you got stuck in the kid row."

"Don't apologize." He wasn't sorry in the least. Stickers and all.

They reached her car and she buckled Josie and then Sage. Isaac put the backpack in the front seat. He met Katie at the back of the car. "Any updates on the case?" he asked.

"Good news, actually."

"Yeah?"

"I had to get a psych assessment and apparently I'm not totally nuts. I passed."

Isaac chuckled. "Of course you did."

"My lawyer said there's no reason for CPS to keep this case going. A couple more weeks and I should be cleared."

"That's great news."

"It is. We're going to celebrate," she said.

"Do you celebrate everything?"

"Is there anything wrong with that?"

"I guess not," he said.

"I'm taking the girls to the aquarium this afternoon. We're stuck in Ridley Bay, we might as well do whatever fun things we can find."

Isaac frowned. "It's busy on the weekends."

"Some of us aren't afraid of crowds."

He wasn't *afraid* exactly, more like uncomfortable. And Katie needed a few natural fears. "Are Suzanne and William going with you?"

"No, they're going to a charity event with JP and Tricia. I'm allowed to take the girls out, you know."

"I know. But... Are you sure you should take two toddlers to a busy aquarium by yourself?"

"Isaac," she laughed. "I've been doing this by myself for years."

"They're getting bigger and faster though."

"Oh my goodness," she said, pressing a hand to her forehead. "If you're worried, come with us and help me chase them."

The invitation gave him pause. She didn't think she needed his help, but she did.

"Or do you have plans with your eighty-four-year-old neighbor?" she asked.

"I don't like the way you said that."

Katie laughed again. "I've got to get these kids home for lunch. Let me know if you want to come. We could even give you a ride in this sexy mom-mobile to save on parking." She waved a hand over the car like a product model.

He sighed and shook his head. "I'll text you."

Chapter Thirty-One

Katie pulled up in front of a yellow house in an older part of town just as an elderly woman exited the house next door. Her house featured a similar style with blue paint. Katie thought about calling Isaac and saving herself the hassle of getting the girls out, but her curiosity about his life won over. She corralled the girls onto the sidewalk. The elderly woman stopped puttering in her garden bed when she saw the twins.

"Oh My-lanta, aren't they the cutest things you ever did see?" she said. "Are they twins?"

Katie grinned. This had to be the eighty-four-year-old she had admittedly been jealous of this morning. "Thank you. They're pretty cute in between tantrums. And yes, they are twins."

"I bet they can get away with murder, with those eyes." She hobbled down the driveway toward them, with a cane to help her.

Katie laughed and agreed. Josie popped up next to Katie, happy to be adored. Sage hid behind Katie's leg.

"What are your names?" the woman asked.

Katie introduced the girls and herself, then shook hands with Vera.

"My son has a little girl," Vera said. "A baby girl with the biggest brown eyes the Lord ever gave a child. He sent me a picture the other day and I about up and moved to Miami."

"What kept you here?" Katie asked. "I'm sure they would love to have Grandma around."

"Oh," Vera waved a hand in the air. "I'm not really 'Grandma.' I don't think I was ever much of a 'Mom.'"

"What do you mean?" Katie asked, watching as Josie and Sage slipped toward Vera's garden to inspect the fall blooms. "Girls, look but don't touch."

Vera looked back at them. "Let them pick a few," she whispered, conspiratorially. "It needed to be thinned anyway."

Katie didn't have to pass that on to the girls. They would do it regardless. "What do you mean you weren't a 'Mom'?"

"I wasn't around much for my son, and now I don't think he wants to be around much for me."

"But if you moved to Miami…"

"I'd be a great big burden," Vera huffed and put her hands on her hips. "I won't be doing that. I am still good for something."

"Obviously, you are. Look at that garden. I can't even keep a plant alive, yet God gave me two kids."

Vera laughed and waved to something behind Katie. With a quick glance back, Katie saw Isaac walking over to them.

"Are you here to see Lauren?" Vera asked Katie, whispering again. "She never comes out of the house anymore."

Katie didn't know a Lauren here. She shook her head. "Isaac, actually."

He reached her side and squeezed a hand on her shoulder. "Katie, it looks like you've met my church date, Vera."

Katie turned to him and instantly noticed the change. "Hey, where's your sling?"

"Physical therapist said to take it off for a few hours at a time."

"How's it feel?"

"It's a little rough."

"Mommy!" Josie interrupted, running to them with a golden flower in hand. Sage followed empty-handed.

"Thank you, sweetie, that's beautiful."

Vera peered at the flower. "Marigold is good for your skin, you know. Good pick. Where's yours, little one?" she asked Sage.

Sage quickly hid behind Katie. Kneeling, Katie informed Sage she had permission to pick one.

"I pick yours," Josie said, already scampering back to the garden bed.

"Let Sage do it," Katie called after her.

"Are they twins?" Vera asked again.

Katie nodded with a smile. "Yes," she repeated. "They're three-and-a-half."

"I can't imagine," Vera chuckled. "I thought one would break me. If I could go back though, I'd have another."

"Well, I have a couple for sale, if you're ever interested." Katie wrinkled her nose and laughed at herself. Old jokes like that didn't sit well right now. "I'm kidding. I'm pretty fond of them."

"I'm sure Lauren would love those girls too," Vera said. "You should meet her."

"Who?" Katie asked.

"We need to get going," Isaac said over her. His tone said enough. It might be some memory of Vera's that Katie shouldn't dig into.

"Right. Aquarium." She glanced at her watch. Keeping track of time was not Katie's strong suit. Since CPS started questioning her schedule, she used alarms on her phone to stay on task. "So nice to meet you, Vera."

Vera clasped her hands. "Oh, you too, sweetie. Thank you for bringing these girls by. They keep a woman young."

Katie wasn't sure she agreed, but she passed Vera the two golden flowers she now held. "Thank you for letting them pick these. Would you mind hanging onto them for us?"

"My pleasure," Vera said, grinning at the flowers. "Isaac, I like this one. Make sure she comes back soon."

He gave Vera that single nod of his and didn't say a word.

•   •   •

Katie circled through the packed parking garage at the aquarium. Isaac took a deep breath. Events like the fall festival were bad enough, and he was fully geared up and paid to be at those. Here, he only had a small sidearm, a barely functioning right hand, and no backup.

He helped Sage out of the car and set her down. She reached a tiny, warm hand into his and tugged on it. She frowned and pointed to his arm.

The bandage and sling were gone, but a brutal scar hid underneath his sleeve, and his muscles felt like they shriveled around it. He knelt down. "I get to take my sling off for a little while," he said. "You will too soon."

Sage reached up to remove the strap of hers and he gently covered her hand to stop her. "Can you keep it with you today? If my arm starts to hurt, I might need a little help. I don't want yours to hurt too."

Sage nodded as Katie came around the car with Josie in her arms. She still wore the green top from this morning, and in the bright sunlight, it made her eyes practically glow.

"That top looks great on you," Isaac said. "Brings out your eyes."

A smile flashed across her face, accompanied by a slight laugh. "Thanks." Her eyes fell to the girls. "Their outfits are matched on purpose, by the way," she said, pointing to the matching pink tops and floral pants.

Isaac grinned at the subject change. She was too confident to be bashful, but he didn't mind seeing a small chink in the armor occasionally.

"Dressing them alike makes it easier to spot them in a crowd," Katie said. "I know exactly what I'm looking for if I lose track of one. See? I do know a few tricks."

"Not bad," Isaac said. Dropping his newly-freed right hand onto her back, he guided them to the ticket booth at the front. He didn't care anymore if he was playing with fire. For once in his life, he didn't want to overthink this.

At the entrance, Isaac pulled out his badge to sidetrack the metal detectors while Katie and the girls walked through. Katie smirked at him when he finished checking in with the security guard. "Couldn't leave it behind?" she asked.

"No way. Not in a place this crowded."

"With preschoolers."

"And their parents." Some of whom were probably gang members. And anybody else could show up, suddenly railing against captured animals, or field trips, or whatever else set off the most deranged members of society. Against a madman, security guards and metal detectors were paper walls.

She patted his arm. "Okay, Officer. We're glad you're here to keep us safe. Now let's find some animals."

The girls voted on jellyfish first and they soon entered a dark hallway, lit only by black lights. People milled about the room, but it wasn't terribly crowded. The darkness lent to a hushed stillness, and glowing, floating creatures filled the tanks around them. Sage dropped his hand and ran up to one of the tanks. Josie joined her, both mesmerized.

Sage waved her mom over and Katie knelt with her in front of one tank. Sage whispered in Katie's ear.

"I don't know." Katie leaned back to look at the sign about jellyfish. She glanced at Isaac. "Let's ask the walking encyclopedia."

He rolled his eyes. "What's up?"

"Do jellyfish have eyes?" Katie asked.

Isaac squatted down to join them. "I think they can sense light, but they don't see quite the same as us."

Sage's eyes went wide. "Can they hear?" she asked, her curiosity overcoming her reservation.

Isaac grinned. He loved the sound of her voice. "Not with ears like you. But they feel movement in the water with their tentacles."

Katie smiled at Sage. "I told you he would know."

She might be right about the walking encyclopedia thing.

Josie wanted to hurry off to the next room, but Sage wanted to watch the jellyfish more.

"I'll stay with her," Isaac offered. This is why he was here. So Katie wouldn't be outnumbered and they could enjoy the aquarium.

Katie hesitated, Josie pulling on her hand. "Don't take your eyes off her."

Isaac raised his eyebrows, tempted to repeat the warning for Katie and Josie.

"I know, I know. You won't." Then Katie disappeared around the corner.

Isaac read the sign about the jellyfish to Sage. He pointed out the different colors and how they moved. He just wanted to hear her open up again. "Which one is your favorite?"

She glanced around the room of tanks and pointed to the one holding small, pink-hued floaters.

"I like those too," he said.

She smiled at him, the textbook definition of a cherub.

They wandered around the room a little more. At her pace, Isaac thought Katie might need to spring for the aquarium membership and take Sage to see one animal per visit. But they needed to compromise with Josie. "Ready to catch up to your mom and Jojo?"

Sage nodded and put her hand in his, implicitly trusting. He would do anything to be worthy of it.

They wound through the dark maze until the last section, where they found Josie trying to imitate a squid. From there, they explored the rescue animal section, admired the sharks, and then found the ultimate kid-magnet: the touch tank.

People packed the room, and at least two layers of kids crowded around the low, open tank. Isaac lifted Josie into his good arm and Katie held Sage so they wouldn't get crushed. A staff member loosely supervised, more concerned about the animals than the impending human casualties.

"This is ridiculous," Isaac said.

"Come on," Katie said. "I want to touch a starfish." She led the way into the fray, weaving and waiting until a single spot opened. She edged into it and soon cleared enough room for Isaac too. They set the girls down in between them, Isaac moving to shield them from the crowd that could easily trample a toddler.

Josie splashed a hand in, while Sage stood on tiptoe to peer into the water. Katie found a hermit crab and scooted it closer to the girls so they could touch its shell. She stroked a finger over it then suddenly jerked her hand back and gasped. Katie yanked Josie back and Sage followed of her own accord.

"Did it pinch you?" Isaac asked.

"There's a stingray in there," Katie said in horror. "Those things have killed people. Why on earth is that here?"

Isaac laughed and spotted a small stingray drifting in wide circles. "That thing is not a killer. I'm pretty sure they remove the barbs anyway."

Katie took a step back, losing their spot. "I think we've had enough touch tank." Josie started to whine, though the general din in the room covered her protest.

Was she serious? Isaac caught Katie's wrist and stopped her. He tugged her closer. "You are not afraid of anything. Stop scaring your girls and go touch the stingray."

"I'm afraid of stingrays and geese."

Well then. He tried not to laugh at her. He had never seen a fearful side of Katie. "We'll pet a goose another day. Come on. You haven't even touched a starfish yet." He put his hand around her back and edged them to the tank again. "Girls, it's okay." Sage looked between him and her mother with wide green eyes. Josie eagerly reclaimed her spot at the tank.

"Isaac—" Katie said warily, as the stingray circled toward their side.

"You're honestly scared of it, aren't you?"

"It's not normal for something to move like that."

He reached into the water as it came around and one slippery wing slid underneath his fingers. His other hand held onto her waist and he had no intention of letting go.

"Just do it, Katie," he said.

When it came back around, she leaned back into him, stretched her arm out to its full extension, and let one fingertip graze the creature. Katie jerked her hand back, sprinkling them both with water.

"You survived," he said.

"I didn't like it."

"You don't have to. You only have to face it. Now tell Sage it's okay."

Josie petted an anemone, but Sage still watched her mom for some promise of safety. Katie sighed and bent down to talk to her daughter. Isaac couldn't hear her words over the white noise of the crowd and the dull ringing in his ears. Soon, Sage stepped up to the tank.

"There's a starfish." Katie pointed to the middle of the tank, though her eyes were on the stingray. With the longest reach, Isaac gently moved the starfish closer to the edge of the tank so the girls could touch it. Katie traced a finger down it.

"Stingrays and geese, huh?" he said, close to her ear. "Not anything normal, like sharks or bears?"

"I didn't pick them, they picked me." The stingray circled near them again and Katie leaned back again, bumping into his chest. She reached out for the girls' hands. "Are you sure—"

"I'm sure."

With Katie's tentative permission, Isaac helped Josie feel it the next time it swooped around. The moment he set her down, she turned and patted her wet hands on his pants. "I'm hungry."

Isaac grinned at her as his father's voice played in his head. *Hi Hungry, I'm Dad."* He wondered if Katie ever pulled those moves.

"Already?" Katie asked. "Lunch wasn't that long ago, Jojo. I didn't bring any snacks."

Josie stomped. "I'm hungry!" she shouted, much louder this time.

"They have concessions in the main hall," Isaac said.

"That works." Katie kept her eyes on the stingray on the far side of the tank. She pulled Josie toward her and put a hand on Sage. "Let's go get snacks."

Sage didn't move from the conch shell she studied. Josie turned back to the tank. "No, I stay here," Josie said. "Mommy get snacks."

"Last I saw, the line looked pretty bad," Isaac said. "Why don't you get a head start and we'll meet you out there in a few minutes?"

She looked more than ready to leave the touch tank, but she hesitated. "I don't know if we should split up."

At that moment, Isaac realized she might not be as fearless and confident as he had always thought. Maybe she had been once, but CPS had shaken her. Or did it go back further to Aaron's death? Right now, she wasn't everything she could be. And Isaac wanted to fix it. "Katie, I won't let them out of my sight for a single second."

Her eyes flicked up to his. "Promise?"

He put his arm around her and brought her close. "I promise," he said, into her hair. "They're okay."

She pulled in a deep breath before straightening away. "Okay. See you in five?"

"Yes. We'll be fine."

When she left, another family pressed in closer and Katie disappeared in the crowded room. The moment he lost sight of her, doubt flashed across his mind. Maybe they *should* stick together. Before he could move out though, Sage tugged on his hand. He bent down to hear her.

"What's that?" she asked, pointing to a horseshoe crab, her eyes round with wonder.

Isaac smiled at the sound of her voice. The crowd made him uneasy; they were fine.

Chapter Thirty-Two

Weaving through the crowd around the touch tank, Katie reached the edge of the room right as a tall, fair woman stepped in front of her.

"I saw you with your girls, they are so cute," the woman said. Long, caramel hair fell in waves to her ribs and she wore a strapless sundress that barely reached her thighs. Who wore dresses like that around kids?

Katie paused at the odd comment. The woman saw her all the way from here? Perks of being tall. "Thank you," she said with a smile. She tried to take another step forward, but the woman moved in front of her and spoke again.

"I can't help but ask—are you dating Isaac?"

At Isaac's name, Katie's spine stiffened. Cops could garner all kinds of enemies, and this gorgeous stranger didn't give off a friendly vibe. More of a Victoria's Secret vampire vibe. "I'm sorry… How do you know Isaac?"

The woman laughed and extended her hand. "I'm Lauren. His ex-wife."

Lauren. That's who Vera had been talking about. Katie suddenly realized how little she knew about Isaac. Ignorance now felt more dangerous than blissful. Katie returned the handshake. "Katie Kaminski."

Lauren's eyes lit up. "Kaminski? Did you know Aaron Kaminski?"

Katie's forced smile vanished. Her mouth fell open as she raced to make sense of what was happening. She snapped her mouth closed. "How did you know Aaron?"

"We went to high school together, I loved Aaron. I'm so sorry to hear he passed. Are you related?"

These were the ghosts of Ridley Bay. The beautiful, cold ghosts in this haunted town. "Aaron was my husband."

Lauren had a face made for reality television—gorgeous features and over-the-top reactions. "Shut up. Aaron Kaminski got married and didn't tell *me*? How have I never heard of you?"

Katie's shock faded and annoyance replaced it now. She knew everything about her husband's handful of dates before her, and Lauren had no claim to him, despite her pretentious familiarity. Two could play at it. Katie put on a coy smile. "I'm wondering the same thing about you."

Lauren seemed happy to find her match. "And the girls, I'm guessing they're Aaron's? Poor things, never knowing their father. Aaron would have been such a wonderful dad. You must be an amazing mother to do it all yourself."

Katie's ears burned. This woman found her weak spots fast. "Thank you," Katie said. Though usually talkative to a fault, she wanted to disengage from Lauren. A red warning light practically emanated from her.

"I guess Isaac's enjoying playing house. He always wanted a wife who could be a perfect mother like his own. He hated me after I lost our baby."

Their baby? Katie tried to hide her shock. She lacked crucial details, engaged in a verbal tangle with someone who knew far, far more than she did. "I'm sorry." Would Isaac really hate his wife for having a miscarriage?

"It wasn't meant to be." She shrugged. "And his job is so risky, I think it might have been for the best. I wouldn't want to do that to a child."

Right. Aaron had a perfectly safe job working for an insurance company. Clearly a safe job didn't equal a long life. And apparently Katie "did that" to her children. Her jaw clenched.

"I have a one-year-old now," Lauren said, gesturing to a man and baby not far from her. "And it looks like Isaac has found replacements too. How old are your girls?"

The word 'replacements' boiled Katie's blood. Children couldn't be replaced, nor be the replacements. She fought the urge to make a snappy reply, stepping to the side instead. "That reminds me, I'm heading out to grab snacks for them."

Lauren laughed. "Okay, I get it. Nobody wants to hear from the ex-wife. I'm just surprised, I didn't think Isaac ever wanted to marry again."

Neither do I. And yet here she was, soaking up every minute and every touch with him. What was she doing? "We're not together."

Lauren's perfect eyebrows arched as her eyes drifted over Katie with clear disapproval. "That makes more sense."

Only insecure women put down other women, but Katie wouldn't bow to the queen of insults. She smiled. "Isaac *is* smart enough to learn from his mistakes." She returned the same look to Lauren and stepped past the woman. "Nice to meet you, Lauren."

"You too, Mrs. Kaminski," Lauren called after her.

It's Katie.

·　　　·　　　·

Isaac's snake alarm went off before he saw her. He lifted his head, sensing something wrong. Someone was watching him. Placing a hand on each girl's head, he took his eyes off them to scan the area. It took less than a second to spot Lauren, holding a baby boy on her hip, strolling toward him, with a dodgy man following not far behind. Isaac braced for impact.

"Cute kids. Are they yours?" she asked, smirk firmly in place.

Isaac's eyes locked onto the little boy as a sick feeling spread through his blood. "Funny. You know exactly where my child is."

She sighed and shifted the boy on her hip as he played with her necklace. "Are you going to hold onto that forever?"

"Some things last forever."

"Well, our marriage wasn't one of them. And our divorce would have been even worse with a child in the middle of it. You know I'm right."

Isaac felt Sage turn and look up at them. He gently eased her head back toward the touch tank. He needed to make a quick escape that wouldn't set off a Josie tantrum.

"Who's he?" Isaac asked, studying the baby.

"My son."

The words hit Isaac like a sledgehammer. A metallic taste filled his mouth as his eyes flicked back to the man behind Lauren. He stood an inch or two shorter than Lauren with a beer gut. "And his father?" he asked, dipping his head in the man's direction.

"My fiancé, yes. And no, I won't give you a name."

This little boy, this little life in her arms—why him? Isaac's mind ciphered out the boy's features—which were Lauren's, which were the other man's. "What made his worth keeping?"

As soon as he said it, he regretted it. What an ugly thing to say about any child. He had stooped to playing her games, and he would lose. She could find any sign of weakness and attack, like a dog smelling fear.

Lauren's eyes flashed with irritation. "He's actually around and involved."

Somehow, it was always Isaac's fault. He had never been enough, though in exactly which way changed, depending on Lauren's mood. Thus the abortion he never wanted would always be partially his fault. The air deflated from him.

"I'm sorry," he said, surprising them both. Call it a newfound conscience or call it the Holy Spirit, he wanted to release this. She didn't deserve his apology, but he did. "I'm sorry if anything I did or didn't do contributed to your decision. I'm sorry I couldn't be enough."

"I'm not sorry for any of it," she snapped.

Abortion, cheating, divorce—none of it. It shouldn't have surprised him, but her words still cut. He hoped she had doubted it at least once. Then she leaned too close to him. His body stiffened the woman who once enticed him now repulsed him.

"But please stop lording it over me," she whispered into his good ear. "Please."

Isaac pulled back and caught the brief earnestness in her eyes. He had loved her long enough to know this was the closest he would ever get to an apology. For the first time in their relationship, Isaac realized he might hold some of the power. And they both needed to be free from this. He needed a break from the anger and she needed forgiveness.

"Okay," he said. It seemed to drop like an anvil to the ground between them. A weight that would never truly disappear. But he was tired of carrying it, of holding it over her head. Suddenly, he saw her as someone who needed Jesus as badly as he did. "I'm done."

She swallowed and turned her gaze to the twins. Isaac's hands kept them firmly facing away. He didn't want her anywhere near them. "I met their mother," she said. "Small world. I knew Aaron Kaminski in high school."

The ringing in his ears picked up and Isaac's eyes darted past Lauren, but he didn't see Katie anywhere. Of course Lauren would know Aaron. Lauren knew everybody's weak spots.

"Very small," Isaac muttered, before leaning down to the twins' height. "Come on, girls, let's go get a snack." Josie wrapped her arms around his neck and jumped onto him. He held Sage's hand on his weaker side.

"This is cute," she said, with an insincere smile. "You're getting to play house. How long do you think it will last?"

The weight he so recently dropped seemed to suddenly hitch a ride on his shoulders again. He took a step closer, counting on her instinct to move out of the way. She stepped slightly to the side.

"You know it'll end when you go back to work," she said, eyeing the twins. "And you don't want to hurt them."

Lauren giving advice about children left a sour taste in his mouth. He ignored her and maneuvered out of the room. He needed to find Katie.

They made their way to the small food court and he spotted Katie at the front of the line and caught her eye. He pointed to the last open table, then sat down with the girls, trying to ignore the pulsating ring in his ears and the buzz in his veins.

A minute later, Katie came over with two popcorns and two pretzels. "Pick your poison," she said, with an overly bright smile. She busied herself setting out napkins and waters for the girls and wiping their hands.

He felt poisoned already, but it didn't stop him from reaching for a pretzel. "Are you okay?" he asked, watching Katie.

"I'm great. The line wasn't too bad."

Isaac narrowed his eyes and tugged on his ear. "Anything interesting happen?"

Katie met his eyes and smiled. "Not really."

So that's how she wanted to play this. Not a word about Lauren. She wanted to lie. The ball of anger he had tried to unwind now spun tighter and tighter in his gut. *Fine.* Two could play this game.

•   •   •

Everything changed after they ate. The rest of the aquarium trip, Isaac was sullen and quiet, nothing like the steadfast man who had first joined them. Obviously he had spoken to Lauren, but Katie couldn't find the nerve to ask. Not while she was still processing it herself.

They left the aquarium earlier than she planned. The girls might have been able to stay longer, but both adults had lost the heart for it.

When they got to Isaac's house, he climbed out of the car without a word. Katie hated the silent treatment.

"Hey," she called, throwing the car into park and getting out as well. She shut the door behind her and met him in the yard. "Are we gonna talk about this sometime?"

"About what?"

"Seeing your ex-wife at the aquarium."

He grunted. "So you decided to tell the truth."

"Excuse me?"

"You lied about it earlier."

"I wasn't lying," she said. "I didn't want to talk about it in front of the girls."

He shrugged like it was the same thing, which bothered Katie.

She blew out a breath and pressed her hand to her head. "Can you come over later so we can talk?"

"Why would we talk, Katie? We're nothing."

Ouch. She felt the impact of his words and glanced down, fighting to regain some confidence. It ran low ever since meeting Lauren. "I mean, we're friends." A decade ago, he had promised to be her anything, and nearly became her everything.

He shook his head. "I'm not doing this again."

"Doing what?"

"You're smarter than that," he said, though it didn't sound like a compliment. "Don't ask questions you know the answer to."

While she wasn't exactly hot-headed, no one called Katie mild either. She marched the few steps between them and closed in on his space. "You're letting her get in your head. You can't give her this much control."

"She's not in control. But she reminded me of what I already knew."

"Which is what, exactly?"

"That you can't trust anybody."

Katie's hands raised in defense. "What have I done? You learned that from her, but it doesn't apply to everybody. You know it doesn't apply to me."

"You lied about not seeing her. You could have said something."

"I was having a hard time!" she said, a bit too loud. "I didn't know what to say and she kind of got in my head too, okay?"

"Fine," he said, perfectly level, perfectly cold.

Internally, she stomped her feet, pounded her fists, and screamed like Josie. She spent too much time around toddlers. "I hate when you do this. You clam up and shut everybody out. I've told you everything. I told you about my pregnancy, my husband, the stupid CPS case, and you told me nothing. I wouldn't have even known you were divorced if it weren't for Zoe."

"That's *you*, Katie. You talk too much. Why would *I* tell you any of that?"

Because we're friends! she wanted to scream. "Because that's what people do. They share things. They see someone being vulnerable and they return the favor."

"I don't."

"I know and it's not fair. Lauren caught me totally off guard. I didn't know her name, I didn't know about the baby—"

As soon as the words left her mouth, Isaac's head jerked back as if she had slapped him. "She told you about that?"

"Yes, but I still have questions."

"Save them," he said and immediately turned around and stalked toward his house.

Katie was torn. She wanted to go after him and shake some sense into him, but she had kids waiting in the car and a schedule to stick to. Letting out a groan of frustration, Katie raked her hands into her hair and forced herself to turn around and get in the car.

Hurt ran through her like a tornado. They had been having a perfect day and then Lauren—no, Isaac—ruined it. She got into the car, her eyes stinging, and tried to calm herself with a deep breath.

"Mommy, what da matter?" Josie asked.

"Nothing," Katie said, her voice strained.

"No, what da matter with Wewoo?" Josie asked again.

Sage's soft voice answered her. "His arm hurts," she said.

Katie nodded, her hand pressed against her forehead. "Yeah. His arm hurts. He needs to go rest." She pulled away from the curb with a glance at the clock and debated whether they had time to get ice cream. She desperately needed a dose of happiness, but Katie had to finish an online parenting class before the day ended. She swallowed the knot forming in her throat. "God, please be my joy," she whispered. The world around her was shutting it out. God was her last resort; maybe he should have been her first.

Chapter Thirty-Three

Isaac burst into his house and ripped off his shirt, ignoring the stinging sensation in his arm. He changed into workout clothes, grabbed his shoes and chest pack, and headed out the door. He hit the sidewalk already at a jog. He needed sweat to cleanse all of this out of his system.

Every slamming step into the concrete reverberated through his arm and pounded into the bullet hole. The pain had him sweating long before the effort. He barely made it a single mile before his chest threatened to explode and his arm burned like fire. Even running had been taken from him.

With a cry of frustration, he bent over, his left hand on his knee, his right cradled against his chest, struggling to breathe. Pain flooded his senses until he couldn't tell where it came from, what was internal and what was external, what was physical and what was emotional. The anger trapped in his chest crushed him.

"Why, God?" he said aloud, bent over on the sidewalk.

Isaac was saved—he had been forgiven and he should be able to forgive too, but he couldn't. His anger formed a prison cell. If Jesus bought his freedom, why was he still locked in?

"God, help me out," he whispered, scrubbing a hand over his face. He straightened and the raw pain in his arm blacked out his vision. Isaac dropped down into a squat to catch himself before he passed out right there on the sidewalk. Regret took over the anger now. How much damage had his stupidity done—both to his arm and to Katie?

This time he stood more slowly, pulling in oxygen to steady himself. The pain seared from his arm across his chest and back. He could hardly walk and he was a mile from home. His fingers were numb and he didn't have the strength to hold his arm up. Isaac sighed and pulled his shirt off, rearranging it into a temporary sling. If he looked like an idiot, he deserved it.

The mile home turned into a hundred. A hundred miles of thinking about Lauren and that little boy on her hip, the baby that never grew up, and Katie and her lies.

By the time he got home and into the shower, the pain dulled to a throbbing ache. Isaac leaned forward in the shower, letting the hot water pelt his back while he pressed his forehead against the cold tile.

For a moment, he thought he could forgive Lauren. If he was a prisoner, he had glimpsed the key. But he couldn't reach it. Then Katie lied about seeing her—or delayed the truth, or whatever she did—and Isaac watched the key sail straight out the window. Could he find it again? He tried to pray, but his words weren't coming out right, and no answers came to him.

He flipped the water off, dried and changed clothes, and popped two painkillers for the arm. Then he grabbed his phone, dropped onto his bed, and called Penn. He thought about calling Micah, but Micah was too good. He wanted somebody who might be able to relate.

"Hey man, what's up?" Penn answered.

Isaac cut to the chase. "Hey, I've got a question about this whole Christian thing."

"Hit me."

"You ever still get angry?"

Penn laughed. "What do you mean?"

"Like really angry. Or is that supposed to stop when you're a Christian? Am I doing this wrong?"

"Man, Jesus flipped some tables. I don't think anger is wrong."

"It doesn't feel right though," Isaac said. This wasn't like Jesus's righteous anger. This anger brought pain and no resolution. "How do you know what's okay and what isn't?"

"The Bible says, 'Be angry and sin not.'"

The anger at Lauren broke away for a moment and Katie filled his mind—and her face when he called her nothing. "Is hurting someone sin?"

"Probably," Penn said. "What do you mean by hurt?"

"I said some things I wish I hadn't."

"Yeah, there's a verse about that too," Penn said. "Speak only what builds others up and gives grace. Something like that."

"I definitely didn't give any grace."

"Well, that's why we need Jesus."

"But that's the problem," Isaac said. "I have Jesus. I'm supposed to be saved now, but I still screwed it up."

"I mean, we need him every hour," Penn said. "We have to turn to Christ with every single difficult emotion and situation, and we'll find his grace. But it's not a one-time thing. It's a constant supply for a constant need."

Isaac was silent for a moment. He had glimpsed grace for one fleeting moment with Lauren, only to turn his back and let anger take over. "I need this anger to go away. I can't live like this."

"You don't have to. Go nail it to the cross. But let me tell you, it's probably not going to feel good. Grace isn't always a nice, happy feeling. Sometimes it's eating your humble pie, or facing all the ugly emotions the anger's covering up. Grace is freely given, but it isn't cheaply taken. Sometimes it requires hard work."

Isaac rested his hand on his eyes. He wasn't sure he understood, but he wanted to. "Thanks, man."

"Anytime. I'm praying for you."

"Thanks, I need it."

"We all do."

Isaac hung up the call and rubbed at the sore spot on his arm. This grace would cost him. He had been afraid of giving his life over to Christ, afraid of what it might change. And now he faced the changes. Grace asked him to let go of the anger, to forgive Lauren, and possibly to risk letting others in again. Those kinds of changes wouldn't happen overnight. They were going to take days—possibly years. But he wanted to change. He had to.

•   •   •

Water splashed out of the bathtub and onto the already soaked towel on which Katie knelt. "Keep the water in the tub, Jojo," she repeated. Motherhood was spent on her knees anyway, so Katie sent up a quick prayer for patience and joy.

She wanted to enjoy this—the way Josie and Sage giggled in the tub right now. Why could it not break through? Why did stress always cloud it? She needed to focus on the good. On how Sage opened up more after every therapy session. On the squid dance Josie invented at the aquarium. On the cookies she planned to eat once the girls went to bed.

When another splash landed on Katie's jeans, she sighed and grabbed two towels. "All right girls, pajama time."

They made it through a round of wailing and begging and she finally got the girls dried off. The routine felt particularly long tonight, but she eventually tucked the girls tightly into their beds and sang a few songs. As Katie gave the girls a final goodnight kiss, Sage began to whine. "I'm scared," she whispered.

Katie sighed and knelt next to the bed. She brushed back her daughter's hair. Sage might be more open now, but Katie wasn't sure good things were coming out. "Why are you scared?"

Sage pointed at the door.

"That's just the door sweetie, I'll be on the other side of it."

Then Sage pointed at the dresser in the room. Then the window. She kept pointing until she covered every spot in the room. Then she decided she feared her own stuffed animals.

"Sage, you're not scared. You're fine." Katie wanted nothing more than to take a hot shower and collapse on the couch with that plate of cookies.

"I'm scaaaared," Sage whined.

Katie dipped her head, pressing her forehead against the edge of the bed and digging into her soul for a little more to give. Some nights these struggles ended with Katie walking out and slamming the door.

"Scoot over." Katie climbed into the bed next to Sage.

"No fair!" Josie shouted.

"You're next," Katie said.

"No, me first!"

Overwhelm threatened to smother Katie. There wasn't enough of her.

She got out of Sage's bed, which started Sage crying now too. "One minute," she promised. "Hang on tight, girls." Completely ruining the sleepy atmosphere, she flipped the lights on, moved the nightstand from the middle, and pushed the beds together. "There." Katie laid down in the middle, right over the crack between the beds, pulling one girl into each side.

Both girls quieted quickly. Katie stared at the ceiling, thinking about their heavy heads on her arms, the to-do list she needed to get to—anything except for Isaac. He had called during dinner and she ignored it. If he wanted to apologize, she didn't want to hear it. Because he was right—they were nothing. Hearing him say so shouldn't have hurt her.

Katie wished she could go back in time and change all of this. Maybe she would never come to Ridley Bay. She would never reconnect with Isaac. The world's worst counselor, Holly, would never meet her. The CPS case would never happen.

But then Katie would have stormed out of this room and slammed the door tonight. She wouldn't be laying here right now, praying blessings over her children. She wouldn't have seen Sage's eyes light up over a starfish, or watched Josie touch a stingray with Isaac's help. Her heart gave another dangerous squeeze. Yes, there were challenges in Ridley Bay, but there was so much good too. Like weeds tangled around the roots of beautiful flowers, every good and terrible feeling was locked up together.

Josie fell asleep first; a soft snore escaped as drool dripped onto Katie's arm. Sage squirmed a little longer. Their eyes met when Katie looked at her. Sage blinked at her, long and slow, half asleep. Katie smiled and brushed a finger down Sage's nose. The blink got longer. Katie repeated the motion, then brushed her finger over each eyebrow. Sage's eyes closed.

Katie studied her. Sage and Josie both had the same little dip in their chins like Aaron.

This love had only ever brought her pain, yet she couldn't feign regret. Aaron and these girls were the best things that ever happened to her. If love and pain were wrapped up in each other, she had to learn to accept them both.

Katie kissed each little girl's forehead and decided to forget about work for tonight. For one, tiny moment, she would savor her babies.

Chapter Thirty-Four

The next evening, Katie had just finished brushing Josie's teeth when she heard a knock on the door. Her heart leaped into her throat. CPS visits taught her to dread that sound. They had already been here today though, shortly after Katie returned from a scheduled photo shoot, and she assumed they were in the clear. In the hours between their visit and bedtime, she let the toys overrun the house and the dinner dishes fill the sink.

The knock sounded again.

Katie rinsed Josie's toothbrush and told the girls to stay in the bathroom, leaving them with a video on her phone. "I'll be right back," she said, slipping out. Her heart pounded and her eyes roamed over the space—couch cushions askew, toys on the floor, apple juice spilled on the countertop.

She peered through the peephole in the door and her thudding heart skittered on ice when she saw Isaac. She pulled the door open. "You scared the heck out of me," she said.

"Sorry," he said, with the audacity to smile. "You weren't answering my phone calls."

Because we're nothing, she wanted to snap. Instead she stared at him for a second, biting her tongue. "So you decided to drop by at 8:30?"

This time he at least had the courtesy to look chagrined. "You didn't want to talk in front of the girls, I was hoping to catch you after they went to bed."

"Well, we're running late tonight, they're not in bed yet." The drowning pressure of Lauren's comments about perfect mothers splashed all around Katie.

"I'll wait," he said, leaning against the doorframe.

Katie wondered what it must feel like to be able to fill a doorway. She sighed and glanced behind her at the wrecked apartment. If clean-freak Isaac wanted perfection, he would soon realize it wasn't here. "It's a mess in here. CPS already came today so I let it go… I was planning to clean after bedtime."

"I'll help."

"I'm not asking for help." The words came out sharper than she intended. "I'm saying you expect perfection and you're not going to find it here."

"I don't—" He stopped himself and lowered his voice. "Katie, I'm sorry for what I said."

It looked like it hurt him to admit that. *Ugh.* She wished she didn't care, but she did. She sighed. "Fine. Give me ten more minutes to get them into bed. Good luck finding somewhere to sit that isn't sticky."

She turned and walked toward the bathroom without a second glance back, unwilling to see his judging face. She stopped outside of the bathroom door, listening to the girls giggle over the show, and sent up a quick prayer. With a deep breath, she entered the fray.

After a few more nightly antics, and Sage's routine fearfulness, Katie finally got them in bed and asleep. She stopped at the soggy mess of a bathroom, sighed, and swiped a bath towel over the whole room and hung it over the curtain rod.

In the living room, Isaac held a stuffed elephant over his head like a basketball player. He sank the elephant into the toy basket in the corner. He already had the living room tidied.

"You didn't have to do all that," Katie said, taking a rag to the spilled apple juice. She carried a stray cup to the sink and flipped on the water.

Isaac joined her and leaned onto the countertop. "Can we talk?"

The air deflated out of Katie. Yesterday, she asked him to talk about it. Today, she didn't want to anymore. She wanted to leave it all behind.

Overwhelm creeped up on her like the tide. "I need to get this place cleaned up in case CPS drops by in the morning."

"Then I'll do these," he said, taking the scrub brush out of her hands.

"You're not doing my dishes."

"Yes, I am. Because we need to talk, and you won't talk until after the dishes are clean, and I'm not talking to you until after you've sat down. No offense, but you look like you need a minute."

"Offense taken."

"Sit," he said.

"I'm not a dog," she grumbled. But sitting sounded better than arguing, so she plopped onto the couch. She leaned her head back and hung her arm over her eyes.

By the time she heard the sink turn off and the dishwasher close, her nervous system had calmed down and the overwhelm eased back. She could do this.

"Hey," he said.

She opened her eyes. Isaac stood in front of her, holding a hand out. She put her hand in his and let him pull her up.

"You okay?" he asked.

"I'm good." She nodded at the dishes. "Thank you."

He held her gaze a moment longer than normal. Katie wondered if he had telepathic abilities she didn't know about. "Can we sit outside?" he asked.

"Sure." She followed him to the patio door. The small patio faced the parking lot; not a nice view, but the salty, coastal breeze revived her spirit.

Isaac sank into one wicker chair and Katie took the other in the well-worn set that came with the apartment. The night air swirled around them, cool and quiet. Katie waited for him to wade in first. It took longer than she was comfortable with, but he called this meeting, and for once she didn't want to be the one talking.

Finally, he laced his fingers behind his head and looked upwards. "I bet Lauren had great stuff to say about me."

"Rave reviews," Katie said.

He snorted.

"Actually, she said more about Aaron than you," Katie said. "That surprised me."

He glanced over at her. "I'm sorry. I guarantee whatever she said wasn't true."

"That seems harsh."

"It's not."

"Well *I'm* not a liar," she said, turning to him. "I'd appreciate if you didn't call me one."

He studied her. "I know. I'm sorry. It's a learned response."

"After meeting her, I think I understand."

"I hate that she caught you," he said. "If I had known, we wouldn't have split up. You shouldn't have to dance with the devil too."

She doubted Lauren was the devil. Isaac had married her for some reason; she must have some redeeming qualities, but Katie didn't want to discuss them right now. "It's okay," she said. "I know a few moves."

Isaac grinned at her. "I'm sure you do."

Quiet settled around them again. Katie waited, biting her tongue. Was he going to make her bring it up? Based on his response when she mentioned the miscarriage yesterday, she wasn't sure she should mention it.

"What did she say about the pregnancy?" he said, his voice quiet and distant.

"That she lost a baby."

Isaac swore under his breath and looked away. He rubbed his hands over his face. "You don't *lose* a baby. That's like saying you lost a bullet from a gun."

Katie shifted in her chair, sitting sideways to face him better. "What does that mean?"

Another long silence. He studied his hands. "She had an abortion."

All the wheels in Katie's mind stopped turning. *What?* And Lauren said he hated her afterwards? "Did you both want that?"

He shot her such a dark look, for a moment she thought he might get up and walk away. "I begged her to keep that baby," he said.

Katie's heart sank. For both of them. For the lies and hurt that had torn apart a marriage, and the hurt he still carried. "I'm so sorry."

He leaned over, elbows on his knees, chin on his fists, staring at the ground. "She said she wasn't ready. She threw the pregnancy test at me and said she was getting rid of it." He shook his head. "She asked me to take her to the clinic and I refused. One day we had a huge fight about it and I said she could take herself, so she did." He pressed his palms over his eyes. "Maybe I should have been there for her, but I couldn't do it."

"Sounds like a lose-lose situation," Katie said softly. She suddenly remembered his questions at the burger diner, when he asked about her decision to keep her surprise pregnancy. He wasn't questioning her; he was questioning his ex-wife.

"I was so angry afterwards. When the due date came around, I told her about it. And she told me she was sleeping with someone else. At that point I probably deserved it. I made a last-ditch effort to get marriage counseling but she wouldn't go. She was already checked out. Maybe if I had gotten help sooner… I don't know."

"Do you know why she did it?" she asked.

He shook his head. "She gave a lot of reasons. I don't know if any were true. She has a baby now with somebody else, so I guess it was just me."

Katie reached over and squeezed his hand. "People change their minds." And sometimes, they do things out of guilt.

They sat in silence for a minute. "By the way, nobody knows this," he said. "Micah Sanford is the only other person who knows. I thought it was between me and Lauren. Please don't tell—"

"I wouldn't."

"Thanks."

They sat and listened to a few late-night bird calls, and the occasional car puttering through the parking lot. "Not even your family knows?" Katie asked.

"I don't want it to hurt them too."

"I don't think that's how families work. You and your mom are close, you should tell her."

"My mom thinks I'm some golden family man," he said. "I don't really want to ruin it for her."

"You are, I see you with my girls. Why would this ruin it?"

He snorted. "My ex-wife killed my baby and cheated on me. That doesn't reflect well."

"I'm sorry, but your ex-wife is a cover model and pathological liar."

Isaac laughed. "That about sums her up, yeah."

Katie studied him for a minute, chewing on the inside of her lip. "When did this happen?"

"A little over three years ago."

That number slithered down Katie's spine. The humidity stuck to her like a wet blanket, pinning her hair to her neck. "Lauren called the twins replacements."

A sound rumbled in his chest. "Of course she did." He pushed up from his chair and moved to the patio railing, gripping it and leaning over. He turned his back against it and faced Katie. "That's not true, Katie. Yes, your girls sometimes make me wonder what my life would look like if things were different. But you can't replace people and I'm not trying to."

She stood and joined him. "I know."

He glanced down at her and lowered his voice. "Don't let her in your head. You were right that she got into mine. She's great at finding people's weak spots and digging in."

"Good thing I don't have any weak spots," Katie said.

Isaac laughed and wrapped his arm around her waist. "Good thing."

His warmth overpowered the chilly night air and Katie sank into his side. "You have to forgive her. And yourself."

He shifted her so he had both arms around her now. "I'm working on it."

Being held like this was intoxicating, and Katie could easily drown in it. She took a step away. "See, this is the problem with smaller towns."

He grinned. "What is?"

"Everybody knows everybody. You don't run into ghosts in big cities. I think I should go to Houston next. Guaranteed, I could spend a year there and never run into anybody's ex."

He chuckled and reached both hands out to her hips and pulled her closer to him again, his eyes fixed on her. "Please don't go to Houston."

His touch and his eyes created a heady mixture of hormones that left her feeling like a high schooler with a first crush. Should a formerly married woman still get feelings like this? "Why not?"

He moved one hand to cup her face and all her bones turned to putty. "Because I like having you here."

Her heart thumped around like a drunk Energizer Bunny. "You do?"

"Yes." He leaned a fraction closer to her and Katie struggled to find rational thoughts.

"But you said we were nothing," she whispered.

"I was wrong." Then he closed the gap and kissed her.

Katie responded the exact same way she had ten years ago—with everything in her. Her arms wrapped around his neck and she never wanted it to end. This feeling, this closeness, was better than she remembered. It returned to her like a tidal wave. She hadn't felt it in years. Not since…

Aaron's name flipped a switch on the tracks and everything came to a screeching halt. Katie pulled back and put a hand on his chest—a barrier between them. "Isaac," she breathed. "We can't."

"Yes, we can."

For a second, her dopey brain believed him. Katie raced to find solid ground again. "Neither of us wants to get married again," she blurted.

He grinned, undeterred. "You're kind of jumping the gun there."

If they were the people they used to be, she might smile back and let him kiss her senseless. But they weren't. She was a widow and a mother, not a carefree twenty-something. Katie took another breath and leaned back. "We know it's a dead end. We've walked down it before and we both got hurt. Now I have two kids along for the ride. I can't do that to them."

Isaac's lips pressed into a thin line, parted, and closed again. Never in her life had she wanted someone to argue with her as much as she did right now, someone to prove her wrong. To tell her the dead-end road went somewhere wonderful. She desperately wanted to stay in his arms, yet that very desire brought immense guilt.

He dropped his hands from her. The night air hit her, colder than before. "You're right," he said.

Oof. That hurt. Which is exactly why she shouldn't have let herself care too much in the first place. Katie pulled on the most confident smile she could muster. "I usually am."

One corner of his mouth barely lifted. "Sometimes I wish you weren't."

Katie stared back into those eyes, intense and dark, and laser focused on her. "Me too."

He sighed and reached out, tracing his hands down her arms until he reached her hands and gave them a quick squeeze. "I'd better go. Thanks for the talk."

Words fled her. "Anytime," she managed. What else could they say?

Chapter Thirty-Five

Thanksgiving crowds at the airport reminded Isaac exactly why he didn't travel for the holidays. He usually worked on holidays so the officers with families could have the day off, and to avoid the masses clogging up the walkways. He made it outside to an exhaust-filled pick-up area before reading Sara's text that she was running late. Isaac found an empty bench and plopped down with his tan rucksack next to him.

Now that he had a signal again, he needed to text Katie. It had been on his mind through the flight. He didn't know exactly what to say, but he felt like a cad for kissing her and walking away. He could apologize for the impulsive move, though it would be a lie to say he was sorry. To kiss Katie was to know her: her passion, her joy, her strength and fragility. He would never regret it.

Isaac: In Phoenix with my family for the week
Hope you have a good Thanksgiving

He looked at his text, as dull and dry as possible. He could have at least added an exclamation mark or emoji or something.

Saving him from any more analysis, Sara pulled up in a minivan and waved him over. Isaac tossed his bag in the back and climbed in.

"Do you still travel with that bag to prove something, or would you like a suitcase for Christmas?" she asked, giving him a quick hug over the center console.

"To prove something."

Sara laughed. "At least you're honest."

Isaac glanced into the empty back of the minivan. "Where are the kids?"

"Figured I'd give you one quiet drive before they all bombard you for the next several days."

Isaac nodded. "Much appreciated."

Sara updated him on the plans for the week as they drove—when Oscar would get into town, how Andres and Mia were hosting Thanksgiving, and the leaderboard the nephews built for backyard football games. All too soon, she parked in front of the small historic cottage, perfect for empty-nesters.

"How is she?" he asked, still buckled. Andres kept him updated on her cancer treatments and progress, but he felt unprepared.

"She's your mom, Isaac. Just talk to her."

"I don't know what to talk about."

"All the normal stuff. Ask her how she is. If she wants to talk about cancer, she will. I have a feeling she wants to talk about you though. We brought lunch on Sunday and all we heard was *Isaac this* and *Isaac that*."

Isaac nodded. "Okay."

Sara sighed and shook her head at him as they got out of the car.

His dad greeted him at the door. For seventy-four, he still looked as good as ever, if a bit thinner and perhaps an inch shorter. Isaac gave him a hug and entered the house.

His mom sat in the living room. Thanks to their virtual book club of two, Isaac recognized her head wrapped in a cap, instead of her former salt-and-pepper hair. She stood with a cane when he walked in. He wrapped her in a loose hug, afraid to squeeze what felt like a fragile, ninety-pound frame underneath him.

"My goodness, when did you get so tall?" she asked as she reached up to pat his cheek.

Isaac laughed. "About twenty years ago."

"Well, I'm used to it with the others, but I don't see you enough to believe it."

"That's because he's the baby," Sara said. "I have a feeling he'll never grow up in your eyes."

"He was the babiest of my babies. You probably wouldn't care for that nickname anymore."

"I don't think I ever cared for it," Isaac said. And for the record, he was now one of the tallest, tied only with Andres.

After a few more minutes catching up, his dad showed him to the guest room, where Isaac dropped off his backpack. He had the Medal of Valor with him, to give to his mom later, and the arm sling tucked into his bag if needed. But mostly, he wanted to avoid talking about it too much. He had heard more than he ever wanted to hear about the shooting.

Sara left to get her kids from school and his mom retired to her room for an afternoon nap, so Isaac went to help his dad in their garden. They chatted about local news, baseball, and Isaac's work. His dad had retired five years ago from a long career in the medical field and always asked for Isaac's best stories. He liked the weird medical emergencies Isaac sometimes stumbled upon.

"How are you holding up with all the cancer stuff?" Isaac asked.

His dad waved a hand. "I'm fine. I have more energy than Andres and Cristian give me credit for. And your mom is the strongest woman I've ever met. She about has cancer kicked."

"Really?"

"Your mother only looks weak next to you boys. You should see her at the cancer clinic. She's doing laps around everybody else, telling them to cheer up and keep moving."

Isaac laughed. He could almost see that.

His dad's phone beeped and he held it at arm's length to read the text. "My visiting time is up. Your mom wants you. She says to bring her a cup of tea."

Isaac headed inside and washed up before delivering the tea to his mom's room. She sat propped against pillows, their latest police novel on the bed next to her. She patted the side of the bed and Isaac took a seat, passing off the tea.

"I didn't like this one," she said, pointing to the book.

"Why not?"

She shook her head, pressing her lips together. "Too much death."

Isaac shrugged. "The main character didn't die."

"Yes, but the side characters have mothers too," she said, sipping her tea.

He grinned. "You and your bleeding heart."

She harrumphed at him. "Speaking of your mother's bleeding heart, what happened to your hand?"

A faint scar ran along the outside of his palm, reminding Isaac he hadn't been here since last spring. "Some crack addict bit me."

"Excuse me?" His mother's voice pitched higher.

"Probably pay back for all the times I bit Oscar."

She leaned her head back against her pillow with a chuckle. "My goodness, I was glad when you outgrew that."

"Because Cristian taught me to 'fight like a man.' I don't think that was much better."

She smiled. "It's a miracle you survived your childhood. Any of you, really."

"Times were different then."

"Oh, quit sounding so old," she said.

"I'm getting there. Almost forty."

"No, don't say that. If you're getting old, then I'm way past old."

"Dad says you're doing great though. Kicking butts at the medical center."

"Of course I am," she nodded. "I'm not going anywhere until I meet all of my grandchildren."

That gave him a dip in the gut. "All of them?" All his brothers were done. The youngest grandchild was six by now.

"I'm waiting on you. I know they're coming, one of these days."

Isaac stared at his hands, thinking of the one she would never meet. "I don't know. I'm getting a little old for that too."

"Oh, men don't age out as fast. You've got time. And so do I. A little, at least."

Silence fell in the room, heavy like a blanket. Katie had suggested he tell his family. Tell them how close he had come, and how he failed. It seemed like more pain his mom didn't need to carry. If the hope of grandchildren kept her around, maybe it was good. Or was it unfair to leave her with a false hope?

Mom patted his knee and faked a cough. "You know, I think my time may be running out after all. You better tell me what's on your mind before I go."

Isaac gave her a gentle push. "That's manipulative."

She laughed. "Well, you've always needed a bit of prompting."

Bottling it all up hadn't done him much good over the years. Maybe releasing the story helped release its power too. Katie said that's what people do—share stories, be vulnerable together.

"I see the light," his mom said in a faint voice. "I'm coming, Lord."

"Good grief." Isaac huffed out a laugh. "It's about Lauren."

"That woman," she scoffed. "What else did she do?"

He blew out a breath and studied the swirling pattern on the bedspread. These weren't nice words to say aloud and he didn't really want to. "She had an abortion while we were married."

His mother drew a sharp breath and let out a heavy sigh. "Oh, Son."

He told her the same story he told Katie, and it wasn't quite as brutal this time. He even told her about the pregnancy test. It might be a stupid thing to keep, but it was all he had, the only proof it had been real and not just a nightmare.

"I'm so sorry, sweetie. Come here." She opened her arms.

Like a child, Isaac leaned over into her embrace. He knew they didn't have many more years of this and he would miss her sorely.

"I think you need to bury it," she said at last.

"Bury it?"

"The pregnancy test. Your baby deserves a proper burial. Buy an outfit and a nice box and bury it. You need some closure."

It was weird, but it sounded right. He or she deserved more than an old test and a dumpster. "That's not a bad idea."

"I know, I had it," she said, with a grin. She reached for his hand. "Why didn't you tell me sooner?"

"I didn't want you to have to carry that as well. Plus, you already hated Lauren."

"Mmm and this does not help. But a mother needs to know these sorts of things. I'm busy praying for you anyway, I might as well know what to pray for." They had already celebrated his salvation over the phone. His mom said she always knew it was coming, no way could he resist the mountains of prayer she heaped on him.

Isaac leaned over and kissed her forehead. "You're a good mom."

"And you'll be a wonderful father one day."

Isaac shook his head. "You're still sticking to that? My wife refused to have a child with me."

"Lauren did that because of her own problems, not because of you. There are women out there who would have a child alone if they had to."

One such woman came to mind. Katie may not have chosen it, or known she would be on her own, but she was doing it: raising two kids, because they deserved to live, as she had put it. His mom spoke truth. Some women were different.

"So tell me about her."

"Her?" Isaac asked.

"Your friend. The woman who thinks you would make a fine dad."

"Who are you talking about?"

His mother sighed and lifted her eyes toward heaven. "You sent me those photos of that after- school program—you looked very handsome, by the way—and said a friend took them. Not a photographer, a friend. And you usually use first names for your friends. So I knew you were trying to hide that this was a woman. And the only reason you would hide that is because you have feelings for her."

Isaac laughed, both impressed and thoroughly amused. "I think you read too many detective novels."

"And based on the photos she took, she thinks you're wonderful with children."

"She's just talented," he said. His mom raised her eyebrows smugly as if he had admitted something. Isaac grinned. "Her name is Katie."

"Yes. Now tell me about her children."

"Okay, how did you know about her kids?"

"Grace Church posted one of the photos, credited to *KKam Photography*. I found her social media account."

"You stalked her? Wait, and my church?"

His mom made a face of disappointment. "Of course I follow your church. And this was all public information, no stalking required."

"You're turning into a great detective." Isaac dragged a hand down his jawline and let out a long breath. "Yes, she has twin daughters, Sage and Josie. They'll be four in March."

"And I haven't seen a man in those photos."

Isaac chuckled. "Maybe we should write a book about you."

He told his mom how he met Katie years before, the little he knew of Aaron, and how they reconnected at Grace Church. She studied his words with her detective-smug grin, reading between every line he spoke.

"She was quite mature to not date an unbeliever," Mom said, referencing his time in Alaska.

He had never seen it that way. "Really? You're taking her side?"

"I take the right side."

"Thanks a lot."

She patted his hand. "Now God has given you a second chance. Are you going to take it?"

"I'm not sure I'm cut out for relationships." Try as he might, trust took time and he still had concerns about Katie. Even if she wasn't a liar, she was flighty—she could up and move to Houston at any minute.

"You can't let one bad experience ruin the rest of your life."

"Katie doesn't want a relationship either."

"Why not?"

Isaac shrugged. "I think she's scared to do it again. And the stakes are higher, with the kids involved."

"Well then, I guess you'll both have to start living by faith instead of fear."

"I'm still new to this faith. I probably need to figure it out more first." Isaac couldn't risk letting Katie and the girls down.

"You know, I got saved when you were a kid," his mom said. "You're the one who broke me down."

"Hey now—"

She chuckled. "I'm teasing. But trust me, I felt like I was starting out too late. Thankfully God's timeline is different than ours. Pray about it, but don't wait for perfection. You're no spring chicken."

"You said I wasn't old yet."

"I didn't say you were young either," she said, her eyes twinkling. "But you still have so much life ahead of you."

"So do you, Mom."

She smiled. "Yes, I do."

Chapter Thirty-Six

The Sunday after Thanksgiving, Grace Church held a church-wide potluck following the service. Katie assumed it was either a chance for people to clear out their leftovers, or an outreach for anyone who might have spent the holiday alone.

She dropped off mashed potatoes and took the girls to the athletic field to run off some energy while the other adults set up tables in the green space out front. Picnics in late November were one of Katie's favorite things about the south. Snow already coated Juneau, while Ridley Bay rested under a blanket of clouds and a light breeze.

Both locations held mental space now. Thanks to a recommendation from Patrick, she hired a real estate lawyer and started communicating with the company interested in the land in Juneau. She had become a woman who could say things like "let me talk to my lawyer" and mean it. Katie didn't recognize herself.

"Hey, I saw your post about Christmas photo shoots," Zoe said, bumping her arm as she joined her. "Can you squeeze us in? Now that Serena's adoption is finalized, I want some real family photos. If you're not afraid to work with all four kids."

"Congratulations again," Katie said, giving her a quick side hug. "And I'm not afraid at all. I think my record for a single session is thirteen kids—cousins."

Another mom from the church asked about Katie's photography. Zoe gladly filled her in and brought up her social media account. "She's probably the most famous person at Grace," Zoe said.

Katie grinned and swallowed a sudden, hard knot. The chasm between her online presence and her personal life deepened daily. Thanks to the personal events of the last month, her photography business ran late on Christmas photos. Other photographers had started posting this year's results, already shot, edited, and printed. She needed to catch up, and promised a quick turnaround on photos. Half of her sessions were filled already, but she needed a few more.

When the other mom wandered off to chase a kid, Zoe turned her full attention to Katie. "How are you feeling about the CPS case?" she asked.

She was one of the few at Grace Church who knew about the CPS case. Zoe agreed to be a character witness if needed, along with Isaac and a couple of Katie's older friends from Baton Rouge. Patrick planned to threaten a harassment lawsuit if CPS didn't drop the case soon.

"I'm okay," Katie said. Photography and the land sale were her mental distractions—the thoughts she ran away to between every CPS visit and appointment. Though there was never quite enough happiness to overtake the darkness chasing her. *Who am I kidding? It's caught me.*

At night it gripped her; her mind raced, reviewing every detail, wondering if she missed anything. Every night, she told herself to prepare for the worst, like Suzanne did. She tried to mentally release the girls. But each mental goodbye failed and she landed in their room, kissing sweaty little heads and singing old hymns. The exact opposite of shielding herself.

The holidays only added to the weight pressing down on her and she sank a little further every day. She wasn't okay at all.

"Food's ready!" someone yelled.

Zoe gave Katie's arm a quick squeeze and began rounding up her own kids. Katie blinked and tried to pull herself out of the void. "Jojo, Sage! Come on, girls!" she called.

Josie's game of tag ended and the kids all scattered to their parents. Sage brought Katie a handful of dandelions and grass. Katie smiled and kissed her cheek. "Thank you, sweetheart." No matter how much she might wish she had a heart of stone, these girls didn't allow it. They kept her soft.

"I hear Isaac's going back to work this week," Zoe said, catching up to her with Serena on her hip. "Ready to see him in uniform again?" She wagged her eyebrows at Katie.

Katie laughed and tried to ignore the effect his name had on her. They had texted a few times since he kissed her, and neither ever mentioned it. "Shut up, you're married," she said.

"You're not," Zoe replied in a sing-song tone.

"I was," Katie sang back.

Nobody understood widowhood. Katie never stopped loving Aaron, and he never stopped loving her—he simply wasn't here anymore. And now she had kissed Isaac, and while the memory made her toes curl, it also sent waves of grief through her for what she had lost. Her heart rode a rollercoaster and she couldn't find the exit.

JP prayed for the meal and everybody started down two long lines. Suzanne joined Katie in one to help load the girls' plates. They chatted, but Katie couldn't relax. Her shoulders knotted up as she tried to stay friendly.

Things had been weird with Suzanne ever since Thanksgiving dinner at the Kaminski house, when Josie said "Wewoo" showed her the turtles at the aquarium. Suzanne's eyebrows had shot up and Katie tried to explain she needed an extra set of hands and he had offered. Of course, that only upset Suzanne more. "I was free the rest of the week, you couldn't have waited a day or two?" she had asked, as if one outing without her threatened her entire existence as a Nana.

So now, when Suzanne asked if Katie had any plans this week, it seemed like a test. Was Suzanne really asking if she had plans with Isaac? She didn't, but would it be so wrong if she did?

Katie didn't care for the growing awkwardness between her late husband's mother and the guy she kissed last week. Her brain cringed. That was a sentence she never even wanted to think.

"Nothing special," Katie said with a smile. Just the therapy merry-go-round—family, physical, speech, play—if they added one more, she might get a bingo. "Sage has a doctor's appointment though and then she should be sling-free."

Suzanne congratulated Sage, who smiled shyly, instead of hiding behind Katie's legs. Maybe the therapy was helping.

When they reached the food, they each took an extra plate and Katie filled Sage's while Suzanne took over for Josie, piling the plate with more food than a three-year-old could ever eat. When they reached the desserts, Josie pointed to every single one.

"Pick one," Suzanne said.

Josie patted at the plate Suzanne held. "Put dat food back to make more room." She nodded, completely sure of her logic.

Katie chuckled and glanced at Suzanne, but Suzanne didn't look up. No cute kid appreciation when it came to the serious matter of desserts.

"We can do one, Josie," Suzanne said. "No more."

Josie peered at the table, eye level with the dishes, and finally picked two desserts, to which Suzanne caved. Then they all followed Suzanne to a table where William and another older couple sat. Katie's eyes roamed over the picnic area, the other young families, and the single adults before she realized what she was doing. She was looking for Isaac and he wasn't back from Phoenix yet. Katie cleared her throat and took a seat at the table with a bright smile. "What a beautiful day," she said, greeting the other couple there.

And to answer Zoe's question, yes, Katie did want to see him in uniform again.

•   •   •

The next week, Isaac came back to the Ridley Bay Police Department on light duty, stuck with desk work for the first few days. His physical therapist had him on a regular routine of torture exercises to regain strength.

The uniform felt like an old skin. It restored a sense of purpose and identity, but it no longer fit the same way—Isaac had previously worn it with anger; now he had to find a way to wear it with hope.

He carried the camouflage Bible in his bag and focused on one of Micah's highlights. *"Speak up, judge righteously, and defense the cause of the oppressed and needy." Proverbs 31:9.* If he could do that, he would count his days a success, regardless of what they looked like. It didn't matter what the world did or didn't see.

By the end of the week, he passed a psychological evaluation and a shooting test. The physical didn't go as well. But he managed to pass it, with excruciating pain. His captain was sick of Isaac pacing around the department building though, so he agreed to allow Isaac to ride with someone else for now. Saturday evening, he and Officer Zapata were patrolling the northside when Katie texted him.

Katie: How's it feel to be back at work?

Isaac: It's good, staying busy

Crime always ramps up at the holidays

Katie: Nothing says love like a stolen gift!

Isaac: All they want for Christmas is a free, all-inclusive trip to the slammer

Katie: Go make those dreams come true, Officer Santa

Isaac grinned and pocketed his phone. Between his vacation and current work schedule, nearly two weeks had passed since he last saw her—long enough to realize she had taken up permanent residence in his brain, in a spot that might have always been hers.

Just before their shift ended, they found a group of teens at a park, gathering well past the city curfew. Zapata parked and Isaac silently prayed the kids wouldn't start anything. Most of them scattered as they approached, a few shouted derogatory terms, but thankfully none stood their ground. A couple of kids were left behind, completely stoned.

"Their parents can deal with them," Zapata said, as he and Isaac helped the teens into the car.

It took a bit, but they finally found their houses and took them each home. At the second house, a woman opened the door in a rage. She took her son into her arms and berated him in Spanish, telling Isaac exactly what she thought of the police.

"Don't you ever touch my boy again," she said.

"Should I leave him there next time?" Isaac asked calmly.

"Better than in your hands," she spat.

He silently disagreed. Gang shootings happened near that park far too often. He would keep bringing the kid home and maybe one day ask if the kid had a better place to go. It was all he could do.

The whole incident pushed his shift late and he didn't get home until well after midnight. He washed the day off and collapsed on his bed, finally sleeping well again. Work was both the disease and the cure.

The next day, Isaac showed up to Grace Church as both a believer and the security guy. It felt right. He chatted with Micah and greeted people at the door, scanning for any unfamiliar faces, and waiting for Katie.

The first worship song ended as Josie ran in, shouting, "Wewoo." He squatted down to give her a high five, but she stopped short, completely distracted by the clear coiled wire leading to his ear. She tilted her body sideways trying to see to the earpiece in his ear. "What dat?"

Isaac pulled it out and let her listen. Her eyes went wider than the moon when she heard the media team chatter. She held it out for Sage, pulling the wire straight across his throat and yanking up his shirt in the process. He unclipped the radio and untangled himself from the chokehold as Sage stepped closer and took a tentative listen, keeping her eyes on Isaac. She smiled at him when she heard the voices.

"Just gonna let your kids maul me?" he asked Katie, straightening his shirt.

"They're about sixty pounds combined. I figured the big, tough security guy could handle it."

"I'm outnumbered."

"Welcome to my life," she said with a laugh, as she swung an arm out to stop Josie from bolting down the hall. "Not that way, sweetie." She herded them toward the auditorium doors.

Isaac reached a hand to her back. "I'll be out front and can keep an extra eye out for them if you want to use childcare."

Katie hesitated and glanced down the hall. "Thanks, but they could still get hurt. I can't risk it."

The church didn't mind parents bringing their kids into the service, but Katie wasn't doing it of her own free will. Isaac existed to make sure people felt safe, and she didn't. He hated it. "Any updates?" he asked.

"We're done with drop-in visits. We still have to follow their rules and check in weekly, but no more waiting around, dreading a knock."

"That's worth celebrating, right?"

She lifted her chin. "You're right. What should I do today, to prove I can?"

A plan formed rapidly in his head. "You should come over to my house this afternoon."

"Use all my newfound freedom to go to your house?" she asked, with a teasing grin.

"Hey, I can be fun. I have a good yard the girls can play in, and I can grill something for dinner."

"Are you sure you want the tiny tornadoes at your house?"

"Positive," he said.

Her eyes danced around his for a moment. "Okay. We'll come over."

"Good."

She smiled and dipped her head in a rare flash of bashfulness. "Are you gonna let us in, Officer?"

Isaac pulled open the auditorium door for her and she walked in, giving his hand the briefest touch as she passed. The girls followed her like ducks in a row.

He had sworn off marriage to prevent getting hurt again, but a life without Katie and her girls in it might hurt him even more. He had to decide which one he wanted to risk.

Chapter Thirty-Seven

Large trees lined Isaac's street, filled with quaint homes of a similar style though never perfectly identical. Katie parked in front of the yellow house again, this time with no elderly neighbor in sight.

Isaac answered the door wearing dark jeans and a cream henley. "You made it." He swung the door open wider and squatted down. Josie returned his fist bump and skipped down the front hall, while Sage stood staring at him.

He smiled at her. "Look at you, no more sling. Feels good, doesn't it?"

She reached both arms up and stepped closer to him.

Isaac glanced at Katie. Her eyebrows shot up and she shrugged. Honestly, she wasn't expecting that at all.

He picked Sage up. "Hey little monkey," he said, grinning at her. Sage looked tiny in his arms as she smiled back.

Instant doubt hit Katie. Was she letting her children get too attached to him? Maybe they shouldn't be here. Every single choice she made affected two little people, depending solely on her for their entire wellbeing. Every choice could be evaluated by a counselor or a caseworker. How she missed having autonomy.

"You okay?" Isaac asked, reaching his free arm around her shoulders.

Katie smiled. They were already here. She wanted to enjoy today, she could worry about the rest tomorrow. "Yeah, but I think Jojo's already destroying your house."

"Sounds like it. Come on." He led the way into a sparsely furnished living room, where Josie had stopped at the coffee table. She flipped the pages on a Bible there. Isaac joined her, watching. "Careful, kiddo. That's my favorite book."

That was possibly the cutest thing Katie had ever heard him say.

"I is careful," Josie said, at almost the exact moment she turned a page and tore it. "Uh-oh."

"I'm sorry—" Katie said.

Isaac laughed and picked up the Bible. "I'll fix it later. Let's go outside, I got bubbles."

"Bubbles!" Josie cheered.

Still carrying Sage, Isaac opened the back door to a concrete patio and a large, landscaped backyard. The patio held a set of two metal chairs with cushions, a small deck box serving as a side table, and a gas grill. Perfect square bushes lined the fence and thick green grass carpeted the yard, one large tree dominated the back of the yard, and a smaller, thinner one stood closer to the patio. Everything was so pristine, Katie doubted the girls should be anywhere near this house.

Isaac set Sage down, opened the deck box, and pulled out a pack of bubble bottles and wands, and two bright green bubble guns.

"You had to get the guns, huh?" Katie asked.

He took a second look at them. "I figured it'd be easier than blowing bubbles."

"Makes sense that 'Wewoo' would be the first person to introduce them to guns."

"I'm sure I'm not the first. Don't they have toy guns?"

"No," Katie laughed. "Why would they?"

"No foam dart guns? I mean, they at least have water guns, right?"

Katie shrugged. "I'm pretty sure they've never seen a trigger before."

He dropped his head and sighed. "Katelyn."

"What? I'm not teaching them violence." Some single parents talked about being both mom and dad, but Katie found being a mom to be plenty of work. She felt no need to play the roughhousing dad role too. Lots of kids survived without fathers. *Right?*

Isaac shook his head at her and didn't answer. He loaded a bottle of bubbles into one gun and demonstrated for the girls, complete with a two-handed grip and sound effects. Josie ate it up, imitating him immediately. Sage took a tentative hold of the bubble gun and gently pressed a few out at a time. In a matter of minutes, they were running around the yard giggling and shooting bubbles at each other.

Katie scooted to the edge of her seat, ready to intervene if needed. "What if they tell CPS they played with guns?"

Isaac laughed. "You'll tell them it was bubble guns and I'll testify to it."

"Should they be pointing guns at people though? Is this where their life of crime begins?"

Isaac gave her a look with one eyebrow raised. "Find me a criminal who got started with a bubble gun and I'll give you a million dollars."

She harrumphed and sat back in her chair. She knew he was right, and the girls were having a blast. "You don't have a million dollars."

He grinned. "No. But I hear that's what you charge for photos."

Katie pressed her lips down to hide a smile. "Who'd you hear that from?"

He kept his gaze set ahead on the girls. She had a great view of his profile from here—strong jaw lined with dark stubble and a slightly crooked nose. "Your website."

Katie feigned a gasp. "You snoop." Her photo sessions weren't cheap, but neither were her results. She had filled her Christmas spots and finished shooting yesterday, then stayed up far too late last night editing. "Well, if you were snooping, can you admit my photos might be worth a little more than someone's living room cell phone shot?"

"Need some validation?" he asked.

Katie turned her nose up. "I'm quite confident in my skills, thank you. It's your art appreciation I'm questioning."

He flashed a grin at her that could turn weak women into gloop. Katie had to remind herself she wasn't weak.

Before she could gloop, the girls came running straight for her. Sage and Josie made a joint attack, spraying her with bubbles. Katie squealed dramatically for them, pulling her knees up to shield herself, and waving a hand to pop the bubbles around her. Then they darted back into the yard. "Hey! Why didn't you get *him*?" she shouted after them.

A few minutes later, they got brave enough to attack Isaac too. He grabbed a bubble bottle and wand, muttering about having a knife in a gun fight, and blew a few back at them, while bubbles peppered his hair and shirt.

When they started to run out of ammo, Sage sidled up to Isaac and slowly reached a hand out for the bubble bottle he held. She seemed to think if she moved slow enough, nobody would notice. Isaac grinned, watching her. "Do you want a refill or the wand?" he asked. Sage ran away and Isaac laughed.

The girls approached together the second time. "We wanna blow bubbles," Josie said.

"Hey, first, what do you say to Mr. Isaac for getting the bubbles?"

"Tank you," Josie said, politely. Sage's lips moved but Katie couldn't hear her.

"You're welcome," he said, handing them each a bottle of bubbles.

"Girls, why don't I hold the bottles?" Katie asked.

"No, I do it," Josie said.

"You guys will spill them in about two seconds."

"That's okay," Isaac said. "I have more."

Katie leaned back. "If you don't mind a soapy yard." Josie and Sage skipped off into the yard. "You didn't have to get anything. They're usually happy enough just running around."

"Well, I realized I did invite you to the most boring house in Ridley Bay after all."

"No, possibly the cleanest though. But the girls are here now, so they'll fix that."

Right on cue, Sage stepped backwards, tripped over her own feet, and fell, dumping the entire bottle of bubbles down the front of her dress. She sat on the grass for a moment staring at her dress, then glanced up at Katie and burst into tears.

"Oh, Sage." Katie headed toward her, but Isaac beat her there. Sage raised her arms to him and he picked her up, soaking his own shirt in bubble solution now too.

"Here—" Katie reached for her daughter but Sage shied back, crying into Isaac's chest. *Really?* She tried not to take the rejection personally.

"It's okay," he said, maybe to both of them, as he rubbed Sage's back. "My fault, kiddo. We should've listened to Mom."

"My dress," Sage wailed.

"I have extra clothes in the car," Katie said, her stress response instantly ticking up. "You're not hurt, Sage. Don't cry."

"She's just upset. She'll get it out of her system," Isaac said, patting Sage's back, completely unfazed.

Katie glanced at Josie and back to Sage. "Are you okay with them for a second so I can run and grab another outfit?"

"Sure."

Leaving the crying behind, Katie hurried through the house and bounded out to the car. Ten seconds of quiet helped her calm down too. She grabbed the plastic bag with backup outfits and made it back outside. Already, Sage had stopped crying and Isaac held her in one arm while blowing bubbles for Josie with the other.

"Here, sweetie, let me get you into a dry shirt," Katie said, reaching for Sage.

Isaac turned. "Which one of us are you talking to?"

Katie swatted at his arm. "Quit."

"Assaulting a police officer could land you in handcuffs." A smirk curled on his lips as one eyebrow lifted.

Katie laughed. "Shut up and give me my child."

Isaac passed Sage to her and she carefully carried her so as not to soak her own shirt. They made it to the guest bathroom inside where she swapped Sage's dress out for a sequined shirt with a unicorn-cat on it. "There. Feel better?"

Sage nodded.

Katie hugged her. "Are you okay?"

She nodded again. "More bubbles?"

"Yes, there are more bubbles. Let's go."

When they reached the yard again, Josie had abandoned the bubbles to chase a butterfly, and Isaac sat on a patio chair watching—his cream shirt soaked with bubble solution and clinging to his chest, nearly transparent now. Underneath it, a series of dark letters ran down one side of his chest.

"You have a tattoo," Katie realized out loud. They had gone swimming enough in Alaska for her to remember his bare, untattooed chest.

"A couple."

"What are they?" she asked. When he grinned that mischievous smile again, she put a hand up. "Leave your shirt on."

"Then you'll have to wait and see them another day."

She shook her head. "Go change."

He walked inside and closed the glass door behind him. Then he peeled off his shirt, revealing a small blue striped flag on the left side of his back. And he flexed. Katie whipped her head back to the yard. *The jerk knew I would watch him.*

When he came back in a black "RBPD" shirt, he held a platter and large tongs. "I'm not much of a chef. I hope hot dogs and hamburgers are okay."

"Perfect. Hot dogs are one of the three main food groups for the girls."

"What are the other two?" he asked, while lighting the gas grill on the porch.

"Chicken nuggets and pizza."

"They sound like me."

"For shame," Katie said, with a laugh.

The girls squatted in the grass, studying a bug they found, while Isaac set to work on the grill in silence. Katie sat in a chair and watched the girls. "How does the crying not faze you at all?" she asked.

He shrugged. "I deal with screaming psychos at work. Toddler fits aren't that bad." He threw another gloop-inducing grin over his shoulder. "Probably helps that I'm half deaf in one ear."

Katie laughed and shook her head.

Isaac put down the tongs and turned toward the house. "Can I get you anything to drink?"

"Whatever you're having."

He walked inside and returned with two beers. He passed her one and sank into the chair next to her. "Katie…"

The sentence seemed to end there. She glanced at him, but he kept watching the girls. "Yeah?"

His mouth pressed into a thin line for a moment. "Do you remember when you said we were the right people at the wrong time?"

That came out of nowhere. Katie nodded slowly. "Yes."

He took a drink and watched the girls chase a butterfly, pausing long enough to make Katie's nerves fire up. "I think we're still the right people," he said, turning to look at her. "And it might be the right time."

Everything on the outside of Katie stilled, but everything inside began to race. Her mind. Her heart. Her breath. "The right time for what?"

His eyes ran over her. "For us."

"*Us*? You're asking me out?" Her thoughts scrambled to catch up. "I thought we were a dead end. Unless you changed your mind on marriage…"

"I changed my mind. I'd rather risk marriage than risk losing you again."

That might be the most romantic thing she'd heard in years, but Katie didn't feel ready for it. It frightened more than flattered her. "Are you serious?"

His mouth pinched and he picked at the label on his beer. "Can you think about it for a minute?" he said, and stood up. He went to the grill and started flipping food over.

Katie stared after him. She had offended him, but she had no idea what to do next. *He changed his mind?* How could they possibly start over? She knew what years of marriage felt like. To start a relationship at square one and build it all again from scratch felt impossible.

She stood, needing to move her body and get out of her head. She should talk to him. But her feet carried her off the patio and to the yard, where the girls played zoo.

Josie held the role of zookeeper, with Sage as a zebra. When Katie joined them, Josie turned into an elephant and Katie became the zookeeper. She wrangled, fed, and put little creatures down for two-second naps, and tried to sort her thoughts. *He's serious.*

"Dinner's ready," he called.

He pulled a couple of dining chairs outside and Katie avoided his eyes as they situated the girls around the deck box as a makeshift table. She retrieved their water bottles, cut hot dogs, squirted ketchup, and tucked paper towels into necklines.

Isaac sat in a patio chair, his plate in his lap. Katie prepared hers, stared at it for a minute, and took the seat next to him. She needed to find the right words, and not let nerves turn her crazy. "I'm sorry," she said. "I'm not good at this. It's been a while."

He reached over and squeezed her shoulder. "It's okay. I'm out of practice too."

Katie's eyes closed as she savored the warmth of his touch. This is what she missed most, more than any grand gestures or kisses—the little touches that said someone stood by your side.

Josie asked for more water and before Katie could force herself up, Isaac got it for her. Various requests kept them moving throughout the meal. When Josie's plate toppled onto the patio, Isaac grabbed a new bag of chips while Katie wiped up ketchup.

"Told you the girls would wear this place in," Katie said.

"It needed it."

When they finished eating, Isaac said he had "I-C-E C-R-E-A-M" if Katie allowed it. They might have a sticky drive home, but Katie never turned down dessert. Besides, she wasn't ready to leave. She still needed to say *something.*

Soon, the girls held bowls of ice cream and sat in the grass eating. Isaac scraped the grill clean and Katie leaned against the house near him. She watched as he worked and the girls dribbled ice cream down their chins. Random insecurities crawled along her spine. Her girls were precious to her, but she knew they were a handful.

"Hey…" she said. He looked up. "You like the girls too, right?"

He set down the wire brush and tilted his head. "I adore them. I never stood a chance against those two."

His statement confirmed what she already saw, but she still worried. "I don't want them to be pushed aside."

"I would never let that happen."

"But you want your own kids," she said.

He groaned. "Always jumping the gun, Katie. Should we discuss retirement plans too?"

"We can't ignore these things."

He moved to stand next to her, facing the yard. "Yes, I want a family. But it doesn't have to be by blood."

After all he had gone through with Lauren, this wasn't an issue they could brush aside. And Katie had never even thought about having more kids. Babies reminded her of the hardest year of her life. She might never get over that. "Are you sure?"

He crossed his arms and sighed. "I mean I'd gladly add one or two. But it's not a dealbreaker for me. I'm not trying to start a cult with half a dozen new kids."

It took her a second to realize he referred to her family. Katie chuckled. "They're not in a cult."

"You know what I mean. I'd be joining your family, and not the other way around."

That gave her pause. She'd never thought of it that way. When her mom remarried, Katie either had to fit the new mold or get out of the way. She always blamed herself for not fitting in. Now, Isaac suggested there was another way to do this.

Katie leaned her head against his arm and he pulled her closer into his side as they watched the girls play in the yard. Every decision she made would affect her daughters. "We might be the right people, but I feel like I need permission or something."

He chuckled. "You're thirty-two. Who do you need permission from?"

"God, I guess. Maybe the kids. Or Suzanne, or Aaron. I'm not sure."

He leaned a couple inches away, turning his head to study her. "Aaron?"

"I don't know," she said.

"It's okay." He moved his arm from her and reached for her hand instead. "I don't want bad timing to mess this up again. We can wait until you're ready."

"But it's been over three years. If I'm not ready by now, maybe I never will be." She had been Aaron's widow as long as she had been his wife. She didn't know what would happen to either of them if she left that identity behind. Would starting over negate what she'd once had?

"Maybe not," Isaac said. "But things can change. I took a few days to think and pray about it. Can you give me that much?"

She nodded. "Of course. I'm sorry I can't give you a better answer right now."

"I mean, it would have been nice if you fell into my arms and kissed me, but this is okay too."

Katie laughed. "Thanks for that."

He wrapped his arms around her again and she leaned into him. It would be easy to say yes to this—to Sunday afternoons playing in the yard, eating ice cream, at Isaac's side. But it meant saying yes to the rest of it—building a whole new life, the inevitable arguments and compromises, and the risk of another heartbreak.

Chapter Thirty-Eight

The CPS court date marked her calendar in capital letters. The night before, Katie hardly slept. When the morning arrived, stars swam in her head. There was only one way to face this. She had to put it in a positive light, somehow. She had to view it as a freedom date. Today, she would regain her freedom, with or without the girls. She told herself that lie until the air in the apartment turned noxious.

She wrestled the girls through hair brushing, into matching dresses, and away from their toys with plenty of time to arrive. This was one day she couldn't afford to be late. Somehow, she still had to drive like a maniac through town to get there. She briefly debated calling Isaac for an escort so she could drive faster.

When she parked, she re-straightened the girls' bows and dresses, with a few less threats than at home. They needed to have their act together here. The girls wore blue dresses, and Katie coordinated with a navy button-down dress.

Rushing into the courthouse, she didn't pay any attention to the officer who opened the door for her until he said her name. The gold *"Torres"* badge was right at eye level and her eyes flicked from there to his face.

He had texted and asked if he could come to the hearing. Other than that, she hadn't seen or heard from him since Sunday. He was giving her space.

"You're in uniform," she said, her dumb brain momentarily forgetting all else besides how good he looked in it.

"I just got off. Swapped shifts."

He swapped to be here?

"Come on," he said. "Let's give some CPS workers a few dirty looks."

Katie couldn't joke right now. "Maybe that should wait until after we're done."

With a hand on her back, he guided her to the right of the entryway. "Nah, it's up to the judge at this point. He's a good guy."

Down the hall, she spotted Patrick, the Kaminskis, and Zoe (sans kids) all standing outside of a door. They were here to support her, but despite all of Patrick's promises, she worried they'd be here to see her lose. To stand there and watch as the black hole devoured her.

They headed inside the courtroom, and for the longest hour of her life, Katie divided her attention between listening to the proceedings and making sure the girls stayed mostly quiet and still. CPS presented the humiliating case and all its evidence. The counselor's concerns, her erratic moves, Sage's injury. They also reviewed the positive steps she had taken since then, like some checklist of becoming a healthy human. Her face burned far hotter than normal and she wished she could melt into the ground. Why did her friends and family have to see this?

After the brief review, they agreed to close the case and the judge quickly declared it finished. But as Katie moved to bolt from the room, Patrick requested the case be immediately expunged from her record, instead of the usual waiting period. She wanted to beg him to just let it go. *Please, just let me leave.*

After a bit more deliberation, the judge granted that as well.

That's it.

For some reason, the declaration filled her head with a rushing wind.

Everyone stood. It was over. And she didn't feel any better.

They all moved into the hall to congratulate her, and Katie's feet followed, but she felt like she was watching it all on replay. Why didn't she feel better?

Suzanne hugged her with watery eyes. "I knew it would all work out."

No, you didn't. You got certified to take my children.

Katie didn't know what to say.

The state had invaded her home and her life, examined and assessed her. They may have found her fit to be a mother, but the fact she had been questioned at all proved her failures. Other mothers didn't face this. What if the court had it wrong? What if Katie still wasn't a good mom? She wanted to scream. Everything felt wrong.

The others looked happy. Her eyes darted over them all, desperate to feel it too. Her hands were sweating. She rubbed them against her dress and then clasped the girls' hands in hers again. Happiness was an ocean away. Regardless of her official record, this had left a permanent mark on her soul. What if she never felt better?

"When's the celebration?" Zoe asked.

Tricia clapped her hands together. "We need a party."

This didn't feel like something worth celebrating. The court said her own children could keep living with her. *Congratulations, Katelyn.*

"No." Katie interrupted Zoe and Tricia in the middle of their planning. "No party."

"You celebrate everything," Isaac said, studying her with a slight frown. "What's wrong?"

"I passed the bare minimum standard for being a decent human being. I'm not celebrating that." She corralled the girls closer to her as Tricia and Zoe protested.

"They put you through a month of torture—"

"We're celebrating you for making it through—"

"Come on, Katie," Suzanne said, giving her arm a little shake. "It's over. Smile."

Things like this never truly ended. The only real change was the return of her freedom. She could leave now. Katie pulled her arm back and smiled her brightest, most photo-worthy smile, just like they wanted. "Thank you. If you'll excuse us though, I should get these girls out of here."

Now Suzanne wore a frown too. "Okay. Are you sure?"

"I'm sure." Katie bent down and whispered promises of lollipops to the girls once they got to the car. She needed them to hurry.

"Can we help you to your car?" Suzanne asked.

"No thanks." Katie started walking, dragging the girls along.

She wanted to run. On her feet, in the car, in an airplane, it didn't matter if it took her away from here and somewhere across that ocean between her and happiness. She didn't have to tell anyone where she went.

The Kaminskis fell behind, but Isaac's long steps stayed ahead of her. He reached the door first and opened it. "Katie, what's going on?" he asked, as sunlight spilled over them.

"Nothing." She fixed her eyes on her car and walked.

•   •   •

The crowd at Grace Church had grown since the fall festival. More visitors came until the ushers had to shuffle people in the aisles closer together, filling the empty spaces in between families and friends. The childcare rooms crowded and they scrambled for more volunteers to help. But as Isaac memorized faces coming in and out, two little faces appeared earlier than he expected.

Josie and Sage arrived in matching vintage sailor dresses, holding hands with William and Suzanne Kaminski. The instant he saw them, he knew something was wrong. Suzanne wore it all over her face.

Isaac sidestepped the crowd to greet them before they reached the doors. He shook William's hand and Josie shouted for "Wewoo." He knelt to give them each a high-five. Sage reverted to her shy self, ducking behind Suzanne. He smiled at her, missing the little girl who had reached for him to hold her last week.

"Where's Katie?" Isaac asked when he stood. William's eyes darted to Suzanne.

"She left," Suzanne said, with a bite in her tone. "Yesterday."

She left. Suzanne might as well have thrown a glass of ice water in his face. But the instant she said it, he realized he should have known. He could always tell which people would show up for their court date and which would run. Despite making it to court, Katie wore the look of someone ready to run.

He had willfully ignored it. He had told himself she wanted to get away from the courthouse. But no, she wanted to get away from Ridley Bay.

"Where to?" Isaac asked, trying to sound casual.

"Juneau," Suzanne said, as if it were asparagus instead of a city.

Alaska? Katie said she would never go back to Alaska. "How long is she gone for?" he asked.

When Suzanne only shook her head, William answered. "She didn't tell us," he said.

The ringing in his ears pitched higher. He pressed a finger to it for a second. "What's she doing in Juneau?"

Suzanne appraised him, seeming somewhat pleased he didn't know anything. "It's personal, I suppose."

He smiled. "Then I'll ask her myself."

Suzanne's happy look disappeared. "Good luck. She isn't answering her phone."

Isaac's eyes dropped to the girls. Katie wasn't answering her phone, thousands of miles away from her children? He remembered the time she said her children might be better off with Suzanne and he suddenly wished he had fought her harder. What did she really mean by that?

With a step toward the auditorium, William excused their group and the Kaminskis toted the girls into the church service. They left Isaac with the remains of everything they had just dumped on him.

He might know the look of someone who would run, but he also knew Katie. Would she really drop off her kids and jet off to Alaska without a word to anyone?

A thousand tiny needles stabbed him all over, worse than the acupuncture he tried for his arm. Yes, she would.

She had been trapped here by the CPS case. She never planned to stay. Had it all been an illusion? Had he made it worse by asking her out? Was she running from him?

While he could have hoped for a better response when he asked her out last week, he understood if she needed time to think about it. He had hoped the CPS case closing would free her from needing permission. He had no idea it would send her running.

Every doubt reared its ugly head. Katie said she wasn't a liar, and he wanted to trust her, but this was a far cry from honest. He had already handed her his heart and now Isaac wanted to stuff it back in. The blood in his veins felt thick and heavy. All of this felt far, far too familiar.

Chapter Thirty-Nine

After an entire day of travel, a rental car dropped her off in front of the gray two-story house Katie once called home. Thanks to living in the south for a decade, she didn't have the right clothes for this climate anymore. She wore her warmest jacket, though it offered little protection against the cloudy skies and wet wind whipping the town.

Katie hustled to the door and stepped foot onto a welcome mat that read "*The Bauer Home*." The door opened before she even knocked. Her mom threw her arms wide. "Oh, you made it, thank you Jesus," she said, wrapping Katie into a hug. She had a matronly figure, with fading brunette hair in a long braid. She pulled back, holding Katie at arm's length and studying her. "My beautiful girl, it's been too long."

Katie smiled at her. "It's good to see you too, Mom."

"I only wish you had brought the girls." Veronica looked around her, as if a couple of toddlers might appear.

"I would have arrived with a head full of gray hair if I had brought the twins on that flight."

Her mom laughed. "Next time, then, please. I suppose Honey needs to make a trip down sometime."

Katie nodded, unsure when or if any of these supposed visits would ever happen. Her mom appointed herself a 'Honey' instead of a grandma. Perhaps because she still had a preteen in the house when the twins were born. At least three teens still lived here. Four, maybe? Raising kids at the same time made grandmotherly affection and trips exceedingly rare.

Her mom ushered her inside and showed her to what had been the baby's room when Katie moved out. "This is normally Mary's room, but she's sharing with Esther while you're here."

"I thought Mary was in college." Katie tried to do some math in her head.

"She is, but she stayed here in Juneau for it. Not all my children left Juneau the second they graduated."

They joined the family in the living room and her mom walked her through everyone's status. "Thomas will graduate high school in May, and then he's going to a trade school. Caleb is a junior. Samuel is a freshman. And Esther is in eighth grade, though she's doing high school math and science." Her mom twittered on about the beauties of homeschooling.

Katie never really knew them and never tried to. Matthew, the oldest, graduated college and now lived in Anchorage. He had been eight when she left for college; Esther, the youngest, had been an infant.

Mary walked in the front door just then and greeted Katie with a hug. She hopped onto the couch opposite of Katie and asked Katie all about her life—her photography, her travels and current location, her land sale. Mary treated Katie like an adored older, wiser sister. Katie answered politely, but she wasn't what they wanted her to be—she was the half-sibling who never fit in with them. She didn't even have Mary's phone number.

When her stepfather, David, arrived a few minutes later, with bags from the grocery store, the awkwardness grew. He greeted her like a long-lost daughter. Katie could only remember the strained, uncomfortable conversations with him that marked her teenage years. She had stayed manically busy through high school to avoid this house—joining the swim team, working a part-time job, and always leading at least two student organizations. She didn't know these people.

"Matthew was so sorry to miss you," David said.

Katie highly doubted that. "This was pretty last minute."

"Next time, with a little more warning, it'd be so nice to have everybody together again," her mom said.

Katie laughed. "Were we ever all together?"

"Right before you left for college," her mom said. "And again at the graduation party."

That's right. Her mom had taken the seventeen-hour car ride with six small children. Katie didn't remember much about that weekend except that Isaac had called to tell her congratulations and she had told him it was a final goodbye. Afterwards, she deleted him from her phone in an effort to move on. He'd been gone a month at that point. That memory pressed into her mind like lemon juice on a paper cut.

"Well, thanks for having me at such short notice," Katie said.

"I've been asking you to visit for years," her mom said. "We would have dropped anything for this."

Katie smiled and excused herself to unpack.

In a perfect world, she might have planned this trip out a little better and even braved bringing the girls along with her. But when she spoke to her real estate lawyer after the court appointment, she realized this trip could prove her freedom. She needed to escape the black hole of Ridley Bay, at least for a few days.

•   •   •

On Monday, the real estate agent led her north of Juneau in a blue pickup truck, and Katie followed in her mom's van. Soon they pulled off the road and onto a snowy, unmarked gravel drive. Only a few yards down, it ended. No house, no fence, no real markers of any kind.

"This is it," Vanessa said, with a wave over the heavily wooded land behind her.

Snow blanketed the ground with no one to walk it down. Katie wore snow boots borrowed from Mary. "Can you show me the boundaries?"

"I can do my best," she said, with a bright smile. The woman wore a pantsuit. Katie felt a little bad about making her trudge through this.

Staying close to the edge of the road, they walked north on the property. The modest driveway marked the southern edge, while a country road lined the western side. Vanessa pointed out occasional visible markers of the eastern edge, though she seemed reluctant to go in that far.

Fairly even land made it a good spot for development, but the real highlight of the property came at the northern edge, where a small lake sat. One end of the lake flowed out to a small river, winding to the channel. The land owner on the other side of the lake had already agreed to sell, and the resort company would own the entire lake.

Sweat dripped down Katie's back by the time they had hiked back to their cars.

"Anything else you want to look at?" Vanessa asked.

"I think I might stay out here a little while, if that's okay."

"Of course, it's your land. Just be careful out here."

"I will."

Vanessa waved and left.

Katie looked around, trying to decide what to do now. This land felt like a stranger's, not hers. She kept waiting for someone to tell her she was trespassing. Preferably not a moose.

Singing to herself and the bears, Katie wandered a little farther east into the property, pressing firm tracks in the snow. She reached a large boulder rising several feet above the ground, with only a light dusting of snow on its bald head. Finding a few footholds, Katie scrambled up for a better view.

From here, she tried to spot something—anything—familiar. She had held out hope that once she got to the property, once she saw it in person, she would recognize it. That the place would trigger some ingrained memory. Nothing came. Katie pulled her knees to her chest as a deep ache rose.

She studied the land around her, hoping to visualize a good camping spot. Trying to remember where they had pitched a tent or found a hole in the trees to stargaze. Katie imagined a dad and daughter around a fire pit, a smoke trail lifting into the sky. Maybe they had carved their initials in a tree trunk, or drank from a stream.

Nothing. Absolutely nothing.

She dipped her head to her knees. The one time she wanted a ghost, there wasn't one. She was truly and completely alone.

The wind shook the pines above her, sending snow plopping around her. The sweat from the hike turned to a chill. Sunlight filtered weakly through the trees and Katie needed to leave. She pulled in a few calming breaths and slid off the rock, landing next to a tree. She ran her hand over the bark, snapping off a small piece to tuck into her pocket.

"Goodbye," she whispered.

She followed her tracks back to the car. Once inside, she took hold of the steering wheel and stared at her hands. The cold had her eyes watering and she pressed her palms to them. She shook out her hands and started the van. Whatever she was looking for, she wasn't going to find it here.

She drove the longest way possible to get back to her mom's house, stopping several times to soak in the views. Texas had its perks, but the glacial landscape here touched her soul. She drove by her old school and a few other haunts before winding back to *The Bauer Home*. She was a Lewis Kaminski.

Inside, her mother stood in the kitchen, wearing an apron and whisking something in a bowl. She looked every bit the part of a homemaking maven. "How'd it go?" she asked.

Katie avoided the question. "I forgot how beautiful Juneau is."

"I never understood why you wanted to leave," her mom said.

"I mean, let's be honest, I didn't really fit in here."

Her mom shook her head, her hand slowing with the whisk. "Why do you always say that? We let you make your own path. Nobody forced anything on you."

"I know. So you lived your life and I lived mine."

Her mom sighed and turned to Katie. "Now I didn't do enough to include you? We offered at every turn, Katelyn."

"Lighten up," Katie said brightly. "It wasn't your fault. I'm just not the family type."

"Yes, you are. You're a wonderful mother."

Katie laughed. "And you know that how?"

"I see all your pictures," her mom said. "You make such lovely memories with those girls."

Katie hadn't said a word about the CPS case and never would. Her mom only knew the filtered, processed, curated version of Katie's life. "Thanks."

"You learned from the best," her mom said, with a wink.

Katie smiled. Her mom wasn't the best and neither was she.

Chapter Forty

Katie excused herself after dinner, claiming the need to work. She slipped away into her room for a couple of hours to finish sending out Christmas photos to her clients and schedule a few posts. She didn't have much to do. Even with all the traveling, she had managed to get a surprising amount of work done without her two little monkeys hanging on her limbs.

The ache of missing them surprised her though. She wondered what they were doing. What they had eaten for dinner. She missed their squishy little cheeks, their giggles, and their wild bath time antics. Suzanne was right—they had never been in her way. Katie just needed to change course.

She flipped through pictures on her phone. Suzanne had sent her a couple, including one of the girls dressed for church like 1920s dolls instead of living children. Katie laughed at it and wondered how long the dresses had lasted.

Despite the ache, she didn't call. The girls were having a wonderful time with their Nana and if she called, she would only disrupt it. They would cry for momma, Katie would feel miserable, and Nana would probably be annoyed. So Katie set her phone down and walked out of the room before she could change her mind.

When she stepped into the living room, she found a quiet space. Only her mother sat on the couch, hand stitching a quilt square.

"Where is everybody?" Katie asked. All day her half-siblings had chattered over one another, filling her in on every activity they did, every new restaurant in Juneau, and all their Christmas plans.

"Mary is babysitting for friends of ours. And David took the rest to a church youth event tonight."

"Oh." Katie stood awkwardly for a moment, feeling useless. "In that case, I might head to bed early."

"Katelyn."

"Yes?"

"You didn't tell me how it really went at the property today."

She shrugged. "Good. It's nice land."

"Your dad loved it so much, he wanted you to love it too."

Katie paused. Veronica never talked about Katie's father. She trailed a hand around the couch, sinking into a seat on the far end. The cushions absorbed her and began to pull out the jet lag, travel, and stress of the last few days. Katie's energy ran low.

"Why did he have it?" she asked.

"Your father knew the previous owner and bought a portion of his acreage when you were born. He wanted to build a house on it one day."

Katie tried to picture him—a young man, married, with a new baby, and dreams of the future. "You think he wouldn't have wanted me to sell it."

"I think you could build a beautiful home on it, if there's any chance of you coming back to Juneau."

She could honor his memory and fulfill his vision. Katie could admit the idea held a certain appeal. But he wasn't the only dead man in her life. She had Aaron too. And Aaron's dreams for his children were in Ridley Bay, not Juneau. She couldn't fix the past for herself, she could only build a better future for her children. "I'm not coming back."

Her mom sighed and set down the quilt square. "Did you remember it at all?"

"No."

"That's a shame."

Katie hesitated. All she had of her father was a wild tract of land with no sign of human life. "Do you have anything from him? A photo, a birthday card, something?"

Her mom shook her head slowly, seeming to think it through. "No, I don't think so."

A river rushed through Katie and she suddenly realized how long she'd held it back. It beat against the dam she had built since childhood. "Nothing?" A crack appeared.

"I'm sorry."

Katie took a deep breath and blew it out. She wouldn't break. Not now. Not over something this old. "How did you do it, Mom?" She asked not to accuse, but with genuine curiosity. "How did you erase Dad and move on?"

"I did not *erase* him."

"You got rid of everything. We didn't talk about him. I don't even know when his birthday was."

Mom dropped her sewing things into a basket at her feet. "June seventh. And why would I keep photos around? That would be weird for David. We moved on because we had to."

Katie struggled to focus, her mind blending her father and Aaron. The mental file on grief had gotten jumbled. "How long did it take you to stop thinking about him?" *Every hour of every day.*

Her mom gazed at the floor. "I never stopped."

The split in the dam grew wider, and Katie raced to hold it up with her bare hands. It should have been reassuring. Isn't that what Katie wanted to hear? That her mother never forgot her father? That she would never forget Aaron? But it cut so deeply, she couldn't bear the thought of carrying this pain for another thirty years, like her mother. "How do you live with that?"

"I stopped fighting it. The more you fight a thought, the stronger it gets. I had to accept it and keep going. Joy and sorrow can occupy the same space if you let them."

"I'm so tired of the sorrow, Mom." Her voice cracked like the dam.

"Oh, sweetheart." Her mom moved closer and wrapped her hand over Katie's. "These men will be part of us forever. It's your shadow now. But you can decide whether you keep staring at the darkness or face the sun."

"I'm trying," Katie said, desperate for an answer. "I've been chasing the sun like mad, but I'm never fast enough."

"I didn't say chase it. You'll never outrun your shadow."

"What if the shadow swallows me whole?"

"I've never heard of a shadow doing that."

Katie shook her head, unable to smile at the joke. She wiped a hand over her face and tried to clear the stone in her throat. "You're stronger than me. To be able to do it all again. Marriage and kids and everything."

"I don't know about that. I just found a person who made me feel brave enough to try again. Maybe you will too."

Katie had found him. Isaac made her hunger for things she had long tried to ignore. "Weren't you afraid of being hurt again?"

"Of course. And caution is wise. But the Bible says guard your heart, not lock it up and throw away the key. At some point, we have to trust God with it."

"He let me down though."

Her mom squeezed her hand. "No, this broken world let you down, but God never dropped you. And if you let him, he'll carry you through every up and down still to come."

Katie only wanted the up parts, but that wasn't how life worked. She had to take it all together, or risk shutting life and love out completely. She had already tried that route, building a stone dam to protect her heart—even from her own children. If nothing else, the CPS case proved her dam was made of paper. And now Prince Charming was tearing it down.

"I think I found someone," Katie whispered.

Her mom scooted her sewing basket under the side table. "Tell me everything."

•　　•　　•

The resort plans the real estate lawyer had forwarded to Katie revealed a beautiful, mountain-style lodge. Its proposed location near the lake required clearing a few trees, but other than a small parking area and a few amenities, they planned to leave the land as untouched as possible. They would host yoga retreats and offer classes on forest bathing. Katie wanted to visit it one day.

First, she had to sell it.

She closed her laptop, grabbed one last piece of bacon from the kitchen, and said goodbye to the teens gathered around the table. Her mom sat with Esther, reviewing a paper together, while Caleb and Samuel each pored over math textbooks. Katie looked back at them before she left. That would have been her, if she had followed the Bauer family plan.

Borrowing her mom's van again, Katie headed to the clerk's office to retrieve the deed. She felt jittery as she drove the few short blocks and parked on the street. Only one person waited in line ahead of her. It didn't give her enough time for the shake in her bones to settle.

Soon the clerk passed her a copy of the document and Katie glanced over it. Her eyes and heart stopped when she saw her father's name, signed on the bottom right.

greg lewis

All lowercase, and his first initials had long lines sliding too far down the paper, while the other letters were small. Exactly how Katie signed her name. Could someone inherit a signature? How had she never known about this similarity? She stared at the paper.

"Is that everything?" the clerk asked.

Katie nodded. "Thank you," she mumbled, heading out of the office. She stepped onto the sidewalk and stopped to brush her thumb over the signature. This was the closest thing she had to her father. She didn't feel his presence at the property, but she felt it here. She could picture him signing it. His hopes and dreams for the place. And it made her stomach hurt.

Katie pressed a hand to her mouth and stared across the harbor. A bitter wind froze her nose and made her eyes water. Was she doing the right thing?

Retreating to the van, she sat inside without starting the car. She had to choose between dead men. Between returning for the life her father wanted for her, or moving forward with the life Aaron wanted for her and the twins. She knew she would choose the latter, but it didn't make the decision any easier. No matter what she did, there would be consequences and pain.

Katie started the van but couldn't make herself drive. She had plenty of time before the closing appointment, and she ran her thumb over her father's name again. Then she grabbed her phone and called Isaac before she could think twice.

"Katie." His tone sounded gruff.

"Hey, do you have a minute?"

"I guess." His words sizzled like bacon in a frying pan. Or maybe that was the breakfast rising in her stomach.

"What's wrong?" Katie asked.

"Nothing." *Pop*.

"Isaac, spit it out, because I need to talk to you, but apparently you have something to say too."

"I have nothing to say."

Katie didn't have the time or patience for petty games. "Fine, then I'll talk." She ran through the brief version: the land she had inherited, her mom's phone call a few weeks ago, and now being in Juneau to finalize the sale.

"And I want to sell it," she said, her voice suddenly struggling to stay even. "I really do. I want to go back to Ridley Bay. But I just picked up a copy of the deed and… I'm having a hard time."

"You don't have to sell it right now. You can wait."

That's why she called him. Because her mom would say don't sell, and the Kaminskis would say to sell, and Isaac would remind her she was free to choose. His integrity kept him neutral.

"The deed has his signature on it. And it's the only thing I've ever seen from him. My mom didn't save anything. I don't have a single card, a photo, anything. This is the only thing I have. I don't even want the land. I want this stupid piece of paper." Her dam was bursting. She sucked in breaths that didn't give her oxygen.

"Katie, slow down," he said, his voice perfectly level and calm. "Take a breath. Are you somewhere safe?"

She opened the car door to let the air cool her face. "Yes."

"Can you sit down for a minute?"

"I am sitting."

"Good. What'd you have for breakfast?"

Katie laughed. "Bacon. You?"

"Eggs and toast. How's the weather there?"

She laughed again. "Isaac."

"You good?" he asked.

Another breath helped calm the rush in her heart. "I'm good."

"Okay. Katie, you can have another copy of the deed made, if that's what this is about. Get a second copy to keep."

She blinked several times and stared across the street to the mountains. "I can do that?"

"Of course you can."

"I don't know why I didn't think of that. I feel stupid now."

"You're not stupid, you're upset. And it's not a stupid paper either, it's important."

"Yeah, it is." She rubbed her hand over her face. "I'll get another copy. I'm sorry for panicking. I probably should have figured that out."

"It's okay," he said.

"Thank you." Katie leaned back in her seat, watching a couple of gulls circle in the sky. Her mind drifted to memories of long-distance phone calls with Isaac years ago and sudden gratitude flooded her. "Isaac, I really appreciate you. I hope you know how much you mean to me."

The line went silent for a moment. Not really the response she had hoped for. Katie double checked to make sure the call hadn't dropped. When he still didn't reciprocate, she remembered the frosty answer she first received when she called.

"Is something wrong?" she asked.

"I'm confused." He chuckled but it sounded dry as cotton. "You say I matter, yet you jet off to Alaska without a single word."

Oh. It hadn't even crossed Katie's mind to tell him. After weeks of CPS watching her every move, she had been completely focused on her own freedom. "I didn't think it would upset you."

"The Kaminskis showed up with your girls on Sunday and said you had left."

Left. That's all they told him? "And you assumed the worst?"

He didn't answer. Of course he had.

Part of her wanted to be annoyed. She didn't have to report to him, and he shouldn't have thought the worst of her. But another part knew they both had their defense walls built a mile high and they had to start breaking them down.

"I'm sorry," she said. "After all the CPS reporting, I wanted to go somewhere without having to alert the authorities."

He sighed. "I'm not the authorities. I'm the guy who asked you out last week."

"You're right. And you're the guy I care a lot about." And even the guy who had texted her when he went to Phoenix. Was Isaac becoming the better communicator? "You could have called me, you know. Instead of assuming the worst."

"Not with my pride," he said.

"Isaac—"

He laughed. "I'm kidding. You're right. Suzanne said you weren't answering your phone and I took her word for it."

Katie rolled her lips in tight. "For the record, I am answering her texts. But I'm worried the girls will cry if they talk to me."

"They might. But you should answer anyway."

"Yeah. Probably so." Katie frowned. "By the way, you should probably steer clear of Suzanne right now. You're on her bad side."

"I noticed," he said. "Any idea why?"

"You went to the aquarium with the girls and she didn't."

"Ah. We might need to talk about that."

"We might." They had a thousand tricky conversations ahead of them. "Isaac, I'm sorry I didn't tell you I was leaving. It's been a while since I've had to check in with someone just because they cared."

"I get it. It's been a while since I've cared."

Katie smiled. God had answered prayers she didn't even know she was praying. He had sent her an anchor when life had set her adrift. "Me too.

But I'm glad you're in my life again. Can we talk about it more when I get back?"

"Definitely. Tell me when."

"I will." Katie glanced down at the deed in her lap. "I better go get that second deed."

"You've got this, Katie."

"Thank you."

"Anytime."

She grabbed her purse and opened the door to go back into the clerk's office. Determination built with every step until she wished she were marching into Holly's counseling office instead. Katie wanted to grab the peg doll from the toy shelf and shove her in the middle of the sandbox, right next to the girls, the Kaminskis, and the church—with a camera and a tombstone or two nearby. And she would add a police officer. She'd add in her mom, stepdad, and half-siblings if she needed to. She would do whatever it took to belong in there, with all the pieces—past and future.

Chapter Forty-One

Days of prayer, asking God to help him release the anger, culminated in the moment Isaac opened a package from his mom to find a classic white baby gown. Isaac finally broke down and ordered a small granite stone with a custom engraving. On his next day off, he spent the morning digging out a tiny spot between two bushes along the back fence.

It took longer than he anticipated, with his dominant arm still recovering, but eventually he had it ready and went back inside. He wrapped the gown around the test and placed it in a tiny wooden box, then grabbed his gloves and headed back outside.

The clouds hung low today and a wet wind lent to truly wintery conditions even here in Ridley Bay. Isaac set the box into the ground. "I'm sorry, little one," he said, the anger finally giving way to sorrow.

He had done his flawed best. Lauren had done hers. It hadn't been enough, but neither of them had to live with the weight of this anymore. One day, he hoped he would see that baby in heaven and find out who they were meant to be.

Without ceremony, he covered the hole and reached for the nearby stone marker that read "*Baby Torres*" along with the year and a Bible verse. *"See what great love the Father has lavished on us, that we should be called children of God!" 1 John 3:1.*

He placed it over the spot and stood there for a while. This was better than keeping the test in a drawer. It made the loss more official, which both hurt and healed.

He had debated long and hard over whether to tell Lauren he forgave her. He decided against it. She didn't want his forgiveness and would likely view his comments as manipulation of some sort. But the next time he ran into her, she would know things had changed. He truly did forgive her. And he wanted her to be free.

He had been through all the what-ifs. What if he had gotten saved sooner? What if he had changed jobs, like Lauren wanted? What if… He mentally took each one and threw them over the fence. He had a fragile hold on peace and chose to accept that peace, moving forward with today.

Before he stepped away, Isaac said a prayer for both the family of his past, and the one he hoped would be part of his future.

The phone call with Katie had helped ease his fears and he realized he had let old insecurities take over. He could trust Katie, even if she handled things differently than he would. And he had a strong feeling Katie was about to say yes to this relationship. He didn't want any of the past anger or hurt to hold him back. God had given him a second chance and he planned to take it. He and Katie both knew how fragile life was; they wouldn't waste a minute.

•   •   •

After the several hours in the air, a delayed connecting flight, and a long drive from the San Antonio airport, Katie reached Ridley Bay after dinner. Suzanne offered to keep the girls for one more night, but Katie couldn't handle another night away from them. The girls ran to her the moment they saw her, confirming she had made the right decision.

Any exhaustion momentarily pushed back as she listened to the girls prattle about their stay with Nana. For the most part, they had high praise, though apparently Nana didn't know Sage liked back rubs at night, or that soda turned Josie into a gremlin.

"How did your trip go?" Suzanne asked, as the girls put on their shoes. Apprehension marked Suzanne's words, as if she feared an imminent move to Alaska in Katie's future.

"It was good," Katie said. "I'm glad it will be a resort. Maybe one day I can take the girls to see it." She preferred that option to losing it entirely to a private buyer.

When the three-year-olds finally had their shoes on the wrong feet—a feat that defied statistical odds on a regular basis—Katie picked up their backpacks. She soon had everyone and everything in the car. Katie adjusted the rearview mirror to peek at them. "Ready to go home, munchkins?"

Sage nodded solemnly.

"Yeah," Josie said. "I miss playing."

Katie laughed. "What do you mean? Didn't you play at Nana's house?"

"Yeah. But she doesn't play as good as you."

Katie wanted to bookmark those words and be able to flip to them anytime she needed them—like the inevitably all-too-soon moment when Josie would shout she liked Nana's house more because Nana made chocolate chip pancakes. Katie shook her head, wearing a smile, and accepted the compliments as they came.

On the drive home, Sage asked Katie about where she had gone and why. Katie tried to explain it in toddler-friendly terms. Josie seemed most concerned about the money and asked if she could get a unicorn now.

"You guys have unicorns," Katie said. They owned unicorns in almost every shape and size available at the store.

"No, a real one!"

Katie glanced back again as they pulled into the apartment complex. "I hear they're hard to find."

"You can do it," Josie said, utterly confident in her mother.

Katie laughed as she parked. She came around to Josie's door and kissed her daughter's forehead. "Thanks for believing in me, Jojo."

Before long, she had the two exhausted girls ready for bed. Washed and brushed hair hung straight down their backs, leaving little wet marks on their rainbow pajamas. They stopped by the beds and Sage tugged on Katie's hand.

"We have to pray," she said.

"Oh. Okay. Yeah, that's a great idea."

The girls knelt side-by-side. Suzanne must have taught them this, and Katie felt a flicker of guilt she hadn't done it first. She washed it away with a deep breath and chose to feel grateful instead that the girls had a grandmother who loved the Lord.

After two rambling prayers, in which the girls thanked God for everything from Nana to unicorns, they hopped into bed. Katie stayed in their room a minute longer than necessary, running her hands over the girls' hair. What a fool she had been. She had been chasing joy when it was right in front of her, waiting for her to slow down enough to see it.

With a sigh, she slipped out of their room and eased the door shut behind her. One day, she would tell the twins she knew she hadn't been the best mother, but by God's grace, she would say she had given it her all.

Chapter Forty-Two

Katie: Hey, I'm back. Need a day or two to recover from jet lag. How about dinner on Saturday?

Isaac: I'm on second shift, would breakfast or lunch be okay?

Katie: Brunch at my place!

He sent back a thumbs up.

It only gave Katie a couple of days to finish what she had started in Juneau the night before she left. She had ordered prints of every single photo she could find of Aaron and purchased a large photo album. She needed to make sure Aaron was never erased.

The next night, after she got the twins to bed, she went into the living room and spread photos out on the coffee table. She sorted photos into a loose chronology. The early days of dating, their wedding, their life in Baton Rouge.

Katie tried to work as efficiently as possible, stuffing photos into pockets and refusing to pause too long on any one. Until she reached the twins' birth. That young and hopeful couple stood in the hospital—Katie with a huge twin belly and Aaron with an equally huge grin.

In the next photo, Aaron held a newborn Sage, his copper hair echoed in Sage's wispy strands. His gorgeous blue eyes and ruddy complexion paled by hospital fluorescents, his hair stood up on one side from sleeping on the sofa in the room.

Katie let the photo fall back to the table and cradled her head in her hands. "God, I miss him." It hurt as much today as it had three-and-a-half years ago. The waves of grief weren't as sharp and bitter as they had been, but they still came. They would always come.

She took a deep breath and stood. She needed a break.

Soon she had the dishes in the sink cleaned, a load of laundry in the wash, and the last few items in her suitcase unpacked. After that, a hot shower helped her relax a little more. Finally, she returned to the couch and sank down in front of the coffee table.

Katie flipped back in the album to a wedding photo about midway through. In the picture, Aaron kissed her cheek, while Katie wore a giddy, lovestruck look. Naiveté shone beautifully on them both. The picture of love, before it was ever proven, and long before it was taken away. Katie knew she would never wear quite the same look again.

If those giddy, lovestruck feelings came her way again, it would be with the heavy knowledge of the risks, difficulties, depth, and richness ahead. It would be with a shadow of grief over what she had lost. Sunlight and shadows went together.

Her thumb ran over Aaron's picture. "Can I do it again?" she whispered.

All the confidence he'd ever had in her was right there in that picture. Of course Aaron would think she could do it. He had believed in her the first time. And maybe it wasn't just Aaron who had made it possible. The girl in that wedding photo had found an eternal love in Christ that made her confident. She had believed the very source of love loved her.

Could she still believe in God's love after losing Aaron? In her head, she accepted that bad things happened. But her heart had gone cold for years. Katie sighed, too weighed down to speak, she trusted God to hear her silent questions.

There may never be an answer. Katie rejected all the cliches about God's timing, and his plans, and things working out. She would never accept Aaron's death as good. But pain did not negate God's love. His love for the world had caused his own pain when the world rejected him. He understood pain. And he cared for her broken heart in this broken world.

Katie glanced at the photos again and knew, whichever path she chose, she would not be walking it alone. She had Aaron and she had God. And some things were worth the risk. She could do this. She wanted this.

·   ·   ·

After another night that stretched too late, she finished the album, and not a moment too soon. Katie called Suzanne in the morning and asked if they could drop by for a bit. Suzanne promised to put on a pot of coffee.

When Katie and the girls arrived, Suzanne shuffled them all into the kitchen where she already had warm muffins waiting. She eyed the photo album Katie carried under her arm, but didn't say anything.

As the girls dove into their muffins, Katie set the album on the table. "I want to show you something I made," she said, refusing to beat around the bush.

Suzanne studied it for a moment, then prepared coffees for the both of them before taking a seat next to Katie. "Okay," she said, in a tight voice.

The moment Katie flipped open the first page, both girls crowded around them, all elbows and blueberry hands, trying to get the prime spot for viewing. Eventually Suzanne and Katie moved the whole party to the living room, where they could gather on the couch.

"Dat's Daddy!" Josie shouted at the first page.

Katie smiled at her, honestly relieved they had seen enough pictures to recognize him. "That's right, sweetheart. Before you were even born."

They made slow progress through the album, stopping to read every caption and answer every toddler question. Interspersed with the photos, note cards filled in the details and funny stories—the kinds of memories that seemed fresh now, but could easily be forgotten in twenty years. When Katie struggled to read, Suzanne stepped in, and together they made it through.

The girls' attention spans began to wane, but they returned when they reached their own baby pictures. It started a fresh round of questioning from Josie and Sage. "Where did Daddy go?" Josie asked.

"Daddy died."

"Will he come back?" Sage asked. Sage spoke her questions more freely now. Therapy seemed to be helping her find her voice.

Katie turned to Sage and reached for her hands. She had answered the question so many times, but never fully. At three, how much could Sage even understand? *Enough to bury her toys.* "Daddy can't come back. But Jesus can. Jesus came back because he's bigger and stronger than death. Because of Jesus, we'll see Daddy in heaven one day."

Katie could see the wheels turning in Sage's mind and knew this would be only the beginning of many conversations about heaven.

Josie patted the album. "I want a picture of Daddy and big Jojo."

"Me too, sweetie." She wished she had a thousand more photos.

At some point during their questions, Suzanne slipped out of the room. Katie didn't blame her. It could be hard to handle. These girls had overwhelmed Katie completely in the early days of grief; she had resented their constant interruptions. Now, she realized they had kept her alive and moving, when she would have otherwise drowned under bed covers and sorrow. The children she once thought to be inconveniences were actually her greatest blessings.

When the girls' curiosity was sated, she sent them off to the playroom and closed the album. A few empty pages at the back waited for the notes and cards she would eventually pull out of her storage unit. It might be time to crack open that time capsule.

One envelope was already tucked at the back, holding a copy of the land deed. Greg Lewis didn't have his own photo album, but at least he had a place.

Suzanne still hadn't reappeared, so Katie headed to the kitchen, where she found her mother-in-law sipping coffee and staring out the window.

"Are you okay?" Katie asked. "I know their questions can be a lot."

Suzanne nodded. "I'm impressed you can handle it all. The album is beautiful, Katie, thank you. I'm glad the girls will have that part of their story."

Katie agreed and edged a step closer, trying to find a way to gracefully jump off the next precipice. Maybe starting with fresh reminders about Aaron wasn't the best way to go about it.

"They're welcome to stay and play if you need to run any errands or anything," Suzanne said.

Apparently they had both grown uncomfortable in each other's presence. Katie needed to work on that. "Actually, could we talk for a minute?"

Suzanne crooked her head and her posture opened. "Of course."

Katie stared at the coffee mug in her own hand. There was no right way to do this. "It's about Isaac."

She glanced up at Suzanne, whose head lifted and fell in what could only be resignation. "I see."

"He asked me out."

Suzanne didn't meet her eyes. "I had a feeling that was coming."

"You don't like him?"

"That's not true. He's a good man…" Suzanne shook her head. "I'm sorry. I suppose I should be happy for you."

"I haven't given him an answer yet."

Suzanne's eyes shot up to Katie. "Why not?"

"Because I don't know what to do."

"Yes, you do."

"But you're not okay with it." And that meant something to Katie.

Suzanne looked out the window for a long moment. "I'm just selfish," she said finally. "I'm afraid of losing touch with the girls. They're my only connection to Aaron."

"Why would we lose touch?"

"Oh—" Suzanne waved her off. "You won't need me anymore. I'll be an ex-mother-in-law. Nobody has room for that."

"Suzanne, no one can replace you. The girls will always be little Kaminskis. And you will always be their Nana."

She chuckled and softly brushed a finger under her eyes, checking her mascara. "I still wish it was Aaron, you know? Here with you, raising his girls."

"I know. But it can't be."

"No, and you shouldn't be alone forever because of it. I should look on the bright side. This might keep you in Ridley Bay a little longer."

"We're staying, regardless of what happens with Isaac," Katie said. She had faced the ghosts in this city; they didn't haunt her anymore. "Being here has been so good for the girls. And me. Your love for the girls is the example I want to follow." Even if Suzanne sometimes set the bar a little high.

"Oh, Katie—" Suzanne reached for her hand and clasped it. "Your courage is what I needed to see."

Katie couldn't help but snicker. "Everybody says I'm brave, but they're wrong. I'm terrified of losing someone again. I used to be fearless."

"Fearlessness is for the naïve, sweetheart. It's bravery that knows what it stands to lose and fights for it anyway."

Katie gave Suzanne a wry look. "But did it have to be with the guy who just got shot?"

Suzanne chuckled. "Hey, he proved he could survive it."

"True." She wanted promises and guarantees that nobody could give her. She could only walk the path God had given her, one step of faith at a time.

Suzanne leaned forward and gave her hand a little shake. "Katie, not everybody gets even one great love story. If God gives you the chance to have a second, then you go for it. Only promise you'll let me babysit on date nights."

"Deal. And promise we'll always be family no matter my relationship status."

"Nothing can change that."

Katie reached out for a hug with her late husband's mother, who would watch her kids while she went out with her future hunky boyfriend. The thought made Katie laugh at herself. This life—this second love story—would be as messy as it was beautiful.

Chapter Forty-Three

Rain washed through the town Saturday morning and Isaac's truck splashed through puddles on the way to Katie's apartment. He had squeezed in a workout and shower first, as well as a quick visit with Vera. Her son had plans to visit for Christmas and Isaac was glad for it. He hoped to meet the man and at least swap contact information in case of an emergency.

He reached the apartment and climbed out of the truck, zipping his utility jacket against the cold. At her door, he could hear the girls making zooming noises inside while he knocked. When Penn had said his quiet nights could end anytime, Isaac thought he meant a warning about mortality. Maybe he meant they were about to get louder.

It took two more knocks before Katie opened the door. She slipped outside, holding onto the handle behind her. "Hey, I'm sorry, I lost track of time," she said. "The girls are playing airport and it's a mess inside, and I meant to change into something besides a dinosaur Christmas shirt, and I haven't started the pancakes yet." Her shirt sported a green T. rex with string lights and the phrase "Tree-Rex."

Isaac smiled. "Airport sounds fun, I like your shirt, and I have plenty of time."

"If I get the girls down for quiet time after lunch, do you have time to talk then?"

"That works. My shift starts at two."

"Okay, perfect," she said. "It's all good things, I promise."

"I know. Nobody gets rejected over pancakes."

Katie dropped her head back in a laugh. "You are so cocky."

He shrugged. "If I'm right…"

She smiled at him, then turned to push the door open. Katie gasped as soon as they stepped inside. "Josephine Erin Kaminski!"

Over her shoulder, Isaac spotted Josie standing on a chair next to the countertop, holding fistfuls of bacon. Katie rushed over to her, trying to rescue the bacon from her greasy toddler. "Are you sure you want to be around this?" Katie called over her shoulder.

"I'm positive," he said. He'd had a clean, quiet house for long enough. He wanted the chaos that came with building a home.

Isaac joined Sage at the coffee table, where she worked hard to copy a picture of an airplane from a children's book. Near her sat a photo album with a picture on the front cover of Katie, newborn twins, and a man who must be Aaron. Isaac eyed it for a moment, wondering what he would find inside, if she ever offered to show him. Like the stone marker in his yard, pieces of their past would always be part of their lives.

He redirected his curiosity to Sage. "I like your picture," he said.

She glanced up at him, somber as ever, then went back to coloring.

"So, Josie's middle name is Erin," he said. For her dad. "What's yours? Katelyn?"

She shook her head, her eyes still on her drawing.

"Hmm. Is it Sparkle-Shoes?"

She looked at him with a closed-mouth smile and shook her head again.

"Sage Twirly-Girly Kaminski?"

She giggled.

"No? What about… Sage Elizabeth?" Katie's middle name.

She nodded and passed him the airplane picture.

"Wow, you did great on this. Got both wings and the tail, even the windows."

Sage set it on a couch cushion. Half a dozen such pictures decorated the living room. A de-greased Josie came running over to them and flew onto a pillow pile. Pretty soon, they boarded Isaac onto a couch cushion airplane for a flight to the grocery store. A stuffed panda rode first class.

The girls had just served him a plastic banana for an airplane snack when Katie announced dinner was ready. She had changed into a red-and-white striped sweater and the table featured half of the Waffle House menu, loaded with pancakes, french toast, eggs, bacon, sausage, and more.

By the time they finished their meal, the girls were syrupy messes. Katie wiped their faces and hands clean while Isaac cleared the table.

"Okay girls," Katie said. "It's quiet time."

"Mommy!" Josie stomped her foot. "You said park!"

"Oh shoot," Katie mumbled, looking out the window. "You're right, I did. How about after quiet time, Jojo?"

Josie melted into a puddle on the ground. "Nooo!"

Katie gave Isaac an apologetic look. "I'm sorry, I promised them a quick trip to the playground this morning."

"A promise is a promise," he said. He desperately wanted to hear her say yes sooner than later, but a few more minutes wouldn't kill him. "Everything is pretty wet, though."

"We'll bring a towel," Katie said, flashing him a grin. "Can't let a little rain stop us."

She soon had the girls in shoes and a towel in her arms. They headed for the door and Isaac stopped to grab his jacket. "Do they need coats?" he asked.

"They've got Alaskan blood," Katie said, with a smirk. "Besides, it's not that cold, weak Arizonan."

Isaac snickered and held the door open for them all. "Whatever you say, crazy Alaskan." She nudged him with her elbow on the way out.

They crossed the parking lot to the playground in the center of the complex and Katie swiped the towel over the slides before the girls could soak themselves. She stepped back to his side and they watched the girls clamber over the small playground. Despite the sun rays bursting through the clouds, the coastal wind had a bite to it and Isaac reached an arm around her waist to keep himself—and her, regardless of what she said—warm.

"You know, I've heard I shouldn't introduce my kids to any new dates until we're pretty serious," she said.

"Hmm. Too late, I've met them and I'm pretty serious."

She smiled up at him, and her smile could send any man to his knees. "Kids can be a lot. It's more of everything. More noise, and laughter, and tears, and joy. It's life filled all the way to the brim and sometimes sloshing all over the place."

Isaac kissed her temple. "If you're trying to scare me off, it isn't working."

Katie laughed and leaned into him. The girls chased each other down the slides for a few more minutes before Josie came running full hilt toward them and threw herself at Katie's legs. "I cold," she whined.

Katie picked her up as Sage joined them and reached for Isaac. He lifted her and her icy cold hands wrapped around his neck. "Me too," she said.

"Alaskan blood, huh?" he asked Katie with a grin.

She frowned. "Raised in the south. How about we go inside for hot chocolate, girls?"

Sage nodded, her copper waves tickling Isaac's face. Josie simply rested her head against Katie's shoulder.

Inside, Katie directed the girls to tidy their airport while she made hot chocolate. They each picked up a single item before getting distracted playing zoo, and Isaac tossed the couch cushions back into place. The girls giggled and squealed in the other room.

Katie walked over to him with two plastic mugs with lids. "Thanks for your help. I'll try to settle them down quickly so we can chat."

"I've got time. If I'm late, I'll complain about my arm and get away with it."

"Perks of getting shot," Katie laughed.

Before she finished her sentence, both girls came streaking out of their room and into the living room. Katie side-stepped, lifting the mugs out of the way as Josie screeched at the top of her lungs and flung herself at Isaac. "Help me!" she screamed, scrambling up his legs like a monkey up a tree. "Sage a tiger!" Judging from the look in her eyes, she truly believed it too.

Sage caught up to them, and with a growl she leaped for Josie, who shrieked in a pitch Isaac didn't know humans could reach—momentarily clearing the ringing in his ears. Isaac swung Josie up into his arms while Katie set down the mugs and pulled Sage off him.

"Hey, hey," Katie said. "Sage, we said no more tigers. It really scares her."

Holding Josie was like holding a honey badger. She clambered on top of one shoulder, her arms wrapped around his head like a vice. Isaac reached up to steady her. "Josie, I'm pretty sure you could take on a tiger," he said.

Josie folded her body over his head, tucking her face into his hair. "No tigers," she sobbed.

Sage growled at them both and Isaac laughed. He pulled Josie down into his arms, freeing his hair from her grip. "So Josie got your fear of random animals?" he asked Katie.

"That is not a random fear," Katie said, lifting her chin. "That is normal and healthy."

"Maybe for a kid who lives in rural India."

She tried to scowl at him, but a smile betrayed her. Katie squatted down to Sage. "Little tiger, it's time for you to go. I have hot chocolate, but it's only for people."

Sage looked between her mom and the mugs for a moment. She roared.

"I'm going to try magic and if that doesn't work, we'll try calm down time." Katie pointed her finger at Sage, waved it around her, and said, "Abracadabra kaboom, tigers go back to the zoo, give me Sage."

Sage popped up and smiled.

"Oh thank goodness, there you are!" Katie said, hugging her. "You wouldn't believe the tiger we saw." Sage giggled.

Isaac rubbed Josie's back. "Hey Josie, the tiger's gone."

She pulled back and stared into his eyes, shaking her head. "I don't wike tigers."

Isaac brushed her wild blonde hair out of her face. "It's okay, there are no tigers in Texas, I promise."

Josie perked up. "I wike Texas."

Isaac grinned and glanced at Katie. "Guess you'd better stay."

She laughed at him. "Come on, you wild things."

Isaac followed her down the hall and dropped Josie off in the room with Sage. Katie situated them both onto their beds with books and hot chocolate. Isaac stepped out as she sang the first lines of a hymn to them. Only a few minutes later, she joined him in the living room, with two empty mugs.

"That was quick," he said.

"They don't always nap anymore, but I think they might today. They were both exhausted." Katie walked into the kitchen and poured two more cups of hot chocolate. She hoisted herself onto the countertop and held a cup out to him. "Want some?"

"Of course," he said, reaching for it. "My Arizona blood needs it."

She swung one foot out to him and nudged him to stand in front of her. "You were right. I am going to say yes. But I need to say something first."

He put his hands on her hips. "Okay?"

"I'm not moving on," she said, lifting her face to him. "I'm moving forward, and that's with Aaron. I can't erase him. He made a permanent mark in my life. And I won't let the girls forget him either; they're going to have his pictures and know his birthday and all that."

Isaac shook his head, confused. "I never expected you to erase Aaron."

Her eyebrows pinched. "Really?"

"Of course not. Aaron is part of your story and I'm not trying to rewrite any of it. Everything that happened in the last ten years—the good and the bad—made us who we are now."

"We're not the same people we were," she said.

"Thank goodness."

She smiled and reached her arms around his neck. "But we're still the right people, and it is the right time."

Hallelujah. Isaac cupped her face in his hand. It felt like he had waited a lifetime to hear those words. "Finally," he whispered as he leaned down to kiss her. He wanted to hold onto her forever but he couldn't do it with his own strength. She had re-entered his life by the grace of God, and by it he prayed she would stay.

Katie tilted her forehead to his. "Do you think we'll argue about stupid things like thermostats and toilet seats one day?"

Isaac laughed. "If we're lucky," he said. And he would count every moment a blessing.

Acknowledgments

This third book was actually the first one I wrote, but it took years to untangle Katie's motherhood journey from my own. While our lives and circumstances are very different, I struggled to embrace motherhood, much like Katie. I had to learn to see the beauty and the blessings amidst the sleep loss and chaos. Thus, my primary thanks for this story must go to those who helped me grow as a mother.

To my husband, with whom I share those daily "aren't-they-cute" parental looks.

To my mother, who taught me to sing hymns and speak life over my children.

To my mother-in-law, who is quick to serve, eager to help, and often reminds me: it's just a season.

To my siblings who laugh with me, weep with me, and show up to every birthday party.

To the rest of my family, who dote on my children, who give advice, and who help me see all the goodness in front of me.

To my church, the moms group, and the women who brought me casseroles after each baby—they have all taught me so much about living and loving well.

Truly, the names are endless—I could credit every author, podcaster, and kind stranger who has encouraged me along the way. Yet it is all the handiwork of Christ, calling me to model the ultimate Father through parenting.

Of course, this wouldn't be a story at all if it weren't for my amazing publishing team and supporters. For that, I would like to thank the entire team at Black Rose Writing and my editor, Denise Harmer, as well as those who read early drafts and helped me refine this story, including Cam Torrens, Lena Gibson, and Barbara A. Luker.

Finally, thank you to my readers for taking this journey with me. I pray this story blesses you!

About the Author

Anna Daugherty is the award-winning author of the best-selling *Grace Church Series*. She holds a journalism degree from the University of Texas at Austin and spent several years as a freelance journalist before rediscovering her love for fiction. Now, Anna writes Christian women's novels with grit and grace. Her books have won the PenCraft Award and the Next Generation Indie Book Award.

Anna lives in the Texas Hill Country with her husband and three young daughters. When she isn't writing or chasing a toddler, you'll likely find her homeschooling, enjoying the outdoors, or reading a book—often all three at once.

For updates and bonus materials visit her website at annadwrites.com.

Grace Church Series

Note from Anna Daugherty

Word-of-mouth is crucial for any author to succeed. If you enjoyed *Before Grace*, please leave a review online—anywhere you are able. Even if it's just a sentence or two. It would make all the difference and would be very much appreciated.

Thanks!
Anna Daugherty

We hope you enjoyed reading this title from:

www.blackrosewriting.com

Subscribe to our mailing list – *The Rosevine* – and receive **FREE** books, daily deals, and stay current with news about upcoming releases and our hottest authors.
Scan the QR code below to sign up.

Already a subscriber? Please accept a sincere thank you for being a fan of Black Rose Writing authors.

View other Black Rose Writing titles at www.blackrosewriting.com/books and use promo code **PRINT** to receive a **20% discount** when purchasing.